The Search For *Peter Hunt* ♥

By

Lynn C. Van Dine

Lynn Van Dine

Pittsburgh, Pennsylvania, USA

The Search For Peter Hunt
Copyright © 2003 by Lynn C. Van Dine

All Rights reserved. No part of this publication may be reproduced, stored in a retrieval system or transmitted, in any form or by any means, electronic, mechanical, photocopying, recording, or otherwise, without the prior written permission of the publisher.

Published by
The Local History Company
112 North Woodland Road
Pittsburgh, PA 15232-2849
www.TheLocalHistoryCompany.com
info@TheLocalHistoryCompany.com

Cover design by Navta Associates, Inc.

The name "The Local History Company", "Publishers of History and Heritage", and its logo are trademarks of The Local History Company.

Library of Congress Cataloging-in-Publication Data

Van Dine, Lynn C.
   The search for Peter Hunt / by Lynn C. Van Dine.
      p.   cm.
   Includes bibliographical references and index.
   ISBN 0-9711835-4-6 (alk. paper)
    1. Hunt, Peter, b. 1896--Fiction. 2. Children of immigrants--Fiction. 3. Cape Cod (Mass.)--Fiction. 4. Artists--Fiction. I. Title.

PS3622.A6S43 2003
813'.6--dc21
                      2002012103

Printed in USA

Dedicated to my Dad,
Alan Van Dine,
For believing.

With special thanks to
Tim
For your endless patience and love

"To tell the truth, rightly understood, is not to state the true facts, but to convey a true impression; truth in spirit, not truth to the letter, is the true veracity."

Robert Louis Stevenson

Peter Hunt 1896-1967. Sketch by Jack Amoroso, 2000. Courtesy of Jack Amoroso. *Hunt is portrayed as he appeared in his sixties.*

Table of Contents

Acknowledgments xi
Author's Note xiii

Prologue 1

1. A Birth In Jersey City 5
2. In America 9
3. A Drubbing and a Dream 15
4. Art and Artifice 27
5. Fledgling Bohemians 35
6. War Wounds 47
7. Madame Makes Up Her Mind 59
8. Disguises 69
9. Leaving That Life Behind 79
10. The Tip of Cape Cod 95
11. Provincetown: New Life, New Art 103

Color Plates *and*
How To Paint Peter Hunt Decorations 115-124

12. Pa's Legacy 139
13. Hurricane Lessons 161
14. Peasant Village 175
15. Perils of Print 187
16. Hustling and Bustling 207
17. Alone for the First Time 213
18. Peacock Alley 221
19. A Fine Day for April 229

Afterword 237

Bibliography 241
Index 245

Lynn C. Van Dine

Acknowledgments

My heartfelt thanks to the following for their valuable contributions to this book:

Nancy Whorf Kelly, Carol Whorf Wescott, Wendy Everett, Walter Hyde, Berta Walker, Hattie Fitts, Harry MacLure, Barbara Weller, Gordon Weller, Lucius Gordon, Antoinette Gordon, Lucia Gumaer, Robert Eldred, Steve Tyng, Jack Amoroso, Helen Rydell of the Santa Barbara County Genealogical Society, Goleta, CA; Penny Duckworth, Minneapolis, MN; decorative artist and instructor Priscilla Hauser;

Goleta Train Depot Museum, Goleta, CA; *Boston Globe*; *Washington Post*; *New York Times*; Boston Public Library, Boston, MA; Archives of American Art, Washington, D.C.; Drake Hotel, Chicago, IL; Ellis Island Archives; Mormon Genealogical Library; Decorative Arts Collection, Wichita, KS; the United States Library of Congress;

Detroit Public Library; Eldredge Public Library, Chatham, MA; New York Public Library; Marysville (MI) Public Library; Port Huron (MI) Public Library; Provincetown Public Library; Provincetown Heritage Museum; Pilgrim Monument Museum; Provincetown Art Association; Smithsonian Institute, Washington, D.C.; Jenny Tobias of the Museum of Modern Art, New York; and Addison Gallery of American Art, Andover, MA.

Very special gratitude to my dad, Alan Van Dine; my mom, Joan More; my brother, Mark Van Dine; and especially my husband, Tim Weller, for being kind and smart readers and editors. Also, a bow to family friend Reginald Aubry for his encouragement and suggestions.

With special thanks to my sons, Donovan and Dock, for their patience. Also, thanks to my eighth grade English teacher, Charles Masters of Finley Junior High School, who taught me that good writing is more than stringing a bunch of words together.

And, of course, my humble gratitude to my editors and publishers at The Local History Company, Cheryl Towers and Harold Maguire, for taking a chance on me.

Lynn C. Van Dine

Decorative motifs by Peter Hunt.

Author's Note

Peter Hunt was a terrible—and wonderful—liar.

A Cape Cod folk artist from the 1920s through the 1960s, he was wildly popular across the United States for decorating furniture with whimsical designs he culled from European peasants. With inexhaustible charm, he told stories of a royal heritage and of adventures around the world to manipulate his way into New England's poshest circles. His pieces made their way into the finest homes and, soon after, they were displayed at the best department stores in New York.

All the while, Hunt was working and playing in the midst of a cultural upheaval in America. In his Bohemian circle sparkled famous and almost-famous artists, actors writers and eccentrics—playwright Eugene O'Neill, novelist Somerset Maugham, French actress Cecile Sorel, screenwriter Colin Clements, political writer John Reed, singer Ganna Walska and the glamorous Helena Rubenstein, among others.

A genius at reinventing himself, Hunt maintained his high profile through the years by sharing his painting techniques for "making old things new" with features in *Life* and *House Beautiful* magazines, an idea seized upon by women trying to keep up their households through the Depression and World War II. After the war, he held command of center stage by publishing two books on decorating furniture and by selling his designs to mass market manufacturers of china, linens, paints, fabrics and home accessories .

But in the end, he was undermined by his own success. His designs so saturated the market, the collectors and discriminating buyers eventually lost interest. His fondness for self-indulgences soon depleted his fortune. As his money evaporated, so did many of his friends. He died alone in a tiny, three-room cottage.

Peter Hunt climbed to the top on the strength of his charm, talent and an endless supply of complete fabrications. He told every story but his own. In almost ten years of tracking down his work and talking to anyone who could remember him, I was able to glean bits of truth beneath the camouflage.

I wrote articles about his designs, his painting techniques, about the current surge of interest in his work, as evidenced by the impressive prices his pieces command at antique shops and auctions. But the real Peter Hunt, the man, remained a mystery.

Still, there were clues. The true rags-to-riches ascent began in a New Jersey tenement just before the turn of the century. Obscured by Hunt's embellishments on his life and art were traces of reality: public documents, newspaper articles and, bless them, people like his former apprentices who stumbled upon elements of his background that Hunt had taken pains to hide.

Eventually, I found enough of these clues to hazard an enlightened guess at the rest. This book is the result. A few of the characters are fictional, and those few are not included with the real people and places in the index. Some parts are imagined, including dialogues invented to explain or launch real events or situations.

But, true to Peter Hunt's style, his real story is somewhere in this story. A tale, I believe, he would enjoy.

> Lynn C. Van Dine
> Cape Cod, MA

Prologue

"I hate the way I died," he said.

Not again.

"I mean it. I loathe my last bow, as it were."

There he was again, lounging in the wicker chair by my bed, toying with the white silk scarf around his neck. "Go away. I was sleeping," I moaned.

"It was so disappointing," he said, ignoring me. "Such an uninteresting end to such a fascinating life."

"Yes, you've told me a thousand times. Now, leave me alone."

"I know, I know. I brought it on myself. I wanted to die quietly. Just slip away in my sleep." He sighed. "But why couldn't it be in my living room chair, dressed in, say, my dinner jacket? Why did it have to be when I was wearing my ratty blue pajamas? My hair was a mess and I forgot to brush my teeth."

I opened my eyes and stared at the dark wall. There would be no more sleeping tonight.

"And, my God, I laid like that for days! I smelled terrible when they found me!" His voice cracked.

I sat up. This was new. He'd never said anything like that before.

"Why didn't anybody find me sooner? Where were all my friends?"

"Maybe they didn't know you were sick. You lied about everything. Maybe you lied about that, too," I said.

He smiled and plucked at the crease in his white slacks. "'Lie' is such an ugly word, don't you think? I'm not really a liar. I just embellish. It makes me more interesting."

"So, where were your friends?"

He straightened in the chair and frowned. "My death, now that was a lie," he said. "It had nothing to do with the truth, with who I really am. I mean, who I was. It was all wrong, don't you see? The funeral, too. So many didn't come. Where was everybody?"

He leaned forward, bringing his face within a breath of mine. "You have to write a book about me. To tell the truth about me. To tell everyone."

"We've been over and over this," I replied, drawing back from the chill that surrounded him. "You don't want me to write the truth. You want me to write down your lies. As if writing them somehow will make them true."

He sat back, his chin jutting out. *"It worked while I was alive. You saw the newspaper and magazine articles. I'd say I was royalty, and they would write all about Peter Lord Templeton Hunt. I'd tell them I moved in the best circles, and they'd print that. Then all of high society would read it in the newspapers, and they would come running. I'd say my furniture decorations were sought out by the finest households in New York, and the same day the article came out, designers and decorators were fighting over pieces."* Peter shrugged. *"People believe what's printed. It makes them happy to believe it."*

"Well, I'm not going to write your lies and tell them as fact. Forget it. Find someone else," I said.

I pulled on a robe and stumbled down to the kitchen. Peter was waiting for me there. He leaned against the counter and watched as I poured a glass of water.

"That's a shame. After all that research, you think you have all the facts about me," he said. *"But you don't. You don't know everything."*

I put down the glass. "Like what?"

Peter shrugged.

I knew this game. "I know enough. You made up an entire personal history. Your business, Peasant Village, was built on whole cloth."

"And it did rather well, didn't it?"

It always came to this. He'd come every few days and nag. "I won't do it, Peter. I won't write that way."

I thought he'd vanish in a huff again, as he usually did at this point, but he didn't.

"All right, let's try it another way," he said. *"Why don't you write everything, all of it. The truth you see, and my truth. Together."*

He was on to something.

Perched on the edge of my desk, Peter tossed his head back. *"I was born . . . are you taking this down? Good. I was born to a Russian prince and princess, who lived in a beautiful castle . . . ."*

"Oh, please," I interrupted.

Peter turned slowly toward me. *"Excuse me?"*

"This is a biography, not a fairy tale, Peter," I said. "The Russian royalty story was exposed while you were still alive."

Peter frowned. *"But I like that version. It's my favorite."*

I shook my head. "C'mon, Peter. You can do better than that."

"You're right! I most certainly can!" he said, grinning. He resumed his dictation pose. *"Ahem. I came into this world a privileged child, the illegitimate son of a French courtesan and her highly placed lover, who must remain nameless, but I heard was connected to Buckingham Palace."*

"Peter!"

"No good? Let me try again."

1

A Birth in New Jersey

April 1896 - New Jersey

"Mr. Schnitzer! What are you doing out in this weather? You'll catch your death." Mrs. Knappenberger rested her beefy arms on the windowsill of her apartment as she peered at her neighbor. Edward Schnitzer huddled on the stoop in his soaked coat and hat, mustering the will to go inside.

He turned to the sound of her voice and nodded, causing the rainwater puddled in the crown of his hat to cascade over the rim and down the front of his threadbare coat. "Mrs. Knappenberger," he spluttered.

"What did I tell you?" she said, laughing. "Terrible weather, terrible. The rest of the world, it's Spring. In New Jersey, more winter rain. What an awful day."

"Awful," Schnitzer agreed. He stared at Mrs. Knappenberger, trying to think of something to say. All he wanted to do now was go upstairs and sip a hot cup of tea.

Suddenly, a shriek pierced the air, coming from his apartment window, two floors above Mrs. Knappenberger's head. Another shriek, like an injured animal. It was Anna! Schnitzer gaped at his window.

"Mein Gott, Schnitzer! Is that Anna? Is it time already?" Mrs. Knappenberger jumped up, tipping over her wooden chair. "Why didn't you say anything?" She disappeared from the window, and in moments Schnitzer could hear the steps protest under her weight as she heaved herself up the stairs. "Anna! I'm coming, you poor thing."

Schnitzer shivered. Such a depressing day. Such a depressing street. So dreary. And upstairs, well, this should be a time for joy, yes? Celebration?

Ah, but here he was, alone in the rain, his hopes for hot tea dashed. Soon, the baby would arrive. Twilight deepened and Schnitzer shuddered. It was fast becoming too late to be out here. Good people were already locked in their homes, safe from the ruffians and the prostitutes that swarmed over Clark Street at night. Schnitzer heard the groan of a door opening on the vacant house across the street, and stepped back into the shadows of the porch so he couldn't be seen. A large, hulking figure carrying a pack on his back stepped out from the blank, leaning doorway and shuffled down the street.

Schnitzer watched the figure go and exhaled when he vanished from view. Such a neighborhood. Just last week, some poor wretch had been found dead and naked on the sidewalk, not thirty paces from Schnitzer's stoop. He'd seen the body himself, pale and crumpled, surrounded by a ring of curious passers-by. Thin, so thin, and blue-tinged, the dead man was curled on his side, like a child sleeping.

The sweaty detective who came said it looked as if it was "natural causes," starvation or the cold, and then the body was picked clean of whatever clothing and shoes he might have been wearing. Natural causes? That wasn't natural, Schnitzer wanted to scream. Even a man with nothing had something for the vultures here.

Schnitzer was tempted to walk back to the corner where several menacing men huddled around a sputtering fire blazing in a garbage can. There, he could warm himself away from the lengthening shadows. But, no, any of them could be the one cruel enough to strip a dead man. And the rats were coming out. Schnitzer could see their shadows as they dashed from one building to the next, or back and forth across the street.

Anna screamed again.

She was in her glory right now. Here was the culmination of months of demanding attention, indulgences, allowances, citing her "condition." While other women never even spoke of their pregnancies, scrubbing and working without a whisper of complaint, delivering their babies with barely a pause in their lives, Anna, well, Anna.

Anna must rest. Anna must eat the freshest of foods for her delicate stomach. Anna must weep and rail at what her husband had done to her. And what of her perfect figure? And where was the perfect life he promised? The house, the luxuries? Where was the dashing young man she married?

Where indeed? Schnitzer stuffed his hands in his pockets. Where, indeed?

Life was full of promise when they met. He'd just arrived in America, excited about the stories of adventure and wealth. He'd left behind a good job as a banker, certain his skills would help him quickly land a job. Bookkeeping and money-counting were the same anywhere, right?

Anna Lowe sailed to New York with her mother a few weeks later, going directly from Ellis Island to stay with relatives in Jersey City. That's where Schnitzer met her, at a dance. He'd come with friends from the warehouse where he worked as a clerk. He wasn't much of a dancer, but the instant Schnitzer saw Anna, demurely sitting on a folding chair, her blonde hair tied back with a blue ribbon, and her small hands folded in her lap, nothing would do but he should hold her in his arms and whirl her round and round.

Schnitzer could barely utter the words asking Anna to dance when her wide blue eyes met his. He tripped over his own feet as he led her to the dance floor, and Anna's raucous laugh surprised and delighted him. Before the music stopped, he was in love with her.

They married in a rush. Schnitzer promised Anna he would work hard, get a more prestigious job, and give her a fine life. They were in America, a country bursting with opportunity. He would go to the banks, get hired, and all would be well, even sublime, because everything happened so fast in the land of freedom.

Freedom. Yes, freedom, all right, cloaked in soot and misery. Freedom to be turned away again and again. No work, not for foreigners. Freedom to live anywhere, as long as they could afford it. They took a dingy flat in Jersey City, "just until I find a better job," Schnitzer had promised. That was six years ago, and they were still here, barely scraping by, living on his meager clerk's salary.

Who would now believe he was once a bank officer, respected as a leader in his village? Here, he mattered less than a stray dog. And this, this dismal place, so far from the hills and pastures of Germany, this dank, gray place where they were free to live. Ah, freedom.

Schnitzer's shoulders sagged. He'd come so far down, dragging his beautiful Anna with him. She did not belong here, a flower trying to bloom in concrete. He remembered their blushes and kisses when they were engaged, dreaming about their home, the family they would make.

Anna had been so eager, so supportive in the beginning, so certain Schnitzer could make all their dreams come true. But time had tarnished their shining hopes. Their years together had taken a toll on Anna, making her face drawn and her eyes hard. And now, a baby. Schnitzer was a fool. A failure. He failed himself. He failed Anna. He even failed the one not yet born.

A protracted scream echoed over the tenement bricks. Then a smaller, lighter wail. A baby's cry.

"A boy! A boy!" Mrs. Knappenberger crowed. She poked her head out of the window as Schnitzer looked up, his hat brim funneling rain water down the back of his coat. "Hear that, Schnitzer? You are papa to a baby boy!"

Schnitzer smiled and waved. "Can I come up now?"

"A minute. We'll call you in a minute." Mrs. Knappenberger's head disappeared.

A boy. They had agreed, if the baby was a girl, she would be called Dorothy. A boy would be Frederick, after Schnitzer's father, and Lowe, to keep Anna's family name. Frederick Lowe Schnitzer.

Schnitzer's smile faded. That's all he had to give his son: a name. A name tainted with his father's failures.

2

IN AMERICA

JANUARY 1900 - NEW JERSEY

The rattle of the kettle woke Freddy from his fevered sleep. Through half-opened eyes, he could barely make out Pa across the room, still wearing his coat, starting the water for tea.

Freddy shivered and groaned. Every muscle in the four-year-old's body ached, and his sheets were soaked from sweat. Schnitzer glanced at the boy, grunted, and turned back to the kettle.

"Still with us, Frederick? Well, that's good," Schnitzer said in a tired voice. "This is your third day with the influenza. Maybe tonight your fever will break. Maybe Ma will feel better, too."

Schnitzer pulled off his worn coat and hung it on the hook on the door. From its pocket, he pulled a package. "See this, Freddy? Springerle from Mrs. Knappenberger. And good, strong tea for Ma. Don't you want some?"

Freddy shook his head and rolled over. If his arms weren't so weak, he could almost touch Ma, sleeping soundly in the overstuffed chair by the dirty window. The curls around her forehead were damp, and her cheeks were deeply flushed. The fever made her look almost pretty, with her lips softened from their usual frown.

Freddy shivered. "Pa," he said weakly.

Schnitzer rushed to the bedside and pushed the enamel basin under Freddy's chin just in time for the heaves and trickle of vomit. He wiped the child's face with his handkerchief and helped the boy lay back on the bed. "It's a wonder you have anything to spit, little Frederick. You haven't eaten for days and days. The springerle can wait, eh?"

Anna moaned then, and twisted in the chair. Schnitzer extended his hand, as if to pat her shoulder, then quickly withdrew it. "Anna? Anna? You want some tea? Yes?"

Anna nodded groggily and put her hand to her face. "So hot," she sighed. Schnitzer brought her a steaming mug, and she took a tiny sip. "Mmmmm. Nice."

Anna turned to Freddy. "How is my son?" She lifted her hand in a weak gesture, as if to say she would reach to hold him but couldn't. "Good, Ma," Freddy whispered. He erupted in a fit of coughing that shook every bone and made him cry out from the painful rips through his lungs. Anna watched him, her eyes glittering with fever, until he quieted.

"Good, eh?" she said. "Or maybe not so good?"

A heavy rapping shook the door. "Anna? Freddy? Mr. Schnitzer?" Mrs. Knappenberger pushed open the door before Schnitzer could get to it and peered into the dark room. "Sheets!" she said in her brassy voice.

"Sheets?" asked Schnitzer.

"Sheets. Sheets. Sheets. For the sick, you must change the sheets," Mrs. Knappenberger barked. "Haven't you changed their sheets in all this time?"

"Change their sheets?"

Mrs. Knappenberger harrumphed. "I would help, but I can't risk the influenza."

She shoved a bundle of sheets into his arms. "Look, you must change their sheets, old for fresh, and wash the dirty ones with boiling water and lye. Hang them on the fire escape, and when they're dry, change the sheets again. And wash the dirty ones again. You got to draw the fever away. They can't stay wrapped up in their sweat, or they'll never get better."

"Oh," said Schnitzer. "I see."

"You? You see nothing. You give Anna some tea and springerle?"

Schnitzer nodded.

"She eat a little something?"

Schnitzer shook his head. "No," he whispered.

Mrs. Knappenberger looked hard in Schnitzer's eyes. "Mr. Schnitzer! You look scared!"

He ducked his head.

"Stop that! You mustn't let them see," Mrs. Knappenberger scolded. "If they know you're afraid, they'll be afraid, too. It will be all that much harder getting well. Now, go. Go change the sheets. Now."

Freddy nestled in his mother's limp arms like a damp rag doll as Schnitzer stripped the bed. With his head against her chest, Freddy could hear Anna's dry, harsh breaths, and the burbles of coughs to come. "Ma," he whispered.

Anna stirred from a doze. "Freddy?"

"Tell me," said Freddy. "Tell me about before."

"Ah, before, before," murmured Anna. Schnitzer paused for just a moment, imperceptibly sighed, and went back to his work.

"Before I came to America, life was so gay," Anna said softly, as if chanting the lines from a favorite poem. "I wore dresses with all the colors of the rainbow, and wreathes of flowers and ribbons in my hair. I would run through the fields barefoot without a care.

"In our village, we would sing and dance for almost any reason, a birth, a wedding, a good harvest. Apples grew, and grapes, and carrots, and wheat, so even though we had little money, we were never hungry. We had lots of peat, so we were never cold."

Anna stopped to give herself over to a wracking coughing spell. Freddy listened to her lungs creak as his head bounced against her chest. Schnitzer edged toward Anna, stopping at the weak gesture from her hand. When the coughing stopped, Schnitzer lifted a glass of cooled tea to her lips and she took a delicate sip.

"Everybody in the village had to work, but I always thought it was fun," Anna said in a raw voice. "The mamas would work with the papas in the fields or the orchards until it was time to go back to the houses and make the meals. The children would work, too, helping the mamas and the papas. We pulled carts that we had decorated in the winter, painting swirls and flowers and designs in so many bright colors.

"When I was a young lady, it was all my mama and papa could do to force me inside to bathe and dress and put on shoes to receive suitors. Such handsome young men! Such games we played! Cards, guessing games, riddles. Such fun!"

Anna sighed. "But Mama didn't approve of any of the village boys who came to call. She said she wanted more for me. That's why she brought me to America.

"Oh, I was so sad to leave my village. I cried and cried the whole trip across the ocean. I was so lonely and America seemed so strange.

"It was like a miracle when I met your Pa. We'd only been in America a few days, and Mama made me go to a dance. I didn't know anybody. I was so shy, I could only look at the feet of people as they danced past me. Then, a pair of brown shoes stopped right in front of me, and I looked up to see your Pa.

He was so handsome and so much fun. He made me laugh all the time and brought me little presents."

Freddy smiled. He like to imagine Ma and Pa dancing together, laughing together. He'd never seen that.

"How could I not love such a man?" Anna continued. "I thought I would go crazy waiting for him to propose. Mama didn't approve, of course. He didn't make enough money. But I didn't listen to her. I loved your Pa too much. We ran off together."

Anna opened her mouth, and closed it. Her arms tightened around Freddy. "And here we are."

"Here we are," said Schnitzer. "Now why don't you two crawl between these nice clean sheets and get some sleep?"

Peter paced the front porch as I stretched out on the glider, taking a break from the keyboard.

"Are you out of your mind? I can't believe you wrote about that," Peter sputtered.

I yawned. "What's wrong with it?"

"What's wrong with it? Readers will be bored out of their minds. It's so depressing. Nobody wants to read such dreary stuff."

"I think you're wrong. I think it's interesting. Besides, now they know your birth name, not the one you made up."

Peter stopped in front of me. "But it's all so stark, so cheerless. If you're going to tell them about New Jersey, the least you can do is put us in a nice house. My God, struggling families were a dime a dozen back then. You should give me a little more comfort, so the readers can be comfortable."

"But that wouldn't be true."

"You're impossible," he said, turning on his heel to cross the porch and sit stiffly on a wicker chair. "Can we at least get on to the New York years now? That was lots of fun."

I rose to head back inside. "I'm not done with this part yet. It's time to put in Tebbs."

Peter frowned. "Tebbs? Is that absolutely necessary?"

"You know it is."

3

A Drubbing and a Dream

December 1907 - New Jersey

Not again. On Christmas Day, yet.

Freddy sighed and slouched against the Lucky Lady's brick wall. Pa had been in the tavern for at least an hour and Freddy had just tried for the third time to convince his father to come home. Pa wouldn't budge. He shouted at Freddy to leave.

Now Freddy was caught between a rock and a hard place. Ma sent him out in the bitter cold to find Pa and bring him home. Pa wasn't going anywhere. Freddy decided to hang around outside. Either the old man would come out, or he wouldn't. But Freddy wasn't going home to Ma without Pa.

Freddy pulled his cap down and crossed his arms to ward off the cold. He was tall for his 11 (almost 12!) years, and his wrists poked out of the worn jacket. His blond hair was in need of a haircut and his pants were an inch too short. Maybe he'd get new clothes for Christmas, he thought. His shabby appearance made him self-conscious and shy.

Unlike other days, the street was quiet. Everyone was probably home with their families, Freddy guessed. The Lucky Lady seemed to be the only place with any life. Sam, the beefy owner and bartender, knew his hard-bitten clientele well enough to open for business, even on Christmas. Especially on Christmas.

Animated voices down the street drew Freddy's attention. A few doors down, a tall gentleman wearing a fur-trimmed greatcoat and a broad-brimmed hat was standing at the bottom of a stoop of a worn brownstone, taking his leave of a tiny elderly woman standing at the top of the steps. She was shaking her finger at him and he was laughing.

Like the other homes in the neighborhood, the brownstone had a sagging grandeur. Once a street of upper middle-class families, it was now several blocks of immigrants who could barely afford to keep up the sooty facades and peeling trim. Despite its decline, this was still a far better neighborhood than five blocks over, where Freddy lived.

The laughing gentleman must have visited his mother for Christmas, Freddy guessed. The youth fished in his pocket and pulled out his small tattered pad and a nub of a pencil, and quickly sketched the scene. Freddy liked the way the woman used the top step to tower over her son and the way the light stuck the man's upturned face. They leaned toward's each other, seeming to make an arch which Freddy rapidly outlined on his pad.

Suddenly, just past the laughing gentleman, Freddy spotted Tebbs, heading his way. His throat tightened and he quickly stuffed the pad and pencil back in his pocket. Freddy straightened, every muscle tensed.

"Yo, Shits-ner. Whaddya doing?"

Freddy flinched, but kept his eyes trained on the ground, trying to ignore Tebbs as the youth sauntered closer. Inside the tavern, Pa flinched, too, and kept his head down, hunkered over an ale at the bar.

Tebbs. Two years older than Freddy, he was built like an adult, square and muscular, with greasy black hair and wisps where a beard was beginning to grow. Hardened by a brutal father and indifferent mother, Tebbs was the school bully. Worse, he had a deep and abiding hatred for Freddy. The feeling was mutual.

They were complete opposites. Tebbs had small eyes and a hawk-like nose on a large head that seemed flattened on the back. His clothes were soiled and stiff with grime. Tebbs ruled the neighborhood children with force and fear. Quick to anger and more than a head taller than the principal, Tebbs would pounce on anyone who crossed his path, terrorizing the other students for money, lunches or for the sheer fun of pounding them.

Freddy was popular at school, charming teachers and classmates with a combination of industry and fun. Fair-haired and slender, Freddy drew pictures of his classmates, much to their delight, and volunteered to help the teachers clean up after classes. Tebbs loathed the way the students were drawn to Freddy, and how the teachers seemed to fawn over him.

By and large, Freddy managed to stay out of Tebbs' way, never straying far from the side of a teacher or a cluster of kids. But the few times their eyes locked, hatred blazed.

Freddy saw Tebbs' worn leather shoes before his eyes traveled up and up to the other boy's squinting eyes. Tebbs was holding a covered pail, obviously headed to the tavern for some beer for his old man. "Tebbs," Freddy said in a low voice.

Tebbs stopped at the tavern's doorway and glared at Freddy. He went inside and Freddy could hear him order the beer, and the sound of the tap filling the pail. Down the street, he could see the elderly lady accepting a kiss on the cheek from the gentleman. After returning the kiss, the gentleman watched the woman go back inside before he turned and raised his cane to signal a horse and carriage.

"I said, Shits-ner, whaddya doing?" Tebbs shoved Freddy with his shoulder as he came out of the tavern. Tebbs looked suspiciously at Freddy and leaned closer. "You ain't hanging around this dump hoping to roll drunks, are you, Shits-ner? Haw Haw!"

Freddy shrugged and dropped his eyes to the pavement, wishing Tebbs would just move along. He could almost feel Pa listen to Tebbs, but Freddy heard no stool scraping or footstep on the threshold. He was on his own.

Tebbs set down his pail and grabbed Freddy by the collar and shook him like a dog. "You wouldn't roll a drunk on Christmas, would you Shits-ner? That wouldn't be nice."

Tebbs slammed Freddy against the brick wall and pushed his face close to Freddy's nose. Freddy went almost cross-eyed trying to return the stare, and concentrated instead on a thin line of spittle running from Tebbs' thin lower lip to his chin.

Tebbs shoved Freddy against the wall again, and a bolt of searing pain shot through the boy's head to his eyes. "Where's your fucking Christmas spirit, Shits-ner? Lemme hear you ho-ho-ho."

A sob wrenched itself from Freddy's chest. Tebbs backhanded Freddy across the face. "Shut up!"

Where's Pa? thought Freddy. He can hear it. He can probably see it. Why won't he help?

Inside the tavern, Sam wiped his hands and bald head on a towel and spoke to Pa. "Seems like your kid's got some trouble on his hands."

Pa shrugged, still staring into his ale. "It's a tough world. He's gotta learn," he said. "I can't help him."

Sam moved down the bar to better watch the ruckus. He rolled back the sleeves of his shirt, revealing arms well-muscled from lifting countless kegs and bouncing countless drunks. Sam yanked off his stained apron and slipped his hand under the counter to make sure his iron pipe, generally used on belligerent customers, was in place. Just in case.

Freddy's nose was bleeding and his eyes were swelling shut from the pounding. Tebbs pinned the boy to the wall with a knee to the gut while he methodically punched Freddy on the face one fist, then another. Neither boy said anything. The only sound was Tebbs' grunts with each blow, and Freddy's grunts as he received them. They seemed almost lost in the rhythm of the beating.

Suddenly, Tebbs' right arm was stopped in mid-air.

"Say there, young man," said a deep voice. "I believe it's time for you to go."

Tebbs whirled around. Holding on to his arm was the gentleman Tebbs had passed earlier. Under a rakishly tilted hat, the elegant stranger had a small pointed beard and dark, piercing eyes hooded by great black eyebrows. His grip on Tebbs wrist was like iron. Tebbs snarled "Who the fuck are you? This ain't none of your business."

Freddy slumped to the ground and stayed on all fours, watching drops of his blood splatter on the concrete.

The gentleman waved his gold-tipped walking stick under Tebbs' nose. "I'm the fellow who's going to give you the worst caning of your life if you don't leave now."

"And I'm the guy that's gonna help him." Tebbs turned to see the Sam filling the tavern door, tapping his iron pipe on the palm of his hand.

"All right," growled Tebbs as he snatched his arm away from the gentleman. He thrust his jaw in Peter's direction. "I better never find you alone, Shits-ner. You're gonna pay." With that, Tebbs ran down the cobblestone street and vanished into an alley.

"Lad? Can you stand?"

Strong hands took Freddy by the shoulders and propped him against the wall. An odd scent of turpentine and wet wool filled Freddy's nose. A silk handkerchief dabbed at his face, causing him to cry out.

"Take it easy, Freddy," said Sam, standing on the other side. "You don't know how lucky you are, that Mr. Waugh came by when he did."

Freddy tried to get a look at the face hovering over him, but his eyes were swollen and filled with tears. "Mr. Waugh?" he said weakly.

"I'm glad I came by, too. Freddy is it? I'm a Frederick, as well. Surprising that Sam here didn't see that thug beating you right in front of his own establishment," said the voice, edged with reproach.

"Aw, Mr. Waugh, I was just on my way out when you got here," Sam stammered. "Why don't you come in for a drink?"

The handkerchief stopped daubing at Freddy's face. "So, Freddy, how are you doing? Are you ready to stand?" asked Mr. Waugh.

"Sure," said Freddy, struggling to his feet. He felt the gentleman and Sam lifting him by his arms on either side. "I just can't see very well, that's all." He started making out a blurred picture of Mr. Waugh's face. "Thank you very much, sir."

"It was nothing, young man. You need to get yourself home now, get those cuts looked after. Do you need help?"

"Oh no, Mr. Waugh, Freddy'll get home just fine," said Sam. "His pa's right inside."

Mr. Waugh and Sam exchanged a dark look that Freddy just barely made out. "I see," Mr. Waugh said, his voice hard. "How fortunate."

Sam shrugged.

"Well, Freddy, I'll be off then," said Mr. Waugh. He fished a silver dollar from his pocket and handed it to Sam. "Sam here will see you find your way home. Good luck to you."

"Yes, sir. Thank you sir," said Freddy, squinting to see the man turn and start walking down the street to his carriage, his cane tapping the sidewalk every other step.

Freddy and Sam watched Mr. Waugh open the carriage door, turn with a wave and disappear inside. Sam put his large hand on Freddy's shoulder. Freddy flinched.

"Do you know who that was, young Fred?" Sam asked as he led Freddy to the tavern door. He didn't wait for an answer. "That was Frederick Waugh. His old nurse, the lady that brought him up, lives near here. You know what he does, to earn enough money to wear such fine suits?"

Freddy shook his head.

"He draws pictures, paints 'em I guess," said Sam, disbelief echoing in his voice. "He paints pictures and people pay lots of money for 'em. Can you believe that?"

Freddy stopped in his tracks. "Really? He paints pictures?"

Sam nodded and pointed to an oil painting hanging on the back wall. "Like that one, see there? He painted that one there. He gave me that some time ago, in trade for, what was it? Hell, I can't even remember now. It was years ago."

Freddy walked towards the picture at the rear of the bar, oblivious to the rowdy talk bubbling around him and unaware as Pa snuck a look over his shoulder to watch the boy. All Freddy could see was the painting, and he had to see it close-up.

Sam shrugged. "Personally, I can't see throwing money at a picture. Some folks just have too much money to spend, if you ask me. Keep your shirts on," he bawled at his customers.

The bar was dim and Freddy's vision was still blurring in and out, but he was drawn to the painting, a picture of wild waves flinging themselves on craggy rocks. It was all there, the cloud of mist, the dark underbelly of the curling wave, the roiling clouds in the background. Freddy traced his finger on one of the long, strong strokes. Thick sweeps of paint gave texture to the waves and the rocks. Streaks of gray, white and green, even red, gave the waves movement and form.

That man, he painted this! Freddy felt himself filling with awe. Somehow, that man, that gentleman, saw this image in his head and miracle! created it with paint and brush and canvas. And that's how he made his living! Like Pa scratched numbers as a clerk, like the vegetable peddler who sang his wares as he walked the street, like Sam and his bar. That man, Mr. Waugh, painted pictures for a living!

Freddy closed his eyes and rocked on his feet. It was all too much to take in. First Tebbs, then his rescue, and meeting a man who made pictures for a living.

He heard Pa approach from behind. "You like that, do you?" Pa said, plucking at Freddy's sleeve. "Don't stare at it till you wear it out."

Without a word, Freddy turned and followed his father's unsteady steps. He felt like his mind was whirling, twirling and overflowing.

Freddy blinked in the pale winter light as he followed Pa out the door. Pa steadied himself with one hand against the building, and Freddy moved around to help from the other side. Something caught the corner of his eye and he stopped.

A beer pail. Tebbs' beer pail.

Slowly, Freddy cast his blurred eyes around the street. Tebbs was sure to be nearby. He couldn't go home without that beer, or his father would beat the daylights out of him. Freddy guessed Tebbs was waiting for a chance to grab the pail unseen and race home.

There he was. Freddy could barely make him out, peering around the corner of a building on the alley nearby.

With his eyes trained on Tebbs, Freddy stooped down and slowly unscrewed the lid of the pail. Then he quietly, deliberately put the can on its side and let the beer flow onto the street, pungent and foaming. Tebbs took a step and stopped.

"Freddy?" Pa called. "Help me out here."

Freddy quickly moved to his father's side and pulled Pa's arm over his shoulder. He held his breath against Pa's sour stench as he leaned heavily on his son. "You all right?" Pa asked.

Freddy's eyes stayed on Tebbs. Tebbs, his fists clenched at his sides, didn't move. "Good, Pa," Freddy said. "Let's go."

Pa pushed open the door to the flat with Freddy close behind him. The room was dark and cold. "Edward? Freddy?" Ma was sitting in the rocking chair by the window.

"Yeah, Ma, it's us." Freddy groped for the lamp, clumsily lighting it. Ma was rocking the baby, wrapped like a Christmas package in a red wool blanket. "You shouldn't sit here in the dark, Ma. How's the baby?"

"Fine, Freddy, fine. Dottie is the sweetest child. Never a whimper." Ma stroked the baby's cheek. "See the lovely blanket Mrs. Knappenberger gave her?"

Pa groaned from the other side of the room. Ma and Freddy turned to watch as he let his coat fall to the floor, and with his cap still on his head, tumble into the bed. Ma pursed her lips and shook her head. She turned to Freddy and stifled a gasp.

"Freddy! What happened to you?" she said.

He turned to start the kettle for tea. "Nothing, Ma. Just took a fall."

"Took a fall, indeed!" Ma rose, the baby snug in the crook of her arm, and stood next to Freddy, turning him towards her. She dipped the corner of her apron in the water and delicately swabbed his face.

Freddy's stomach tightened. The swirling colors and whirling ideas about the picture gentleman that had so filled his mind on the way home dimmed in the gray, barren flat. Even with the lamp lit, the room was so dark, furnished with battered sticks of furniture fished up from sidewalk cast-offs, and the bed smelled as if it hadn't been aired in years. He had to hold onto to the amazement he'd felt outside, to make it real somehow.

"Ma, you'll never guess what happened," Freddy said, trying to dodge the damp cloth. "I met a man who makes pictures for a living! He paints them, and people pay him money for them."

"Oh, Freddy, the stories you tell," Ma tutted. "There are no artists in New Jersey. Artists live in New York, or Paris."

"Well, this one used to live here. That's what Sam said." Freddy bit his lip. Ma knew who Sam was, and now she knew where Pa had been. He watched her face darken, and then she composed her features.

"Ah, Sam," she said evenly, taking the cloth from Freddy's face. "Sam knows about artists, does he?"

"Really, Ma! The man, Mr. Waugh, he's a Frederick, too, and Sam has a picture he painted hanging on the wall." The words spilled out of Freddy's mouth before he could pull them back.

Ma scowled and turned away. Freddy followed her to the chair by the window. "No, no, Ma, it wasn't like that," he said, horrified by what his mother must be thinking. "I was only in there a minute, just to see the painting, nothing else. I just looked at the painting."

Ma harrumphed as she settled the baby on her lap. "I believe you only because I can see who used our last nickel on ale," she said, angrily gesturing at Pa, who was snoring softly into his hat. "You mustn't ever go inside that place again, Frederick. You know my rules."

Freddy nodded sheepishly and turned back to making the tea. As it steeped, he closed his eyes and deeply inhaled the fragrant steam. "That's what I want to do," he said, as if talking to himself. "I want to paint like that. I want to be an artist, and get paid for my paintings."

"You might as well want to be the man in the moon," Ma said.

The two were silent for several minutes. The only sounds were the remote voices of people in the other apartments and Pa's snore. Freddy poured the tea and placed Ma's cup on the table within reach.

"Ma," he began.

Ma raised her hand. "No, no," she said, her voice soft and sad. "Don't listen to me. We're in America. If that's what you want to do, you must work hard at it, all the time. And you must make your luck, yes? You must make your own luck."

Freddy took her hand. "Yes, Ma," he said. He didn't know what to say. Ma had let him keep his flicker of hope. She pulled her hand away. "Enough talk," she said. "You're still a boy, yet. Enough time for that. Don't you want your Christmas present?"

Switching Baby Dorothy to her other arm, Ma fished in her apron pocket and pulled out a small package. Pa snorted and rolled over, his cap falling to the floor. Ma pushed the package across the table toward Freddy, "Open it."

Freddy worked the paper open. "Don't expect too much," she warned.

A *Bible*. Freddy marveled at the soft grain of the leather cover, and traced the words in gold lettering, "*Holy Bible*," with his finger. Even the pages were edged in gold. Freddy had never held anything so fine.

"Oh, Ma," he said breathlessly.

"Open it, something's written," said Ma.

Inside the cover was written in flowing script, "Frederick Lowe Schnitzer."

"I had the priest write your name, so it would look pretty," said Ma proudly. Pa snored. She sighed. "It's from Pa and me."

"It's beautiful, Ma," said Freddy, gingerly turning the thin pages.

Ma nodded. "Now put it away so we can eat."

Freddy rose and carefully placed the *Bible* in the corner, under his bedroll.

"You read that, a little each day, yes?" said Ma. "It helps somehow. It's good for you to know it. Maybe if you know your *Bible*, God will help your luck."

Ma sighed. "Now let's start dinner while our Santa sleeps it off."

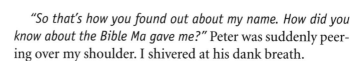

"So that's how you found out about my name. How did you know about the Bible Ma gave me?" Peter was suddenly peering over my shoulder. I shivered at his dank breath.

"Your mother must have sacrificed a lot for you and your sister," I said.

Peter straightened and walked round the desk. He turned to face me. A lighted cigarette appeared between his long fingers and he inhaled deeply, then exhaled. *"She did,"* he said in a level voice.

"She must have been very strong."

Peter tapped his ashes. Nothing fell into the ashtray. *"She was,"* he said, his words controlled.

Why so reticent? I wondered. "So why did you have to make up those stories about her?"

Peter looked away. *"Stories?"*

"Yes, stories! You know the ones . . . Ma came from a fine family, Ma went to a finishing school, Ma had royal blood. Peter, she sounds like a terrific woman without the stories. Why not tell the truth?"

"The truth! What do you know about the truth?" Peter cried. *"Don't you see? My stories were a kind of truth, too. That's how Ma carried herself. Dignity. Strength. Grace. When I said those things, people believed it. She WAS all those things!"*

I shook my head. "She was better than that."

"Of course she was," Peter said. He flicked away his cigarette and it vanished at the top of the arc. *"But do you think she would have been treated with the same regard, the same esteem, if I told people where she came from, how she struggled? It just didn't work that way. Not then. Respect was accorded to pedigrees, not accomplishments."*

Suddenly, he was at my side, and I jumped. "Jeez, I wish you wouldn't creep up on me like that," I said.

"No more talk about Ma. It's your turn," Peter said. *"Now you tell me something."*

"What?"

"How did you know about the Bible?" His voice had a forced lightness.

"I saw it. I looked through it," I said, backing up.

"Where is it?" asked Peter as he leaned closer.

"In a box with all the pictures and things left over after they cleared out your cottage," I replied.

"And where is this box?" His eyes locked onto mine.

I blinked. Once. Twice. Then I grinned.

"I'm not telling you," I said.

Peter scowled and vanished.

4

ART AND ARTIFICE

1913 - GREENWICH VILLAGE

"Oooh, what's happened to me?" moaned Freddy as he put his throbbing head in his hands. A waiter approached, the coffee cup clattering in the saucer. Wordlessly he put the coffee at Freddy's elbow and withdrew.

The gray March mist clung to Greenwich Village like a tattered veil. A woman wearing a sky blue smock, her red hair trailing down her back, ambled past his cafe table, and only when she was a few steps further down the street did Freddy see she was barefoot.

He shook his head, trying to focus his thoughts. The throbbing intensified and Freddy stilled himself. He gingerly wrapped his cold hands around the warm coffee cup and sipped, hoping no one would notice he needed both hands to get the rim to his mouth.

But then, why would anyone notice? Compared to some of the things he'd seen these past few days, an 18-year-old man clutching his coffee cup with both hands was comparatively normal.

Maybe it was a dream, or some gin-induced hallucination? Freddy set down his cup and pulled his coat close to ward off the chill. The coat! Baron Willy's coat! The coat was real enough, thick, scratchy wool, that Baron Willy wore on his shoulders, so debonair! And he whirled it off and onto shivering Freddy in a gesture so grand and gentle, Freddy could barely utter his thanks. The coat was real, so everything else must be real, too, he reasoned.

Focus, Freddy told himself. Focus. I must put it all together. I want to make sense of it, and then remember it always. Freddy nodded as the waiter refilled the coffee cup and withdrew. All right. Let's start with the coat. With Baron Willy. How did all that start?

The Armory Show, that was it. He met Baron Willy at the Armory Show. He'd made Freddy laugh. What was it he said?

Freddy felt lost in the marvelous painting that commanded his attention the moment he entered the Armory Show. He knew he would see something new. He was counting on it. But this was so much more than he could have imagined.

The rumors about the first exhibition of modern art had been flying for weeks, even into the cramped shipping office where Freddy worked as a clerk. His boss peered from behind his newspaper and said, "Word is you're some kind of artist, Fred. You're not one of them perverted modern artists, are you?"

Freddy could honestly answer that he had never seen modern art, much less painted it. He was still working on landscapes and still lifes in his weekend art classes. "Not even a nude model," he quipped. His boss grunted and went back to his reading.

It was the first time Freddy had visited New York on his own. The tall buildings, the waves of bustling people and the deafening noise of the city filled him with excitement. Even though he was wearing his best houndstooth jacket with a clean white shirt and silk tie, Freddy felt he looked unsophisticated compared to the businessmen and shopping women that moved deftly through the crowds.

Using a map, Freddy made his way to the Armory. He threw himself onto a trolley and took in the sights as it rang its way through the streets. Up high in those buildings, people worked, he thought with amazement. Down on the streets, well-dressed men and women stepped around hawkers and beggars as if they were annoying pets. Kids raced alongside the trolley, yelling for pennies, and Freddy tossed them a few coins. The hum of the city vibrated with a strange energy.

Crowds milled around New York's Armory, outside and in. Some people looked intrigued, others looked dazzled. Many people frowned, or even barked their outrage. "This is garbage! This is terrible" One man stormed. "This is not art!" He spat at the foot of the huge painting and stalked away, just as Freddy drew close.

It was magnificent, Freddy thought. Strong, passionate streaks of paint created lights and shadows that played down the canvas in an arc. "*Nude Descending a Staircase*. Marcel Duchamp" he read on the placard beneath. Freddy studied the painting. It was a painting of form, he realized, and emotion. And it was almost overwhelming in its power.

"*N-N-Nude Descending a Staircase*, eh," stammered a voice behind Freddy, a gentleman's voice with a British accent. "I c-c-can't say I can make out a nude, or a staircase for that m-m-matter. It's m-m-marvelous, don't you think?"

Startled, Freddy realized the voice was addressing him and he turned to see a fine looking gentleman, a black greatcoat hanging from his shoulders and a wide-brimmed black hat twirling in one hand. The gentleman bowed slightly. "Or am I m-m-mistaken? Are you, too, horrified by this work of art?" He grinned.

"Yes, uh, no," Freddy said. The man's grin broadened. "It's wonderful. It's not that it looks like a nude, but that it feels like a nude."

"Feels like a n-n-nude, eh? No wonder I like it!"

Freddy laughed. "No, no, no, what I mean is . . . ."

"N-not at all. I know what you mean. And it is w-w-wonderful." The stranger extended his hand to Freddy. "But I warn you, I know almost n-nothing about art. I'm B-b-baron Willy Knockblock Exeter Drosse with the *Ch-chicago American*."

"Freddy, uh, Frederick Schnitzer," Freddy replied, shaking his hand. "I'm an art student." He nodded toward the painting. "But I'm just realizing no matter how much I study, I don't know nearly enough about art."

Baron Willy laughed. "Do you mind having a look round with me? A friend of mine has a p-p-picture here, somewhere."

All right, that was how it started. Freddy pushed away the empty coffee cup and idly watched the passers-by. So many different kinds of people here—from dapper gentlemen with refined looking ladies to the toughs who might very well be Hudson Duster gangsters. There were collegiate-looking fellows, wearing Harvard caps, and thin, young women wearing shortened skirts and bobbed hair. And the artists, artists everywhere, looking for all the world like common ne'er-do-wells except for splotches and swipes of paint, pastels or marble dust.

Baron Willy and his clutch of artist friends brought Freddy here, to Greenwich Village, after the Armory Show. What were their names? He could picture their faces easily. Most of them were his age, but one was slightly older, Marsden Hartley, that was it! The chap with the painting at the Armory Show. He was a fine, fair fellow with a knotted smile. That's right, he was heading back to France on the same ship Willy was taking. When were they leaving?

Today!

"Oh, no," Freddy groaned. Had he had a chance to say good-bye? Would he ever see those fellows again?

He realized he would miss Willy. In the few days they had together, Willy had shown him so much, taught him so much.

And last night. Freddy could feel his blood buzzing through his body at the recollection, and his cheeks burned. A small flat with wild-colored murals on the walls that seemed to dance in the candlelight, a small group of people singing, drinking and laughing. Through the hours, the group gradually dwindled until Freddy and Willy were alone. Did he imagine the caresses and kisses? And now Willy was gone!

"Freddy!"

Freddy leapt to his feet and turned. "Willy!" he cried. "I thought you'd left!"

Pain knifed through his head. Freddy groaned and slumped in his chair.

Willy sat next to him and pulled a silver flask from a pocket inside his coat. "Hair of the d-d-dog, friend?" he chuckled, nudging Freddy with his elbow.

Freddy checked to see if anyone was looking before he splashed a jigger full into his empty coffee cup. "Thanks," he said with a rueful grin, and gulped it down. "Much better," Freddy gasped, handing back the flask.

Willy rose. "C'mon, Freddy. Let's go for a w-walk. The air will clear your head." Looking sideways, Freddy admired Willy's aristocratic profile. By the light of day, even with the softening of the fog, Freddy saw that Willy was older than he first guessed, maybe in his 40s, with hamster cheeks about to turn to jowls and large ears. Still, Willy walked with a casual elegance, his coat swaying in rhythm to his even gait.

Together, the two ambled toward the great arch of Washington Square. Freddy felt the fog lift in his brain. Near the fountain, he stopped suddenly and pointed at the concrete. "Am I seeing things?" he asked Willy.

Making their way from the edge of the fountain and down the walk to the other side of the park were the wet imprints of a woman's bare feet. Someone, some female, must have been in the water recently, judging from the dark, small footsteps, Freddy guessed. Someone with tiny feet and high arches.

Willy laughed. "N-no, you're not seeing things," he said. "There's a lovely young w-woman who lives in a flat right off the park, and she takes a daily dip in the fountain. Without c-c-clothes, of course. She's well-known around the Village."

"I'd imagine so," Freddy replied, grinning. "What's her name?"

Willy tilted his head as he thought. "D-don't know I ever knew her name. I m-m-must have been distracted when I met her. She'd just come out of the fountain then, and was shivering from the cold. We didn't g-get much of a chance to talk."

Freddy laughed. "It's so good to see you, Willy. I thought you'd already left for France."

"Actually, the ship leaves this afternoon," Willy replied. "I was hoping to find you. I want to know how to r-reach you when I get back."

Willy gestured to a wrought iron bench facing the massive white fountain, and the two sat down. "Huh," said Freddy. "I don't know."

"You don't know? You don't know w-where I can reach you? Or you don't know if you want to be reached?" asked Willy, hurt edging his words.

Freddy's head jerked up as he realized what Willy was thinking. "No, no, Willy. That's not it. I want you to reach me. It's just . . . ."

"Just what?" Willy asked, his expression guarded.

Freddy shrugged. "Everything's changed. These last few days, the world is different for me." He shook his head. "I can't go back. I won't. But I don't know what to do."

A smile spread across Willy's face and he tipped his hat back on his head. "Why F-f-freddy, it sounds like you want to start your life f-fresh, is that it?"

Freddy nodded and looked down at his hands, which were clutching his knees like eagle talons. He relaxed his grip and deliberately flexed his fingers. "I want more. I want this, this . . ." He groped for the right words, and couldn't find them.

Willy clapped Freddy on the back, nearly sending him tumbling off the bench. "Excellent," Willy crowed. "Nothing better for a soul than a complete life ch-change."

Freddy looked at Willy, bewildered. "A life change?"

Willy laughed. "Hell, Freddy, I do it all the t-t-time. It keeps things interesting. Get up and let's walk. Tell me what you want to d-do."

Freddy took Willy's proffered arm, and pulled himself off the bench. "What I want to do?"

"Certainly. Not what you sh-should do, but what you want to do. Not who you sh-should be, but who you want to be." The two men fell into step and made their way along the walk.

Freddy listened to the sound of their footsteps. Willy's was softened by fine leather and the satisfying little click of the metal taps on his heels. Freddy's step was more of a shuffle. Self-consciously, he lifted his feet as he walked. Willy didn't seem to notice.

"So?" said Willy.

Freddy's mind jerked back to their conversation. What was it? Oh. He blurted the first thing that came to his mind, the first thing that always came to his mind.

"I want to be an artist. I want to make money at it, so I can work on my art and live comfortably," Freddy said. He flushed. "I know that sounds ridiculous."

"N-nothing of the sort!" said Willy. "That sounds like a fine life. A wonderful life. Now you must d-decide to do it."

Willy's ebullience was frustrating, Freddy thought. He had no idea of the poor living Freddy could barely eke out (if he still had a job! he remembered with an inner groan). Willy had money, breeding. He could do anything. "It's not as simple as that," Freddy said.

"Of c-course it is!" Willy said.

Freddy stopped. "You don't understand, Willy. You don't know a damn thing about me!" His voice had started out plaintive, but he finished almost shouting.

Willy faced him. "Don't be a f-fool, Freddy. I don't need to know a d-damn thing about you. You're the one who decides. Th-that's the hard part. Changing is easy."

"Easy. Right."

Willy's face grew thoughtful. "You have to be w-willing to let everything, everyone else go. You have to b-become what you want. You have to immerse yourself in who you intend to be, what you intend to do. You m-must believe it. You have to create a new r-reality."

Freddy shook his head. "Create a new reality?"

Scowling, Willy pulled a silver cigarette case from the folds of his coat, opened it and pulled out a cigarette. He replaced the case and extracted a black cigarette holder from the same pocket in a smooth, elegant flourish. Willy lit his cigarette and began pacing the walk, striding through his own cloud of smoke. "Look, Freddy, look around you. W-what do you see?"

"Fog, a fountain, a pathway," Freddy said.

"N-no, around us!" Willy exclaimed. "What is all th-this?"

Freddy looked around, taking in the huge marble arch, the stretches of grass and the grand houses that ringed the open space. "Oh. You mean, Washington Square?"

"That's it!" Willy exclaimed. "B-but it's not really Washington Square. I m-mean, underneath, is it?"

Freddy shrugged helplessly. "What are you talking about? You're bringing back my headache."

Obligingly, Willy fished out his brandy flask and handed it to Freddy. As Freddy sipped, Willy talked. "Do you know what Washington Square was b-before it became a park? It was a cemetery, old boy, a p-potters field. More than

10,000 s-souls were buried here, m-many from a penitentiary close by. And it was a hanging g-grounds, where offenders were executed."

Willy waved his cigarette holder. "Before that, this was a marsh, a smelly m-marsh."

Freddy capped the flask and handed it back to Willy. "So?"

Willy put his arm around Freddy's shoulders. "So now, when you look around you, w-what do you see?"

Freddy groaned. "I'm sorry, Willy, all I see is Washington Square."

"P-precisely!" Willy exclaimed. "That's it. What it was before has nothing to do with what it is n-now! It's not a swamp, not a graveyard, none of that! What it is now is w-what it's been made into!"

The idea began to glow in the back of Freddy's head. "You're saying that I can be what I choose to be, that it has nothing to do with who I was, where I came from? Is that it?"

"Yes, yes, yes! Be who you are, r-regardless of whom you were. The Freddy you create is yours, yours only. Is it really you? Of course it is!"

"Damn!" Willy looked stricken. He pulled a gold pocket watch from his vest.

"What is it?"

"The b-boat! I have a thousand things to do before it leaves," said Willy. "Look here, Freddy, I'll let you know where you can reach me through General D-delivery here in New York, all right?"

Freddy nodded, tears stinging his eyes.

"W-what did you say your last name was?" Willy asked.

"Schnitzer," Freddy said, his throat aching.

Willy stared at him. "Sh-sh-Schnitzer?"

Freddy nodded.

Willy shook his head. "W-word of advice, my friend? The first thing you need to do is find a new name. Freddy Sh-Schnitzer? That's not you at all."

"Change my name?" Freddy said, startled.

"Certainly. Everyone does it. I d-do it," Willy shrugged.

"You?"

Willy laughed and patted Freddy on the cheek. "You're so innocent. Of course I m-made up my name. For f-fun. And to p-protect my reputation."

"For fun?" Freddy asked, perplexed.

"Of course. D-don't you see? It's a pun, old man, a p-play on words. For my special gentlemen friends. 'Baron Willy.' Get it?"

Freddy blushed a deep red. "Oh."

Willy embraced him. "You'll think of s-something, my dear, I'm sure. Au revoir."

Freddy watched Willy walk away, until the fog swallowed him at the great marble arch.

Freddy slumped onto a cold iron bench.

"I'll think of something."

5

FLEDGLING BOHEMIANS

1913 - GREENWICH VILLAGE - SIX MONTHS LATER

Swathed in a silk robe, Freddy leaned back and laughed at the antics of the other artists at his table, almost losing the turban he'd knotted on his head. A fellow wearing a paper crown and a bed sheet for a robe had climbed atop Freddy's table, declaring, "I am the Poet King! It was I who put historical poems in the Grand Opera and the Nobel Prize contests! Gather around, revelers, and I will sing you one of my songs!"

"Sing, Poet King!" "Silence! His Majesty will amuse us with a song!" "Wine for His Royal Highness!" Shouts rose from the crowd pressing in for a better view.

Polly's Restaurant, Freddy's favorite haunt in Greenwich Village, blazed with color, lights and gaiety. Freddy was exhilarated by a feeling of stolen joy.

It was all so much easier than he could have ever imagined.

Within hours of Willy's leave-taking, Freddy had been swept up by a clutch of young Village writers and artists who pounced on the fresh face in their midst. He'd been walking the streets of the Village for hours, mulling over what Willy said and not really sure what to do with the advice. Change his name? Change his life? Freddy knew, deep down, that this was exactly what he wanted to do. The prospect of returning to life in Jersey City now galled him.

But how? When? He needed some sort of a plan.

Freddy was so absorbed in his thoughts, he didn't sense the hours slipping by or see the shadows lengthen. He walked past people without really seeing them. He paused at store windows without registering what was displayed.

Freddy was jarred from his thoughts when a cluster of laughing young men and women overtook him on Christopher Street and swarmed around him with a great deal of friendly jostling and joking. At first, Freddy was frightened a little, but their voices were jolly and they generously shared their flasks of whiskey and gin with him.

"Hullo! Who is this? A new fellow for our band of merrymakers?" announced a tall fellow with wild brown hair, an untucked flannel shirt and a wide grin. He clapped Freddy on the shoulder. "Have we a new neighbor?"

Without waiting for Freddy's answer, the large man took Freddy by the arm. "You look a little lost," he said grinning. "Come with us. We're going to the Home for Working Women."

Freddy's mouth dropped open. Working women? Prostitutes? But there were ladies in this noisy group! A slight young woman with a blue beret perched on her blonde, bobbed hair took his other arm. "Don't looked so shocked," she said in a melodic voice. Her cheeks were rosy from the cold air and likely a few pulls of whiskey. Her gray eyes danced as she turned her head to better see Freddy. "That's the name of a bar. It's not really a home for working women."

She looked to Freddy like a pixie dressed in street clothes. Her nose and chin were aristocratic and delicate, but her mouth was wide and sensuous. Her blonde curls bounced as she walked, her pace somehow a combination of a stride and a skip. She wore no makeup, unlike the other women in the group, and looked to be no more than eighteen years old. She warmed Freddy with her sunny expression and a little squeeze to his arm.

"Don't be taken in by Cookie," warned the large man. "Everyone loves Cookie and we are helpless to the magic of her charms." He and Cookie laughed. "I'm John, John Reed," he said. "And that silly little siren is Cookie Cook. What's your name?"

Before Freddy could answer, John jerked his head in the direction of hooting from across Christopher Street. "Well done! Rehearsal's out early! Now this will be a party," he said, his oversized shirt flapping as he waved them over.

Name? Name! Freddy's mind raced, remembering Willy's advice. He wracked his brains trying to think of something elegant or clever. Nothing. All that came to him was that he was hunting for a new life. Maybe Searcher? Seeker? No. Hunter? Hunt? That could work. Hunt who?

Luckily, the celebrants were too busy jostling, drinking and joking to press him. They entered a shabby tavern and the shouted greetings and drink orders were almost deafening.

Freddy could barely keep up with all the goings-on. As people danced in the center of the room—men and women, women and women, men and men, and a few dancing by themselves but somehow with everyone—other couples huddled off to the sides, some talking, others necking. "It's all laughter and love, laughter and love," Cookie sang out to Freddy from the dance floor as he watched her gaily move from one partner to the next and the next.

Freddy didn't know a soul, but everyone sitting nearby drew him into conversations, arguments, songs and pranks as if he was a regular. His mug was never dry of beer and there was always someone shaking his hand or asking his opinion of almost anything: the Armory Show, the Communist Party ("Hey, if it's a party, I'm all for it," Freddy joked to the howls of the others around the table), free love, argyle versus silk socks, and which ocean liner had the best double-berths.

Freddy glowed in the camaraderie, soon chiming into the raucous chatter. He'd never had so much fun. When Cookie, exhausted from dancing, finally plopped into the chair next to him, Freddy greeted her with a smile blurred by too much beer. She pulled off her blue shoes and tossed them onto the table. "That's enough dancing for this little girl," she said, laughing. "Darling, give me your beer."

She drank thirstily and smiling happily, handed the empty mug back to Freddy. "Deee-lightful," she said. "Now, I must ask you something. Something of terrible importance." Her grin belied the somber words.

"Yes?" said Freddy, grinning back.

"Your name, darling. I can't call you 'darling' forever, you know. Unless, of course, that is your real name," Cookie said. Freddy sensed a pause in the tavern, as if others were listening, waiting to hear the handle to apply to the newcomer. He saw Reed looking at him and grinning.

"My name?" said Freddy, stalling.

"Yes, darling, your name," Cookie replied. "We all admire your mysterious persona, but it's past midnight. Time to unmask. Tell little Cookie your name, please."

Freddy paused. Nothing came to mind. He opened his mouth, with no idea of what might come out. What had he come up with earlier?

"Hunt?"

"You don't sound so sure." Cookie giggled.

"I'm not."

Cookie turned to better see John Reed as he teased his current love interest, Mabel Dodge, a sculptor, someone told Peter. Mabel stood regally at the center of the restaurant, wearing an emerald sari and a gold silk turban.

"Ah, Sri Dodge! And where have you hidden your asp, my little snake charmer?" John bowed and stretched his hand to the hem of Mabel's sari, which she snatched from his reach.

"My asp is quite safe in my Forbidden Temple, you wretched mongoose," Mabel retorted. "Forbidden to you, at any rate."

The onlookers roared with laughter. How quickly the two parried their cruel double entendres! Freddy recalled Willy's advice about using a name with a double meaning. Freddy was stuck with "Hunt" as part of his name. Hunt what? Hunt Club? Hunt Rabbits?

Freddy shook his head. Stupid, stupid, stupid. Why couldn't he come up with anything? The drinks fuzzed his thinking.

Hmmmm. What if Hunt was the last name, not the first? Witch Hunt? Man Hunt? Freddy grinned. No, too obvious. Duck Hunt? Aha! How about Dick Hunt? Freddy could call himself Richard Hunt, Dick to his special friends.... No, too obscure. It had to be something else.

Freddy's mind was like a bloodhound on a chase, racing frantically for a while, then suddenly stopping, only to gallop at full speed without warning. He couldn't let go of his vulgar train of thought. If he could just get it right. What other names for his.... Pecker? Prick? No. Willy already had Willy. What about Johnson? No. Manhood? Freddy snorted. Too ridiculous.

What else? What else? He ransacked his brain. When he was small, what did Ma call it? What was that?

"Wash everywhere, even your peter," she'd sing out at bathtime.

Peter!

Freddy tried it out, rolling it over in his mind. Peter Hunt. Peter Hunt. Peter Hunt. Yes! That was it!

When Cookie turned back to the table, Freddy smiled. "As I was saying, my name... it's Peter Hunt."

At 3 a.m., Peter stood outside the door of the Home for Working Women wondering what to do next. He had no place to stay now that Willy was gone, and was too shy to ask any of the partygoers he'd just met. He pulled his collar up around his neck and decided to find a bench in Washington Park when a small gloved hand slipped into the crook of his arm.

"Oh, Peter, here you are, darling! I've been looking all over for you!" Cookie beamed up at him and nudged him with her elbow. "See, John? Peter's taking me home." Reed's large frame filled the doorway. "All right, little siren. But I take you next time," he boomed, and turned back into the bar.

"This way," said Cookie, leading Peter down MacDougal Street. "John's sweet, but he won't take 'no' for an answer," she said when they were out of earshot. "And I don't want to make an enemy of Mabel. She's very jealous."

Cookie looked at Peter from the corners of her eyes. "I saw you with Willy and his friends last night, and decided you would be a much safer escort."

"Oh," said Peter, confused. "Oh!" he exclaimed when he realized what she meant.

"It's all right, you know. I accept people for whoever they are. Don't worry about me," said Cookie.

"But, but," Peter groped for words. "But I don't know!"

Cookie stopped and studied Peter's face by the dull glow of the streetlight. "Oh dear," she said after a long pause. "That was tactless. I'm so used to all this 'free love' stuff, I forget my manners. I'm so sorry." Her large, gray eyes filled with tears.

"No need to apologize," Peter said. "I mean, I understand the confusion. I was with Willy, and ... oh, I don't know what's happening to me!" He smiled weakly. "But you're perfectly safe with me. I'm not, uh, interested in romance right now."

"Neither am I!" Cookie said, her face brightening. "You're a good sport. Let's go on, shall we?"

By the time they stopped in front of the Cookie's slumping rooming house, she'd told Peter her life story. The youngest of 10 children born to struggling eye doctor in St. Louis, Cookie was five years old when she was sent to live with her father's sister in Chicago. "It was the best thing that could have happened to me."

Auntie Rae was a milliner with an exclusive clientele that visited her shop on State Street only by appointment. A tall and imposing widow, Auntie Rae "was more of a snob than the snobs were," said Cookie. "She was so intimidating, Mrs. McCormick and Mrs. Armour, the richest ladies in town, would practically fall over themselves in gratitude when she accepted one of their orders. Of course, she also made absolutely gorgeous hats."

As Cookie grew, Auntie Rae made it her business to school the child in manners, social demeanor and the finer arts, such as embroidery and landscape painting, in which Cookie (Auntie Rae insisted on calling her by her Christian name, Elisabeth) especially excelled.

As a widow and a businesswoman, Auntie Rae was the quintessential pragmatist, insisting on hard work, simple meals and few luxuries. "She didn't think much of any show of emotion, especially anger or affection," said Cookie. "But I could tell she had a soft spot for me. I did for her, too."

Using her connections, Auntie Rae managed to have Cookie enrolled on a scholarship into one of the better private schools in the city, "Not on the north side, but still pretty good," and planned to send her ward to college. "You'll have much better prospects of marrying well," Auntie Rae said.

Cookie rebelled. She had her heart set on art school. "Since my grades weren't all that terrific, Auntie Rae agreed, but only if I attended school in Boston, where the best families lived."

"Here we are," said Cookie as they rounded the corner to Carmine Street. "I have a room up in the attic for weekends in New York. My aunt has no idea that $2 of my monthly 'pin' money goes for that. Over there, across the street, is where a bunch of Harvards share a place."

"Havards?" asked Peter.

"Harvard students. They're the cream of the crop as grooms go," said Cookie, dropping her voice to a loud whisper. "Here, I can keep my eye on them, and they can keep their eyes on me."

"Oh!" said Peter. He walked Cookie up the steps and began to take his leave.

"I can't believe I've talked so much. And you barely said a word! Not that I'd let you get a word in," Cookie said as she rummaged in her purse for her keys. "Where's your flat?"

Peter shrugged.

Cookie's mouth dropped open. "Oh my dear! You don't have a place yet? Well come in and stretch out on the porch." She quietly closed the door and put her fingers to her lips. "Just don't make a noise so my housemates don't know you're here. Try to leave before dawn," she whispered. "And don't you ever, ever tell Jack!"

The next few weeks carried Peter rapidly, relentlessly into his new life. He felt like a child's rubber duck, bobbing in a churning tub, laughing all the while.

Ma and Pa were confused when Peter told them his plans while packing his few belongings, but neither could hide the relief in their eyes. Peter moped when he was in the apartment, and whiled away the hours on his bed, making sheet after sheet of drawings. He seldom went out, and never brought friends home.

Still. "You're going to New York and you don't have a job?" said Ma, worry lining her face. "How will you live?"

"Cheaply," Peter answered. "I've got some savings and I hear the new theaters in the village need people to paint sets and design costumes. I'll get along."

Pa shook his head. "You know, I can't help you." His eyes searched Peter's face. The boy was a young man now, standing a little taller than his father. Peter's face was mature, with a wide forehead, thin nose, and a determined chin. His straight, honey-colored hair was tousled, and Pa absently brushed it out of Peter's eyes. Overcome by a swell of emotion, he hugged Peter, hard. "Do well," he said. "Don't fail."

Ma's mouth was set in a straight line across her sad, lined face. She clutched her son in a fierce embrace and suddenly pushed him back. "You must come to see your Ma now and then," she said brusquely. Peter nodded.

Six-year-old Dorothy was devastated, and wailed once she understood he was moving out. "Please don't leave, Freddy," she begged. "It won't be fun here without you."

Peter knelt in front of her and held her close. "Dear Dottie," he said soothingly. "Be a good girl, go to school, and once I'm settled, I'll bring you to have fun in the city, all right?" She ran away from his arms and flung herself on his bed.

Despite the raw emotions he left behind in the apartment, Peter whistled happily to himself as he almost skipped down the stairs and out onto the street. "That wasn't so bad. If I do well, I'll send them money," he promised himself.

Peter took a small room in Greenwich Village, the spare bedroom of an aspiring sculptor and his girlfriend, who both strode around the flat nude all the time (ever-ready for sudden inspirations, Peter supposed).

He scrounged around for work, and soon found jobs painting scenery for the small theaters scattered throughout the Village. He didn't make much money, but it was enough to pay for his room, art supplies and a modest meal every day. Peter joined an informal "community" art class, where Village artists gathered to work, critique each other and swap ideas. Soon, Peter's small room was filling up with his canvases and sketches.

But his days weren't spent entirely on work. The evenings in the Village were bright and lively, with hundreds of young people from across the country set on shrugging off the social inhibitions of their former small town lives. On every street rang the sounds of impromptu parties and merrymaking. Weekends were even more crowded, as students from colleges all over New England took the train to the Village, ripe for fun. Sprinkled through the throngs were knots of well-to-do partiers from the tonier parts of New York, "slumming it" in the Village.

Peter was soon aware of the huge divide between the Village Bohemians and the reserved moneyed set living further up Fifth Avenue. The adjoining neighborhoods could just as well be separated by an ocean, they had so little truck with each other. Peter could see, too, that success in the Village wouldn't necessarily guarantee success in the rest of the city. In fact, being a Bohemian would likely work against any long term aspirations.

After a couple months, Cookie started a campaign to convince Peter to move to Boston. He could share a flat with a friend of hers, a playwright named Guy Jones, she said, and attend classes at the Boston School of Practical Arts.

"You're not sure what you want to do, but you know it has to be in art, right?" Cookie said one evening at Polly's Restaurant, talking underneath the usual clamor. They huddled over a small table by the glowing fireplace. "Well, take some classes, try out different things, and make friends and contacts, too. I've met all sorts of folks, and they're so talented."

"I don't know," Peter said.

"Well, it's a lot easier to find work in Boston," Cookie argued. "It's like a big little city. Dozens of rich people like to hire college artists as waiters and house painters and things. They feel they're supporting the arts or something."

Peter nodded. His interest was piqued.

"C'mon Peter, be a sport," Cookie implored. "Boston would be so much fun if you were there. We can come back to the Village every weekend."

Peter laughed. "What does it matter, Cookie? Why should my coming to Boston make any difference?"

Cookie shrugged and looked down into her beer.

Strange. Peter just couldn't figure out Cookie's feelings for him—or his feelings for Cookie. Every time they stumbled into one another, they fell into easy conversations. They both roared at ribald jokes and bawdy limericks, and they both leapt to join in spontaneous hijinks, like when a group of Provincetown Theater folks decided to perform an impromptu street rendition of King Arthur. Peter was an unconvincing dragon and Cookie an irrepressible giggling Guinevere.

They had so many unspoken things in common, Peter thought. They both watched everyone and every activity around them with intense scrutiny, each trying to better understand the people and situations they witnessed. Peter paid close attention to gestures and greetings and mannerisms, selecting those idiosyncrasies he thought added a touch of elegance to his own repertoire. He wasn't quite sure why Cookie looked so closely at people from beneath her eyelashes. Her attention was often fixed on the most fashionable women and the most elegant men.

Neither showed any interest in intimate relationships, either with each other or the people that giddily floated around them. In the Village's climate of exuberant "free love," Cookie and Peter joined in on the jokes and innuendoes, but managed to hold themselves aloof from any encounters.

"Cookie," Peter said.

Cookie's head jerked up and she frowned. "I like you, Peter. That's all. But, for me, that's everything. I've never had a friend like you, and I don't want to pull it to pieces to see how it works. Can't we just see how it goes?"

The move to Boston was exhilarating. Cookie was waiting for Peter at the depot when his Monday night train arrived. After an enthusiastic embrace, she handed him a yellow rose "that I pilfered from one of the nicest yards in the city." They lugged his bags to Beacon Street, where they stopped in front of a genteel-looking apartment building with ivy crawling its walls up to the small wrought-iron balconies.

There, Cookie introduced Peter to his new roommate, a serious bespectacled fellow named Guy Jones who barely looked up from his typewriter to nod. "I know Guy's old roommate, and he couldn't take the constant racket from the typewriter," Cookie whispered to Peter. "That's how I heard about the room."

Early the next morning, Cookie rapped on the apartment door to whisk Peter off to sign up for classes at the art school. With Cookie's effusive introductions and his own charm (conveyed with words and expressions he'd picked up by watching people in the Village and along Fifth Avenue), Peter had a raft of friends by the end of the week.

On a whim, Peter signed up for classes in batik and Russian art, and was astonished at how greedily his mind ate up the concepts and techniques, how readily his hands replicated images, and expanded them into his own. When he wasn't in class or at one of the innumerable parties his friends threw, Peter was working with the independent theaters, volunteering to paint sets and, later, dream up costumes to go with the sets. The directors and the audiences raved about his designs, likening them to sets they'd seen at the Ballet Russe in Paris.

It seemed to Peter that almost all really promising artists or writers had been to Paris. "Someday, as soon as possible, I must get to Paris," Peter decided. "I must see the artists, hear the music. And I must see the Ballet Russe."

In the meantime, he began to develop a small side business in batik fabrics using traditional wax and dye methods. A couple of fashionable women saw costumes Peter had made for a friend's play, using cottons he'd batiked in Russian designs. They asked him to create similar robes, but with much finer materials. He happily obliged, working hard to make the textures and shades fit their personal coloring. The women were delighted. As their wealthy friends inquired about the new fabrics, Peter's clientele grew. His easy manner and occasional flirtatious jokes made him a favorite "extra man," and he was often called on to "lighten up" a tea or cocktail hour.

It wasn't too long before more and more upper-crust clients came to Peter for fabrics made especially for their walls, curtains, and furniture. When they asked his price, he would say only "whatever you think it is worth, Madame." Peter was astounded by the wads of bills they pressed into his hands.

He stashed away the money for his passage to France. He enrolled in more classes, both in techniques and European designs. Every new pattern or stroke Peter learned in class he took to his batiked fabrics, and his clients demanded to see his latest decorated silks, satins or tapestries.

This popularity allowed him to cultivate a certain eccentricity of style, good for showing off his work and for demanding the attentions of people—well-moneyed or not—who welcomed less conventional tastes and ideas. In the evenings or on his weekend trips to New York with Cookie, Peter would wear his luxuriant fabrics like a sheik's tunic with a scarf knotted at his neck, or wrapped on his head like a turban. People recognized him immediately and greeted him with enthusiasm.

The avant garde painters, writers, sculptors and poets Peter met in the Village filled him with creative energy and an unending sense of fun. They loved to play, and play hard, each trying to outdo the other in outrageous behavior.

Men and women who lived in the Village sensed a tenderness in Peter. Many shared their ideas, their dreams and their plans, along with details of blooming or lost loves, while huddling with him at a cafe table or in a corner at a party. Peter listened with all his heart and did his best to encourage them or console them.

Peter could be so receptive and so comforting, nobody realized that despite the confessions of their deepest souls, he remained distant from them, still not ready to share his own dreams.

Peter saw Cookie almost every day. They often spent long, quiet hours in the Beacon Street apartment he shared with Jones. Leaving the door ajar to appease the landlady, Cookie would sketch or paint or write poetry while Peter hovered over the hot kettles of wax and dye simmering on the small stove.

"We're the perfect couple," Peter once announced to Cookie. "We expect nothing and get great comfort from each other."

"Too bad I'll never have a husband as easygoing as you," Cookie replied with a grin.

One day, as Peter was helping Mrs. Elliot, one of his rich patronesses, into a cab outside the Ritz Hotel on Newberry, he saw Cookie walking towards him with a short, cherub-faced young man, a college student, Peter guessed. He froze. Cookie hadn't noticed him yet, and, for some reason, Peter didn't know if he should greet Cookie or stay quiet. She glanced up and saw him just a few steps away, and a warning flicker of her eyes was all he needed. Peter turned and bent over Mrs. Elliot, fussing over her comfort.

Assured that Mrs. Elliot was settled and the driver paid, Peter straightened and closed the cab door. He didn't see the gloved hand waving in the cab window. He was watching Cookie lift her face to something the young man was saying. She gleamed at him a radiance Peter had never seen before, an expression that was inviting, enthralled and, yes, deliberate. Peter's throat tightened. He knew that look.

It was the same expression he wore when he charmed the wealthy women who came to him for fabrics. Peter so beguiled his affluent clients that they actually competed with each other in offering him favors: a seat at the opera, an invitation to dine with the latest royal arrivals from Europe, a weekend at a country estate. With a few words, a light hand on a wrist, Peter made them feel that they held a power over him, a power that commanded his attention and admiration.

That's all the women really wanted. They didn't need lovers and their complications. They didn't need the endless write-ups in the society columns. What these lonely, rich women needed, Peter divined, was affection, fond appreciation of their abilities, their efforts or their better attributes. Peter never failed them. He lavished each woman with gallantry and praise, careful that each compliment was always rooted in truth. Mrs. Elliot, for instance, was delighted when Peter commented on her bright, green eyes, and she demurred that the boys who courted her long ago had said the same thing.

In response, the women were unfailingly generous with Peter, not only with cash, but with cachet. As they drew him into their circles, his business expanded from fabrics to consultations on interior design or assessing bargains in artworks and antiques.

Sometimes, Peter wondered if he was too calculating with these kind women. But, in the end, he always reasoned that everyone benefited. "Everyone's much happier," he'd tell himself. "Isn't that what's really important?"

Now, in the flash of a moment, Peter saw that Cookie had the same effect on people. She'd simply never used that charisma on anybody, at least not in Peter's presence.

Not until now.

Cookie, Peter sensed, had found her quarry.

6

War Wounds

1917 - France

It was like a nightmare, time and reality were so distorted. He was in Boston, and then on a ship. France! He was finally in France! But what kind of country was this? Deep, gray smoke, exploding bombs, bullets tap-tap-tapping, hideous screams, blood. What was he doing here? Surely, he was dreaming. And he couldn't wake himself up.

"P-peter Hunt, eh? My that IS clever. So much better than Schnitzer, eh?"

That voice! Nasal, British. Peter knew it immediately. But he couldn't seem to swim up from sleep. He couldn't open his eyes. Or his mouth. What was happening?

"Here, now, is that any way to g-greet an old friend? Let's shake hands. Can you feel my hand? C-can you squeeze it?"

Peter tried to squeeze back.

"Well, now, I saw your fingers m-move! Give it another try. Squeeze my hand."

Peter strained, putting every ounce of will in to squeezing the warm hand.

"Excellent! You should be c-coming round soon. I'll drop in later."

Vexed, Peter tried to cry out, but his mouth still wouldn't obey. How could it be? Was he imagining things?

Was that Willy?

Peter clung to Willy's arm as he stumbled out of the hospital into the gray day. Blinking, he looked around. Everything was dismal and colorless: rubble coated in gray dust, gray skies, a tree's skeleton tilted over a trench. Peter gagged on the dust and the acrid smell that reminded him of burning garbage.

With his free hand, Willy lit two cigarettes and passed one to Peter. Peter's hand shook uncontrollably as he tried to take it, until, finally, Willy placed it between his fingers for him. Peter nodded his thanks.

"So what b-brings you here, to this charming corner of the world?" Willy asked, politely averting his gaze until Peter managed to put the end of the cigarette in his mouth.

"I might ask you the same thing," Peter said through clenched lips, trying to keep the cigarette in place.

Willy shrugged. "Just doing my b-bit for Britain. Did you know I used to be a doctor?"

Peter shook his head. The cigarette waved from its precarious perch, and he spat it to the ground in frustration.

"I was horrible, mind you. I could do the w-work, but had no taste for it," Willy said. "I gave it up to write." He held his cigarette to Peter's mouth to allow a long, satisfying drag.

"Thanks," said Peter. "I didn't know you were a writer. I guess I don't know much about you at all."

"Ah, who knows anything, really, about anyone?" Willy said. "It doesn't matter now, anyway. N-now, I am an orderly." He flicked away the cigarette butt and led Peter to a low stone wall. "Sit here, and t-tell me how I came to find you in my hospital."

Peter sat with a grateful sigh. "You know, I'm not quite sure," he said. He reached to the back of his head and felt the damp bandage there. "Last thing I remember, let's see, I was near my ambulance. I'm an ambulance driver, you know."

Willy nodded.

"I signed up a few months ago. It was quite the thing to do back in the States. All the young men of position in Boston and New York were eager to help out. So, I went, too." Peter chuckled ruefully. "Of course, these chaps could afford cars and knew how to drive. I had to have someone teach me after we arrived. Here I was trying to learn how to shift gears as bullets flew by. Qu'elle catastrophe!"

Willy chuckled. "I c-can imagine. It must have been quite a sight."

Peter grinned. "Oh, it was. And I had no idea what war is really like. I think we all set off like this would be a lark, an adventure." He shook his head. A bitter sorrow flickered across his face. "Many of the fellows I came with have been hurt or . . . worse," he said. His body trembled even harder. "Willy, how long does this damn shaking last?"

Willy patted his arm. "It'll get b-better, old son. You'll see. Head wounds take their own time to mend. Now t-tell me how you were hurt."

Peter frowned, "I'm not sure I remember," he said. "I was struggling with something." He straightened suddenly. "Dear God, it was Tebbs!"

Peter leapt from the ambulance and crouched at its side for a moment, waiting for a break in the shelling. He didn't know who was firing, and he didn't care. It was too close, much too close, to the small medical tent less than a mile from the front.

A shell hit a few yards away, and Peter covered his head with his arms as fragments and shrapnel rained around him. Nothing for a moment, and still nothing. Crouching, he ran around the back and gestured to his partner, ducking on the other side of the ambulance. "C'mon Max! Let's get out of here!"

Max, a dark-skinned Alsatian who spoke almost no English, made a stooping run behind Peter. Already, the medics were piling stretchers of wounded outside the tent flaps.

Peter seized the handles on the nearest stretcher and Max took the other end. Awkwardly, they tried to carry the wounded man close to the ground while hurrying to the ambulance. Once in the back, protected by little more than a canopy of plywood and two-by-fours, they strapped the victim in place and ran back for the next fellow.

The shelling started again, but some miles off. They still had time. Peter and Max hustled the second, then the third patient into the ambulance, Peter closed his ears to their groans, their screams, and refused to look at their ravaged faces, their bloodied sheets. If he looked, Peter knew, he would falter, and he couldn't afford the time or the emotion right now.

Finally, the last stretcher. Peter ran low to its foot, while Max ran to the head. Silence. Peter took a breath. That meant a shell was on the way, headed for who knew where. He nodded and Max and he gripped the handles.

"Fucking Schnitzer!"

Startled, Peter tried to make out the mangled face. Tebbs! Peter's stomach seized up and he dropped the handles. Tebbs screamed. Peter's eyes traveled down the stretcher, and he saw a bloody bandaged stump where Tebbs' once had a right leg.

"Get the fuck away from me!" Tebbs yelled, thrashing in the stretcher so hard that Max lost his grip and dropped his end. "I'd rather die here than have you touch me!" Tebbs cried.

Stunned, Peter straightened. Tebbs! He couldn't believe it. Peter and Max exchanged a look. A shell shrieked through the air above their heads. Max bent down to pick up his end.

Then nothing.

Peter shook his head and glanced at Willy. "We were picking up wounded. A shell landed too close, I think," he said.

Willy nodded. "Well, you're g-going to be all right. You're faculties are coming b-back," Willy said, standing. "Let's get you back in to rest a bit."

Peter allowed Willy to help him up, and paused as he tried to regain his balance.

"Willy, tell me something," he said as they walked back to the hospital. "Did you check in other wounded when I came in?"

"About 10 in your group, I'd g-g-guess," Willy said. "You're wondering about M-max? You were the only ambulancer in the lot. Max must have found a new p-partner."

"Good," said Peter, embarrassed that he hadn't thought to ask about Max at all. "But the others. Do you remember an American soldier, lost his leg? His tags would have said Tebbs."

Willy frowned. "I don't recall. But, so many people come in all the t-time. I could check. F-friend of yours?"

"No." Peter said sharply. He controlled his voice. "Don't bother. I just wondered."

"Hurry up, Willy! We don't have much time!"

Willy harrumphed and continued to pick straw from his uniform's pants leg. "L-look at this! I just had the sweetest French lad clean these for me! And already it's c-covered with hay and smells like a c-cow."

He straightened and smoothed the front of his jacket. "What have we come to? Traveling in the back of a w-wagon. Oh!" Willy looked at Peter and grinned. "Well, you're certainly feeling b-better, aren't you?"

"Oh, hurry up, Willy. I want you to see what we've been working on."

Willy looked about. Another village mutilated by war, he thought, taking in the mangled buildings and debris on the street. Men and women with grim faces worked slowly in the ruins. Children pawed wordlessly through a smoking pile of rubble, scavenging whatever they could. As they saw Peter, many of the villagers smiled and called out greetings, which Peter returned, addressing every one by their names.

"Bonjour, Monsieur Balotte! How is your knee today?" "Alors, ma petite Stephanie! Watch out for sharp edges." "Madame Ormay! Bonjour!"

Willy smiled and nodded in Peter's wake. Dear Lord, he knew everybody!

"Peter, what's the n-name of this village?" Willy called to Peter's back.

"Arras," Peter called back without turning. "We're not far from Marseilles." He hurried through the town square and ducked into a small alley alongside a stable. At the rear of the stable, Peter turned again.

Close on his heels, Willy almost ran Peter down as he rounded the corner.

"Whoa, old fellow!" Peter laughed. "We're here! Help me with this."

The two put their shoulders to the huge door that ran the height and half the width of the stable. "Wait here!" Peter ordered and vanished into the darkness inside.

Soon Willy could see a lantern flicker, then another, and another.

"Good Lord," he whispered.

There Peter stood, in the middle of an empty stable wearing a golden turban with a large ostrich plume, his arms outstretched. A magenta sash was wrapped around his waist, and a curved sword was tucked in it. He stood by a tall, brightly colored santos of the Virgin Mary and a satin canopy. Behind him stood strange, stylized pictures of an elephant, a camel and palm trees. "I'm an Arabian warlord, ready to protect my oasis from nomad marauders," Peter proclaimed.

Willy approached slowly, his eyes traveling from side to side, up and down, trying to take it all in. "W-what is all this?" he finally said.

Peter laughed, and spun around. Willy saw he was wearing yellow slippers with curled toes, each trimmed with a red tassel. "Do you know anything about pageants?" Peter asked.

"A little," said Willy.

Peter tugged his turban until it perched on his head at a rakish angle. "Well, a bunch of us in the Ambulance Corps were on leave in Marseilles, and we stumbled on this village. The people were awfully nice, and were fascinated by Americans."

"I wonder w-why," Willy said dryly.

Peter elbowed him. "They made us a wonderful meal, a feast, with real lamb, a few vegetables, food we hadn't enjoyed in a long time," he continued. "It was wonderful, and we ate like pigs. But, by the time we'd stuffed ourselves, we realized the villagers weren't eating anything."

"Ah ha!," Willy interrupted. "They'd p-poisoned the food!"

Peter gave him a withering look. "No, you cynic. Worse. They'd given us all their food, the best they had, and even killed their last lamb to feed us. They had nothing left."

"W-w-why?" Willy asked, incredulous.

Peter shrugged. "They were kind-hearted, to start with, and maybe they hoped we'd have something to give them. They were much too proud and polite to let on. And we didn't have much." He sighed. "We felt terrible."

"You should have," said Willy.

Peter grimaced. "Right. Well, we did. So we gave them everything we had on us—chocolates, rations, cigarettes, even military scrip, which we hoped they could use on the black market. Still, we could tell the people were trying to hide their disappointment."

Willy nodded. "All right. B-but what did that have to do with this?" he asked, gesturing at the stage and sets.

"I'm getting to that. We tried to talk with the villagers in our fractured French, and learned that they were about to celebrate the holiday of some saint or another, but had little left in the village to put on a proper pageant. That gave us an idea."

Peter and the other Americans set about building a shrine for the saint's image—which had so far survived intact, if not the worse for wear—using bits and scraps of lumber and metal from the piles of debris, and tools from their truck. Peter, using some odd pots of paint from the villagers, carefully restored the chipped paint on the saint. Then, ripping out the lining of his jacket, he used somebody's needle and thread to stitch a satin-like robe for the statue and bunting for her alter.

The villagers were delighted with the ambulancers' efforts and set about helping, making a crucifix with banded pieces of timber they then decorated with paint. Peter watched their work in fascination. Though crude, the designs were bright and cheerful, with embellished swirls and curves.

"It was so startling and uplifting to see colors, especially after months and months of nothing but the ashes of what was once a beautiful country," Peter recalled. "And to see such designs, made with such simple joy."

He complimented one of the men decorating the cross, and the man nodded, almost understanding Peter's bad French. He then led Peter to the stable, empty of horses, all the way back to a corner lit only by sunlight coming through the cracks in the outer wall. There, Peter saw a canvas-covered something, and he waited with anticipation as the villager pulled off the tarp.

Peter blinked at the sudden brilliance of color and shapes. There stood a little cart painted in a rainbow of colors with fetching little figures, roughly drawn, in various acts of celebration—drinking wine, eating food, holding flowers.

Peter walked slowly around the cart, taking it all in. "It was amazing. The designs were primitive, but very clear, and some quite detailed. You could tell what the characters were doing. It reminded me of the Russian designs I studied, but these were less structured, more emotional." He paused. "They were happy."

At the wide back of the cart, Peter could discern a man and a woman, sharing a bouquet of flowers, all created with a minimum of strokes. Around them swirled hearts in every color.

Peter turned to the man who was standing a little away, beaming at Peter's fascination. Peter pointed to the image on the back. "Pour de mariage?" he asked.

A cloud crossed the villager's face. He frowned and nodded. "Ma femme," he said, his voice catching. He shrugged and hung his head. "Mort," he said.

"Le guerre?" Peter asked.

The man nodded, his eyes still cast down. "Un bombardement."

Peter sighed. So sad. Such lovely cart, a wedding cart, carefully stashed away in hopes it would survive the war, unlike the beloved wife pictured on its side.

"Triste, comme ça," Peter said, wincing at his mangling of the language. "Mais, la charrette est tres magnifique."

The villager lifted his head and smiled sadly. "Je retinir pour les memoires de temps heureux."

"To remember happy times," Peter said. "Oui." He helped the man lift the tarp and drape it over the cart. "Comment t'allez vous?" Peter asked. "Je m'appelle Peter."

"Je m'appelle Etienne," replied the villager.

"Etienne, voudrez vous, uh," Peter faltered, his vocabulary failing him. He gestured to the tarp. "Instruire? Moi? A decorer? Will you teach me?"

Etienne nodded, a smile slowly spreading across his face. "Oui!" he said simply.

"After that, I went to Arras whenever I could," Peter said to Willy. "So did the others. Whatever we could find—fabrics, sewing things, buttons, anything that might work for their pageants, we'd bring to the village. And we always brought something to eat, something good. I once brought celery from Marseilles. Today will be even better."

Before Willy could ask, a large silhouette of a man filled the opening in the wall. "Peter!" he bellowed, the name sounding like "Pee-tair." "Bonjour!"

"Etienne!" Peter shouted back, and dashed across the length of the stable. "Regardez! Poissons!"

He pulled a bundle wrapped in paper and string from beneath his tunic and handed it to Etienne. Carefully, the peasant unwrapped the package. Under several layers of wrapping were several cooked fish.

"Where in the world?" said Willy, gaping. "How d-did you get your hands on fish?"

Peter laughed as Etienne wrapped him in a bear hug. "Didn't you hear the shelling last night? Over the water?"

"Yes," said Willy, still confused.

"Once in a while, if a shell hits at just the right distance—close, but not too close—it blows the fish out of the water. Everyone scrambles and the fastest ones have fish for dinner! I traded my long underwear for these," Peter said.

As Etienne re-wrapped the fish, Peter emptied the pockets of his coat. Willy gaped. How did he stash away all this stuff? Bandages, pencils, gauze, even a dented tin plate. Etienne laughed in delight, scooped up the booty, and swept out the door.

"He's off to tell everybody, give everyone a share," Peter said. "Too bad I couldn't bring more fish. The parents will give theirs to their children."

"P-peter." Willy shook his head. "You give them bits of nothing, yet, in all this horror, you give them joy!"

It was just past dusk when Willy and Peter made it back to the rooming house next to the hospital. Willy reached around the doorsill and tugged out his duffel.

"You're leaving?" asked Peter.

"T-time to help someone who's really sick, old man. Not a lazy fellow like you," Willy said.

Peter held out his hand, and Willy saw it tremble. Willy seized the hand and shook it heartily. "I leave for England t-tonight, and then, who knows where they'll send me."

Peter nodded, his face drawn. "I'll miss you."

"Pah, you'll forget me the instant I'm gone," said Willy. He slung the duffel over his shoulder. "T-time to be off."

"Will we see each other again?" Peter asked, lightly touching Willy's arm. "Please."

Willy paused and thought. "Tell you what. If we both survive this b-blasted war, look for me in Paris. On the Left Bank, you'll find cafés. They'll know where I am."

He quickly hugged Peter and turned to go. Peter watched him walk away. He remembered watching Willy walk away before, so long ago, in Washington Square.

Suddenly, he called out, "Willy! Is that your name in Paris?"

Willy stopped, but didn't turn around. His voice was rough. "Oh, of course. Yes, it's Willy there. Ask for Willy Maugham."

"Outrageous! That's what it is! Outrageous! Take that monster out of our book! Immediately!"

I could hear Peter yelling, but I couldn't see him as I struggled to get the shampoo out of my eyes.

"Get out of my bathroom! Now!" I yelled, rubbing at my stinging eyes. "Talk to me after I'm dressed!"

I'd just curled up with a hot tea in the den when Peter appeared, lounging on the easy chair opposite me. His body was turned slightly away and he wouldn't look at me. Sulking, I guessed.

He sighed. *"I don't like the book anymore,"* he said. He dragged on the cigarette that appeared between his long fingers. *"I want you to stop."*

Stop? "Why?" I asked.

Peter shrugged. *"You focus too much on all the negative things, the sad things. That's not me."*

"It's the truth!"

"But it's not me. It sounds so sordid. Contrived."

"Well?"

Peter grimaced. *"None of it is necessary."*

"Peter, it's all part of what made you. Your beginnings, your family, your friends. People want to understand not just what you became but how you got there. Why you made the choices you did. What influenced you. Who influenced you."

"And that's why you feel it necessary to drag in that scoundrel, that poseur?" Peter flicked his cigarette away and crossed his arms. His face was creased in a scowl.

"Willy? Yes, that's why."

"Don't even say his name!" Peter shouted. *"He betrayed me, betrayed all of us. He was completely out of my life long before I died. He has no place in my story."*

Peter rose and stalked to the window.

"You know Willy has a place in your story," I said. "He was there at the beginning. In fact, he encouraged you, didn't he?"

Peter didn't move.

"Willy was there during the war. After you came back from the war, there were a number of years where you two had a lot of fun, remember?"

Peter said nothing.

I paused. "You don't remember? Why, there's even that picture."

"What picture?" Peter snapped.

Got him. "You know the one. You were dressed up like . . . ."

He rose five feet off the ground and stayed there. *"Dear God, not that picture."*

"Yes, and he'd written on the back, remember . . . 'To Peter . . . .' "

Peter covered his ears. *"Stop it! I can't stand it!"*

" . . . 'A man . . . who isn't one.'"

Peter vanished.

7

Madame Makes Up Her Mind

April 1918 - New York

Peter stood a few steps away from the brownstone and tried to compose his face and his thoughts. All his friends' rejoinders from the night before danced like champagne bubbles in his brain. When he came close to recalling some bit of advice, the bubble would pop. Did he have to drink so much last night?

Of course he did. A quiet cafe, frothy beer and bubbling wine helped loosen Horace's tongue, so Peter could get a better sense of his mother, the powerful Helena Rubenstein, who had commanded Peter's visit today. Then Crocker and Clements chimed in with hilarious accounts of past meetings with her, which, for the most part, unnerved rather than bolstered Peter's confidence.

A few more drinks, and they'd developed a plan of action for this morning's meeting.

"First, you need a title," Horace advised. "Mother likes titles, even though she knows most of them can be had for the price of a good horse. Still, she loves the sound of a good name, especially if it's royal."

"And you'll need to wear a well-made suit. Something fashionable," said Crocker. "She'll notice. But nothing too grand, either. She'll want to be better dressed than you. And leave your damn turban at home."

"Take her a little present," suggested Clements. "Say, one of your scarves. She loves getting something for nothing."

"And don't be shy about dropping names. Start with your wealthiest clients," Crocker said with a mischievous grin. "Just be selective. Don't use the name C. Templeton Crocker, for instance. My reputation could work against you."

Horace laughed. "Listen to me. When it comes to money, ask for twice what you hope to get. My mother loves to dicker. She insists on it."

It was past two in the morning before they said their good-byes, Horace, Clements and Crocker loudly wishing Peter good luck and clapping his back so hard he almost fell over.

"Fine fellows," Peter thought. Colin Clements had crossed his path the year before in Paris. After Peter mustered out from the ambulance corps, he tramped around Europe for several months, visiting Poland, Germany, Alsace, Italy, Sweden and even the Ukraine. He loved the glimpses of fine cities and sweeping countryside he found between the savage, blackened swaths of war.

In every country, he'd seek out some charming village where the peasants, amused by his horrible French or his awkward pantomimes of greeting, welcomed or, at least, tolerated him. At his prompting, many showed Peter their gaily decorated homes, wagons and furniture. Flattered by his interest, they'd show Peter how they painted their designs, and would explain the meanings of some of their symbols. Then they'd share their meals and their wine with him, before he set off on the road again.

After eight months of traveling, Peter decided to go to Paris, find a cheap loft, and work on developing the designs he'd collected in his travels. He had saved enough money before the war to stay at least a few months and still afford boat passage home.

Peter found a cold-but-clean walk-up in the Latin Quarter. Although it was furnished with only an uncomfortable bed, a table and a chair, it had a large window that brought in enough of the gilded French light so he could work.

Every evening, Peter took his meal of the day at one of the crowded cafes, filled with artists, musicians, poets and writers from all over the world. Peter asked around for Willy, to no avail.

One night, Peter stepped under the awning of the Rotonda Café, and found every table taken. As he turned to go, a chap sitting alone caught his eye and gestured for Peter to join him.

"Hullo, sport," said the fellow, who stood to reveal a tall, heavyset body clad in a worn dinner jacket. His black hair was wet and slicked straight back, and his mustache was curled with wax. He put a monocle in his eye and gestured for Peter to sit. "The place is packed and I don't know a soul," he said in a flat, Midwestern accent. "Tell me your name and we'll be dinner partners."

That's how Peter met Colin Clements. He found out later that Clements met a lot of people in a similar fashion. "I enjoy being surprised by strangers over a meal or a drink," Clements explained. An aspiring playwright from Nebraska, Clements, too, had served in the war and was traveling though Europe before returning to the States.

They took to each other immediately. Clements could talk at some length about anything and nothing, pontificating and opining in an affected theatrical voice, using the most stultifying language imaginable. Peter could listen for hours, entranced by the rapier wit and the pomposity of Clement's casual soliloquies. One day, after Peter unveiled one of his works, an interpretation of a peasant design, Clements intoned, "I'faith it is romantic! Very symbolistic! What crystal clarity! What admirable restraint! Surely this must be classical. Yet, there are strange gods in yonder world, garden pleasances, languorous queens, Pierrots and Pierrettes and moonlit nights. This is an apparition! intriguing, elusive and subtle." Clements continued in that vein for another 10 minutes before, weak with laughter, Peter interrupted him.

"So, then, old man, you like it?"

Clements laughed. "Buy me a drink and I'll tell you more."

Clements introduced Peter to C. Templeton Crocker a few days later, declaring, "You must be twins, tragically separated at birth, as evidenced by your uncannily similar visages." Indeed, Crocker was about the same height and had a slight build like Peter, and both had straight blond hair they combed to the back in a similar fashion. However, Crocker had the tan of an outdoorsman and affected a pipe, which he almost never lit.

"You may call me Templeton if you wish, but most find Crocker less of a mouthful," he said, shaking Peter's hand. He had a soft voice and elegant manners, Peter saw, but somehow looked out of place at the Rotonda. He seemed too polished, Peter decided.

"I know Crocker from the Portmanteau Theatre," Clements said, elaborately gesturing for a carafe of wine. "He's a librettist, in fact, working on America's first libretto of merit, a momentous endeavor for our country's anemic cultural offerings, bringing his exceptional vision to New York from far-off San Francisco."

"Clements, shut up," Crocker said with a grin. "You're sucking up all the air."

"What do you do in San Francisco?" Peter asked.

Crocker shrugged. "Write. Read. Dream. Spend my father's fortune," he said.

"He's from the Union-Pacific Crockers, don't you know," Clements offered before downing his wine in several loud gulps.

The three of them got along well, and often gathered for dinner or drinks at various cafes in Paris and, some months later, in taverns in the Village or on lower Fifth Avenue. So, when faced with a momentous meeting with none other than cosmetics queen Helena Rubenstein, who'd summoned Peter quite out of the blue through her dour son Horace, Peter summoned Clements and Crocker as reinforcements.

Their evening went well, perhaps too well, thought Peter as he straightened his tie and smoothed his hair before approaching the brownstone. His ears buzzed and the bright light gave him a headache. His best suit, a close-fitting gabardine he wore only when trying to appear like a successful businessman, smelled faintly of mothballs, a scent that tightened his stomach. Or was it nerves?

He took a deep breath and pushed open the door. Immediately inside was the secretary, a voluptuous woman with straight, red hair pulled back into a severe bun, wearing what appeared to Peter to be a nurse's dress over a voluptuous figure. She snapped shut the novel she'd been reading, discreetly hidden on her lap.

"Peter Hunt, calling for Helena Rubenstein," he said.

"Madame's expecting you," the secretary said, as she shoved the book under the desk. "Please follow me."

"Of course, Miss . . . Miss?"

The secretary smiled coolly. "How kind of you to inquire," she said formally. "I am Hildie Hopfer." She shook Peter's outstretched hand. He held onto her hand, turned it, and kissed it gallantly. She blushed. "Madame calls me Hoppy," she said.

Peter made a mental note of her name, and how she referred to Mrs. Rubenstein. He'd learned when he first began working with wealthy clients that it was the secretaries and head butlers that held the keys to their employers' kingdoms. A few well-placed attentions to the right staff kept him on the better invitation lists and apprised of the latest gossip, invaluable tools for anyone with little money and a lot of ambition.

Hoppy led Peter through the salon. Peter was struck by the walls, one painted a deep magenta, another a burnished yellow, and another a lime green. A Russian combination of colors, he thought. But wasn't Madame Polish?

On the second floor, Peter heard Madame before he saw her. "This is not right! You must do it again! Why can't you work as I do? You must work more, talk less," came through a partially opened door in a throaty, accented voice. A middle-aged woman, clutching a sheaf of papers and several small boxes scurried out, nearly knocking over Hoppy and Peter. "Your turn," she said through clenched teeth to Hoppy. Hoppy signaled for Peter to wait outside, and she entered Madame's office to announce him.

Peter tried to run through all the suggestions made the night before. He'd worn his best suit, check; he'd brought a gift, check; he'd considered what names to drop and in what order....

Oh, no! He hadn't come up with a title! Horace seemed to think that was very important. Peter had to think of something, quick!

Hoppy appeared in the doorway and motioned for Peter to come in.

Peter hesitated for an instant, then entered the office. "Lord Templeton, Madame, at your service," he said, bowing over Madame's hand while sneaking a wink at Hoppy. "Peter Lord Templeton Hunt."

A snort came from behind him, and Peter turned to see Horace hunched down in a straight-backed chair. Horace made coughing noses to hide the laughter that had almost escaped. Wait until Crocker heard about Peter's use of his name!

"Ach! My artist! Lord Templeton, is it? Come in, come in!" Peter was taken aback. Although her face was familiar, with dark, heavy lidded eyes, a thick nose and a wide, cruel mouth, framed by her trademark chignon, she stood a full head shorter than he. She wore an impeccably tailored suit of red brocade—French, Peter guessed—with half a dozen strands of pearls obscuring the collar. Her wrists and fingers were laden with jewelry, and dangling diamond earrings bobbed as she spoke.

Peter bowed again. "Madame, I must apologize," he said. "I took this dear girl away from her work to lead me to you. She was so busy! Working, working. But she was very gracious, nonetheless. A fine representative of your company."

"What? Hoppy? Yes, she's a good little girl," said Madame, waving Hoppy out as she took her seat. Hoppy darted a smile to Peter before she closed the door.

"You've made a friend for life," Horace said under his breath as he pulled a seat up for Peter.

"You know Horace, of course," said Madame. "He fancies himself an artist, too, I'm afraid." She scowled at Horace and he ducked his head. "What am I to do with him?" she said.

Madame turned in her seat to fully face Peter. "So, Lord Templeton, is it? You come from where?"

"Why, from Petrograd, Madame," Peter said, improvising. Were there lords in Russia? he wondered. "Actually, I am the son of English parents, from Gloucestershire, who happened to be traveling through Russia when I was born."

Madame's eyes narrowed with suspicion. "They traveled through Russia? While your mother was expecting?"

Peter froze his pleasant expression as he groaned inwardly. He hadn't thought of that. "They were on their way home when I arrived a month early."

He frowned slightly at Madame, pretending to be perturbed by her doubts. "My mother is a very remarkable woman."

Madame nodded, appearing satisfied. "All women are remarkable, Lord Templeton. Especially the clients of Helena Rubenstein."

She burped loudly, and waved her hand in front of her mouth. "Pardon," she said. "Too much black coffee."

Peter fought to keep an uncontrollable giggle from erupting. He refused to look at Horace, who was shifting in his seat. "You, your company, have some business to discuss?" Peter said.

Madame tilted her head to one side. "You tremble, Lord Templeton. Your hands are shaking. Do I make you afraid? Little me?" she asked coyly.

Peter folded his hands and felt his cheeks flush. "Oh no, Madame. Ever since the war . . . I suffered a small injury, and now my hands seem to need to dance sometimes." He attempted a smile.

"You've been to the war, and still you can blush! How darling! But doesn't such shaking affect your work?"

"Actually, no," Peter replied. "It's funny, really, but once I lift a brush, my hands do exactly what I want. It's only when they're idle my hands shake so."

Madame smiled. "Your work! Yes, I have seen your work, you know," she said, picking up a brochure from her desk and holding it up for Peter to see. It was from a show at *Le Petit Gallerie* in the Village, hosted grudgingly by the owner, whose wife had insisted on meeting Peter after seeing his fabrics at one of Mabel Dodge's evenings. The owner's wife wanted to see more batiks and his other work, so he showed her his paintings and experiments with white-on-black drawings. The gallery owner's wife was taken with Peter's depictions of peasants, angels and hearts, delighting in their whimsy.

However, the gallery owner, was not impressed with Peter's work, saying it was unrefined and uninspired. But his wife was relentless, finally convincing him to stage a small show after pointing out that some of the most prominent women in Boston and New York were Peter's clients.

The gallery owner was so disgruntled, he left all the promotional efforts to Peter. Undaunted, Peter silk-screened posters, talked with the newspapers and printed invitations. Guy Jones and Clements wrote glowing copy for the show's brochure. Guy signed himself as editor of the *Mentor* magazine, a position he'd taken only a few months earlier; Clements signed his effusive, far-ranging article—which featured a playlet within its pages—"Colin Campbell Clements."

Peter inclined his head at Madame. "You flatter me. Such a small show for a woman with such a well-known collection of art." The newspapers often reported on Madame's ever-expanding art collection. She had a fondness for

Matisse and Picasso, personally and artistically, but she would buy only medium-quality works, scoffing at the high prices of the best pieces.

"It was Horace's idea," Madame said. "He tells me you work for mutual friends in Boston and New York."

"I work for no one but myself," Peter replied. "And I have more than one hat, Madame. I design stage sets and costumes, I decorate rooms, homes, even tea rooms. And, of course, I paint." He paused and saw Horace and Madame exchange a glance. He was selling too hard. He had to let Madame do the pushing.

"I'm sure you are acquainted with some of my clients," he said. "You know Mrs. Parrish in Massachusetts? Mrs. Sennett on Park Avenue?"

"Yes! Yes! Yes!" Madame barked. "But you aren't telling me about the fabrics!"

Peter blinked. "The fabrics? You mean, the batiks?"

"Of course! I want to see the fabrics I hear so much about. They say you have the touch of a Russian."

Peter beamed and withdrew a thin, narrow box from the pocket inside his jacket. He quickly fluffed its flattened ribbon and handed it to Madame. "As a matter of fact, I happened to bring you one of my batiked scarves as a token of admiration," he said.

From the corner of his eye, he could see Horace nod slightly. Good. Madame tossed the box to the side as she held up the scarf. Made of gossamer thin silk, it was one of Peter's favorite batiks. He had dyed the silk a deep purple and used brilliant reds and yellows in his whimsical designs of cavorting horses, with a scattering of stars, suns, and flowers.

Madame held the scarf up to the light. "Magnifique," she cooed.

She carefully folded the scarf and put it to the side on her desk. "You make bigger ones, too? You use different materials?"

Peter nodded. "Of course." His heart started beating harder. Now that he knew she liked the design, the proposition would come soon. Imagine! A commission with Helena Rubenstein could advance him a lot, financially and by reputation. "Satins, muslins, even rugs. What did Madame have in mind?"

She waved her hand casually, but her eyes glittered coldly. "Only if you think you can do it, a few small things."

"Yes?"

Madame opened a desk drawer and took out a paper bag. After some rummaging, she pulled out an apple and bit into it fiercely. She continued, a chunk of apple tucked in her cheek. "A dress, of course, with a stole, I think. Like what you did for Yvette Guilbert, yes?"

"But she's an actress, Mother," Horace blurted.

"She's a woman," Madame said, annoyed.

"Elegant and dramatic?" Peter supplied.

"Yes, yes, that's it," Madame replied. "With a headdress, too. Also . . . ."

"Also?"

"My new salons in Chicago and Toronto. They need something new, something stylish, but something no one there has seen before," said Madame. "Can you bring these colors, these designs," she delicately lifted the edge of the scarf, "to my salons? Will the creations of Peter Lord Templeton Hunt make them trés chic?"

Peter sat forward eagerly, "Oh, Madame . . . ."

"Wait!" she commanded, holding up her hand. "Before I can know if you will do this, we must first settle on a price."

"Here we go, sport," Horace whispered.

"Well done!" Horace said two hours later, as he escorted Peter down the stairs.

Peter grinned bleakly. "Goodness, I hope so. Your mother is . . . quite a woman.

"That's an understatement," Horace said, chuckling. "But, really Peter, you two square off pretty evenly. That's something."

"Perhaps, but now I'm all wrung out," Peter replied as they made their way through the salon.

"Too bad, though," said Horace as they approached the front door.

Peter bowed slightly to Hoppy before turning to ask, "What's too bad?"

"You're really in for it now," said Horace, opening the door. "She's taken a liking to you."

"Here it comes," I crowed. "The biggest whopper of them all. The most audacious, most extravagant, embellished and oft-quoted lies of one man's lifetime. This, Peter, is my personal favorite."

For once, I was talking to myself. "Too bad you couldn't be here."

"Oh, I'm here all right," Peter said. "I wouldn't miss this part of the book for the world. It's my favorite story."

"Go for it," I said, my fingers poised to type his words.

"I first saw Provincetown quite by accident," Peter said. He eased into the overstuffed chair, his head tilted back and his eyes closed. "I literally blew in. I was on a pleasant excursion with Scott and Zelda Fitzgerald, on their yacht, when a storm suddenly blew up."

My fingers flew over the keys. "Go on."

His eyes still closed, Peter smiled. "Well, we had to put in at the nearest port, which, as you know, was Provincetown. What a charming village! I walked the cobblestone streets, my large black cape billowing as my two afghan hounds strained against their leashes. Behind me ran my valet, a curious fellow, a red-headed dwarf. Oh, we must have been such a startling sight for the villagers!"

"I'll bet," I muttered. Peter ignored me.

"The place was enchanting! Portuguese women, with their dark hair and their bright, black eyes hurried through the town, shawls wrapped tight around their shoulders. Fishermen, dark and rough from years on the sea, repaired their nets with flying fingers or worked on their boats. Fish were everywhere! Drying in the sun or stored in barrels to send to Boston or New York."

He paused. "Are you getting all this?"

"Oh, yes," I said, not looking up. "Every word. Leave nothing out."

Peter cleared his throat. "Well, you know how I admire industry. These people worked so hard! At the wharves were docked ships from almost every country: France, England, Germany, even Russia! The world was at their doorstep, and they were very casual about it.

"The town itself reminded me so much of the villages I saw in Europe. Not just because most of the people spoke Portuguese, but they had houses of every style and shape huddled together there. If you looked closely, you could see how almost *every home was decorated with what they could scavenge from the beaches. Why, one house was built around an overturned schooner hull!"*

Peter rose and walked around the desk to peer over my shoulder. *"You know, that part about the schooner house, that is an absolute fact."*

"Really? I thought that was another of your flights of fancy."

He nodded. *"Every story I tell has some hard fact inside."*

"That makes sense. Throw a few facts in, and they give the story credibility."

"Exactly," he said, straightening. *"Shall we go on?"*

"Whenever you're ready."

"Well, even back then, there was an artists' colony, led by Charles Hawthorne. You've heard of him, surely?"

I nodded.

"Writers lived there, too. Mary Heaton Vorse would come during the summers at first. Later she settled there. Gene O'Neill lived in an abandoned life saving station. After a few years, it seemed like all of Greenwich Village summered in Provincetown. Or Truro."

"But you were talking about the first time you saw it," I interrupted.

"Oh, yes," he said. *"So, there were a few artists there, but it was primarily a quaint fishing village. I was enchanted. I immediately decided I had to stay."*

"Excellent!" I said. "I've got it."

"Let me see," said Peter, walking around the desk. He peered at the screen, and gradually his smile fell.

"What's wrong?" I asked.

"Hmm? Oh, nothing," he said straightening. A lit cigarette appeared between his fingers and he contemplated it. *"It's all there, just the way I like to tell it. But . . ."* his voice trailed off.

"But?"

"I was just hoping something, once this part was written. I thought then . . . ." His voice trailed off again. He began to fade. *"Then I'd know."*

"Peter! What is it? What did you want to know?"

He was gone.

8

DISGUISES

1919 - CHICAGO

A sharp pounding on the door startled Peter from a deep sleep. "Who is it?" he mumbled, fumbling for his robe.

"Me! Hoppy!" The heavy door muffled her voice. "Peter, come to the salon quick! Madame's upset!"

What now? Peter wondered as he raked his fingers through his hair. Ten minutes later, he stepped from the lobby of the Drake Hotel and shivered. Even in May, Chicago had a knife-like morning chill. He hurried down the street to the Rubenstein salon.

Hoppy, currently Madame's favorite secretary, was waiting for Peter at the door and nodded toward the shouts coming from the office. Clatters and thumps punctuated the inarticulate tirade.

Forgetting to remove his hat and coat, Peter pushed open the door. "Madame!" he said in a loud, clear voice.

Madame whirled around. Her chignon was loose and her makeup was streaked with tears. The office was in a shambles, with chairs overturned and papers strewn over the floor. By the window stood Madame's husband, Edward Titus, nattily attired in a light-colored business suit. He looked bored.

"That's it! No more!" she shouted.

Stunned, Peter stood still. In the past year, he'd often seen Madame irate, even ranting, shouting at her employees, her maid, and especially her relatives. But nothing like this. She seemed beside herself with rage.

"Madame?" he said again. He tentatively stepped toward her, trying not to leave marks on the scattered papers. She put her hand up to stop him and he froze. "Come back when I call," she said in a hoarse voice.

Madame was composed and her hair was smoothed into place when Hoppy signaled Peter to re-enter the office an hour later. Titus was nowhere to be seen. Hoppy was busily stacking the last of the scattered papers when Peter entered. "Both of you, sit," Madame said.

Peter and Hoppy exchanged a glance as they sat and waited expectantly. Madame's mood was strange to them. Her silence was almost violent. "Children, this is the end," she said in her deep voice. Her mouth trembled. "Rubenstein will be no more."

"Madame?" Peter and Hoppy said in unison. Peter started to rise until Madame gestured for him to sit. "My husband has forced my hand," she said bitterly. "I have to sell the business and move to Europe. I must do it to save my marriage."

"Oh, poor Madame!" Peter knelt beside her chair and took her hand, almost invisible beneath her large rings. "How awful!"

"What can we do, Madame?" asked Hoppy. "We must do something!"

"Nothing can be done," Madame said. The three sat mute. Finally, after a long pause, Madame raised her head, her eyes brightening. "Yes! I know! I will punish him! I will run away."

Baffled, Peter rose. He'd never seen Madame run away from anything. She was a dynamo of relentless determination. She would take on even the most disagreeable negotiations, the most dismal dinner parties. "Run away?" he asked.

"Yes, and you will come with me!" Madame laughed at Peter's expression. "I must not let Edward do this to me too easily, darling. I can't sign papers if I can't be found, yes?"

After Hoppy left to make the arrangements, Peter and Madame walked slowly through the salon. Madame tapped the rolls of batiks stacked on a table in the center of the salon. Peter had planned to hang them on the walls that day. "Such a shame, darling, but we can't use these now. Why waste them on the Lehman Brothers, my poor company's new owners, eh? We will find them a good home."

"Helena!" A woman's accented voice carolled from the front of the salon.

"Ganna!"

Helena broke away and sailed to the slim young woman standing in the entryway. She was dressed in a well-tailored orange walking suit that flattered her figure, and her light brown hair was tucked under a matching velvet cloche hat. A large sapphire surrounded by diamonds glittered on her finger.

After an enthusiastic embrace, the two chattered in a foreign language. Polish, Peter guessed. After a few minutes, Madame turned and spoke in English. "Ganna, you must meet the most talented artist. We have been talking about his batiks just now, as a matter of fact." She drew Ganna forward. "Peter, Lord Templeton Hunt, this is my dear friend, Madame Ganna Walska. She is a singer, an opera singer. When she chooses to sing."

Peter took Ganna's hand and bowed over it. She raised her eyebrows to Madame. "Lord Templeton?" she said in a dulcet voice. Peter saw Madame's slight shrug and smile as he straightened. "Charmed," he said. What was that about? he wondered.

"Tell me, Lord Templeton, what is your artistic medium?" said Ganna, a blend of European languages accenting her words.

"Oh! How lucky!" Madame cried. "Ganna, you must see his work! You will love it!"

Talking to each other in Polish, the two women watched as Peter unrolled his batiks. He waited as they held the fabrics up to the light and their fingers traced the designs. Madame draped one batik over one of Ganna's shoulders, and another on hers.

In a few minutes, Madame turned to Peter. "Done, then!" she said, her eyes twinkling. "Ganna will take all of your batiks and will pay prettily for them."

Peter could barely nod before the two walked past and entered the main salon, chattering away in Polish. After he'd rolled the fabrics and put them away, Peter returned to the salon to find the two women peering into one of Madame's beauty cream jars. Ganna shook her head. "My darling, I am perfectly happy with my creams from Elizabeth Arden," she said. "Harold says my skin is softer than rose petals."

Peter almost flinched. Madame detested Elizabeth Arden with a passion. The mere mention of the name would send her into a fury.

But Madame only snorted. "What does Harold know? He sells farm equipment! Those potions are fine with beautiful skin like yours. But will they keep your face younger, more beautiful? No. Arden knows horses, not women."

Ganna chuckled. "You do despise her, don't you? But I am sure both salons have equally fine preparations."

"No!" Helena shouted. "She only enhances existing beauty. I can create beauty! Why, my Creme Valaze could even make a man as beautiful as a woman."

Peter rolled his eyes. Here she goes again. Ganna seemed to know just how to get Madame going. When he looked back at the two women, he was startled to find them staring at him. "Ladies?" he said.

Ganna and Madame looked at each other and began to laugh. "You must show me!" Ganna teased. "I must see this miracle! You must make a man as beautiful as a woman!"

Madame's eyes lit up. "I will! And then you will leave that horrible Arden and come here, yes?" Her face fell. "Even though, after today, I will be gone. I can never return."

Ganna patted Madame's arm. Peter couldn't stand to see Madame look so sad. Besides, the salon was closed for the day. "I'm game," he offered. "As long as no one else will see me. NO ONE."

An hour later, Hoppy knocked on the door. "Madame? I have your tickets," she said.

"Come in, come in," Madame called. "You must meet our new client."

Hoppy entered and saw Madame standing behind a figure facing the mirror. The woman wore the salon's turban and cover-up.

Ganna was sitting in the next chair, her hand covering her mouth. Madame ignored her. "Lady Faux, meet my girl, Hoppy."

Hoppy crossed the room smoothly and held out her hand. "Bon jour," she said.

"Go to hell," Lady Faux said in a gruff, familiar voice.

Startled, Hoppy's hand fell to her side and she stared at Lady Faux. Seconds slipped by, and still she stared. There was something about that woman, and Hoppy just couldn't place it. Something.

"You got a problem, sister?"

"Peter? Peter! My God, is that you?"

Madame and Ganna howled as Peter at first grimaced, then grinned. Hoppy recovered herself and joined the laughter. "Oh, Peter, you're such a handsome man, but you're an ugly, ugly woman!"

Before the three let Peter go, they insisted on a photograph. As Hoppy dashed up to the public relations office, Madame covered Peter's shoulders with one of his batiks and Ganna fitted her cloche hat on his head. In a twinkling, he was decked out in a pearl necklace and dangling earrings. "How do you women wear all these things?" Peter exclaimed. "I couldn't stand the extra weight!"

Finally, the camera was set up and Peter was positioned for what was to look like a studio shot. "Smile!" said Hoppy.

"No, no, don't smile," said Madame. "Look demure."

Peter tried to arrange his face.

"Ugh! You look like you just had cod liver oil!"

"Try looking enticing," Ganna suggested.

Peter did his best. Madame chortled. "Oh, well, if that's the best you can do. Take the picture, Hoppy."

Madame and Peter looked out the windows of the train in a companionable silence. Twilight had settled over the fields of Illinois, and they could just make out cows sprinkled here and there, and the lights of a lone farmhouse every so often.

They would first travel to New York, where they would catch the train to Cape Cod. Until today, Peter had no idea Madame had ever set foot on the Cape, and tried to imagine the lavish retreat she'd established in Provincetown.

"Tell me about when your were a little boy," Madame said, breaking into Peter's thoughts. Her eyes stayed on the moving landscape.

"Oh, it was so magical," Peter said. "My parents were English, you know, and traveled around the world. Before they sent me off to school, we idled away many months in Russia, Asia and Europe. They knew people all over the world, royals and the height of society, so we stayed in some of the grandest mansions built. Why, one time . . . ."

"You went to France?" Madame interrupted, her eyes still gazing out the window.

"Of course," said Peter. "Many times."

"And when you were in France, did you ever hear of La Grande Therese?" asked Madame. She looked at Peter from the corner of her eyes.

Peter was stumped. Therese? La Grande Therese? "Why, no," he said. "Who is she?"

Madame turned to face him. "In a way, nobody really knows," said Madame. "But who really knows anybody?" She shrugged.

"La Grande Therese was very famous in Paris 10 or 20 years ago," said Madame. "At first, it was good. Later, it was not so good." She pulled a paper bag from her huge purse and rummaged in it until she extracted an apple. She offered it to Peter, and when he waved it away, she bit into it. Peter strained to make out what Madame was saying as she chewed the apple.

"She lived very extravagantly," Madame said. "Therese was the daughter of a wealthy family from Toulouse. She had beautiful mansions, in Paris and in the country. She entertained the richest, most powerful people almost every evening, giving enormous dinner parties with the finest foods served on silver platters. Her dresses were made by the best couturiers and she wore many, many jewels. Everybody wanted to be her friend. She was often in the newspapers as one of Paris's very exclusive high society. That's when she was called La Grande Therese."

"Then something happened." Madame took another bite of the apple, chewed and swallowed. "Little stories started coming out. Nothing much, at first, but there were more and more. At first, some talked about how Therese had many, many bills and never paid them." Madame shrugged. "Not so unusual. Many of the rich did that. Then, after some small embarrassment or another, they would take care of the accounts. But Therese never did."

Madame studied her half-eaten apple. "Well, you know what happens. Merchants become alarmed and start howling for payments. Creditors get worried. Pretty soon, someone took her to court. Ah, then things got really bad. Do you know what happened?"

Peter had been sitting straight up as Madame told her story. A headache began to pound in his temples. A vague sense of panic was knotting his stomach as he slowly shook his head. "No," he said, his voice strangled.

Madame gave him a sharp look and then took another bite of the apple. She shoved the core back into the paper bag as she slowly chewed. She did not speak until after she swallowed.

"Everything fell to pieces for Therese, right there in the courtroom," Madame said. "Soon the whole world knew. She wasn't from a wealthy family at all. No, she was the child of unmarried peasants, and her father was mad. The people she said supported her financially, what was the name? Crawford. Completely made up. No people ever existed."

Madame chuckled. "Paris was aghast. She'd made everything up, everything! And they believed her. She would tell stories, flirt or cry, and she would be extended credit beyond her dreams! The more she exaggerated, the more she was loaned. I suppose the creditors thought that because she looked rich and sounded rich, she was a good risk. She made fools of them. They were outraged."

Madame burped. "Too much black coffee," she said, and fell silent.

Peter waited until he couldn't stand it anymore. "What happened to her?" he blurted.

"Hmm? Oh, she was ruined," said Madame. "So were many of the merchants who extended her credit. And her daughter and husband, too. Therese was sent to jail for five years hard labor. When she came out, she disappeared."

Madame fell silent again. What was this about, Peter wondered. Was Madame trying to tell him something? Or was this just a story to pass the time? No, he decided. Madame was not one for idle chatter. Everything she did and said was directed toward something.

The trembling of his hands worsened until he had to shove them into his jacket pockets. Dread hissed in his ears, but he wasn't sure what to fear.

"You know what she did wrong? Therese?" Madame said suddenly.

Peter shook his head.

"She wasn't smart about her lies. Everything was pure invention," said Madame, her eyes intent on Peter's eyes. Here it comes, he thought.

"She had not one real person, not one little truth in all her stories. Everything was built on nothing." Madame raised a gloved finger. "Had she a real person named Crawford, even if he was a janitor in America, it would not have been so easy to find her out. If she had given a few of her creditors a little bit now and then, they wouldn't be so quick to demand an accounting. You see?"

"I think so," Peter said cautiously.

"Hmph!" Madame sniffed. "Pull down a blanket and pillow for me, will you?" After Peter had Madame settled comfortably and the light dimmed, he slumped in his seat. Madame must know something about his past. Maybe everything. And she was letting him know it, too. What should he do?

Madame's voice floated from her pillow. "We are a lot alike, Peter, you and me," she said softly. "We are creators. We can make much with very little. We work hard. We have ambitions, yes?"

"Yes," Peter said, his voice choked.

"We know what we must do to get what we want." Madame sighed and rolled onto her side, propped her head on her hand. "But we must be smart. Every illusion must have a grain of truth, yes?"

She wasn't angry! That was a relief, Peter thought. But what was she driving at? "Yes," he said. "I see."

"Titles can be traced too easily, darling. If you need a title, marry it, or buy it," Madame said with a smile. "But I don't think you need a title, do you?"

Peter flushed a deep red. "I thought, I thought . . . ." he stammered.

Madame chuckled. "You thought I wanted you to have a title. That's Horace. He says that to everyone."

Peter was mortified. "Madame, I'm so sorry."

"No, no, no," she said, and laid back down. "Just tell me again about your family. Are your parents alive?"

Peter's head dropped. "Yes. They live in New Jersey."

"No!" Madame said. "Don't tell me more than I ask. Do you have brothers? Sisters?"

"A sister."

"How old?"

"Seventeen."

Madame grunted. "A difficult age. Is she in school?"

Peter lifted his head and let a smile slip. "Yes, I enrolled her in Northwestern."

"Good, good. She can stay out of trouble there. You look after your parents?"

"Of course."

"This is all I will say, and then I will sleep," Madame said. "Take care of your family. Let no one want for anything. It's what you should do, anyway. More important, it keeps them quiet."

She was silent after that. Soon, Peter could hear her breathing settle into a soft snore. He stayed up the rest of the night, watching Madame sleep.

By the time they reached Provincetown, Peter was so uncomfortable he didn't care if they stopped at the gates of Hell, as long as they could get off the train and stay off. They'd been traveling for days, and Peter felt rumpled and unwashed.

Madame, on the other hand, almost danced down the steps from the car to the station platform. "Oh, Peter! Isn't it lovely? Breathe the air!"

Peter inhaled and fell into a fit of coughing. Madame laughed and sauntered off, leaving him to struggle with the bags.

Peter couldn't wait to get to Madame's vacation place. A long, hot bath in a huge tub, like the one at her Connecticut house, a nap between fine, thin sheets and then a sumptuous supper, and he'd be right as rain. Madame had already hailed a cab by the time Peter caught up with her, and was leaning forward in the back seat to talk with the driver. She turned to Peter as he slipped into the seat beside her. "Hoppy's here and my little cottage is open," Madame said.

Peter smirked. Little cottage indeed. Madame never did anything on a small scale. He looked out the cab window as they rattled down the narrow cobblestone street. Madame pointed out the bustling wharves, a turquoise sweep of water, tiny shops, and small yards crammed with laden fish-drying racks. Provincetown looked like dozens of fishing villages Peter had passed through in Europe, he thought.

"Here we are!" Madame sang out as the cab slowed to a stop. Gingerly, trying not to aggravate his back while hoisting the bags, Peter stepped out. He looked around until he spotted Madame almost skipping up a shell path to a tiny, tumbledown cottage. Must be the servants' quarters, Peter guessed. But where was her house?

"Come along, Peter!" Madame called. Hoppy was on the tiny porch, waving. "Come see my little retreat!"

Peter stumbled up the steps after her. "This is it?" he said in disbelief.

Hoppy grinned and handed him a martini.

"This is it," Hoppy said, rolling her eyes. "Hovel, Sweet Hovel."

After a few days, Madame's delight in Provincetown began to make sense to Peter. Of course, he could see why she enjoyed long rambles on the beach and climbing the massive sand dunes. The seashore was so wild and remote, the ocean so grand and raw, he felt swept up in the salty power of Nature. At her cottage, Madame was quite self-sufficient, cleaning up, building fires and making simple dinners.

Here, in fact, she was not Madame. She was Miss Helena or, sometimes, just Helena. When, she walked the streets, many of the townsfolk greeted her by name, some stopping to pass the time. But nobody fawned over her as they did in New York, or eyed her critically.

By the end of the week, Peter was reluctant to leave.

"I know, I know," Madame nodded. "Here, you are free. You can be yourself. The only real power here is the ocean, and it has a mind of its own."

Madame sent Peter back to New York a few days before she planned to return. "I will not see this place for a long time, and I want to say good-bye," she said. "But you must come here, whenever you like. I will arrange it with Hoppy."

Peter clasped her hands, tiny without the bracelets and rings she usually wore. His brain teemed with things he wanted to say and couldn't. So much had happened, in Chicago, and here. He felt as if his world had changed, but he wasn't sure how.

"Go, go," Madame said before he could open his mouth. She pulled her hands away. "I have things to do. And you must go back to work."

9

LEAVING THAT LIFE BEHIND

JERSEY CITY, 1926

Ma watched quietly as Peter wolfed down the steaming rabbit stew she'd set before him. She absently plucked at the starched white tablecloth.

Ma didn't like the look of her son. He was thin for a man just turned 30, and his tailored blue suit seemed to hang off his frame. His cheeks were pale and she could see the blue veins just beneath the skin of his temples.

Across the table Pa ate slowly, his eyes fixed on his plate. Now and then, he dunked his bread into the fragrant gravy and chewed. Ma knew every bite hurt him. What teeth Pa had left were cracked or loose, and his gums were raw from an infection.

Father and son both hunched over their bowls in the same way, their backs bowed as if awaiting a blow. They even ate in the same rhythm, scooping up forkfuls of stew at the same time. Yet Peter's hands moved more elegantly, holding the fork between forefinger and thumb. Pa held his fork in his fist, the same way Ma would have held it had she felt like eating.

Such lovely manners my son has, Ma thought to herself with some embarrassment. Where did he learn them? And his clothes, made of fine fabrics and sewn so skillfully. Where did he buy them? How much did they cost?

Ma frowned to herself. Peter had money, all right. But where did it come from? Certainly not those bolts of cloth he created, with loud colors and strange designs. She stole a guilty look at the walnut blanket chest, Peter's present to her last Christmas. The fabrics he'd given her were wrapped in tissue at the very bottom. She couldn't, wouldn't wear anything so garish. And they were certainly too bright for her sober apartment. What would people think?

It was difficult enough trying to tell her friends what Peter did for a living. Ma hated the sarcastic smiles they made when she called him an artist. Nowadays, she never left the house without the tattered brochure from Peter's single New York art exhibit (was it three years since then, already?) and the creased book jacket from *Plays for a Folding Theatre*, which Peter designed, both tucked in her shopping bag should anyone care to look. She hadn't read the *Plays* book all the way through. That Mr. Clements, Peter's friend, wrote lots of long speeches filled with words she didn't understand. It was enough that Peter's name was on the inside flap.

However, Ma hid away the five-year-old article from the Boston newspaper. In it, Peter said, "I was born in Russia, but I'm not a Bolshevik; I'm supposed to be an artist but I'm not a Bohemian." The neighbors would have a field day with that, never let her live it down, so Ma buried the clipping in her top dresser drawer under her nightgowns.

Peter shared his good fortune with his parents, judging from all the improvements he'd made to their apartment. At first, he'd brought rugs and small pieces of furniture. Then, a few years ago, he'd rented the adjoining vacant apartment and had a wall knocked out, doubling their living space. The next day, Peter came laden with buckets and brushes, and worked until long past dark painting the walls and ceiling bright white, and the floor a glossy black. The apartment looked bright and clean, and they no longer had to sleep in the main room.

Over the next few months, when Peter came for occasional suppers, he'd bring his paint box and work painstakingly on decorating the walls. While listening to her gossip about the neighbors, he'd painted tromp l'oeil Doric columns, windows with views of a countryside and an ocean, even velvet-looking drapes.

Ma had been delighted and touched, but all the changes seemed to make Pa even more morose. At first, he complained the place was too big, now, too fancy. But as Pa's health continued to decline, finally forcing him to leave work, he and Ma grew to depend on Peter's generosity. Though Peter never mentioned it, Ma knew he paid their grocer's bill and, until Prohibition started, took care of Pa's tab at the Lucky Lady. Pa was ashamed, Ma knew that, but he'd come to accept his son's benevolence with a sullen quiet.

Could an artist, such a young artist, make enough honest money to support himself and his parents? No, not likely. So what else was Peter doing? Ma wasn't sure she wanted to know. If it was bad or illegal, she would have to stop accepting his help, and she couldn't do that. Not now. For the first time in years, since before Peter was born, she didn't have to worry about where the next meal would come from.

Still, the neighbors talked. Mrs. Knappenberger had once asked, right in front of the grocer, if Peter was a bootlegger, especially with all those trips he made back and forth to Cape Cod.

Ma shuddered the recollection from her head. "Do you want more stew, Freddy? Bread?"

Peter straightened and smiled, and Ma's breath caught at the sight of his sea blue eyes. Such a beautiful young man! "No thanks, Ma. This was delicious," he said, folding his napkin and placing it beside his plate. "And, Ma, it's 'Peter' now, remember?"

"Peter, Schmeeter," Ma said as she rose from the table and took their plates, his scraped clean and hers untouched, to the sink. "With us, you're our Freddy. Right Pa?"

Pa lifted his head and looked from Ma to Peter, surprised at being called upon. He shrugged. "It's his name, I guess," he said indifferently. "We gave him a name from the old country. We live in a new country. He wants his own name. So what?" Pa turned his attention back to his food.

"So what? It's your father's name, and my father's. It's a tradition," Ma spluttered.

"Speaking of names," Peter interjected, trying to derail the topic, "Ma, I was wondering if you had other relatives here in America?"

Ma sat in her chair at the table. "Yes, I suppose, if they're still alive," she said. "Why?"

Peter pulled a newspaper clipping from his jacket pocket and smoothed it open on the table in front of him. "Tell me who."

Ma folded her hands in her lap and thought. "Well, Mama brought me here, but she's dead now. Her cousin came later, with a husband. He was just out of medical school in Hamburg. Let's see, his name was William something."

"And his wife?" Peter prompted.

"What was her name? Ah! Irene, that was it. Cousin Irene. They sent me a letter when Mama died." Ma's eyes filled with tears. "So long ago."

"Did they have children?" Peter asked. Pa cleared his throat and rose from the table, his chair scraping loudly. He took his plate to the sink and then shuffled to the bedroom.

Ma shrugged. "I don't know. I suppose so. They went out West. Why all the questions?"

A strange smile flickered across Peter's face as he unfolded the clipping: "Cook, Lynch Wed," he read aloud. "Elisabeth Irene Cook and Edward Allen

Lynch exchanged vows at St. Mary's Chapel on December 19 in a private evening ceremony. The bride wore a . . . well, never mind that." His eyes scanned the page. "Here! 'The bride is the daughter of Dr. William A. Cook and Irene Lowe Cook of St. Louis.' Could they be your cousins, Ma?"

"They could. They could indeed," Ma said. "Let me see the bride's picture." She pored over the dark image. "My God, she looks just like Mama!" she exclaimed.

Peter nodded. "Well, that explains it."

"You know her, Peter?"

"I've known her for years," he replied, the strange smile returning. "I call her Cookie. Now I suppose I should call her 'Cousin Cookie'. I suspected something like this. It only makes sense. We're so alike, we had to be related."

Ma was quiet as she washed the dishes and put them away. Peter leaned back in the green chaise he'd given Pa. They'd positioned it right over the spot where Peter had slept on a cot as a boy. Peter wrinkled his nose. Already the chair was saturated with Pa's smell of sweat, old milk and sickness. Pa didn't look well, Peter thought. Of course, Pa never really looked well. But he looked especially haggard at dinner. While sneaking glances at his father's sallow face, Peter had decided that tonight was the night. He would tell his parents his plan. Ma would warm to the idea. Pa, though, could be a problem.

Peter watched his mother work. She looked better and better every time he visited. Her cheeks were rosy and her brown hair, threaded with gray, was pinned primly at the nape of her neck. Her angular shoulders and hips had softened with the better meals she'd been eating. With a well-made dress and chic hat, Ma could easily fit in with his patronesses, he realized.

He smiled to himself. In many ways, their roles had reversed. Now he looked after his parents, kept them safe. He enjoyed trying to invent ways to make their lives easier. Peter visited their apartment at least once a month, always bringing with him groceries or linens or small luxuries. Ma's greatest delight was when Peter gave her a bottle of Helena's Creme Valaze. Her eyes sparked and she held the jar close. Even Pa's silent discomfort couldn't dim her elation.

"Look at you smiling there," said Ma, drying her hands on her apron. She untied it and hung it next to the draining board. Peter put his feet on the floor and patted the end of the chaise. Ma sat, sighing. "I have something to ask you," she said.

"Good," said Peter. "I have something to ask you, too."

Ma took Peter's hand and held it, her eyes searching his. "This Cookie, the girl that got married . . . did she? Did she break your heart?"

Peter blinked, confused. Then he chuckled. "Oh, no, Ma. It wasn't like that." He paused, thinking. "This is actually very good news for me."

Ma waited, still holding his hand, as Peter sorted his thoughts. "I do love Cookie. She is my closest friend. No, more than that, we understand each other. It's like we're part of each other. We can be funny together, and quiet together, and work together and never get tired of each other."

Peter paused, musing. "In fact, we're so well suited, I wondered why I didn't have any, you know, marriage feelings about her. Not that she'd ever marry me. She's far too practical." He shrugged. "Cookie always wanted to marry someone who could help her."

"Help her?" Ma asked.

"You know, someone who could give her all the advantages. A gentleman, someone with lots of money and a position in society. She wants to live a better life."

"Ah, I see," Ma said. "She's a smart girl. Not like those others I hear about. Flappers? All their free love and cigarettes. They do everything for fun, for romance. How can they marry to any advantage?"

Peter laughed. "Why Ma! How do you know about flappers?"

"Hmmph!" said Ma. "Your sister is one of those flappers. You think I don't know, but I do."

Almost, Peter thought. They'd almost had an entire evening together without Dottie clouding the room. "Have you heard from her?"

Ma shook her head angrily. "No. I suppose that must be good. She only comes here when she's in trouble, when she doesn't want anyone to find her. You?"

"Yes." Damn. So Dottie hadn't said anything to Ma and Pa. Yet again, Peter was left holding the bag. "She has news," he said. "She's married. To a man in Chicago."

Ma finished crying long before Peter finished giving her the details of Dottie's marriage, and glared at the air in front of her as Peter talked. He'd been startled when he ran into Dottie at the Drake Hotel during his last visit to Chicago a month earlier. He'd traveled to Chicago to look for her, since he hadn't heard from his sister in months, and Northwestern University had sent him a check to reimburse him for her tuition. "Student no longer enrolled," the letter said. What was going on?

Less than an hour after he'd checked into the Drake, Peter arranged for a car to take him to the dean's office in Evanston. Peter had just settled into one of the Victorian chairs in the lobby to wait for his cab when he heard, "Freddy! No, Peter! Darling!" ricochet across the marble floor. It was classic Dottie.

She was a vision of tousled elegance as she crossed the lobby, her steps weaving just a little. She wore a close-fitting pink evening gown elaborately beaded in crystal. Tendrils of her reddish blond hair had sprung free from her matching snood and her rouge was slightly smudged.

"How lucky!" she exclaimed as she accepted his kiss on her cheek. "I've been wanting to see you!"

"Just coming in?" Peter asked as he handed her into the chair next to his.

Dottie giggled. "Oh, you know me. The fun doesn't really begin until an hour before dawn. Peter! You'll never guess!"

"What?"

She held up her gloved hand. Peter stared at the pink satin blankly. "Something about your gloves?"

Dottie looked at her hand. "Oh, no! Here!" She pulled the glove off her hand with a flourish. "See?"

On the third finger of Dottie's left hand was an emerald the size of a marble set in white gold. "Nice," said Peter. "That must have cost some beau a pretty penny."

"Not a beau, silly! My new husband!"

She'd met him at a dance a few months earlier at the Drake and mistook him for one of the guests. She couldn't understand why, when she'd caught him staring at her from the edge of the ballroom, he didn't ask her to dance. She was vexed and intrigued.

He stopped her as she prepared to leave with a few friends. He was one of the managers at the Drake, he said, and asked Dottie and her friends to be his guest for a late supper in the hotel's restaurant.

"But it's closed," Dottie pointed out.

"I shall open it just for you, and cook your supper myself," he said with a charming bow.

Bob Heist had been working at the Drake since a little after it opened in 1920, starting as a desk clerk. His sharp business sense and dignified manner helped him rise through the ranks quickly. Devoted to his work, he lived simply in a small apartment in the hotel and managed to save most of the money he earned. He was perfectly contented, he later told Dottie, until the evening he looked in on the party in the main ballroom and saw her whirling across the dance floor in another man's arms. "I can't explain it. We'd never met, yet I was utterly jealous of your partner."

Dottie enjoyed Bob's attentions and his lavish gifts, but most of all, she was drawn to his confident bearing. He was older than most of the men in her crowd, by more than ten years at a mature 36 years, and he was a bit, well, portly. But somehow that made her feel safe.

"As does his income?" Peter was crude enough to ask.

Dottie sniffed. "I suppose that helps. But best of all, he has to work most evenings here at the hotel, and he's ever so nice about letting me go out with my friends without him."

"As if he could stop you?" Peter frowned. "Have you told Ma and Pa yet?"

Dottie blushed. "Well, no. I haven't had a chance, yet. I've been pretty vague with Bob about them, too. Oh, don't make that face! You don't tell anyone about them, either!"

"I haven't married anyone, Dottie. Surely you had to say something."

"I told him my parents were in the middle of a grand tour through Europe."

Peter told Ma everything but the last bit. That would be too much. He waited for Ma to speak.

After a few long minutes, she cleared her throat. "You think this is a good marriage?"

Peter nodded. "I hope so. In fact, I think Dottie married quite well, despite herself."

Ma shook her head. "That sounds like Dottie. Always lands on her feet."

Peter rose. "I'm making tea, Ma. Want some?"

He waited until Ma had a chance to sip her tea before bringing up his idea. "There's something I want to talk about with you." Ma's face fell. "No, no, Ma, something good."

She stared in her teacup and waited.

"You know how I go to Cape Cod now and then? You know I like it there a lot." Ma said nothing, so Peter went on. "At first, I would stay at a little place owned by a friend of mine. It's so beautiful. I just love to walk the beaches. During the last few years, friends of mine have been coming from New York to stay in Provincetown, and it's gotten to be quite a happy, busy place."

Ma remained silent.

"Well, anyway, I found a wonderful house there, three stories, right on the beach and the main street, Commercial Street. At first I rented it, and you know what I did? I started a little antique shop there."

Ma looked at Peter. "Antiques?"

"Yes, well, I find a lot of nice little things as I'm decorating rooms for some of my clients, and if the price is right, I buy them. Then I take them out to the Cape in the summer, and sell them from a little shop I set up in the house. My house. Our house."

"Antiques. You make money from antiques?"

"During the summer, I do. Enough to pay for the summer house and a fall trip to Paris." Peter couldn't hide the pride in his voice. "I find I'm a fairly good salesman."

"You must be."

Peter darted a look at his mother to see if she was needling him, but she seemed genuinely interested. "Why didn't you tell us about this?"

Peter frowned. "I was afraid I might fail and I didn't want to disappoint, uh, either of you."

Ma knew what Peter was hiding. He didn't want Pa to see him fail. Pa would seize on a failure, blame himself, and shame Peter, not in words, but in silences. She understood.

"But you're doing well? That's good."

Peter leaned forward and took her hands in his. "Well enough to buy the house, Ma. Well enough that I want to move there, live there all the time."

"Oh," said Ma, biting her lip "I see."

"No, no, Ma," Peter said, gripping her hands more firmly. "I want you and Pa to live with me. I want us all to live in my house in Provincetown."

Ma drew back and folded her hands in her lap. She cleared her throat. "I don't know if we can do that," she said. "We're honest people. We can overlook a lot, but that seems like too much."

"Ma?"

There it was. No dancing around the question now. She might as well ask, whether she wanted to know or not. "Where did you get enough money to buy a house, Freddy?"

Peter looked puzzled. "From my work, Ma. You know that. From my paintings, theater designs, decorating jobs. Why?"

Ma shook her head. "No, I need to know. You must tell me. Where do you get so much money?"

"I just told you."

Ma's cheeks flushed and she rose from her chair. "We are simple people, but we are honest. I'm not stupid. You can't make a living making pictures and moving furniture. Where do you get so much money? Are you a, a . . ." Her voice faltered. "A criminal?"

Peter's mouth dropped open and he stared at Ma, dumbstruck. "A criminal? A criminal?"

Ma put her hands on her hips. "A criminal! Yes! Are you? Because Freddy, we won't live on stolen money!"

Their eyes locked for a long moment. Peter's face was pained. "You think I stole my money? That I didn't earn it? Ma . . . ."

Ma held her ground. "Tell me. I'm your mother. I won't turn you in. But I'm not going to pretend you make your money with pictures, either."

"No?" Peter sighed, and put his hands on his knees. "You think I'm lying about my work? Come, Ma. Come and see." He walked to the apartment door and picked up the leather portfolio he'd left leaning against the baseboard. He gestured with it towards the table. "Over here, Ma. See what I do."

He unstrapped the portfolio, opened it and stepped back. Ma looked at the stack of papers inside with a mixture of fear and suspicion. Her hand shook as she lifted the first drawing and held it close to the light on the table.

It looked like a fairy tale cottage, one you might see in storybooks, with a thatched roof and a light glowing from a window. It was drawn with pen and ink and then watercolored. In the corner was Freddy's handwriting: Peter Templeton-Hunt. Ma carefully laid the drawing aside and lifted the next picture. A large black bird, a vulture? Hanging by a noose around its throat. But it wasn't an ugly picture. The wings and tail made elegant curves.

The next two were watercolors of women, one in blue wearing a large matching turban, the other in orange with a large upright collar and a cloche. Peter had scrawled titles for these. Ma could make out only "opera" on one, "casino" on the other. After that, a watercolor of the doorway to a windmill.

"You made these?" Ma asked without looking up. "They're like pictures in a magazine."

Peter had moved to the window and was looking down on the alley. He did not turn. "Yes, I made them. All of them."

Ma turned to the next picture, an almost abstract tempera painting of an angel holding a scarf, surrounded by an ornate border. "What is this?"

Peter moved next to her. "That's for a set design, a background for a theater production."

"And these?" Ma gestured at the remaining pictures.

"All sorts of things. Book illustrations, designs for fabrics. Those two, of the ladies? Costume designs."

"Those for the theater, too?"

"Sure, Ma. I'm pretty good at it, too. I've designed costumes for Yvette Guilbert and Cecile Sorel."

"The French actresses? The ones who make such scandals?"

Peter chuckled. "Yes, Ma. They're actually very charming. You'd like them."

Ma backed away from the portfolio. "I don't think so."

"How about Ganna Walska? The opera singer? She's the one who introduced me to them."

"Ganna Walska! Ganna Walska! She's the one who got that rich fellow to get a monkey gland transplant, right? I read about that in the newspaper."

Peter held back a laugh. "You mean Harold McCormick? Yes, that's Ganna's beau. She's a lot of fun, Ma. I like her a lot."

Ma shook her head. "These don't sound like very nice people. Not nice at all."

Peter shuffled through the drawings and took one from the pile. "They're nicer than you think, Ma. The newspapers just make them sound bad. How about this, though? You know who asked me to design this pattern?"

Ma took the drawing and examined it. Deep, vivid purples, golds and crimsons were intertwined in intricate swirls highlighted with silver. "This is for a costume, too?"

"Well, a dress, actually. An evening gown. For Helena Rubenstein. Have you heard of her?"

Ma gaped, caught herself and snapped her mouth shut. "You know Helena Rubenstein? The beauty woman? From the magazines? She must be rich!"

Peter nodded and set the drawing on the pile. "Do you want to hear more about what I do?"

Ma pulled out a chair at the table and sat next to the portfolio. "Tell me."

After Peter named several of the tearooms he'd redecorated in New York and Boston, then the rooms he'd made over for his better-known wealthy clients, Ma held up her hands. "All right! Enough! So you make an honest living. Who would have thought people would pay for pictures? For decorating a room? But why didn't you tell me all this before? Why were you so mysterious?"

Peter smiled as he straightened his drawings before putting them back in the portfolio. "I guess I was afraid you'd think I was putting on airs. Or that you wouldn't believe me."

Ma grunted. "Yes, it's so much better to let me think you're a criminal. Let the neighbors think you're up to no good." She patted the seat beside her. "Now sit down and tell me about your house."

As he had hoped, Ma took to the idea without too much persuading. The idea of running a house on the edge of the sea "almost sounds like a dream. I keep thinking I'm going to wake up."

But, both agreed, Pa would be another matter.

"Tell him Frederick Waugh, you know, the artist who gave a picture to Sam at the Lucky Lady? He has a place in Provincetown. He even had an exhibit there a couple years ago," Peter suggested. "If that doesn't work, I think I know something that will."

"What, son?"

"Tell him that whiskey washes up on the shore there."

"What?"

Peter laughed. "It's the truth, Ma, I swear. A few years ago, a rum-runner, you know, a ship smuggling whiskey and rum, well, it was called the Annie Spindler and it wrecked just off Race Point, by Provincetown. For days, beachcombers found case after case of whiskey washed up on shore. They counted about 800 cases."

Ma smacked her hand on the table. "Prohibition or no Prohibition, I'll do what I have to so I can get your father to Cape Cod. That rum-runner story, well. You leave him to me."

It was past dark when Peter finally left his parents' apartment. He'd have to hurry to catch the last train to Boston, and good luck hailing a taxi in this neighborhood, he thought. He pulled the brim of his hat down and headed up the street, hoping to find a cab at the corner.

"Ungh!" Peter was pushed hard from behind and sprawled on the sidewalk. He should have looked harder into the shadows, he scolded himself. He lay still, waiting for his assailant to rifle his coat for a wallet, praying just to get out of this alive.

"Fucking Shits-ner" growled a voice above him. "Look at you."

Damn. Tebbs.

Peter struggled to his feet. The last time he'd seen Tebbs was just before Peter had been knocked unconscious in the war. The two men eyed each other. Although they were the same height, Tebbs appeared more sturdily built, despite the missing leg and the crutch he used in its place. He wore a grimy denim shirt and cheap work trousers, one pant leg loosely knotted beneath the stump of his missing leg. His hair was thinning, and a three days' growth of beard shadowed his full face.

"Tebbs," said Peter, brushing off his sleeves. "If you'll excuse me . . . ."

"In a hurry, are you? Don't wanna catch up with your old war buddy?" Tebbs leered. He seized the lapel of Peter's coat. "Or do you think you're too good to be seen with the likes of me?"

Peter grabbed Tebbs' wrist to make him loosen his grip, but Tebbs' hold on his coat was like iron. "Let go," Peter spat.

Tebbs' eyes were locked on Peter, his glare cold. "I know what you did."

Peter returned Tebbs' words with stony silence. The street was dark and empty. Lights glowed from the apartment buildings, but he knew better than to call for help. No one would risk interfering.

"Yeah, if it weren't for you, Schnitzer, I'd still have my leg," Tebbs hissed. "You left me on that stretcher in the middle of a fucking skirmish. One look at me and you refused to take me to the hospital. I had to wait, lying there, shells blowing everywhere. By the time another truck came, it was too late to save my leg."

"That's not at all what happened, and you know it." Fury swept away Peter's fear. "That leg was blown long before I saw you. You didn't want me near you. Besides, I was hit before I could help you." Peter struggled to pull himself free. Tebbs backhanded Peter's jaw with his free hand, sending Peter reeling. Tebbs yanked Peter back in place by jerking at his lapel.

"You wrecked my life," Tebbs said in a low voice. "I can't get a job. I can't get a woman. You owe me, Schnitzer." He jabbed his index finger into Peter's chest. "You owe me big. From the look of you, you can afford it, too."

Tebbs forced his grimey hand into Peter's inside pocket, and Peter could hear the lining rip. Peter tried to push Tebbs away. He never saw the fist flying to his nose. Before he knew it, Peter was sprawled on his back on the cobblestones.

With surprising agility for a one-legged man, Tebbs swooped over Peter and began rifling through his suit jacket pockets until he found a wallet. Standing over Peter, he pulled a fistful of bills and tossed the empty wallet on the ground.

Peter groaned. Tebbs backed up a couple paces as Peter sat up, rubbing his bleeding nose.

"Look at you. Fine coat, fine manners. Talking all proper. I heard you even changed your name," Tebbs said. "But it don't make no difference. You're still a runt named Freddy Shits-ner who comes from the same place I do."

Peter staggered to his feet. He pulled a handkerchief from his pocket and held it to his nose. "I'm nothing like you," he said.

"Yeah? Gimme your coat," said Tebbs, taking a step towards Peter. "Now."

"Fuck you," said Peter. He tried to fend off Tebbs' fist, but it came down hard on his temple. Peter dropped to his knees.

"Gimme the fucking coat, Shits-ner. Or do you want some more?"

His head buzzing with rage and humiliation, Peter shrugged off the coat. Tebbs picked it up and put it on. "Now, gimme your shoes."

Peter sat back on his haunches. "My shoes?"

The crutch cracked against Peter's shoulder and sent him sprawling on the ground. Without getting up, he kicked off his shoes.

Tebbs took his time picking up the shoes. He looked them over admiringly. "Very nice. Course, I only need one, but I'll keep the other for a spare."

Tebbs watched as Peter painfully pulled himself to his feet. Peter's face was streaked with blood and grime, and he shivered in the cold. He lifted his eyes and looked at Tebbs with a black hatred.

Tebbs grinned. "See there, Shits-ner? Now I got the money. I got the coat. I even got the shoes. Does that make me any different? Am I good enough now for your fancy friends?"

Peter swayed. Soon Tebbs would be gone. This would be over, Peter thought. Leave. Just leave, he willed.

"Naw, it don't make me no different. Don't make you no different, either. 'Cept, now I got somethin', and you got nothin'. I know who I am. Who the fuck are you?"

Through swelling eyes, Peter watched Tebbs turn and, leaning on his crutch, move down the street and into the shadows, his tuneless whistle echoing on the brick walls of the apartment buildings. A curtain moved in one of the windows above, but nobody came.

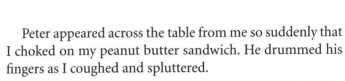

Peter appeared across the table from me so suddenly that I choked on my peanut butter sandwich. He drummed his fingers as I coughed and spluttered.

"Very attractive," he said when I finally composed myself. *"Do all writers eat so elegantly?"*

"Only the ones who hang out with ghosts," I retorted. "Something on your mind, or did you want a peanut butter sandwich, too?"

"Heavens, no," Peter said with a shudder. *"I prefer a, shall we say, more sophisticated cuisine."*

I took a bite of my sandwich. "So? What's up?"

"Good Lord. Don't talk with your mouth full. I want you to tell me what else is in this box of yours."

"What box?" Hah. I knew he'd come back to this.

"Don't play games with me. The box with all my personal items in it. The one you've used to embarrass me." He frowned in irritation.

"Oh, that box. Lots of stuff."

"Such as?"

"Parts of scrapbooks with clippings and pictures, but you already guessed that. Sketches. Designs for fabrics. A lot of your DuPont promotions."

"Ah, DuPont. They were very good to me. Because of DuPont, I became nationally recognized."

Sandwich eaten, I pushed the plate away. "They also gave you an income during the war."

Peter nodded. *"True. We both benefited from that relationship. Besides, it was my contribution to the war effort."*

"How selfless of you."

"Sarcasm does not become you, dear. What else did you find in my box?"

"Let's see. Clippings. Watercolors. Letters. Almost 50 of your Christmas card designs. Letters and cards from all sorts of people. Oh, and almanacs. There were a half-dozen almanacs. And a child's picture book"

"That's all of it?"

"You know about the other things."

"How big was this box?"

I shrugged. "About a foot wide and 18, 20 inches long maybe."

"My whole life in a box."

Peter was quiet for several minutes. I resumed typing.

"It's strange, knowing someone has been looking at the relics of your life. Trying to make sense of them, puzzle out what they mean." He frowned. *"Even I can't make sense of my life. I wonder, just what was that all about? What did it mean? What was the point?"* Peter sighed.

I stopped, confused. "I thought you found out about all that meaning-of-life stuff after you died."

Peter snorted. *"You think somebody gives you some sort of summary, a certificate? 'Successfully completed all requirements for living a full life,' right? Hardly."*

"No?"

"Of course not. I was hoping I could learn something through this exasperating exercise with you. Write down my life, I thought. Then I'll see why I existed. But, no, it's not working. I can't seem to make sense out of it all."

Peter's voice was bitter. *"It just doesn't look like a very important life, does it? I didn't change anything. I didn't affect anything. Why was I here?"*

I didn't know what to say. "I wish I could help you," I offered.

"I wish you could, too."

10

THE TIP OF CAPE COD

SPRING 1930 - SEASHORE OUTSIDE OF PROVINCETOWN

The wind battered Cookie as she stood on the desolate beach and looked out on Provincetown Bay. The waters were gray and agitated, churning up menacing whitecaps. Wind-whipped sand struck her face and hands like a thousand needles.

"This is where you come to relax?" She had to cup her hands around her mouth and lean close to Peter so he could hear. "It's like we're at the end of the world."

Peter looked at Cookie as if he'd quite forgotten she was with him. "It's wild! It's beautiful!" he yelled back.

Cookie laughed and nodded. The same way a tornado is beautiful, or a volcano, or any other terrifying force of nature, she thought.

Two keening gulls careened in front of them, flung by the stiff breezes. The sun pressed from behind the dense clouds, giving the sky a yellowish cast.

"Open your arms to it," Peter yelled as he raised his arms as if to catch the howling wind. Cookie opened her arms, and for a moment she thought she would be blown away. She flung back her head and laughed.

"That's it! Let the wind blow you free!"

In the lee of the squat Woods End lighthouse, Peter and Cookie unwrapped sandwiches from their rucksack and ate with fierce appetites. "It's the salt air that makes you so hungry," Peter said between bites.

"Here, and I thought it was the three-hour forced march we took to get here," Cookie replied. She licked her fingers, then wiped her palms on her jeans. Leaning against the white clapboard side of the light, she watched Peter take the last bites of his sandwich.

With his windblown hair and sunburnt face, he could be another fisherman, except for the pencil-thin mustache he had grown on his upper lip. His long, elegant fingers were spotted with different colors of paints, the same assortment of colors splattered here and there on his dingy duck pants and yellow cotton shirt. Wiping his hands on a handkerchief, he settled next to Cookie.

"All right, it's been ages since I saw you in Chicago. What was it? Two years? Much too long!" he said.

Cookie laughed. "My God, you're right! The last time I saw you was at that jazz club in Chicago, just after I married Eddie. That's when you told me that we're cousins."

"And you wouldn't believe me."

"Can you blame me? It was too good to be true. That's exactly the kind of story you'd make up."

"So, what changed your mind? When did you know I was telling the truth?"

Cookie sifted sand between her fingers. "I wrote to my brother. He got all my parents' papers after they died. When I asked, he looked through them and found letters from your mother, from Ma, to my mother. Just two. I guess they lost touch."

"Well, we won't lose touch. Not ever," Peter vowed happily. "Now tell cousin Peter everything going on in your life. Leave nothing out. Let's start with your husband. How's married life?"

"It isn't."

"Oh." Peter frowned as he considered her response. "That's too bad. Or is it?"

Cookie dug her hand deep into the sand between them. "Not really. I was bored to tears by the end of our first month together."

"What happened? He wasn't who you thought he was?"

"No, not at all. He was very nice and all. I suppose once we married, there didn't seem to be anything else to do."

Peter nodded, his eyes on the sea. "Thrill of the chase? That sort of thing? I thought you knew better."

Cookie drew up her knees and held her legs with her arms. She rocked once, twice. "I do, I suppose. But Eddie gave me a nice settlement, so now I can be quite independent."

Ah, now we're getting to the heart of the matter, Peter thought. He recalled some tension between Cookie and her Aunt Rae in Chicago, politely expressed through their too-straight backs, terse asides and cool stares. Cookie's husband, Edward Lynch, had been oblivious, but Peter knew her too well not to notice.

"So, Aunt Rae didn't approve of your marriage and threatened to stop your stipend?"

Cookie's head swiveled to look at Peter. He kept his eyes trained on the ocean. "How did you know?" she said.

Peter continued as if he hadn't heard her. "You took stock of your situation. You could either make Aunt Rae happy, break things off with Lynch, and maintain an adequate income. Or, you could marry him anyway, knowing it wouldn't work, but well aware that with his substantial assets, you could broker a pretty large settlement, more than you would have gotten from your aunt. You figured either Aunt Rae would eventually accept your decision, or take you back into her good graces after the divorce."

Cookie's mouth had dropped open. She closed it and swallowed hard. "Something like that. But, Peter, really, you make it sound so cold-hearted. I was fond of Eddie."

Peter pulled his gaze from the water and looked at Cookie. Her pixie face had thinned in the past two years, and shadows edged her eyes. Her arms, circling her knees, seemed thinner, too. "I know, dear heart. You're fond of your aunt, too. You were just being practical."

Cookie sighed. "Oh, Peter, you do understand. I knew you would."

"So, have you patched things up with Aunt Rae?"

Cookie's head dropped and she rested her forehead on her knees. "No."

"Why not?"

Peter saw Cookie's shoulders heave before he heard her muffled sobs. "She's dead, Peter, didn't you know? She died a month after the wedding, just after your visit. In her sleep. She went to bed one night, and she just died. Her heart just stopped." Cookie wiped her cheeks with the back of her hand, trying hard not to cry.

Peter held out his arms and Cookie's face collapsed. He rocked her while she cried, smoothing her tousled hair with a gentle hand. "Oh, but Cookie, what a sweet way to die. No fear. No regrets. That's how I would want to go."

Cookie straightened and accepted the handkerchief Peter offered. "Not me," she said, trying to smile. "I want to go fighting."

As if on cue, they both leaned back against the lighthouse. They fell quiet for several minutes, and their ears were filled with the soft thunder of the ocean and the screams of the gulls.

Finally, Peter spoke. "Did I ever tell you about the submarine that sank here?"

Cookie shook her head.

Peter pointed in the direction of Cape Cod Bay. "It was just over there, two, no, three years ago. A Navy sub called the S-4 was doing maneuvers in the bay. Sometime in the late afternoon, the town got word that a Coast Guard cutter, the Paulding, had hit the sub. I guess they didn't know the sub was underneath, and the sub's crew didn't know the cutter was up above. The sub came up at exactly the wrong time and the wrong place. They collided, hard."

"The Paulding ripped a huge hole in front of the conning tower and the sub went down fast, too fast for any of her crew to get out."

Cookie looked out at the water and shivered. "Oh, Peter, how awful."

"Oh, that wasn't the worst of it."

"The worst of it?"

"Help from the Navy didn't come until the next day. Divers, using a hammer and Morse code, discovered that six men were still alive in that dark, brutal cold, trapped in the torpedo room. A gale was blowing pretty hard, and the divers had to come up. After what seemed like forever, the Navy gobs took down a hose to pump air into the ballast tank. But the ballast tanks were blown. They couldn't raise it."

"So, they attached the air hose to the torpedo room, right?" Cookie guessed. "So the men could breathe?"

"They tried. But the weather got worse and worse. The Navy couldn't get back to the sub until the next day. The submariners had been on the bottom of the ocean, in the dark and cold, for two days. They had no food and they were running out of air.

"Even though the rescuers couldn't reach the submariners, they could communicate with them, using Morse code and an oscillator. The six men below asked when help would come. The fellows above tried to keep up the spirits of the men below, and relayed messages from their families.

"As the hours ticked by, messages from below came less frequently. Finally, about dawn on Tuesday morning, came the final message from the sub. 'We understand.'"

"Oh, Peter. How sad."

Peter straightened and began collecting the remains of their lunch and stuffing them in the rucksack. Cookie helped, and in a few minutes, they were standing. Peter took a final look at the spot in the water where the S-4 went down.

"You know what happened when the storm finally let up? The sub had been down on the bottom for four days. The rescue ship had lost its buoy and had to drag to find the sub again. The entire fishing fleet of Provincetown, thinking there still might be a chance to save the submariners, offered to help drag for the sub. But the Navy said no.

"That rescue ship dragged for the sub all day long. When they finally found it and sent down the air hose, it was too late."

Peter slung the rucksack over his shoulder and took Cookie's hand. "So, I like the idea of dying in my sleep, no advance warning, no fanfare. Death can be an agonizing business, and I'm not particularly brave."

Provincetown postcard from the 1930s.

"Me and my big mouth," Peter muttered. *"Be careful what you wish, because that's just what you'll get."*

I could hear his voice, but I couldn't see him. "So, Peter, help me understand. Are you in Purgatory now? Hell?"

"Only when I'm with you, darling."

11

Provincetown: New Life, New Art

Later The Same Day - Commercial Street In Provincetown

Catching her breath from their brisk walk back to town, Cookie stood on the cobblestones of Commercial Street and stared up at Peter's house. It was three stories in all, almost gaudy with its china blue paint and buttercup yellow trim. Cookie counted four gables and admired the small balcony over the front door. From it hung the sign: "PETER HUNT ANTIQUES."

In the plate glass window, vases, figurines and paintings were arranged on highly polished furniture pieces. From the windows hung valances made with Peter's batiked fabric.

"Come on in and take a look around," said Peter. He dashed up the steps and waited for her on the porch.

"Steps? You're going to make me climb steps?" she whined. "You make me walk on the beach for miles and miles, and now you want me to climb stairs? I don't think so."

Peter laughed. "I'll make it worth your while. I'll make us drinks and snacks."

"What kind of drinks?"

"Bloody Marys?"

Cookie brightened. "So, Provincetown hasn't heard of Prohibition? I'm coming up!"

"Oh, darling, we know all about Prohibition. The nice men on the rum-running boats told us all about it."

Soon, Peter and Cookie were sipping their drinks in the breakfast room, their chairs companionably side by side facing the windows that overlooked the beach.

"Yummy," said Cookie. "Peter, this place is just wonderful. Your apartments are right over the shop, and the shop's right on the main street and the beach. You can work and play without ever leaving the block!"

Peter beamed. "Oh, we just rattle around here, you know."

"Speaking of 'we,' where are Ma and Pa?"

"You want to see them? Stay right there." Peter took a pair of weathered binoculars from the windowsill and handed them to Cookie. He pointed down the beach to the right. "See that long dock? That's McMillan Wharf. At the end, do you see that steam ship"

"The *Romance?* Yes."

"That's where Ma is."

"On an excursion steamer?" said Cookie as she peered through the binoculars. "Your mother's on a steamer?"

Peter grinned. "She's quite outgoing now, Cookie. She's simply bloomed since I brought her here. She loves to sit out on our front porch, and makes a game out of chatting up the tourists, rustling up invitations aboard their ships for drinks and cards."

"Ma? Outgoing? She seemed so reserved in her 'Welcome to the family' letter."

"She was reserved back then. But the instant she took her first deep breath of sea air, she dropped at least 30 years. For a little while, I wondered if she was losing her faculties."

When Ma first arrived in Provincetown, sitting straight-backed in the cab of the moving truck next to Pa, she was dressed in her black "good" dress, with a starched white collar and cuffs, and low-heeled pumps. Her black straw hat was small, with just enough brim for a modest veil, and her gloves were dark and short, just barely covering her wrists. Before she attacked unpacking the moving boxes and barrels, she changed into her navy blue housedress and her sensible canvas slippers. She refused all of Peter's entreaties to leave the work and visit the town or stroll on the beach, saying, "I need to get the house settled before I do anything else."

Four days after their arrival, Ma allowed Peter to escort her to the grocery store. She dressed carefully, sensing people would be curious to see Peter's mother. She wanted to look "serious, and nobody's fool," so she put on a deep brown wool skirt with its hip-length matching jacket, a crisp white blouse and a white cotton scarf. She walked slowly beside Peter, watching her steps as she carefully placed her brown oxfords on the uneven cobblestones. "Ma, you're walking like a shore bird looking for clams in the sand," Peter teased.

Ma was shy at first, dropping her eyes as Peter introduced her to the grocer, the postmistress, and the lighthouse keeper who had stopped in town for supplies. But that didn't last long. Everyone they encountered greeted Peter with affection and welcomed Ma warmly. "We've so looked forward to your arrival," said Mary Vorse. "Peter's been bustling about for weeks, trying to get everything ready. He was so excited."

Ma warmed to Mary Vorse immediately. Petite and cheerful, Mary took Ma under her wing to show her the ins and outs of Provincetown. She showed Ma the marine outfitter's shack, which also served as the town hardware store, and pointed out the heavy rope mats made by the fisherman's wives that, when placed at a doorway, trapped the ever-present sand from shoes and bare feet, and in front of a kitchen counter, saved her feet from aching.

Mary pointed out the different fishermen, and told Ma who brought in the best catches. "Dom, there, brings in a tuna now and again. Anton, in the red dory, he's the best lobsterman. If you want the best prices for salt cod, you see Rico, over there." The best bakers were the Portagees, Mary said, and the best of the lot had a tiny shop at the base of McMillan Wharf.

Mary insisted Ma buy herself a pair of leather sandals from a boy selling them on a street corner. "You can't get around Provincetown without sandals. They make walking so much easier, Ma, especially when you have to go from the beach to the house or the street. Your feet stay cool and the sand shakes right out."

To Peter and Pa, the changes in Ma were small at first. One day, Ma was wearing sandals. A few days later, she came home wrapped in a flowered shawl "made by the baker's wife. Can you imagine? She dyed all the yarns herself," Ma marveled. "I see all the women around town wear shawls like this."

"That's because they're all Portagees," said Pa.

A few days later, Ma took her mending basket to the front porch so she could enjoy some fresh air while she worked. "Why, I never had a chance to lift my needle," she told Peter over dinner that night. "Folks are so friendly here. They all stop and say hello and talk, even though most of them don't know me. They weren't shy at all about coming right up and introducing themselves. I told everyone of them to call me 'Ma,' and call again."

"This reminds me so much of life in the village when I was a girl," Ma told Mary. "Everybody knows everybody and all their business. Folks pick up and talk whenever they see each other. I forgot, after all those years in Jersey City, what is was like to be able to go outside and not be afraid."

Ma went on the porch with her mending the next day, and the next. Soon, she knew almost all the people who passed her stoop, and called out to them by name. After a time, she started greeting the tourists that arrived every few days on the excursion boats from Boston. She'd ask them where they'd come from, give them directions if they asked, and, once in a while, they'd invite her back to their ship "for a little nip. Just a taste of sherry."

By the end of a month, Peter told Cookie, it seemed Ma had somehow blossomed with the same gaiety and energy she'd had when she was a young woman. He was thrilled in the beginning, then a little nervous, "especially when it was clear she'd developed a taste for those little nips."

Soon, however, Peter sensed that whoever Ma had become was no stranger. "She's just so much more of herself. Her personality is suddenly singing out loud."

"Peter, that's wonderful! I had no idea this would work out so well."

Peter's face darkened. "Well, Ma's happy." He pointed to a group of fisherman huddled over a tangle of nets and floats. "See there?"

"The fishermen? Yes. They look like they're right out of a painting, don't they?" said Cookie.

"I suppose they do," said Peter. "Especially the one with the green cap."

"Green cap? Which one . . . ?" said Cookie, squinting her eyes to better see. "Oh, I see him. Who is he?"

"That would be Pa."

"Your father?"

Peter nodded. "That's him," he said ruefully. "He's much better now. The sea and sun have restored his health. But he's having a tough time settling in."

Cookie passed the binoculars back to Peter. She saw the tremor in his hand, and her eyes traveled up to see his head shaking slightly. He still shakes when he sits still, she noted. His personal memento from the war.

"Tell me."

Peter sighed. "Pa hardly ever talks. And when he does, it's only with Ma. He never talks with me."

"Peter, it's three years since they moved here! Is he so angry?"

"That's just it. He doesn't seem angry at all. He's calm. He's busy. He fixes things up around the house. He helps out the fishermen. He putters around the beach. But he almost never speaks."

"But I don't understand. Why?"

Peter's face darkened and he busied himself refreshing their drinks. "I don't know."

Cookie watched Peter. She could see the hurt on his face. "But your father likes to be around the fishermen?"

Peter gave her drink a final stir and offered it. "Yes, in fact, he gets along quite well with them. They speak only Portuguese, you know. And he doesn't speak it at all. He just steps in and lends a hand when they seem to need it. It's wonderful, really, because now and then they send along fish or their wives bake up marvelous dishes, just for him."

"Does he help around the shop?"

"Not really. He stays away from the tourists."

For a few minutes, they said nothing, both watching as Pa tugged at a huge net, helping a rough-looking fellow spread it out to dry on the sand.

"So, Peter, why an antique shop?" Cookie asked.

"Actually, it's something I always wanted to do. You know, I worked with dealers quite a bit in New York. So when I decided it was time to come out here, I simply used the connections I already had. Plus, I have a good eye for separating the wheat from the chaff at tag sales."

"And is business going well?"

"It's all right, but it could be better. But I have other projects. I'm still pulling together rooms and apartments in Manhattan, mostly for Helena's friends. And, there's the Drake Hotel."

"The Drake Hotel?"

"Didn't you know? Dottie's husband commissioned me to decorate their lounge. I'm doing a Cape Cod motif for them ... nets, lanterns, floats, the whole thing. For lots of money, too."

Cookie laughed. "I guess that means Dottie's forgiven you for kidnapping your parents."

"Is that what she said?" Peter laughed. "I think she's just happy I've taken Ma and Pa as far east as geographically possible." He sipped his drink. "How is Dottie? She hardly ever writes or calls, and has only visited once."

"She's in her element! Dottie positively sparkles in Chicago! Her husband seems to give her a pretty free rein, which somehow seems to have settled her a bit. I see her now and then, especially at Art Guild functions. That reminds me ... what about your art? Are you still painting?"

"Am I still painting? Wait until you see! Madame?" Peter stood and offered his arm to Cookie with affected gallantry. With mock coquetry, Cookie averted her face and accepted it, rising slowly. "Oh, mon Dieu, monsieur. Je rougirais!" They laughed.

Peter led Cookie to a room at the back of the house, sunlight streaming in its large windows. The studio was a jumble of bright colors—daffodil yellow, rose, scarlet, bright orange, and teal. But no easel or canvas was in sight. All the paintings were made on pieces of furniture.

"Oh, Peter! This is like walking into a fairy tale!" Cookie said, her voice hushed.

Dominating the room was a heavy wooden hutch that filled the far wall. It had been painted a deep green, and then decorated with colorful images of peasants on the cabinet doors. Around the frame and on the edge of each shelf were patterns with hearts, flowers and curlicues. Although designed to look almost primitive, Cookie could see Peter's deft strokes and stylish edge in the work. At the base, she could see written "*Anno Domini 1929.*"

Peter leaned against the door frame and watched as Cookie explored. She knelt at a blanket chest with a yellow background and decorations of angels holding baskets of flowers and hearts. Next to that, a blue writing desk had a stylized painting of a quill, an inkpot, an envelope and a piece of paper with the salutation "Dear John." Cookie found a signature on the desk's side, "*Ovince, Anno domini 1930.*"

"Ovince?" she asked without looking up.

"My nickname for Provincetown," Peter said. "I'm trying to give it a continental sound. I dropped the 'P' and 'R' at the beginning and the 'town' at the end.

Cookie nodded and examined a dining table decorated with his avant-garde tromp l'oeil pictures of colorfully edged plates, wine glasses and platters of fruits and vegetables. Peter saw Cookie smile at the red and yellow stripes he'd painted around the legs.

"It's almost like Pennsylvania Dutch, but the colors are European," she said. "I've seen peasant paintings like these where? Italy? Not France, although, almost. Like the characters they draw on the pottery in Brittany."

"Germany, with just a pinch of Italy," Peter said. "You're doing very well. Go on."

"These spray patterns, these came from the French *étouches*?"

"The spacing of them came from France. The form is a blend of Spain, Romania and Portugal."

Cookie pointed to a barrel half Peter had decorated with peasants riding horses and carrying hunting rifles. "I'd know those horses anywhere. You were working on them in Boston. Russian, yes?"

Peter nodded. "And the flowers?"

Cookie put her forefinger to her mouth as she thought. The flowers were painted balls with lighter comma shapes to denote petals.

"Romania?"

"Poland."

Cookie examined the decoration on a wardrobe. On a cream background bordered in orange was an ornately attired woman holding a bird, attended by a small servant holding an umbrella. Facing her was a young man on a horse, a dog at their feet and another servant with an umbrella. "*La reine Saba et Soloman,*" she read aloud. Further down the wardrobe, two drawers were painted with the same characters in different scenes. In one, the queen lifts up a heart; on the bottom drawer, the man offers a house to the woman.

"I see! It's the story of Soloman and the Queen of Sheba," said Cookie. "Here's where she travels to meet him, then she offers her heart to God, and Soloman givers her a palace. Am I close?"

"You're on the nose," Peter said. "I find I enjoy trying to depict stories from the *Bible*."

"I didn't realize you were religious," Cookie said, looking at Peter.

"Oh, I'm not. I loved reading the stories in the *Bible* when I was a child. This is one I especially liked. Besides, how can I live here, right by the glorious ocean, and not feel a little closer to God?"

Cookie stood next to Peter and surveyed the room. "You've given up your pen-and-inks? Your woodcuts? Your costume work? This is what you're doing now?"

Peter opened the door. "I still do my other art work, but I want to explore this for now. I like the idea of true, simple designs to tell true, simple stories on pieces that have true, simple functions. The peasants I met in Europe, they had a very pure faith. It was simple and pragmatic. Do right. Work hard. Trust God. I'm trying to get to the heart of that sense."

They turned at the sound of a clattering on the stairwell. Down bounced a red handbag, followed by an assortment of cosmetics, coins and papers. "Damn!" said a feminine voice.

A pair of white sandals on tanned feet followed. They were attached to long, tanned legs, white shorts, a blue tee shirt and a grinning, sunburnt face framed by straight, red hair.

"Hoppy! What an entrance!" Peter laughed. He held her hand to help her around the scattered contents of her purse and the two stooped to pick up her belongings. As Hoppy's head bent near his, Peter kissed her cheek.

Hoppy returned his kiss and wiped off the lipstick she'd left on his cheek. "Is this your friend from Chicago?" Hoppy extended her hand to Cookie.

"I'm Hildie Hopfer, but everyone calls me Hoppy. Peter stole me from Helena Rubenstein."

For a fleeting moment, Peter saw Cookie's mouth set, her jaw square and her brow wrinkle. Almost as soon as he glimpsed her expression, it was gone, replaced with a charming smile and laughing eyes. "What a nice surprise. I'm Cookie. I had no idea Peter had a housemate."

Several days later, Pa helped the fisherman lay out the last of the day's waterlogged nets. He stretched his tight back, nodded to the fishermen, and began making his way up the beach. The shadows would be stretching out from the dunes by now, and he could make his way up the shore to the hills at Mayflower Heights and look out at the ocean.

As he walked his eyes scanned the sky, the water and the beach. Now and then he would stop, examining the odds and ends that washed up to see if there might be something useful. He seldom found anything, once an old china cup he kept next to his bed. But he couldn't help looking.

Pa walked in an easy rhythm, no hurry, no dawdling. Gulls pecking in the wet sand eyed him suspiciously and decided they did not need to fly away. A brisk wind whipped through the wild oats, moving the grasses in their own dancing currents. He pulled his cap tight to his head and pushed on.

Too bad that nice young woman wasn't around. She'd accompanied Pa on a couple of his afternoon walks and he enjoyed her company. Hell, aside from the fishermen, she was probably the only person in Provincetown he could stand.

Why was that? What made Cookie different from those others? Was it because she was related somehow?

The first time she'd walked with him, he wasn't having any of it. Pa had been around enough of Peter's friends from Chicago and New York to know they were a noisy, silly lot, filling the air with unnecessary chatter and loud parties. Even Helena Rubenstein, who was easygoing enough when she was on her own, got caught up in all the raucous carryings-on of the actors, artists and writers when they arrived in the summer.

Peter had fussed over Cookie even more than he fussed over his other friends, throwing a dinner party her first night, taking her all over town to meet everyone. Cookie was a charmer, all right, laughing and teasing until even the Portagee wives, who held tourists—especially female tourists—in deep contempt for their loose ways, waved and called her name when she passed.

Pa kept his distance, as he always did, hoping Cookie wouldn't notice him and try to draw him in, as Peter's friends seemed to feel compelled to do. Sure, he was polite, passing plates at the table or nodding when they passed each other on the street. He just didn't want the bother of pulling himself free from some well-intended but unwanted attention.

Cookie was sitting on steps of the deck at Peter's house, gazing at the ocean, when Pa came out for his walk that day. Her small hands were folded on the empty page of her sketchbook and her pencil was tucked behind her ear. She seemed to be lost in thought. Pa stepped around her and down onto the sand, heading for the Mayflower hills.

After he cleared the edge of town, he'd gotten a funny feeling and turned to see Cookie following him, about twelve paces behind. She'd tied on a blue scarf to keep her hair from blowing, and a white sweater was knotted around her waist. Was she following him? She was looking straight at Pa when he turned and she smiled.

Now what should he do? Invite her along? Was that what she wanted? Did she think it was time to make nice with Peter's old man? Pa tipped his cap to her and, before she could catch up, resumed his walk. He hurried his pace, just a little, to keep her at a distance.

Cookie didn't try to catch up, so Pa settled back into his old rhythm. What was she up to? What did she want? She was probably expecting him to stop and wait for her, but no. Not today. He was going to walk in peace.

Peace. That was all he wanted, ever since Peter brought him to Cape Cod. The place was nice enough. Hell, it was beautiful. And the Portagees, well, they were good, hardworking folks.

But Peter, his life, his friends, that was unsettling. Pa didn't want to know so much about his son, now a grown man of 34, and how he lived his life. This business of antiques and art. What was the fascination? Peter could spend hours, even days, painstakingly restoring some beat up old dresser or ugly chair, raving about its "lines" or "provenance." And when Peter turned to his painting, especially since he'd taken to covering every article of furniture he could find with those wild, bright characters and flowers, why, he'd work through the night and into the next day, with no sense of time passing.

When Peter wasn't working, he was carrying on with his friends, throwing parties, acting crazy. One night, Pa caught of bunch of them, men and women, in full evening attire—top hats, tails and gowns—standing waist-deep in the harbor, toasting the moon with martini glasses. They were laughing and shouting so much, that soon, it seemed every light in Provincetown had been turned on and a bunch of folks from town stood on the shore, laughing and shouting back. It made Pa uneasy, not just because Peter and his friends were drawing attention, but because he knew some of those fellows with Peter were, well, queer. They were obvious about it, too, with their effeminate gestures and clothes. Pa wasn't too sure if Peter was one of them, even though he'd shown some interest in Hoppy. Pa searched the faces of the frolicking group, and, sure enough, Hoppy was out there with them.

Eventually, even Ma, who nowadays slept like the dead, came out in her nightgown and wrapper to see what was going on, her gray-streaked hair in a long braid down her back. What did she do? Why, she started laughing and said we all should go out and join them!

Pa was unnerved by the changes in Ma since they'd moved to Provincetown. She hardly ever stayed in the house, and left all the chores to Hoppy. Instead, Ma would put on the big straw hat with silk flowers that Peter had given her, and she'd sit on the front porch, talking to everyone and anyone who passed by. And when a tourist steamer came in, well! She'd fly upstairs and put on one of those bright-colored dresses she'd taken to wearing and head up the street to the wharf. Pa wasn't sure how she did it, but Ma would greet folks and talk them up until someone invited her on board to look around and have a few drinks.

Who was this woman? She'd reverted to the way she was when they were first married, full of life and fun. Pa felt too old for her.

He rounded the sandy spit and the hills came into view. Pa frowned. What would he do when he got there? Was Cookie still behind him? He didn't want to turn and look and have her see him. Should he keep walking past Mayflower Heights, hoping she'd give up and turn around? That was too far to go, even for Pa. He'd have to stop. With his luck, she'd probably make him talk, too.

When he climbed the hill, he turned to face the sea, refusing to watch Cookie approach. When she drew near, he could hear her scarf flapping in the wind.

"Hello, Mr. Hunt."

Pa blanched. He couldn't get used to that name. He and Ma dropped "Schnitzer" when they moved to Provincetown, at Peter's request. German names drew hard looks since the war, "and this is simpler," Peter said. "One big, happy family."

"Hello, Cookie. You can call me Pa. Everyone else does." He kept his eyes on the whitecaps dancing on the surface of the ocean.

"Look what I found."

Pa turned and his eyes widened. Cookie held out to him a battered, but still intact and capped bottle, whisky judging from the color of the amber liquid inside. "Well, now, this is some kind of find."

"Do you think it's whiskey? From a rum-runner?"

Pa turned the bottle over in his hands. "Stranger things have washed up on this beach. One way to find out. Open her up."

Cookie nodded and Pa pulled out his penknife to scrape off the wax sealing the cork. He held the bottle to Cookie, but she shook her head. "Help yourself," she said.

Pa took a small sip. "That's whiskey all right. Good find." He corked the bottle and tried to hand it back to Cookie.

"You can have it if you want it. I'm more of a vodka person, myself."

"Why thank you." Pa uncorked the bottle, took a long pull and replaced the cork. The warmth of the whiskey flooded his chest and loosened his shoulders. "I'm heading back now. Care to join me?"

Cookie's blue eyes locked onto Pa's, as if she were searching for something. "That would be nice."

They fell into a leisurely pace and walked along the shore. Pa waited for Cookie to start the conversation, the way all Peter's friends did. She'll remark on the weather, or the view or ask what he thinks of this or that, Pa guessed. Cookie looked out to the sea as she walked, her hands in her pockets. The two strolled on the long stretch of beach and rounded the spit.

Cookie said nothing.

Pa waited. Any time now, she's going to start up, he thought. Peter's friends just couldn't stand quiet. They had to fill it up with talk. What about this one? Ma said she was a cousin, or was it a niece? Family. She probably feels obliged to make nice, Pa thought. Yep, she's probably figuring out what she wants to say right now.

They walked a mile, and then two, past the sandy dunes and the scrubby pines. The sun began to set, making the bay glow crimson.

Cookie said nothing.

Pa waited. What if she didn't say anything? Was she waiting for him? Well, she'd have a long wait. Of course, if she was waiting out of courtesy, that made him appear rude. Still, he liked the quiet on the beach and he didn't intend to ruin it himself.

They passed the lifesaving station where Eugene O'Neill lived. Gene wasn't a bad sort, Pa thought. A little moody, maybe. He got pretty melancholy when he drank. Still, when Gene sat next to Pa at the house or a party, he didn't say much. An admirable quality in a fellow.

Cookie looked with interest at the houses backed up to the beach. Her eyes roamed over every little thing, clothes drying on a line, a seashell on a railing, a child throwing sand at a playmate, an overturned dory.

Now she'll say something, some little remark about the village, or the people. Pa waited.

Cookie said nothing.

Finally, they reached the house. Cookie sat on the bottom step of the deck and looked up at Pa as he started to climb around her, her blue eyes locking on his. "Thank you, Pa," she said in a mild voice.

He held up the whiskey bottle. "Thank you."

They walked together again the next day. Cookie kept to herself. Pa began to relax, and started to enjoy the fact that here he was, an old man, walking up the beach with a pretty girl. No thinking up bits of conversation, no trying to puzzle out what was being said. This is all right, he thought. She's not like those others after all.

After they reached the Mayflower hills and started walking back, Pa decided to break the ice, just a little. "How long will you be at the Cape?"

Cookie turned and beamed. Pa felt something in his gut tighten. Lord, she was a beautiful girl. "Funny you should ask. I'd booked my room at the hotel for a week, but Helena's invited me to stay at her cottage. I'm having such a good time. I'll be staying here for the summer."

Pa nodded. Now what? He'd already run out of things to say. "You're an artist," he managed.

Cookie shook her head. "Oh no, Pa, I'm no artist. I just like to paint."

"There's a difference?"

"To me, there is. A painter paints things for fun. An artist has skill, talent, and paints from his soul. Sometimes it's very difficult."

Pa stopped. Cookie took another step before she realized he was no longer at her side. She halted and turned.

"You're saying they way they throw those blobs and blots of paint around is difficult? Difficult? You go up to that art school, Hawthorne's. He's supposed to be a teacher, but his pictures don't look at all like what he says they are. They look like he was holding the brush with his toes! Hell, a monkey could do better."

Cookie tried to suppress a giggle, but couldn't. Pa saw her expression, smiled back and they both burst out laughing. Cookie slipped her hand in the crook of his arm as they resumed their walk, and Pa felt his cheeks grow hot.

"You know, Mr. Hawthorne is very well respected in New York and Boston," she said. "I think what he's trying to do is paint how something feels."

Pa grunted. "It must not feel so good. I guess I just don't get it. Now, take those pictures Mr. Waugh makes, you know the artist down the street in the big red house? Why, he paints beaches and coasts so well, you can almost smell the ocean, taste the salt in the air. That's good art."

"I've seen some of his paintings here and in Chicago. He's very famous. Did you know that?"

Story continues on page 125.

Above: *Peter Hunt demonstrates his technique at his Peasant Village shops in Provincetown. This photo appeared in* Life *magazine November 2, 1942. ©1996 Time Inc. Reprinted with permission.* ***Below:*** *Peter Hunt's Peacock Alley, Orleans, Massachusetts. Print by Richard Ellsword, collection of the author.*

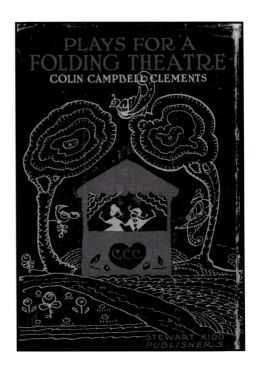

Examples of Peter Hunt's art.

Above: Cover art for Plays for a Folding Theatre. Stewart Kidd Publishers, Cincinnati, 1923.

Left, top to bottom: Watercolor and ink sketches signed Peter Templeton-Hunt, 1920s. Peter Hunt Papers 1788-1968, Archives of American Art, Smithsonian Institution. Photos by the author.

Opposite page top: Print of Don Quixote Owl, one of Hunt's attempts at psychedelic art, 1960s. Collection of the author.

Opposite page bottom: Cape Cod Compass, cover art (1964) and sketch (1963). Courtesy Yankee magazine.

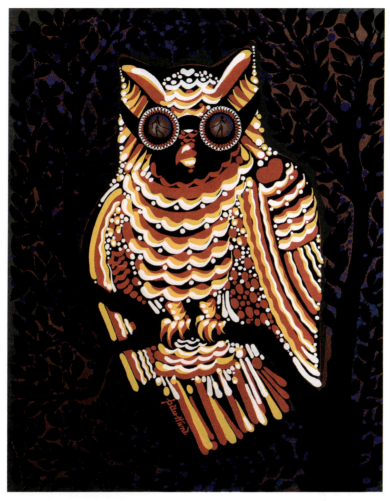
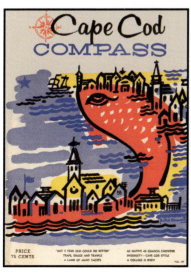

Top and middle left: *Details from a Peter Hunt dining set decorated with the story of King Soloman and the Queen of Sheba, painted in 1952, from the collection of the Provincetown Heritage Museum—Pilgrim Monument collection.* ***Middle right:*** *Detail from a side board in the Museum collection showing Hunt's hearts-and-flowers style.* ***Bottom:*** *On a chest owned by his artist friend Walter Hyde, Hunt painted storybook-type villages and giant fish in the rivers. Photos by the author.*

Some remaining evidence of Peter Hunt's presence showing details of a decorated door (Peter Hunt Lane, now Kiley Court, Provincetown) **above** *and window panels (Peacock Alley, Orleans)* **below***. Photos by Gordon T. Weller.*

Examples of Peter Hunt's Technique

This page and opposite page top right: From Peter Hunt's Workbook, Peter Hunt. Ziff-Davis Publishing Company, New York, 1945.

Opposite page bottom: Examples of furniture decorated in Peter Hunt's style. Hutch and blanket chest, collection of Barbara T. Weller, and coffee table, collection of Lucia G. Gumaer. Photos by the author.

How to Paint Peter Hunt Decorations

Almost all of Peter Hunt's designs are composed of variations of the basic stroke. Use a pointed brush and acrylic or oil-based paint. Hold the brush nearly vertical to the surface. Rest your little finger on the surface to steady your hand. In one smooth motion, bear down to create the wide part of the stroke and lift the brush as you pull it towards yourself. The paint should grow thinner and thinner until it makes a point. Don't do it too slowly, or too much paint will come from the brush.

Once you master the stroke, you can tilt or bend it or make a line of curved strokes for a swag or a border. Diagonal strokes make a heart. Try one of the following designs excerpted from *How to Transform Outdated Furniture* by Peter Hunt for Dupont Nemours. See below and facing page for instructions.

How to Paint Peter Hunt Decorations
(Numbered steps illustrated on facing page)

1. Straight diagonal lines make a wavy, angular, decorative stripe.

2. Curved lines make a flowing decorative stripe.

3. Dots and hearts placed above and below lines 1 and 2 make a more decorative motif. Use dots and hearts alone or together.

4. Practice this simple stroke. Bear down on the brush as you start the swag and lift up as you complete the stroke. This stroke forms the petals which are painted onto the background of the rose in 4a.

5. A commonly used "spot" made like 4 but kept straight. See 5a and 16 for application.

6. Cross-hatching—See 6a for application.

7. A variation of stroke 4—used to form the leaves in 4a. Combine as in 7a to make leaves as in 7b.

8. Paint names and mottos in your handwriting to "personalize" your things. Writing is much easier than printing.

9. Vari-colored lines and dots form one design.

10. A continuous swag—(stroke 4 in reverse) with tear drops added (stroke 5).

11. Multi-colored wavy lines make novel band effect.

12. Asterisk of straight lines.

13. Star—use individually, in rows, or all-over patterns.

14. Continuous ribbon—bear down and lift up on brush as you move along with the wavy line. For 14a (Maypole design), first make 14, then add overlying strokes.

15. Valentine heart—Many designs embody two or three hearts, one within the other. 15a is a Pennsylvania Dutch heart.

16. Decorative design made from stroke 5 in graduated sizes. See 16a for variation.

17. Ivy design—draw leaves first then vine.

18. (Top of Sampler) This is called a "feather edge." Use little paint. Brush over the edge so that the bristles create the informal and pleasant irregularity shown.

Right: *Carol Whorf watches Peter Hunt demonstrate his painting technique. From* Peter Hunt's Workbook, *Peter Hunt. Ziff-Davis Publishing Company, New York, 1945.*

Above: Peter Hunt's How-to-do-it Book, *Prentice-Hall, 1952. Nancy Whorf is the child on the left.*

Below: *Hunt created two booklets for DuPont. After the success of* Transformagic *(1943), he was asked to do the second longer booklet on the right (1944).*

Continued from page 114

"Must be why he works so hard. He's at it every day," said Pa. "For him, painting is a full time job."

"Well, for me, it's a way to relax. To have fun."

"Fun?"

"Sure. I paint things I like to look at or think about. Things that matter to me. I use my favorite colors." She bent to pick up a small, white scallop shell that had been washed up on the beach. She held it up and looked closely at its surface, turning it one way, then the other. "I guess artists are trying to share their ideas with other people. Me, I do it just for myself. I don't try to be perfect. I just like the painting of it, I guess."

No sir, she wasn't like the others, Pa thought. Once the topic of art was brought up with Peter or his friends or the other artists in town, people would get excited and argue and sometimes even come to blows. He liked the way Cookie looked at things. At least, he liked the way she talked about art.

Pa was up early the next morning. He went out on the deck with a hot cup of coffee, and was startled to see Cookie already there.

She wore an old plaid men's shirt over a pair of rolled up dungarees with a hammer dangling from a loop at the side. In front of her were arranged mitered pieces of new wood so they made four squares. Pa watched with interest as Cookie unrolled a bolt of cloth, held it over one of the squares, and then swiftly cut it to size with a pair of oversized shears.

Cookie looked at Pa with a mischievous glint to her eyes. "You want to help me a little?"

Together, Pa and Cookie hammered the wood together to make frames. They stretched the canvas over the frame until it was taut, and then nailed it into place. They worked in an easy silence, building one after the other until four canvases were assembled.

Just when Pa thought the work was done, Cookie handed him a can of glue-smelling stuff and a worn brush. "Now we have to size them." They worked methodically, carefully covering each canvas with even strokes. Just as they finished, they heard the clatter of a skillet come from the kitchen. Then came the sound of laughter, Peter's low chuckle and Hoppy's giggle.

Cookie scowled, and darted a look at Pa. When she saw he was watching her, she seemed to smooth out her expression. She put her finger to her lips and gestured for Pa to follow.

"We were having such a nice time," Cookie said when they were out of earshot. She pointed down the beach. "See that little blue cottage? With the white shutters? That's where I'm staying. Would you like to see what I'm working on?"

Her easel was set up in the living room, next to a table littered with tubes of paint, rags, a palette and brushes soaking in a can of turpentine. The rest of the room was tidy and filled with light streaming in from the French glass doors at the front of the house. Next to a straight-backed rocker was a wicker table stacked with books, topped with a jelly glass holding a bouquet of rambling roses, their sweet smell mixing oddly with the fumes from the turpentine.

Pa walked around the easel to look at the painting while Cookie hung back, giving him room. He saw a face, a man's face, sad and long with thin lips and drooping eyes. The entire portrait was painted in shades of blue, purple and green.

"Well now," said Pa, rubbing his chin. "Who's this blue-looking fellow?"

Cookie crossed the room and stood next to Pa. "He's someone I know in Chicago."

"Is that his natural color?"

Cookie's smile was tight. "No. I just find him interesting. I want to understand him. I thought painting his face, but in a different way, would help."

"Did it?"

Cookie shook her head. "Not yet. But I'm getting there." She tapped the portrait's blue nose with her fingernail and joked. "Maybe I'll try yellow and orange next."

"I'll pass on seeing that one."

When Pa left Cookie's cottage a half-hour later, he was loaded down with parcels. One had some sweet Portuguese bread for Ma, another was a book of European folk stories for Peter, and an embroidered Japanese kimono, "because Hoppy liked it when I wore it the other night, so I thought she should have it," Cookie explained, her jaw tight. Under his shirt, so no one would notice, Pa had tucked the package she'd made up for him: paper wrapped around tubes of paint and a few brushes "in case you want try it for yourself."

When Pa stood on the bottom step and turned to say good-bye, Cookie impulsively lifted the bill of his cap and kissed him playfully on the forehead. Pa felt a lingering tingle where her lips had brushed.

Two weeks later, Helena Rubenstein stood in the courtyard of her cottage, arms akimbo and her feet slightly apart, as if she were standing on the rolling deck of a ship. Peter was slumped on a lounge chair, idly stroking Hoppy's hair as she sat on the flagstones beside him, her head against his knee. Ma and Pa hunched over a table in the corner, playing pinochle. Willy, on vacation from writing his plays and books, was pouring another brandy at the brightly painted cart-turned-bar Peter had decorated for Helena. Paolo, the Portuguese teenager Cookie had found for Hoppy, scuttled back and forth, collecting glasses and dishes that Cookie stacked in the cramped kitchen as she hummed to herself.

Helena nodded with satisfaction. "Now that was a Fourth of July celebration. Willy, darling, pour me a drink. Do you think everyone had fun?"

"Without a d-doubt, the soiree of the season," Willy said, bringing her a glass of wine. Helena threw herself in a wicker chair and Willy sat in another near her. He raised his glass to her. "To the most charming, albeit diminutive, hostess on this side of the ocean."

Helena gulped her drink and burped. "You said that when we were in England."

"It was true there, too, my dear."

"Well, I believe you managed to bring every soul in Greenwich Village to the Cape for your party," said Cookie, coming out on the patio. "I haven't seen so many Provincetown Players in one spot since their New York performance last season."

"Even Gene O'Neill came," Peter said. "That's quite a coup, especially since he's been so hard at work on his new play."

Helena burped again. "He didn't say much. I thought he was a wet blanket."

"He never says much," said Peter.

"I liked how everyone set off the fireworks over the harbor," said Hoppy. "We had a show all up and down the shore."

A comfortable silence settled over the group. Paolo approached Hoppy, knelt beside her and whispered in her ear. Hoppy nodded and waved him off. Paolo padded out of the courtyard through the back gate. Willy, Cookie and Peter watched as he darted into the darkness of the lush trees in the yard.

"There's a sweet-faced child," Willy said.

"Behave yourself," Cookie said, wagging her finger at him. "He's too young for you."

Peter laughed, a bit too loudly. Hoppy raised her head, searched his face, and then rested against his knee again. Willy darted a look at Cookie, then Helena. Helena barely shrugged.

"That reminds me!" Willy hastened into Helena's cottage and came out, carrying a large manila envelope. He handed it to Peter. "I thought you might like to have it b-back."

Peter opened the envelope and pulled out a photograph of a plain woman in a cloche. As soon as he saw the face, Peter shoved the picture back in the envelope. "Where did you get this?" he demanded.

Willy laughed. "Why from Helena. One of her best m-models, I think."

"Really?" said Hoppy. "She didn't look so remarkable to me."

"Very funny," Peter said with a scowl.

Willy winked at Helena, who stifled her laugh behind her hand. "When you get a chance, you might want to read the inscription, dear boy," he said.

Helena yawned and stretched. "It's time for my beauty sleep," she announced, rising slowly from her chair. Ma and Pa immediately got up from their card game and thanked her.

Peter hugged Helena. "I'll deal with you later," he hissed into her ear. He put his arm around Hoppy. "Time for us chickens to roost, too."

Willy stood and lifted his Panama hat from where it was rakishly perched on a marble bust of Adonis. "Clearly some of us tire too easily. The night is still young. I'm taking a walk." He turned to Cookie and inclined his head. "Would you c-care to join me?"

They were almost to the end of McMillan Wharf when Willy stopped. "Let's sit here, shall we? It feels like we're out in the middle of the water, doesn't it?"

The lights of Provincetown danced on the water near the shore. Now and then, an errant firecracker whistled and banged. The air was rich with the smell of the sea.

"Peter told me about your aunt. I am s-sorry for your loss," Willy said after a time.

Cookie tensed. "He told you about that? What else did he say?"

Willy chuckled. "Never fear, young one. Peter tells me very little about anyone he c-cares about. Especially you. He's afraid I'll use you, I s-suppose."

"Use me?"

"Make you into one of the characters in my books. He knows I find you especially fascinating."

Cookie turned Willy's words over in her head. "You put real people in your books? Your plays? I thought you made them up."

"Oh, dear me no. Well, actually, I do make up the names, the words they use. But all of the characters I write about, they're based on real people. The situations, the drama, the gestures, all from real life. That's endlessly more interesting than anything I could make up."

"Who, for instance?"

Willy took off his hat and held it over the water by the brim. "Well, m-myself, for example. I show up here and there. My d-darling ex-wife, Syrie, too. She's sometimes a man. I think that's f-fitting. And any number of my friends, acquaintances."

"You just take a person and put them in your books? That almost sounds like kidnapping. Don't they get angry when you do that?"

Willy's laugh was low, almost threatening. "Sometimes. But I'm quite careful. I protect them and myself. I may use a number of mannerisms, or part of their background, or only some elements of an event, not everything. I improve, embellish, exaggerate. That's what makes writing such a demanding craft."

Cookie shuddered. "I'd hate to find myself in a book like that."

"Oh, my d-dear, you'd be one of the most intriguing characters of all! You're very complex, you know. People don't see all the elements at play in you. Not Helena, not Pa, and certainly not Hoppy. Not even poor Peter."

Cookie tossed her head. Willy admired how the moonlight glinted on her hair, the delicate lines of her nose and chin in profile. "I have no idea what you're talking about," she said.

"D-don't play games with me. I was once Syrie's husband you know. And I survived to tell the tale."

"So?"

"My dear, Syrie's mastery of subterfuge and manipulation exceeds that of a p-politician! A courtesan! A homosexual!" He chuckled at his own joke. "The only woman I've ever seen who is more adept at spinning webs is you, C-cookie."

Cookie gave Willy a hard stare. "Really, Willy! Why are you being so mean to me?"

"Mean? Quite the opposite. I'm singing your praises, my girl. You're brilliant. The way you're working Hoppy and Peter this summer, why, it's masterful."

"Willy, I think you've lost your mind. They're my dearest friends."

"You're jealous of Hoppy. I can see that if they can't. D-don't worry, my dear. Your secret's safe with me. I'm jealous, too."

"You? How strange you say that, Willy. When I first met Peter, I thought he was one of your, um, intimates. He said no. But I've always wondered." Cookie watched Willy intently.

Willy twirled his hat in his hands, once, twice. "It's not nice to pry, dear girl," he said in a gruff voice. He put the hat on his head and tilted it. "But there are those who drink from both sides of the cup."

Cookie shifted on the rough planks of the wharf until she could lean against a piling that smelled of seaweed and fish. "You think you understand me, but you don't. I've been trying to be a good friend. Privately, I happen to think Hoppy's all wrong for Peter."

Willy wagged a finger at Cookie. "Now, don't try that tack with me either, young lady. I know that ruse too well. My most disagreeable experience with m-marriage taught me a lot about women. To get what you want, you pretend you don't care and snatch it when no one's looking. C-conversely, the way to get rid of someone or something is to behave as if you care deeply, so you can watch for weaknesses and pounce, n'est pas?"

Fury danced in Cookie's eyes, but she controlled her expression to appear unaffected. "What a fascinating theory," she said in a cold voice.

"Theory? Oh, no, it's fact. Admit it. You can't stand to see Hoppy so close to Peter."

"I told you, I just don't think she's right for him."

"But you are?"

Cookie forced a small laugh. "Don't be ridiculous. We could never be romantic. We're cousins, you know."

"Pah, that's hardly a roadblock. Cousins marry all the time, in Europe and in the States. There's something else at work."

Cookie suddenly stood up. "I think it's time for me to go back."

Willy rose with deliberate grace, then smoothed his yellow shirt and white slacks, checking for dirt. "Very well. I will happily escort you," he said pleasantly.

They walked in silence until they stopped at the bower in front of Helena's front gate. Willy leaned forward to kiss Cookie's cheek. He whispered in her ear. "Before I take my leave, darling, let me just say that bringing Paolo into play was a stroke of genius."

Cookie yanked her head back and pushed Willy away. "I c-can't wait to hear about what happens," he said.

Cookie fumbled with the gate latch. Her hands were trembling hard and her breathing was shallow. She could hear Willy's steps recede, but his whisper rang loudly in her ears.

Cookie ran the brush through Hoppy's hair slowly, admiring the yellow lights in the fine, red tresses. Hoppy sat directly beneath her on a lower step, snapping beans in a colander resting on her knees.

"So your old friend Colin Clements married his co-writer, Florence Ryerson, and now they're writing film scripts in Hollywood?"

"Right," said Peter from the hammock hung from the deck rafters. He'd pulled Willy's Panama hat over his face and folded his hands over his pressed, blue shirt. At the end of his beige linen pants, his bare feet were neatly crossed. "All the playwrights and writers are going to Hollywood—Dorothy Parker, Robert Benchley, even Scott Fitzgerald. They're making a pile of money."

"And Willy's gone to visit them?"

"He's making some noises about having one of his plays made into a film, but I think he really wants to see Scott Fitzgerald flounder at MGM."

"Will he see Templeton Crocker while he's on the West Coast?"

"No, remember? Crocker's off on his boat, the *Zaca*, for a yearlong run around the world."

"That sounds like it could get awfully boring," Hoppy said without looking up from her peas. "Just lots of water and little islands now and then."

Cookie and Peter laughed. "We wouldn't last a week, I'm sure. But Crocker said they'd be busy doing some sort of scientific studies on the plants and people on those little islands."

Ma banged through the screen door, Paolo at her heels with a tray loaded with glasses of iced tea. "Something cold to drink?" she said. "Where's Pa? I'll take him a glass."

She stood at the top of the steps and scanned the beach. "Will you look at that. There's a sight."

Midway between the house and the wharf, a cluster of art students had set up their easels facing out to the ocean. All of the students wore white and each held a palette in one hand and daubed at the canvas with brush in the other hand, as the teacher wound his way around them, stopping here and there to look or comment.

Twenty paces away, facing in the opposite direction, Pa sat on an old beach chair, peering at the canvas on his sawed-down easel. He wore a worn, striped fisherman's jersey and jeans, and an old fedora with paintbrushes sticking out of the hatband.

"Now there's a study in contrasts," Peter quipped as he accepted a glass of tea from Paolo and winked.

Hoppy leaned to set her glass on the step beside her, pulling her hair from Cookie's hands. "You know, every day for the past two weeks, Pa's spent hours on his painting. I've never seen him so interested in anything."

"Or so content," said Peter, sitting up. He watched his mother cross the sand to where his father worked. Ma handed Pa the glass and stood back to look at the canvas. "Have either of you seen any of his paintings?"

"No," said Hoppy. Cookie began twisting the hair in a French knot. "Not me," she said around the hairpins in her mouth.

Cookie deftly worked on the knot, rapidly inserting hairpins in place as she held the hair. "There!" she said.

Hoppy reached back and touched the knot. She turned to look at Peter. "What do you think?"

Peter raised his glass as if toasting her. "Enchanting. You're ready for a dress ball."

Cookie stood and stretched. "Well, I have to get along now. I need to pack."

"Pack? You're leaving?" Peter put his glass down on the floor. "But you were going to stay through next month."

"You can't go," said Hoppy, holding the colander as she stood. "We're having so much fun!"

"What? You're going?" Ma was standing at the bottom of the steps. "Is something wrong?"

Cookie held up her hands. "Nothing's wrong. Oh, no. I'm having the loveliest time with you. It's simply time to go."

Ma frowned. "But we were just getting to know each other. What happend? Is it that man Willy? You two were angry when he left."

"What?" asked Peter.

"Oh, no. It's not Willy," said Cookie.

Hoppy shook her head. "No, Ma's right. You two hardly spoke at all the last two days he was here. Something was wrong."

Peter took Cookie's hands and his eyes searched her face. "You and Willy quarreled?"

Cookie slowly withdrew her hands and dropped her gaze. "No, no. We didn't quarrel."

"What then? What?"

Cookie looked up at Peter, then to Hoppy and Ma for help. Cookie spread out her hands. "Willy was just Willy. He did what he always does. He cuts to the marrow of a thing, and I ended up angry with myself. He made me realize that . . ." Cookie took a breath, then exhaled hard. "That I should be working on other things, that's all. I should be getting on with my life."

Peter frowned. "Cookie, you know better than to take Willy seriously. He's just such a bitch sometimes."

Cookie smiled affectionately at Peter and patted his cheek. "Oh, he's a bitch, all right. But he's a good friend, to both of us. Like it or not, he always tells us the truth."

Just after dawn two days later, Cookie watched Paolo put her bags on the train. She'd said her good-byes the night before and was anxious to leave.

"Everything's on the train," said Paolo. His teeth were white against his dark skin and his dark eyes shone.

Cookie held out five $20 bills, which Paolo accepted with a quick little bow and immediately tucked in his pocket. "That should take care of the rest of the summer. You don't need to stay on with Mr. Peter. Now you can have a little vacation with your family."

Paolo stepped backwards several paces. "No, Miss. No vacation. Mr. Peter already told me to stay." With a small wave, he darted off the platform and around the depot, out of sight.

"No, Paolo!" Cookie called. But it was too late.

"Peter, look here, at my computer screen. Recognize that?"

He appeared at my elbow and squinted at the screen. *"Why, that looks like the hutch I decorated for Vickie Ryder. She was very fond of the birds I painted."*

"How much did she pay for it?"

Peter frowned. *"She got that as part of a dining room set. I painted a sideboard, table and chairs to match. My pieces were considered expensive then, back in the early '40s, but she could afford it. Probably around $700, $800 for the lot. Maybe even $1,000."*

I pointed underneath the picture, to a line that began "Winning Bid." "Look."

"Let's see. 'Winning bid, $9,756.' Good Lord!" He turned to me, his eyes wide. *"For one piece? Can that be right?"*

"Sure. Your decorations are considered to be important artworks and antiques. Robert Eldred, you remember him, the Cape auctioneer? He sold one of your two-pedestal desks for almost $5,000 last year. Look here."

With a few clicks of the computer mouse, I pulled up another Internet web site. There were two images, both of woodblock prints. Done in intricate art nouveau style, one portrayed a woman rising on a pathway to heaven with Pierrot playing a guitar at her feet, and was entitled Jeanne d'Arc. The other had a boomerang-shaped shepherd with curly haired sheep looking into the night sky at a couple of angels. It was titled "And there appeared among them a multitude of heavenly hosts." Both of the pictures were signed "Peter Templeton Hunt."

"Do you remember these?"

Peter couldn't hide his smile. *"Look at that. I did those back in the early 1920s. Weren't they in one of our town art magazines? That's right, the Lorelei. I did the cover, too. Where did you find these?"*

"There's a fellow on the west coast who wants to sell that magazine for almost $1,500."

"You're not serious!"

"I guess that must have been your Aubrey Beardsley-meets-Erté period."

Peter nodded. *"I was using their styles. They were quite the rage, especially in Paris."*

We studied the woodcuts for a moment. I could see his distinctive use of parallel wavy lines to suggest movement. "You gave up this style in the early 30's. Why? Nobody was buying?"

"What a rude question," Peter snapped.

"Oh, don't be so sensitive. Your art was much better when you quit using other artists' styles and developed your own."

Peter crossed his arms and leaned back against the edge of the desk. *"A lot of people would disagree with you. Many artists in New York and Paris said my designs weren't really art, just decoration. Unfortunately, most of the dealers agreed."*

"You didn't believe that, did you?"

"Well, sometimes. I had to wonder."

"Isn't that about the time Pa started painting? What did you say, that you encouraged him to take up a brush and canvas? And later, to show his work?"

"Something like that."

"But that wasn't true. That was another of your stories. Like when you wrote that he lost his fortune in 1920, 'ten years before it was fashionable.' Why did you say that? He never had a fortune."

Peter looked vexed. *"I felt it gave him more dignity to say he'd lost money, rather than he never had it at all. Don't you see the difference? What's important is that when he finally took up painting, he was surprisingly good. Everyone said so."*

"Everyone, except you."

Peter waved his hand as if brushing away my remark. *"That was only in the beginning. We don't have to put all that nonsense in the book. Everything worked out. We don't have to put in every single detail, you know."*

I chuckled. "For instance, I don't have to write about the inscription Willy wrote on the picture of you in drag? I saw it, you know."

Peter lifted his chin and seemed to stare at something over my head. His voice was icy. *"So you said."*

"It said, 'To Peter, a man . . . who isn't one!' What was that all about?"

"None of your business." His eyes flew back to my face, glaring.

I shrugged. "Maybe. But the question keeps coming up. First you seem attracted to Willy, then to Hoppy. And over the years . . . "

Peter shot to his feet. *"You've been looking into that? My God!"* He was scandalized.

"People are curious. A lot of people who knew you when you were alive asked me if I knew anything about your sexual orientation. I couldn't be sure, but one of your apprentices gave me a clue."

Peter was livid. *"You asked my apprentices? I can't believe this!"*

"No, no. Not like that. She brought it up on her own. She said you once told her, what were the exact words? Your 'door swings both ways.' That was it. Do you recall saying that?"

Peter covered his face with his hands and vanished.

12

Pa's Legacy

April 1934 - Provincetown

Peter held Ma's arm as they approached the casket. He wasn't sure if he was supporting her or clinging to her.

How many times had he heard said of a corpse, "He looks so peaceful" or "He looks like he's sleeping"? Not Pa. Pa looked dead. His face was gray, his eyes sunken, his wrists emaciated. His hard life, the cancer of the last year, were written on his face. He looked worse than dead. He looked ravaged.

Ma leaned into the open casket and kissed Pa's cheek. One of her tears fell on his nose, and she wiped it away with her dainty handkerchief, taking with it a comma of pancake makeup applied by the funeral director to make Pa look less dead. She backed away so Peter could say his good-bye.

Rage boiled in Peter's stomach, and he fought it down for the hundredth time since Pa drew his last creaking breath. He bent to kiss his father's forehead, but couldn't bear to actually touch his skin. He quickly straightened and took Ma's arm again to lead her back to the front pew.

Taylor's Funeral Chapel was filled with people. The locals ranged from the artists who encouraged Pa in his last years to the Portuguese fishermen and their wives who welcomed Pa into their tight-knit community. In the last few rows were the dealers and collectors who traveled all the way from New York and Boston to pay their respects to the deceased folk painter.

Folk painter, indeed!

Peter helped Ma into her seat, the one closest to Pa's casket, and sat beside her, next to Cookie. He closed his eyes to the hundreds of flowers surrounding the casket. Thinking Peter was overcome with emotion, Cookie patted his hand.

It wasn't until the funeral procession wound its way to the Provincetown Cemetery and surrounded the gaping hole that would soon receive Pa that Peter dared take an accounting of who had come.

His Provincetown friends were there in full force: Mary Heaton Vorse, her shiny dark hair tied in a careless knot at the nape of her neck, held an umbrella against the misting rain. Ross Moffett, Todd Lindenmuth, Bruce McKain and John Whorf stood in a sad knot, likely anxious to get back to their studios. Frederick Waugh and his son, Coulton, stood on the other side of Ma, their faces serious. Could Fred be remembering the first time he almost met Pa, so long ago, rescuing Peter from a thrashing outside the tavern in Jersey City? More likely, he was replaying in his mind the easygoing talks he and Pa shared as they smoked their pipes on the Waugh porch facing Commercial Street.

Well enough, Peter thought. These people could be a comfort to him, to Ma. But what galled Peter were the others ringing the inner circle of mourners, the high and mighty of the art world, paying their respects to Pa.

Sure, gallery owner Hudson Walker had a house on the Cape, and was among the first to praise Pa's work. But why would collector Sidney Janis leave his fine New York study, or Richard Cameron Beers leave his gallery to take the ferry from Boston? To attend Pa's funeral? Pa? Why should Pa mean so much to them?

Peter wagged his head, trying to shake off the fury that threatened to envelope him. Ma took his trembling hand in her small, gloved one and squeezed. Could she know what Peter was feeling?

This wasn't envy. No, this was deeper, more profound. Peter was outraged.

"I thought I'd find you here." Cookie was silhouetted in the doorway to Pa's room.

Peter was sitting on Pa's bed. He'd flung his jacket in the corner and loosened his tie. His light hair was mussed and his black-rimmed glasses were pushed high on his forehead.

"How's Ma?" he asked without looking up.

"Better than you, kid. She's telling the art dealers about how she met Pa at a dance at her very exclusive boarding school. I hadn't heard that one before." Cookie crossed the room, her high heels clicking on the bare wood floor. The silk of her tailored black suit rustled as she sat next to Peter. One after the other, she kicked off her shoes. Her eyes slowly swept the room. Pa's bathrobe hung from the bedpost as if waiting for its owner to return. A shaving mug and brush shared the dresser top with a framed wedding photo of Dottie. "Dottie couldn't come? Did she send word?"

Peter sighed and leaned to one side to extract a yellow piece of paper from his pants pocket and handed it to Cookie. "She sent a telegram. And flowers." His voice was leaden.

Cookie's eyes continued their tour. Over Pa's bed hung a picture she recognized. He'd roughly framed the painting she'd given him that summer, when was it? Five years ago? When she'd painted studies of Colin in blue, then green, and orange. This was the last of the series, a study in black, gray and white, the most accurate to Colin's somber features.

On the wall opposite the bed was one of Pa's paintings. Cookie rose and stepped closer to it in her stocking feet. It was a painting he'd done of Peter's antique shop. In Pa's simple, naïve style, the shop was minutely detailed, with each item of each display portrayed: the silver chafing dish on the empire table; a Federal clock hanging from the back wall, a potted plant at the side, a painting of McMillan's Wharf (one of Moffett's?) on an easel in the center window, with another painting of a schooner above. Pots, vases and bowls were lined up on a decorated chest in front of the store, and even the neighborhood cat sitting next to the welcome mat was depicted.

Something in the upper left corner of the painting caught her eye, in one of the upper windows. A face! "Oh, look Peter! I found you in Pa's painting! How clever!"

Peter's head rose. "Me?" He slowly stood, as if his muscles were stiff, and joined Cookie in front of the painting. She pointed, and he pushed his glasses back down on his nose and peered at the spot. Sure enough, there was his narrow, pale face peeping around the white curtain, as if he was a ghost. "I never noticed that before."

"Look at all the detail! Wasn't it wonderful how, in the end, he won all that notice for his art? Who knew he was so talented!"

Peter frowned. "Who knew? Who indeed? And who knew he was a bastard and a thief!"

Peter was away in Boston when Pa first brought out his paintings. The Provincetown antique shop was struggling, especially since the Depression had flattened the number of tourists coming to town, so Peter took interior decorating jobs on the mainland to keep the household solvent. It was late fall, after the summer of Cookie's first visit, and Peter was immersed in converting a stale tea room on Boylston Street into a jazz club. Peter had been away for two weeks, and kept up with the goings-on back home from the occasional cheerful postcards he received from Hoppy or Ma, thanking him for money he'd wired or saying how much he was missed.

In the Commercial Street house, Ma and Hoppy were still asleep and Paolo was making coffee in the kitchen when Pa juggled a stack of paintings down the stairs and into Peter's shop. When Ma and Hoppy came for breakfast an hour later, Pa and Paolo were waiting for them.

"Come see, Missus! Miss Hoppy! Come see," said Paolo, taking Hoppy by the hand and practically dragging her into the shop. Startled, Ma watched them go through the door and turned to Pa. He smiled and nodded.

"Oh, Ma! Look!" Hoppy cried.

Propped up in various places throughout the shop were Pa's paintings. Even Ma hadn't seen them up close. Pa insisted she let him keep his "blobs and streaks" to himself. Her hand covered her mouth as she tried to take in what she saw.

The images were simple and stark. Leaning against a Victorian butterfly chair was a picture of a boat Ma recognized as the car ferry that shuttled back and forth between Provincetown and Boston. The colors were flat, with no shading, but absolutely true, down to the dingy blue and white of her sides. Pa had painstakingly painted in the smallest details, including the rivets on the cabin and the gangway handles.

Ma didn't know what to say. She was surprised that Pa had decided to show his work, and thrilled. But, to her mind, the images looked like the work of a child. She moved on to the next picture, propped against a Louis Quinze settee, a panorama of the goings-on at the town landing, with fat tourists in loud colors, fishing boats and dories crowded near cruise ships and yachts, and seagulls fighting for a place on the pilings.

Pa had painted what he saw exactly the way he saw it, down to the smallest detail.

Nothing was touched up to be prettier or more interesting. He didn't use shadowing and some things looked disproportionately large or small. To Ma, the painting seemed, well, plain.

Hoppy, on the other hand, was oohing and aahing with delight. She practically leapt from one work to the next, exclaiming over Pa's subjects and squealing at some small detail he included. "Oh, Pa, this is wonderful! You even put in the spot with the missing bricks on Commercial Street!"

Ma listened intently to the young woman, but detected no insincerity in her gleeful cries. Maybe Hoppy saw something in the paintings that Ma didn't. Paolo was beaming in front of a picture Pa had placed on top of an Empire chest. It was a picture of the young man cleaning fish on the beach. "This is me!" Paolo told Ma. "You see?"

Ma nodded. She recognized Paolo's brown, curly hair and the plaid shirt he usually wore. Though she could not see his cheekbones or the planes of his face, somehow Pa had caught his serious expression. Behind Paolo were painted two bare legs with red-painted toenails, cut off just above the knees. "Hoppy, too," said Paolo.

Ma turned to Pa, her eyes full of questions. Pa was trying to stifle a smile. "I thought maybe I could sell some of these. Make a little pin money. Those tourists will buy anything."

"Tourist season is long over," Ma said.

Stung, Pa shrugged.

Ma saw she'd hurt him. She touched his shoulder. "But I guess it's worth a try. You never know."

Pa's face brightened. "That's what I was thinking. See what happens."

Ma turned back to the shop, her eyes jumping from one painting to the next. "Won't Peter be surprised."

Peter was surprised, and tickled, to see Pa's paintings when he came home the following week. "So this is what you've been working on," he said. "These shouldn't be laying around, Pa. We should hang them properly. What's this?"

Peter lightly touched a painting of two fishermen unloading their boat. "This isn't canvas."

Pa reddened. "That's the first one I tried. I used an old bed sheet, and stretched it on a picture frame."

Peter chuckled. "Very ingenious." He felt like a parent whose son suddenly showed an interest in his dad's vocation. He couldn't help smiling at Pa's subjects, his unadorned reflection of the life and sights of Provincetown. "These remind me of the primitive paintings I've seen in Paris," he said.

"Primitive?" Pa scowled behind Peter's back.

"Well, naïve," Peter amended. "Like folk art." He turned to face Pa. "I've got an idea, Pa. Why don't you come with me to the studio, and I'll show you some things about shading and perspective that you could try."

Pa shoved his hands in his trouser pockets and shook his head. "No, son. I thank you. I don't want to be an artist. It's enough just trying to get these right."

Peter was leaving the Portuguese bakery a few days later, his arms filled with long loaves of bread, when Mary Vorse stopped him. "Peter, I just saw your father's paintings. They're wonderful."

"That's so nice of you to say," Peter replied, shifting the loaves. "I'm thrilled he's finally taken up a hobby."

"A hobby? Well, yes, I suppose. I had no idea he was so talented. He's quite good. He's been the talk of the town. The other artists are staggered by his ability."

"Oh, Mary, you don't have to say that. I know his paintings are crude. But I'm so proud of his effort. You're very kind. Now I have to be off."

Peter sailed down the street as Mary shook her head and walked in the other direction.

"Peter!"

His line of sight blocked by bread, Peter almost walked into Hudson Walker. The two men laughed and shook hands. "Like son, like father, eh?" Walker said.

"Ah, you mean Pa's dabbling in art? Yes, we're all quite pleased. Maybe this will bring him out of his doldrums."

"Out of his doldrums, I should say so," said Walker. "What luck to discover such talent so late in life."

"You needn't carry on so. Pa doesn't pretend it's art. He's just amusing himself."

"So, you're not going to do anything? Set up a showing?"

"Really, Hudson, I think that's going a bit far." Peter's voice was edged with annoyance. "Imagine doing such a thing, staging an art show, just to indulge the whims of a weekend painter. Even if he is my father."

Walker tilted his head and considered Peter for a moment. "Let me buy you a cup of coffee, Peter."

For fifteen minutes after they sat down at the cafe, Walker did most of the talking while Peter shook his head in disbelief. Walker gestured for more coffee. They were silent until the waiter left.

"So, you're saying Pa's pictures would be considered some sort of serious art in the city?" Peter said. "There are people who would actually buy what he's painted?"

"You've been to the Salon des Independents in Paris? Yes? Then you know, it's not a school of art, more a group, a category, I suppose, called *peinture d'instinct*. You know the names, I'm sure – Bombois, Vivin, Henri Rousseau."

"Yes, of course, but Pa? He doesn't use strong colors or bold lines. His paintings don't have the least bit of emotion, not even a message. Technique? He has none. How could you group him with them?"

Walker laughed. "You really don't see it, do you?"

Peter shook his head, mystified.

"His paintings are strikingly honest, Peter. They're the truth. Pa's truth. And he's expressed it in his own way, through his own unique approach. Isn't that what art is?"

Peter rose and picked up the loaves of bread he'd laid on a nearby chair. "I don't know, Hudson. To my mind, art should be more than that."

Peter was in Chicago a few months later, working with architect Benjamin Marshall on the design of the Cape Cod Room in the Drake Hotel, when the clipping arrived.

Peter was standing in the middle of the room, trying to decide if planks or flagstones would make a more nautical-looking floor, when Dottie's husband, Bob Heist, the Drake manager who recommended Peter for the project, held out an envelope. "It's from Dottie. Something she saw in one of the New York newspapers."

It was Dottie's habit to scour the newspapers from New York, Boston and Chicago, scissors in hand, clipping out stories or advertisements she thought would be of interest to other people. Peter was about to stuff the envelope in his pocket when Bob arched an eyebrow. "She said to tell you to read it right away."

Bob sauntered over to chat with Benjamin, who was inspecting the wide beams in the ceiling of the room. Sighing with exasperation, Peter ripped open the envelope.

"Pa Hunt's Work on View," said the headline. Peter's stomach flip-flopped. Below, he read: "With native persistence, augmented by good sales, Richard Cameron Beer continues to present to those art lovers willing to journey to the Central Sixties an opportunity to 'discover' new talent if they will. The present show at his Times Gallery differs from the preceding in the inclusion of a fairly large group of paintings by one man – Pa Hunt, the Provincetown primitive."

Peter pursed his lips, stuck the clipping back into the envelope and jammed it into his pocket. Now the art critic of the *New York Times* was praising his father, the man with no taste and no training! Worse, he was showing in a gallery that had twice, *twice* turned down Peter's carefully executed woodcuts for shows on Art Deco designs.

Bile rose in Peter's throat. The irony, no, the unfairness of it all, galled him. Artists he admired, gallery owners he respected, critics he tried to woo were all raving over Pa's paintings. Peter could not even hint at his incredulity and irritation over Pa's success without appearing mean-spirited or, worse, too much of a traditionalist.

Peter just couldn't see what all the fuss was about. Pa's paintings had no elegance, no uplifting message. They were postcards of his life, and badly drawn ones at that. Ma, too, had confided her confusion over the enthusiasm stirred in the art colony. "They're not very pretty to me. But please don't ever tell Pa I said that."

The person most surprised by all the fuss was Pa. He shrugged when Provincetown artist John Whorf asked him how long he'd been painting. "A few months is all," he said. Whorf roared with surprised laughter. When Whorf praised Pa's sense of composition, Pa shook his head. "Now, don't go trying to jolly me, son."

To Pa, the world, especially the art world, was just proving his theory that artists and folks who collected art were either foolish or crazy. Still, if they wanted to throw their money at him, he'd be glad to take it. It didn't much matter. He'd paint whether anyone liked it or not. He enjoyed painting. He liked the smell of the paint, the way it rolled off the brush, and how blending two colors could make a whole new color. He enjoyed taking his time, making sure every detail was right. He couldn't remember enjoying doing anything as much.

To Peter's chagrin, Dottie thought the situation was hilarious. "Who knew that the famous artist in the family would be Pa? Here, we all thought it would be Peter!"

Peter imagined Dottie was laughing right now, picturing his face as he read the article. Maybe she was even hiding nearby so she could watch! He could sense someone standing in the doorway. Peter pivoted. Someone was there al right. But it wasn't Dottie. It was Cookie, arm in arm with her new beau, Colin Campbell.

"I hope we're not disturbing you," Cookie said after kisses were swapped and handshakes exchanged. "I just wanted to see what you're working on. Colin, too."

Colin nodded uncomfortably. He was tall and lanky with coal-black hair and a long, sorrowful face. Peter guessed Colin was shy. He was quiet while Cookie and Peter chattered, catching up on friends she'd missed in New York. Colin only spoke when Cookie encouraged him, blushing with pleasure as she clung to his every word. Yes, he was clearly smitten with Cookie.

Peter wondered briefly why Cookie would choose him. Colin seemed kind enough, caring enough, but not very interesting. His was just another face in the latest pack of Chicago's young entrepreneurs. From a family of Chicago merchants, Colin must have money, a lot of money, Peter decided.

Peter walked Cookie and Colin through the echoing space at the Drake, showing them where the bar would go, and the tables. He opened boxes crammed with fishing nets, buoys and glass floats Peter had scavenged in Provincetown, explaining how he would hang the nets and military surplus portholes to replicate a Cape Cod fishing dive.

"Oh, Peter, it sounds magnificent," Cookie exclaimed. "Doesn't it, Colin?"

Colin appeared to consider his words before uttering them. "Magnificent," he pronounced.

"Now, Peter, kiss me good-bye. I'm leaving town," Cookie said, offering him her cheek.

Peter obliged. "This is sudden. Where are you going? Back to New York?"

Colin shook Peter's hand. "We're going to my family's ranch in California," he said.

"California! A ranch! That sounds fun," said Peter, not sure how one had fun on a ranch, or why Cookie would pursue someone who lived on a ranch.

Cookie took Colin's arm. "Yes, darling. I'm off to meet Colin's mother."

"Ah." He walked the couple to the door and out onto the sidewalk. After taking a few steps, Cookie looked back over her shoulder and winked.

Several months later, just after Peter finished the Cape Cod room at the Drake and returned to Provincetown, a telegram arrived from Cookie. Peter tipped the delivery boy and remained in the doorway, not noticing the damp December day.

He knew from Cookie's letters from California that Colin's mother wasn't, as Cookie put it, receptive to her charms. A dour woman, the plainest of three daughters in a wealthy Chicago family, Mrs. Campbell was suspicious of young women who were too pretty or too cheerful. She'd raised Colin's sisters to her particular standards: their good looks were muted with plain clothes, and they rarely initiated any conversation outside of what was being served for dinner or what the weather would be the next day.

Cookie cut her visit short and fled Santa Barbara, Colin close on her heels. Although she could be certain of keeping Colin interested, Cookie wrote, his mother "could ultimately ruin all our hopes and plans."

The wire was from Chicago. When did she return home? Cookie was not one to send telegrams idly. This was either very good news or very bad.

Peter opened the telegram:

> "DEAR GOD THOUGHT I WOULD FIND YOU HERE HAVE JUST MOVED INTO AWFUL PLACE ARE YOU COMING BACK JUST HEARD FROM DRAKE HOTEL YOU WILL BE BACK YOU MUST HELP ME DO A MINIATURE VICTORIAN APARTMENT WILL NEED LAMPS AND SO ON THINK YOUR OYSTER BAR IS MARVELOUS COME SOON IT WILL BE SUCH FUN I AM MRS. COLIN CAMPBELL NOW AMBASSADOR EAST WIRE ME COLLECT CHEERIO = COOKIE.

A few days later, an envelope arrived, addressed in Cookie's loopy handwriting. Peter found no letter, just three Chicago newspaper clippings. One was from a few days earlier, a top-of-the-society-page wedding announcement of the nuptials of Elisabeth Cook and Colin Campbell. The other two clippings were obituaries. One was for Colin's mother, dated in February; the other for his Uncle Joseph, who was appointed guardian of Colin's trust after his mother died.

Peter's eyebrows shot up as he read. It seemed Cookie was in the good graces of either Lady Luck or the Grim Reaper.

Two years had passed since Cookie married Colin and Pa had his first one-man art show. Peter managed to pay the bills with a number of decorating jobs, including the Brunswick Cellar and the Argonaut Club in Boston. He tried to generate interest in his woodcuts, but spent most of his creative time developing his own version of a peasant painting style. Peter put several of his decorated pieces out in the antique shop, and they sold right away to campy New Yorkers summering on the Cape.

Peter soon realized a side business had been born.

Pa, in the meantime, was the focus of an exhibit at the Provincetown Art Association. Now known in the New York galleries as a "Provincetown painter," his works were often included in shows on naïve art or regional artists. Dealers like Sidney Janis, Hudson Walker and Max Weber not only encouraged Pa and brokered his growing sales, they bought several of his paintings for their private collections.

Pa didn't like taking their money, after all they'd done for him, but each insisted. Walker suggested he use the money to buy Ma a present, which Pa thought was a fine idea. During one of his trips to New York, Pa had Janis take him to Tiffany's. On the way, they saw a policeman shoo away an itinerant artist set up on the sidewalk. Pa and Sidney stopped to look at the paintings, crudely drawn images of stages with actors, Egyptians, and Grecian maidens with bits of costume jewelry and lace affixed here and there. Here was an artist Pa could understand. He painted as if it didn't matter how it looked. It mattered only that it got painted. "What do you think?" Pa asked Janis.

"Quite inspired," Janis replied, nodding.

"How dare you manhandle the Poet Prince!" The artist was dressed in a worn three-piece suit. Judging from the gray hairs in his walrus mustache, Pa guessed he was around forty or fifty years old. The police officer spoke too softly for Pa to hear. Huffing and puffing in indignation, the Poet Prince gathered his paintings. "Writer of eight plays, 150 poems and 40 songs, and this is how I am treated," he muttered. "The world needs to see my paintings, learn from them. And I'm treated like a common vagrant! He brushed away invisible hands tugging his sleeves. "Stop it girls, stop it."

The Poet Prince straightened and saw Pa and Janis. "I'd like to buy one of your paintings," Janis offered.

"Girls! Shameless! The man's trying to talk!" The Poet Prince pushed the air around him. "They won't leave me alone," he said to Janis. "Now, what do you want? Speak!"

"A painting, I'd like to buy a painting," said Janis, unruffled, as if he ran into artists surrounded by invisible women every day.

"Never!" shouted the Poet Prince. "You aren't good enough for one of my masterpieces! Be off or I'll summon a constable! Come along girls." He stalked away, head held high.

Janis and Pa looked at each other and laughed. "Now, that's a real artist," said Pa.

At Tiffany's, Pa bought a tea service of the thinnest, most delicate bone china. Back in Provincetown, without saying a word, he left the package on Ma's bed for her to find when she went upstairs to sleep.

The next morning, Ma was waiting for him, his coffee steaming in one of the china cups. Her eyes were bright with tears as she kissed his freshly shaved cheek. "Thank you, Edward."

Pa blushed. "Why Anna, someone might see." He took a sip from the cup. "Doesn't coffee taste fine in such dainty cups?"

Ma chuckled. She had been uneasily pleased with Pa's success. While delighting in the praise lavished on her husband, she kept expecting someone to realize that his paintings weren't all that good. Her anxiety was heightened by Peter's barely suppressed antipathy. Even if Pa was never exposed as a fraud, Ma didn't think Peter would ever forgive his father. But, for what? Wasn't Pa finally doing what Peter had always wanted, bringing pride and money to the family?

It was almost more than Ma could bear. Too often, she found herself shuttling back and forth between Peter, glowering in his studio, to Pa, who was entertaining some art dealer or buyer in the parlor. Sometimes, she'd just throw up her hands and take a walk to the wharf, where she was sure to find or make a friend.

Cookie ignored Peter's outburst and continued her deliberate tour of Pa's room. She paused at his wardrobe and opened the door. There hung Pa's shirts, his pants, a weather-beaten jacket and rubber fishing pants. She took a deep breath. "I can smell him."

Peter slumped on the edge of the bed. "Oh, Cookie. I'm sorry."

Cookie was facing the corner, studying two fishing poles propped there. "Want to tell me what that outburst was all about?"

Peter picked at the chenille of the bedspread. "Pa stole my life."

"Your life?"

"He stole my dreams. He took them over."

Cookie moved to a small, handmade bookshelf. She knelt to examine the titles. "How did he manage to do that?"

Peter lay back on the bed, keeping his feet on the floor. He threw one arm over his eyes. "I know it sounds childish, but, dammit, I'm the artist. We moved here so I could work with other artists. I'm the one who's been painting all my life. I took thousands of hours of classes. Then he . . . he." Peter drew a long breath and let it out slowly. "Pa paints for three months—no instruction, not even decent materials, and every art dealer in town is knocking at the door, begging for his work. His work! Those crude, ill-formed images, and they couldn't get enough. The same dealers who wouldn't even look at my work!"

Cookie had taken a book on shipbuilding from the shelf and was flipping through its pages. "Keep your voice down. Ma might hear." She stopped to examine a diagram. "Sorry, kiddo. Pa's the artist and you're not? That whine won't wash with me."

Peter pulled his arm off his face and raised his head. "Pardon me?"

Cookie put the book back on the shelf and slowly stood. She faced Peter. "You're not being honest, Peter. You're not angry about his 'living your dreams,' as you say. You're furious that Pa was able to tap into the source of whatever it is that's at the heart of any great art while you're still trying to find it. You think you're too blind, too timid or—and this is what really scares you—not talented enough to discover just what that is." Cookie walked to the window overlooking the harbor. Pa's straight-backed chair stood next to it, and she sat down.

Peter was sitting up, his face distorted with anger. "What are you talking about?"

Cookie raised her hand. "Calm down. You've got to find a way to make peace with your father. Or the memory of him."

Peter didn't answer.

"Peter, do you know why we get angry? Do you?"

Peter shook his head. "I don't understand your question."

Cookie leaned forward. "People get angry as a way to cope with pain or fear. Have you ever heard that? Think about it. Whenever you get angry, ask yourself, 'what is it that makes me hurt so?' Or, 'what's making me so afraid?'"

Peter crossed his arms. "You think I'm afraid? Afraid of Pa?"

Cookie tilted her head. "No, I don't think you're afraid of Pa. I think you're afraid you'll never be a real artist. I think you're afraid that you don't get it, and won't ever get it. And I think you're afraid Pa knew the secret to great art and didn't tell you. But that simply isn't true."

"What makes you such an expert on Pa?"

Cookie shrugged. "I'm not. I'm an expert on you. We're cut from the same bolt of cloth, remember? Not just as cousins, but as pragmatists." She took a deep breath. "Tell me something. The truth. When you work on your woodcuts, what are you thinking about?"

"What does that have to do with anything?"

"Just tell me."

"I'm thinking about the image, placement of the figures, the message it should have, the technique."

Cookie leaned forward, her elbows on her knees and her hands clasped. "What else?"

Peter scowled. "What do you mean, 'what else'? Nothing else."

"You mean, you're not giving even the tiniest thought to who's going to see it, who's going to like it, how it will compare to similar works?"

"Well, of course I do. Don't you?"

"No."

"No?"

"Not at all. I just paint for myself, for my own amusement or to sort things out. So, it doesn't matter what other people think. What matters is the doing of it."

"But you don't even want to be an artist. If you tried to paint professionally, it would be different."

"Maybe. Maybe not. The point is, Pa wasn't painting to show off his work. He wasn't painting to compete with you. He was painting for himself. That's all."

"Well, it didn't work out that way, did it?" Peter didn't try to hide his bitterness.

Cookie steepled her fingers, forming a point that she wagged as she talked. "Peter, I think that's why people like his works. He's all there, every bit of his ability, every part of his being. When he painted, that's all he did. He was completely involved, painting what he saw. I think people are drawn to that kind of honesty. You know all this, right?"

Peter had lowered his head and was staring at the floor. He said nothing.

"You hold yourself back when you work, Peter. You can't seem to stop watching yourself, rather than surrendering to your work. You'd rather paint in other people's styles, styles that have already won approval, than trust your own style. Are you hearing me?"

Peter kept his eyes on the floor. "So?"

Cookie rose from her chair and stood squarely in front of Peter. "So, that's the secret to the greatness of Pa's art. He couldn't have put words to it. But he showed you everything he knew in every painting he made. He was able to begin with the kind of openness that you've been working years to achieve. It makes you crazy."

Peter lifted his head and glared at Cookie. "Yes, it makes me crazy. It will always make me crazy. Is that what you want to hear? Fine. I can't stand that, in one day, one try, he was attuned to whatever it is that makes a painting a work of art, and I can't get there. Satisfied?"

Cookie eyes blazed. "You silly idiot. Do you hear what you're saying? One day? Your father didn't get there in one day."

Peter frowned, puzzled.

"Peter, it took Pa sixty-four years to get to the place where he could open up that way. Sixty-four years of living, suffering, failing, never succeeding. He knew he was near the end of his life. He had nothing to lose. All he had left was what was in his heart.

"You're half his age, Peter. You've got a way to go. Maybe if you learn from his experience, you can get there faster. Accept the legacy Pa left you,"

Peter's head was reeling. "Legacy?"

Cookie sat next to Peter on the bed and patted his hand. "Legacy. Yes. Now, thanks to Pa, you have some great contacts in New York. You can use his name and his paintings to keep those contacts open while you take your next step." She stood and smoothed her skirt. "Where are my shoes? It's time to go downstairs."

Peter shook his head, trying to catch up with Cookie's sudden change of mood. "Wait."

Cookie stood in the doorway. "What? You're still angry at Pa?"

Peter sat very still. He could feel his heart thump in his chest, the gentle waggle of his head. But the rage was gone. The blackness was gone. In its place was a deep sadness. "No," he said in a faltering voice. "Now, I just miss him."

Peter reached across the bed for his jacket. "You know what you said about using his name with the dealers?" He put on his glasses and straightened his tie. "Cookie, it's so sad. Hunt wasn't even his real name."

The harbor was uncommonly calm as Peter and Cookie sat on an old wooden bench on the wharf, waiting for the ferry. A full moon glowed bright and large in the clear sky and was mirrored in the calm water. Every now and then, a beam of pale yellow from the lighthouse sped across the water towards them, then vanished. Only a few people were sprinkled around the landing.

"I wish you'd stay, at least for the night," Peter grumbled. "You come all the way from California for Pa's funeral and stay for only a few hours. You turn my head upside down, then you leave."

"I didn't turn your head upside down. I set it straight." Cookie kicked off her shoes. "By the way, where's Hoppy? I didn't see her today."

"You had to ask, didn't you?" Peter tried to keep his voice light. "She's in Paris."

"Oh, how nice! When will she be back?"

Peter sighed. "She won't. She's back working with Madame. She lives there now. With Paolo."

Cookie felt the blood drain from her face. "Paolo?"

Peter's smile was grim. "Yes. I seem to be losing people left and right. Just before Pa got sick last fall, they left."

"But Peter, I thought you and Hoppy . . ."

"So did I. But I was away a lot last year, working, avoiding Pa. I shouldn't have been surprised. But I was."

Seven minutes.

It had taken seven minutes for Hoppy to tell Peter she was leaving and Paolo was going with her. They were standing at the end of the wharf. She was going to board the ferry Peter had just taken in from Boston. Paolo was stowing their bags on board. Hoppy spoke in a low voice, her eyes shadowed by the brim of her pink traveling hat. As she spoke, Peter stared past the hat and fixed his eyes on the clock face at the top of Town Hall. He couldn't bear to look at her. If he did, he would break in two.

Seven minutes. One by one they ticked by as she ticked off her reasons for leaving. Peter was gone too much. She had been lonely. She'd fallen in love with Paolo. She wanted to move to Paris. She wanted to work for Madame.

Three minutes, so far.

Then Hoppy mentioned Willy.

"Willy?" Peter whispered, his eyes clinging to the clock. Four minutes had already slipped away. Gone, forever.

"Willy told me about his marriage to Syrie," Hoppy's voice dropped to a whisper. "He was very discreet, but made it clear he prefers young men. He told me how he needed to quell any whispers about his homosexuality. That kind of gossip could ruin him."

Besides, Willy reasoned, Syrie loved him. He liked her well enough. They even had a daughter. But, in the end, Willy and Syrie were both miserable, angry prisoners of a lie. Surely, Hoppy didn't want that to happen with Peter, Willy said. Could she ever be certain that Peter loved only Hoppy, or if he loved her just "well enough" to mask his true desires? How long could that kind of marriage last?

Five minutes. Gone.

The blood rushed in Peter's ears. His heart was pounding. He could no longer make out Hoppy's words because he was dying, right there, at the end of the wharf, looking for all the world like he was involved in a conversation with a pretty woman in a pink suit.

Six minutes.

He felt his life ebb away as she patted his arm and kissed him on the cheek, the brim of her hat momentarily hiding the clock face from his view.

Seven minutes.

She was gone. Paolo was gone. In seven minutes, his heart had been ransacked and destroyed.

For the first few days after they left, Peter was numb with pain and sorrow. The house didn't make sense to him anymore. It was all wrong. Where was Hoppy? Paolo? Oh yes. Gone. He cried, cried until his ribs hurt, until his face was raw from tears. He couldn't see any end to his searing grief.

Seven days. That's how long it took Peter to finally find the edges of the pain so he could begin to roll it up like a carpet, the better to carry it. He never doubted the pain would stay always, bowing his shoulders. That's when the anger took hold.

Willy. Damn Willy.

The anger forced the pain to the side, so Peter welcomed it. He reveled in it. He fed his fury until he could think of nothing else. His rage gave him a reason to breathe.

Peter found strength in his anger. Determination. He would go to New York. He would confront Willy. He would punish him. As soon as the idea came to Peter, he left the house and got in his car without stopping to shave or change his clothes. He barely noticed the miles flying under his wheels, the city traffic. His anger was a steel cocoon.

Willy was startled to see Peter, and annoyed. Once seated in Willy's sumptuous drawing room, Peter started speaking in a low, cold voice. Before long, though, Peter left his chair and strode back and forth, across the room, his words rising to shouts of anguish and wrath.

Willy appeared unmoved. Instead, he watched Peter with interest. "You're quite mistaken, old chap. It wasn't me that drove Hoppy away. It was Cookie. She's the one who brought Paolo."

"No, Willy, it was you. Cookie may have brought Paolo, but if he hadn't arrived, there would be someone else. Isn't there always someone else?" Peter retorted.

He pushed his face close to Willy's, and spoke in a low voice. "It was you, Willy, who made Hoppy unsure about our love. You made her feel that the end was inevitable. And you did it because you could. We're just puppets to you, not friends. You play with us, torment us, just to see what we'll do. We're like characters in one of your savage little books. You keep us only for your amusement."

Willy feigned a yawn. "Perhaps. But, when you get down to b-brass tacks, darling, you simply couldn't keep her. Your love wasn't strong enough."

Peter stopped. The truth in Willy's words stunned him. Peter shook his head. Willy was right, of course. But what he did to Hoppy and Peter was wrong. Willy had played with their hearts, their lives. The anger fizzled to nothing. The pain condensed to the size of a bullet centered in his heart. Peter had had enough.

He walked out of the door and, for all intents and purposes, out of Willy's life.

"Oh, Peter." Cookie's stomach clenched. "You must have been devastated."

"I was."

"Why didn't you let me know? I would have come right away."

"Oh no, darling. Separate the newlyweds? No, I couldn't do that. Besides, I had a long talk with Willy. That was very helpful."

Cookie felt sick. She recalled her conversation with Willy that long-ago Fourth of July, just a few steps from where she and Peter now sat. A sob escaped, and she covered her mouth with her hands.

Peter pulled out a handkerchief. "You silly thing! Look at you. A day devoted to death and funerals and not a tear is shed. The mention of a broken heart, and the waterworks come on."

Cookie wiped her eyes and clutched the handkerchief. "Peter, this is all my fault."

"Because you hired Paolo? That's what Willy said. Don't be ridiculous. You didn't tell Paolo to steal Hoppy from me."

"No, but . . ."

"Not another word. No more talk about my broken heart. Let's talk about you and your affairs of the heart."

Cookie blew her nose. "There's not much to tell."

Just when Cookie had all but given up hope that she and Colin would ever marry, his world turned upside down. Colin's mother, the battleax, had suddenly died of heart failure while on a trip to England. Cookie would never hope for anyone's death, of course, but she couldn't ignore the convenience of Mother Campbell's exit.

Still, there was another obstacle to their happiness. Joseph Leiter, the battleax's brother, would take the reins of Colin's considerable inheritance, just as Mother Campbell had instructed in her will. Uncle Joe told Colin he didn't think Cookie had the position or wealth to marry his nephew. Besides, she was a divorcee.

Cookie was ready to walk away, to re-open her search for a husband, but something held her back. She was startled to realize that her feelings for Colin ran deeper than she imagined. She loved him! When did that happen? Against her better judgment, she stayed with Colin, in a sort of shamed limbo.

Uncle Joe obligingly died a few months later, "Just before we were furious enough to kill him!" Cookie joked to Peter. Cookie and Colin were finally free to marry.

It wasn't until after their notary public nuptials that Colin began moping around the Chicago apartment Peter had decorated for them. "Colin didn't want to go anywhere, do anything. And he started complaining about my friends. He said they were too silly," Cookie said. "I tried to cheer him up, encourage him on picnics or golf, but he wouldn't have any of it."

Cookie eventually realized Colin was only now beginning to grieve for his mother. His grief was deep and enduring, more than Cookie thought reasonable. Still, even when he was morose, Colin was sweet-natured and indulged her every whim. "He tried so hard to make me happy, even though he was so sad," said Cookie. "So, when he told me he wanted to go to his mother's ranch in California, well, I couldn't say no. Besides, I thought going to the ranch would help him get over his loss."

Campbell Ranch wasn't a ranch, exactly. Colin's mother had built a huge Scottish castle, with furnishings and luxuries fit for royalty, smack in the middle of Nowhere, California. Just like Mother Campbell to have so much opulence surrounded by nothing but rocky terrain and the Pacific Ocean, far from the warmth of a city, Cookie thought. But she bit her tongue.

The place reeked of Mother Campbell. Rooms were jammed with heavy Empire furniture, grim portraits and dark, heavy velvets. Colin wouldn't hear of changing a thing. So Cookie read a lot, rode horses every day and waited for Colin to come to terms with his mother's death. Then they could go back to having fun.

Days passed, then weeks. Problem was, Colin didn't want to leave. Ever. He liked living at the ranch. We'll stay here a while longer, he told Cookie. There wasn't much Cookie could do about it, either, now that she was expecting.

"Expecting what?" Peter asked.

"A baby, you twit."

"Cookie, that's wonderful!"

Cookie shrugged. "I hope so. Maybe a baby will help Colin see that we need to move to a place closer to civilization, and away from his ghosts."

Peter put his arm around her shoulders. "I think it's wonderful! Another little Cookie! What more could you want?"

Cookie looked at Peter thoughtfully. "Actually, a lot more."

The lights of the ferry rounded Long Point, followed by the low thrum of her engines. The steamship's whistle bounced across the water.

Cookie used her foot to feel for her shoes. "I'm just beginning to realize that getting everything you want isn't always enough."

"What more could you possibly want?"

Cookie pulled on her jacket and tugged at its cuffs. "I don't know. More. Passion. Excitement. Fun." She looked up at Peter. "You should want more, too."

They watched the ferry glide to the end of the wharf as one of the crew tossed a rope to a dockworker to tie to a mooring.

Peter and Cookie watched the few passengers disembark. "More? I should want more than to be an artist? And make money at it?" Peter said with a chuckle.

"I mean it. You've spent years on your art and you're not happy."

"Cookie, I'm perfectly content."

"Maybe that's why your woodcuts aren't generating more interest. Did you ever consider that?" Cookie's eyes were sparkling with excitement. "Think about it! When an artist is excited about what he does, inspired, doesn't it show in his work? Add some talent and skill, like yours, and the work is bound to be outstanding."

The first mate signaled to Cookie that she could board the ferry. "I don't know, Peter. I'm just thinking out loud. But, I remember when we were students, and even for a while after the war, you were so excited about your work. You were creating your own version of a peasant design, remember? Why did you stop? You were so happy."

Peter picked up her suitcase. "How many peasant designs have you seen at any of the New York galleries, Cookie? That's not what they sell. If I'm going to make money, I have to make what people want to buy."

"Have any of the gallery people seen your peasant designs?"

Peter shook his head.

"Well, silly, how do you know if you don't try? What you're doing now isn't working. What do you have to lose?"

Peter laughed. "Cookie, that's not art. That's craft! It's just decorations!"

Cookie kissed Peter's cheek and wiped her lipstick from his face. Her smile was sweet and sad. "Oh, Peter, I don't know what counts as art and what doesn't. All I know is life should be more than contented. You have a wonderful talent. You should do what you love. I bet it will shine through, just like it did for Pa."

Cookie stood on the deck of the ferry, waving and blowing kisses to Peter until the ferry disappeared from view. Peter stood on the landing for several minutes, looking out on the water. He shivered.

Time to go home. Ma was alone.

The Cape Cod Room at the Drake Hotel in Chicago is shown in this old postcard. Hunt designed the room in the 1930s, and it remains virtually unchanged.

"*Going through your pictures from Provincetown?*" Peter leaned on the back of the couch to look over my shoulder. "*Not exactly a professional shutterbug, are we?*"

"I guess not. This one's my favorite, see? There's still a door with your decorations where Peasant Village used to be. Say, where have you been? I haven't seen you in a while."

Peter craned his neck to see the album better. "*I've been busy. Turn the page.*"

"Busy? Doing what?"

"*Thinking. Are you going to turn the page?*"

I turned the page. "Thinking? Thinking about what?"

Peter looked at me over the top of his glasses. "*Nosy, aren't we?*"

Ah. This game again. I closed the album and stood. "Well, I've got to get back to work."

"*Where are we now?*" Peter was sitting on the back of the couch, his feet planted on the cushion I'd just vacated.

"We are about to enter Peasant Village." I sat at my computer. "I need to concentrate now, if you don't mind."

"*Not at all.*" Peter fell silent, but he didn't leave. After a few minutes, I was typing so fast I forgot he was in the room.

"*Ahem.*"

"What? Oh, Peter, yes? What do you want?" I knew he'd finally give in and tell me. He always did.

"*I've been thinking about the book. It's not going at all the way I'd hoped.*"

"No?"

"*No. It's not fun enough. It should be breezy and gay, but you keep weighing it down with sad and unhappy parts. I don't want people to think of me that way.*"

"Peter, you weren't born happy, much as you tried to tell people that. You became happy. You went through some difficult times, but you always worked to be happy. It was a process. People will want to know how you got there."

"*I highly doubt it. People want to feel uplifted. This isn't uplifting.*"

"Sure it is. If you overcame so many obstacles, maybe they can, too. That's uplifting."

"Why dredge this up? I haven't thought about most of this since the moment it happened."

"You went over it when you died, didn't you? When your life flashed before your eyes?"

"Excuse me?"

"You know, they say when you die, your life flashes before your eyes."

"I wouldn't know. I was asleep at the time."

"Huh. Do you think that's why you're a ghost?"

"I don't know why I'm a ghost. For all I know, that's just the way death works."

"Think about it. If that were true, the world would be choked with ghosts. But you don't hear about hauntings a lot. Usually it's a spirit who's got unfinished business."

"And you think this depressing review of my life is my unfinished business."

"I don't know. But I wonder if maybe you spent so much time creating an illusion about your life, you never really reviewed it, saw the big picture."

Peter scowled. *"Why would I want to do that? What a waste of time! It was bad enough when I went through it."*

I shrugged. "Got me. Perspective maybe?"

Peter frowned. *"Why would I want perspective? What difference would that make now?"* He tapped his lower lip with his forefinger as he thought. *"Why am I a ghost, anyway? What unresolved business could I possibly have?"*

13

Hurricane Lessons

September 1938 - Provincetown

The wind howled around the house, rattling the windows and blowing cold air under the doors. Now and then, it would gust down the chimney, flattening the sputtering fire. Rain pelted the clapboard and windowpanes like shotgun pellets. Waves pounded relentlessly at the house's pilings, making its timbers shudder. The ocean rumbled and roared.

Peter parted the kitchen curtains with his forefinger and peered outside. The sky was a deep gray, and the ocean looked black. The beach was submerged in swirling water.

"Looks like we're in for a bit of a blow," he said as he returned to the task of mixing martinis. "I believe you girls will be staying in Provincetown tonight."

Carefully, he poured out four martinis and added olives to three of them, an onion to the fourth. "For Ma," he explained.

"A blow? You call this a blow? Seems more like a hurricane to me," said Judith as she accepted her drink with a grateful nod.

"I think it *is* a hurricane," agreed Vickie Ryder. "I think that the big storm that was supposed to blow past us decided to come here instead."

"Could be," said Peter. "I'm taking this upstairs to Ma. I'm sure she's nervous with this weather. I'll be right back."

As if on cue, both Judith and Vickie crossed their left legs over their right, prompting a burst of laughter. "If we get a few more moves down, we could do a vaudeville act," said Judith, her blue eyes shining. A tall, 30-ish woman with blonde hair and a long nose, Judith smoothed the front of her crisp yellow dress. Her skin was bronzed and freckled from a summer spent boating, picnicking and shopping all over Cape Cod. Her husband, Drummond, a quiet, lean man with a deep fondness for the sea, had taken their children back to Rochester in time for the start of school. Judith was, ostensibly, closing up their summer home in Chatham for one delicious week on her own at the Cape.

Judith and Vickie had been friends for more than ten years, since the moment they met at the Beach Club in Chatham. Vickie was Judith's physical opposite, a petite brunette about the same age (which neither would ever reveal), dark eyes and pale skin that, rather than tanning, blotched with red patches. She, too, had shooed her husband, Sid, a Grosse Pointe financier, and their children back home so she could cruise the Cape with Judith.

The two women carried themselves in different ways, too. Judith held herself tall and regal, like a queen, walking with even, unhurried steps. Depending on the situation, Vickie either scampered or lagged, but could never manage to move at a steady pace. Judith had a way of continually scanning her surroundings, always aware of what was going on around her. Vickie, on the other hand, often forgot herself when focusing on anything that captured her interest, and several times a day caught herself wondering just what had she been doing before she was distracted. Judith, when amused, had a low, undulating laugh while Vickie's laugh was a sharp, high bark.

Judith came from a wealthy German family that could trace its lineage back to the 1600s. Vickie's family fortunes had skyrocketed when she was a young girl, and she often felt guilty for all the money she spent. "Although not so guilty as to make me stop," she told Judith.

Neither woman could imagine spending a summer at the Cape without the other.

"Well, Ma's a basket case, but she's soldiering on," said Peter as he sailed back into the room. "I told her that if the weather got any worse, I'd take her to the other house."

A huge wave crashed under the house, pounding the pilings. The walls shuddered and creaked. A floorboard was forced out of place by the surge of wind and water, and a spray blew up through the floor. Judith and Vickie squealed.

"Things just got worse," Peter announced cheerfully. "I'll go get Ma."

The four dashed through the driving rain across Commercial Street and down an alley, Peter hurrying Ma by tugging at her hand. The wind whipped their raincoats and pulled at their plastic rain hats. Judith and Vickie shrieked as they ran through puddles.

Thirty paces down the alley, Peter and Ma veered through an arched gate, and dashed across a courtyard and up the side stairs of a large clapboard house. Peter unlatched the door and the four stumbled inside.

They startled Sam, Peter's carpenter, as they piled inside. He had been dozing in front of the kitchen fire. "Are you crazy? Gallivanting around while a hurricane blows? You're dripping all over the floor! I thought you were going to stick it out on Commercial Street," he said.

"Oh, Sam, we're so sorry," Judith said in her low, soothing voice. "We didn't mean to burst into your home like this."

"T'aint my home," said Sam in a flat Cape Codder accent. He inclined his head at Peter. "T'is."

Once they were all settled in the keeping room, hands warming around mugs of tea "sweetened" with brandy, Judith said, "I had no idea you were landed gentry, Peter."

Peter laughed. "Not quite 'landed,' darling. I just think real estate is a good investment. Besides, we'll probably want to move out of the shop so I can expand the business."

"Maybe we won't," Ma muttered into her tea.

Peter patted her knee. "My business manager. She prefers to keep an eye on things."

"I'm comfortable there," she said. "I feel closer to Pa there."

A silence descended on the small group. Sam reached for the radio and turned it on. An announcer spoke in sharp staccato about Neville Chamberlain meeting Hitler in Germany. "The war," Sam said softly. "We'll be in it soon enough."

Peter's expression was remote. After a moment, he brightened. "Did you girls hear? Pa's paintings are on tour with the Museum of Modern Art!"

"How wonderful!" "You must be so proud!" Judith and Vickie exclaimed. Peter and Ma exchanged a smile. Ma's hair had lightened to a steel gray since Pa's death, and she'd plumped up considerably. Her face was lined, but her cheeks, rosy and soft, made her look younger than her age.

"It's a show on what they call 'self-taught' artists," Ma said. "They call it *Masters of . . . Masters of . . .*"

"*Masters of Popular Painting*," Peter said. "It's all very thrilling. They have two of his paintings, and you'll never guess what one of them is!"

"What?" asked Judith.

"It's a painting of my shop! The sign's on it—*Peter Hunt Antiques!*"

"What fabulous publicity," Vickie blurted. Judith burst out laughing. "Yes, darling, he's going for the erudite but thoroughly modern antiques shopper," she said.

"Peter's in the painting, too," said Ma. "Peeking out the window."

"We went to see it at the opening reception," said Peter. "Imagine Pa on display at MoMA! I wonder what he'd think."

"He'd think you and those art friends of yours are crazy," said Ma.

"Art friends?" asked Judith, accepting a refill of brandy from Sam.

"Oh, yes! That's how it came about. You remember Hudson Walker and Sidney Janis, the art dealers? I introduced you when we went to New York last summer."

Judith and Vickie nodded.

"Well, they were the ones who 'discovered' Pa, as it were. They put his paintings in their galleries. They cultivated a following for Pa."

Peter sipped his tea. "They've been so kind to Ma and me. When MoMA was started, when was that? 1933? Sidney and Hudson got very involved. I think it was Sidney who suggested the popular artists show. When it came down to choosing the artwork, they made sure Pa was included."

The wind suddenly rose, making talk impossible. Judith and Vickie shuddered at its piercing wail. A sharp banging, then a clatter sounded on the side of the house. Peter looked at Sam and shrugged. "Oh, well, there goes another shutter," he yelled into Sam's ear. Sam nodded gravely.

When the wind died down a little, Peter held up the teapot. "Time for the second round! Isn't this fun?"

"Fun!" said Ma, rolling her eyes. "You think everything's fun."

Peter pretended a pout. "Well, almost everything is."

Vickie giggled, as much from Peter's expression as from the brandy. "You work like you're having fun. I love the room you decorated for Judith's daughter! It's enchanting."

Judith nodded. Little Marjorie was thrilled this summer when, before lifting a brush, Peter sat her down and asked her all kinds of questions about her favorite colors, her favorite stories, and what she most liked to play, especially when she stayed at the Chatham summer house. "We want your room to be just yours, with all the things that make you happy," he said.

Peter stayed in Judith's guest house for three weeks while he worked. Peter started by taking all of Marjorie's furniture out to the stable, where he sanded everything down and painted them a bright yellow. Then he spent days in her room, scraping, sanding and painting, usually humming to himself.

When Judith invited Peter to come to the main house for a cocktail party, he was a delight, chatting with everyone, telling funny stories, and listening to even the most boring guests as if they were the most fascinating people on earth.

It was the same charm that overcame Judith's usual coolness when they first met. Vickie had insisted they go up to Provincetown for the day because she had "discovered the most wonderful artist. He's descended from Russian royalty, quite sophisticated, but he prefers the simple life up there. He calls his place Peasant Village. You'll adore him."

Judith had her doubts. He was probably some ne'er-do-well from Greenwich Village, trying to get what he could from the well-to-do summer people.

Still, Vickie was bubbling with excitement, which Judith enjoyed mightily. When enthused about something, Vickie insisted on bringing all her friends, especially Judith, along for the ride. Even if Judith couldn't share the enthusiasm, like the time Vickie made her go swimming in the freezing water off Monomoy "for a lark," Vickie's eagerness was so earnest, Judith always had fun on their adventures.

She followed Vickie into an antique shop on Commercial Street and was startled by the bright colors and charming images she saw on a chest just inside the door. Further in, she spotted a dining set and a deacon's bench, all vividly decorated in a like style. Before she could examine them more closely, Vickie squealed, "Peter! There you are!"

From the shadows in the back glided a slim, tall man with heavy black-rimmed glasses perched on a long nose. His receding hairline made his face look longer than it was, and Judith noticed his head shook slightly with a tremor. He wore a white shirt and dark tie over dungarees and boat shoes. When Vickie introduced the two, Judith saw his hands were long and elegant.

"Come in, come in," he chirruped. "Ma and I are just settling down to lunch, some lovely chowder. You must join us. It's an authentic Cape Cod meal!"

By the time they'd finished eating, Judith was completely charmed by Peter and Ma. Both were disarmingly plainspoken about their neighbors (Mr. Greeley is a drunk, you know, but a very nice one, and he builds the best fish traps in New England), and gossipy about the town's better-known summer residents (Madame Rubenstein comes here to relax, so we never let on who she is to the tourists).

Peter showed Judith the furniture he'd decorated, saying, "I only took this up to experiment, for fun. This is actually supposed to be an antique shop. But I'm selling more of the amusing pieces than I ever did of the antiques. I never imagined!"

Judith could immediately see the appeal. She and her friends were drawn to the Cape every summer because it was fun letting their hair down. Peter's decorated chairs and tables reflected that feeling of brightness and gaiety.

Peter talked enthusiastically about his works. "See this? This is a young peasant courting his lady fair by taking her for a ride in his carriage. He's even put flowers around the horse's neck to impress her!"

On a writing table, he'd painted an ink bottle, feather quill and a sheet of paper with the words "Dear Jacqueline" written in script. "This is for a friend of mine," Peter said. "She's fond of writing."

Vickie encouraged Peter to talk more about his painting. "It's quite simple. Anyone can do it," he said. "I just think about what a piece of furniture would be used for, or where, and who would use it. Then I try to fill my heart with happiness before I start. That's the secret of the peasants in France and Sweden, you know. Their decorations were always put on something they used, and they decorated it for fun, for pleasure. They didn't care what anyone else thought."

Judith was struck by Peter's easy elegance. He had a Park Avenue polish, and was apparently well-traveled. He spoke with studied casualness about socializing at some of the finest European resorts in some of the most exclusive upper-crust circles. But Judith was naturally suspicious of new people and couldn't help but wonder, was this some sort of posturing, put on to sell to a better clientele? By the end of the afternoon, Judith decided Peter was too charming to care about the details. It was possible he was telling the truth.

The following summer, Judith asked Peter to decorate several chairs and a table for her guest house, and, during those weeks, introduced him to her summer neighbors, all of them well-heeled. Peter's quick wit and easygoing charm made him a favorite of the wives deserted by their husbands, who worked weekdays in the city. "They wear him like a bauble, like a charm on their charm bracelets" to parties, clam bakes and cocktail hours, Judith once told Vickie.

Judith saw Peter every summer, but Vickie would see him more often throughout the year. Either they would meet up during one of Vickie's shopping trips to New York or Boston, or Peter would stop by her home in Grosse Pointe on one of his regular trips to Chicago. During one of his visits to her house, he stayed awake one night and decorated the walls of Vickie's basement with peasant-style images of her, the children and her husband. "When I got up, he was just going to bed. Oh! I was so surprised. Imagine him doing that!"

Vickie was delighted. Judith was certain she would have been incensed at Peter's audacity.

Peter awakened in Vickie a taste for the outrageous. In New York, they went to Harlem for dinner and dancing, and then to the Village "to see who's about,"

Peter said. He seemed to know everyone in the Village, and Vickie drank and talked and sang with them until dawn. In Grosse Pointe, Peter took Vickie skating, something she hadn't done since she was a teenager, and they howled with laughter as they made figure-eights and pratfalls in front of all the young people there.

So it was inevitable when Vickie's serious, studious daughter, Portia, was ready for her debutante season, Peter was engaged to decorate the Somerset Ballroom in Boston for the coming-out party.

Peter and Vickie cooked up the idea of an Austrian Village for the theme of the party. Portia was not at all happy about the idea. Vickie insisted, saying, "Darling, it will be the hit of the season. It will be completely different from any other coming out party! You'll love it!" Seeing that the party was more Vickie's affair than her own, Portia withdrew and would have nothing to with the plans.

Peter spent the better part of a week preparing the ballroom, and Vickie worked shoulder to shoulder beside him, both of them sweating and laughing the whole time. On the big night, the guests found themselves in an enchanted Austrian Village, complete with a little church, shops and a café. Real storks flapped at anyone who came too close. Vickie and a reluctant Portia greeted the guests in matching leather lederhosen and yodelers' caps.

Portia disappeared to her hotel room soon after eleven, having danced the obligatory number of dances and accepted the mandatory toasts. Vickie, Peter and the other guests "had a grand time! We carried on until three or four in the morning!" she told Judith.

The Boston society columns raved about the affair, and the news of the marvelous Austrian Village ball was soon carried in the New York papers as well. "Darling, we made social history," Vickie wrote when she sent a batch of the clippings to Judith.

Over the past few years, Peter was as much a part of Judith and Vickie's summers as their family cottages and favorite stretches of beach. It was only natural that, before finally heading back to their lives on the mainland, Judith and Vickie would want to see Peter one more time.

Who would have imagined that while they were in Provincetown, a hurricane would race up the coast? Or that their families would soon hear that Cape Cod had been swept into the sea?

The radio went out with the lights, so the howling wind seemed even louder as they lit candles that flickered and spat in the drafts.

Judith examined the wooden candlestick Peter handed her and couldn't help smiling. Once a lathed chair leg, Peter had cut it in half, drilled a hole for the candle, glued on a base and painted it to look like a charming peasant girl. "How do you think of such imaginative ways to make things?" she wondered.

Peter was rummaging in a chest he'd decorated with angels flying with draping fabrics and baskets of flowers. He pulled out an armful of blankets. "Hmm? Oh, I don't know. I just look at something and an idea comes. I'll show you tomorrow in the studio." He shoved the blankets at Judith. "Help me, will you? We're going to have a slumber party!"

After Ma had trundled upstairs and Sam went to his room off the kitchen, Peter, Judith and Vickie stretched out in front of the fireplace. Peter had made up a small picnic with a loaf of Portuguese bread, a round of cheese and a bowl of apples. He filled stemmed glasses with "a jovial claret" and passed them to his friends. "Now, didn't I tell you? Isn't this fun?"

Peter and Sam were in the courtyard deep in conversation when Vickie and Judith finally awoke. The courtyard was strewn with limbs, papers and leaves, flung on the flagstones by the strong winds the night before.

"Hello, sleepy heads," Peter called when he saw their faces in the window.

He'd been up for hours and had already been to the town hall to learn about damage from the hurricane and what might be needed.

"It seems you girls will be spending the next day or two with me. The only road out of town has been washed out. You can't get off the Cape," Peter announced over coffee. "I wish I could say I was sorry for the inconvenience, but I'm not. I'm glad I have you all to myself."

"Thank you darling. You're such a sweetheart," said Vickie. "I'll just call home and let them know what's going on." Judith nodded in agreement.

"Sorry, ladies, can't be done," said Peter. "The telephone lines are down. Electric, too. We'll have to get along like the Pilgrims."

"Hardly," snorted Sam. "The Pilgrims didn't have a fine roof over their heads or a basement full of canned foods."

"Bless Ma for all her work last fall," said Peter. "She canned enough fruits and vegetables to feed the entire town." He looked around. "Where is she? Has she come down?"

"Down and out," said Sam. He gestured to the window. There was Ma, wearing a yellow rain slicker and matching hat, lugging a large basket down the alley toward them. "She's steaming this way now."

"I brought the girls some clothes. Mary Vorse lent them to me," Ma explained after she settled at the table with a cup of coffee. "And some necessaries. Candles and the like. Looks like you boys have a few windows to board up at the main house."

"Oh, dear!" said Judith. "The wind blew them out? How frightening!"

"Not at all," said Peter. "We're quite used to it. We always get a blow or two this time of year." He looked in turn at each person seated at the table. "All right, kids. It's time to get to work. Sam and I will tend to the main house and you girls can pick up the branches and things in the courtyard, if you don't mind. After we're done, I'll give you a lesson in peasant painting."

"What about me?" asked Ma.

"You, dear heart, have the most important job of all," said Peter. "You take care of all of us."

After a lunch of bread-and-jam sandwiches, Peter took Judith and Vickie across the courtyard to what looked like a garden shed. Inside was a studio, every open surface painted and decorated with Peter's hearts, angels and flowers.

"Peter, this is charming," Judith exclaimed. "I had no idea."

After the women were seated at a table built around a brick column in the center of the room, Peter put blank green trays in front of each of them. He then pulled out three magazines and squeezed paints on each: bright red, sunny yellow and a royal blue. "Here are your palettes," he said.

"That's clever," said Judith. "No wood palettes to scrape and clean: you just toss them when you're done."

"Precisely," said Peter. He handed each woman a brush and took up one for himself. "Ladies," he intoned in a deep, formal voice. "It's time for you to meet the basic stoke. Once you've learned this stroke, you will be able to create any kind of peasant design you wish."

Loading his brush with red paint and scraping the excess on the edge of the magazine, Peter returned to his normal voice as he demonstrated. "You want a nice bit on the tip of your brush, see? Not too much, not too little." He pushed the end of the brush onto the tray, making a small blob of red appear. "Then draw your brush back toward you while lifting the brush evenly and constantly." As he drew back his brush, the blob stretched at one end, becoming narrower and narrower until it came to a point. "There! What does that look like?"

"A polliwog," said Judith.

"You think so? I always thought it looked more like an exclamation point." Peter dipped his brush in the paint. "Now, watch. You can make them tilt, one way and another." His brush moved swiftly as he painted. "And if you make them so they're touching, you have what?"

"A heart!" said Judith.

"Once you master the basic stroke, you can start curving it one way or bending it another. See? And if you connect one after the other like this, you have a border!"

The tray was filled with red, yellow and blue strokes and borders. "I'll wipe this off and you practice the basic stroke."

Vickie and Judith bent over their trays. "Oh, no, mine look like fat worms," said Vickie.

"Mine look like splotches," said Judith. "How do you make the end so narrow?"

"The trick is to lift your brush smoothly as you move it down," said Peter. "Don't go too slowly, or it will look fat and dumpy."

By the end of the afternoon, not only had Judith and Vickie mastered the basic stroke, they also learned how to draw peasant people, birds and flowers under Peter's lighthearted instruction.

"What fun!" said Vickie. "No wonder you enjoy it so much, Peter."

"That's the true peasant spirit," said Peter. "The peasants decorate things because they enjoy it. It's fun. If you're too serious or deliberate, your decorations look stiff and unnatural. You must have a light heart, like a peasant!"

"Good for you, Vickie," said Judith. "Now you think like a peasant. I can't wait to hear what your husband thinks."

Vickie giggled, and stopped, her face serious. "I hope he isn't worrying. I wish we could use the telephone."

Just after the breakfast dishes were washed the next morning, Sam brought news.

"You'll never believe what I just heard from Tom, the lightkeeper."

"What?" said Ma, Peter, Vickie and Judith together.

"He was working his shortwave radio last night, trying to roust someone on the mainland. No matter who he calls, he can't rouse anyone in New York or Boston. After a while he gets some fellow in England." Sam pulled a bandana from his pocket and blew his nose.

"Fancy that. England, you say," said Peter, trying to sound interested.

"Naw, that's not it," said Sam, shoving the kerchief back in his pocket. "It's what the fellow in England told Tom."

Peter swallowed, trying to stifle his impatience. "And what did the fellow in England say?"

"Well, it's odd, you know, how Tom couldn't reach anyone here in the States on his wireless, but he gets a fellow in England. Funny."

"Funny indeed," said Peter. "So?"

Sam scanned the expectant faces in the room, pleased at the attention. "Well, sir, the fellow in England says Tom can't get anyone on the East Coast because a terrible storm ripped through, killing folks, washing out houses all along the seaboard."

"Dear Lord," Ma said.

"That ain't the strangest part though. Everyone in the States thinks the Cape's been washed out to sea."

The hurricane had devastated much of the New England coast, Sam said, washing out roads, or barricading them with fallen trees, and wiping out electricity and telephone wires in three states. Apparently, when people couldn't reach the Cape because the roads were blocked, and no one could be raised by telephone or shortwave radio, word spread through the U.S. news reports and on to the European press that Cape Cod had been swept out to sea by the wrath of the storm.

"Oh, dear God," gasped Vickie. "Sid must be going crazy."

"My Drummond must be ecstatic," said Judith wryly. After a horrified pause, everyone in the room burst out laughing.

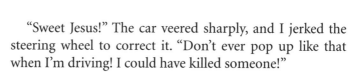

"Sweet Jesus!" The car veered sharply, and I jerked the steering wheel to correct it. "Don't ever pop up like that when I'm driving! I could have killed someone!"

"I know just how they'd feel, too," said Peter, sitting in the passenger seat. "Have fun shopping?"

The traffic light ahead turned yellow. Still rattled from Peter's sudden appearance, I decided not to take a chance and rush through, so I slowed to a stop. "Not really. I couldn't find anything I liked, so I let a saleswoman talk me into buying a dress that's going to make me look like a hippopotamus."

"At least you'll be a stylish hippopotamus. She must have had a great sales pitch."

The light changed and I eased onto the accelerator. "You should know. I read that your artist friend, John Whorf, said you were the greatest salesman of the century. That you could sell anything."

Peter smiled with pleasure. "John Whorf was a brilliant artist. A genius. Terrific judge of character."

"Oh, please."

"His daughters worked for me for a time. Carol was a darling, so quiet and pleasant. Her younger sister, Nancy, well, she was just the opposite."

"Nancy said you fired her after the first few weeks."

Peter straightened in his seat. "Can you blame me? My God, she was like a firecracker – fast, sparkling and loud. She'd dash around, talk and joke, and made me so nervous I couldn't stand it. She was a disruptive influence."

I turned onto River Road. "Oh, Peter, what did you expect? She was only fourteen years old."

The car approached Riverside Park. I pulled over and turned the key to shut off the engine. "That was Nancy in the picture of you and a little girl on the cover of your How-to-do-it Book, right?"

"Well, yes, but that was posed. She wasn't working for me then. There's another picture in there, of the girls working in the courtyard at my Peasant Village. Did you see it? Carol's in that one. Wasn't she pretty?" He paused. "I hired Nancy again, ten years later. She was incredible. She out-painted me."

I chuckled.

"I'm quite serious. She became better at those designs than I was."

"Now, Nancy and Carol are well-known artists in their own right."

"See? Mary Hackett was wrong. She told her daughter, Wendy, that if she worked for me, she would be prostituting her art."

"Well, Mary Hackett was a mother and an artist. Besides, Wendy came to work for you anyway. She said that she was sixteen years old, and didn't have any art yet."

Peter laughed. *"It was so much fun, having all those lovely girls around the place. They'd chatter away, tease each other. Every day, I'd have them take a break in the afternoon for tea. Sometimes those girls drove me a little mad, but we always had fun. I'd almost forgotten."*

He frowned. *"I forget lots of things lately. I can still remember people. I can still remember feelings. But it's like the memories are floating away."*

"What's taking their place?"

"Resonance. That's the only word for it. Resonance."

Peter was quiet for several moments. *"You know what I miss most? Doing things with people. I miss the laughter, the talking, the fun."*

"Hey, what am I? Chopped liver? You talk with me."

Peter snorted. *"That's entirely different."*

"How?"

"Can you imagine what would happen if I suddenly appeared to Carol or Nancy or any of my friends? They'd either be terrified or call for a ride to the funny farm. You, you kept looking for me, even after you knew I was dead. You were glad to see me."

I rolled my eyes. "'Glad'? That's not exactly the word I'd use."

14

Peasant Village

SEPTEMBER 1941 - PROVINCETOWN

"I don't know if we should be eating this," said Ma, looking dubiously at the oversized tuna steak steaming on her plate. "It could be cursed."

"Ma, sometimes I think you spend too much time with the Portagee wives." Peter set down his plate and sat down across from her. "You're looking at this all wrong. If the fishermen catch almost a thousand tuna in one day, that's a blessing, not a curse."

He took a bite of the fish. "Mmmm. So good."

Ma scowled and picked up her fork. "It's strange, is all. So many odd things have been happening. These are strange times."

"Strange and wonderful," Peter said, chewing.

"Tell that to those poor people in Czechoslovakia."

Peter bit his tongue. It was no use arguing with Ma. The years since Pa's death had been difficult for her, and the toll showed in the lines on her face and the stoop of her shoulders. White streaked her steel-colored hair and her eyes had a yellow cast to them.

Ma missed her husband, that much was immediately clear to Peter after Pa died. After the funeral, months passed before she resumed her post on the front porch and then she'd talk only with the people she knew. Instead of her banter and teasing with the tourists, Ma was matter-of-fact with them now, helping them in the shop, but never engaging in conversation with them.

When Peter hired a handful of Portuguese housewives to work in the room above the shop, sewing and embroidering floor coverings and fabrics with his peasant designs, Ma took to sitting with them. The women were remote at first, but when Ma took up a piece of sewing and smartly whipped on an admirable hemstitch, they opened up, trying to talk with their broken English, and she tried to learn a little Portuguese from them.

Ma felt comfortable with the Portuguese wives, she told Peter. They reminded her of the women in her village when she was a girl. Besides, Ma wasn't asking to be paid, so she could do as she pleased.

For the past year, it seemed that all Ma and the wives talked about was the war in Europe. They fretted over each newspaper report, radio bulletin and letter from a far-away relative. The world they knew so well in Europe was being destroyed, and the circle of destruction seemed to grow every day, encompassing more villages, more cities, more countries. "I'm worried for the people in Europe," Ma would bark when Peter asked what was wrong. "You should worry, too. Soon the war will come here."

From all appearances, Provincetown was gearing up for war. Sailors flooded the streets and the taverns when on leave from the Navy cruisers patrolling the Provincetown waters, the outermost U.S. port before Boston or New York. The town turned out for the monthly evacuation drills, so women and children could quickly move out of harm's way, "should the need arise."

At St. Mary's of the Harbor, wives, daughters and grandmothers would gather for sewing and knitting circles, making clothing for the war relief effort. On those nights, before picking up Ma, Peter always stopped to view the creche in the chapel. Peter and Frederick Waugh had painted it back in 1936. Frederick had worked night and day on the little church, assembling artists, begging supplies and even painting the gentle-faced Madonna and child at the alter. Two years later, after a bitter struggle with cancer, the church held Frederick's memorial service and he was buried in the North Truro cemetery.

But for all the dire news and war exercises, Provincetown—and Peter—enjoyed an unexpected prosperity, especially considering the economic ravages of the Great Depression. Because Provincetown's fishing industry was key to food supplies in the U.S., the government returned the beam trawlers seized for war use and the price of fish skyrocketed.

In fact, if it wasn't for the war in Europe and Helena Rubenstein, Peter doubted he would be doing so well. It was Madame who brought her wealthy friends and clients to Peter's shop, extolling the designs of hearts, horses and whimsical people he painted on all manner of things: bureaus, tables, chairs, trays, and even birdhouses. "This reminds me of the peasant decorations back in Poland, but so much more beautiful," she would say. "The peasants, they didn't have the skills of my artist Peter, yes?"

Partly from Madame's pressure, but mostly because they were genuinely charmed by his work, the women would buy pieces, usually the odd chair or occasional table, to brighten their Cape Cod cottages. The matrons always had guests during the summer, and the visitors delighted in the charming decorations and begged to know where they came from. Soon, more and more new customers were arriving at Peter's shop.

Demand for Peter's decorated pieces doubled from one summer to the next, then doubled again the following summer. Not satisfied with just one or two pieces, many of the well-to-do summer people asked Peter to design suites of decorated furniture for bedrooms, dining rooms or guest houses, often asking that he decorate the walls and ceilings, too.

By 1940, when every other artist in Provincetown was struggling to find work, it was all Peter could do to keep the shop supplied and consignments met. He scoured dumps, tag sales and thrift shops for inexpensive pieces of furniture and oddments, even items in sad disrepair, and hauled them home. Ma would protest in vain about the heaps of wood and metal piled in front of the shop as Peter and Sam pawed through the jumble of chair legs, firkins and broken drawers, looking for anything that could be renewed, restored or taken apart to be used on other pieces.

Peter and Sam became quite expert at seeing possibilities where other people saw just junk. The glass from a broken mirror could be removed, legs attached to the back and, with a coat of paint and Peter's designs, voila! A coffee table with a painted image of a tea service, complete with filled cups. Firkins, finials and turned table legs were transformed into lamps with painted ribbons or hearts or swags. A dainty Queen Anne side table missing one leg was cut in half, decorated with yellow, blue and green paint, and attached to a wall as a foyer valet. An old organ was disemboweled and decorated to be a writing desk, with images of peasants holding out pens and papers. In what Peter considered one of his most innovative conversions, he took an old cello case, opened it and hung it at an angle, fitted it with shelves and attached it to a wall as an étagère.

That summer, two things happened that guaranteed Peter's financial security, at least for the foreseeable future.

A New York advertising executive on vacation with his family at the Cape was struggling to find a hook for the latest product of one of the agency's clients, DuPont Nemours. The company had just developed a line of paints to be used for crafts and home projects. Once the adman saw the way Peter took "old things and made them new," inspiration took hold and he asked if Peter would help him develop a brochure to give customers some practical ideas, for a fee, of course. They called it *How to Transform Outdated Furniture*, and Peter agreed to decorate a dresser, a drawer and a headboard for "before" and "after" pieces. Maybe Peter could even do a promotional demonstration now and then?

About the same time, a buyer from Macy's was on vacation in Provincetown when she spotted Peter's peasant designs and immediately ordered several cases of knick-knacks and accessories to be scattered throughout the store's home furnishings department. Shoppers snapped them up almost as soon as they were on put out on the floor, so the buyer placed another order with Peter.

Not to be outdone, Gimbel's and Bloomingdale's soon followed suit and Peter was overwhelmed by the demand. He needed help fast.

Peter asked John Whorf if his daughter, Carol, a teenager already showing a fine artistic bent, would be willing to work for him after school. Intelligent and quiet, Carol quickly picked up on the execution of Peter's designs. She hesitated, though, on deciding what images to paint. "Think of a story you like, a fairy tale or a legend, and make a painting out of that," Peter suggested.

Carol painstakingly painted a princess atop a stack of mattresses. "The Princess and the Pea," Peter said when she showed him her work. He frowned. "You shouldn't be so careful. Peasants never decorated things slowly. Their strokes are quick. This looks a little stilted."

Carol's face fell. "You've picked up the style very well," Peter said. "Your eye for color is good. Try again." He handed the tray back to her.

Peter watched her pick up another tray and consider it. She frowned, picked up the brush and dipped it in the paint.

"Wait!" said Peter. "You're so serious! This should be fun for you."

Carol looked at him quizzically.

"Peasants decorated things because they wanted to, because they enjoyed it," Peter said. "Try this, darling. Approach your work with a glad heart, a blithe spirit."

Carol nodded, but didn't look convinced.

"I have an idea," said Peter. "Come along, let's have tea."

Over tea and cookies, Peter chatted and teased until quiet Carol was laughing out loud. When they were done, he sent her back to the studio. "Now you see? You have a glad heart," he said. "Let's see what you can do."

Carol's brush flew over the tray, and a smiled played across her face as she worked.

"Wonderful!" Peter exclaimed when she showed him her work. "Is that us?" Two peasant characters, one a man and the other a woman, were seated under a fantastical tree, having tea.

Carol nodded.

"That's exactly the way I want you to do things. We'll just make sure to have tea every day."

The advertising agency called Peter from New York. The brochures he'd worked on were so successful, DuPont wanted them redone as a booklet, featuring him. It would be called *Transformagic,* and would feature Peter working with visitors to his shops, Peasant Village. Would he be interested? It would benefit DuPont, and Peasant Village could share in the publicity. That could mean more business.

Soon, Peter hired more of Carol's friends: Nora Haspell and Wendy Hackett. As he promised, he had the girls break for teatime every day. "You must be happy as you paint." They used old magazines for palettes and helped each other with ideas. When the weather improved, the girls worked outside on the terrace, much to the delight of passers-by.

Peter used the sudden infusion of money from Macy's and DuPont to buy the buildings adjoining and across from his alley house, and soon he owned every property on Kiley Court. Some he converted into small gift shops or studios, others into apartments. He dubbed the alley "Peter Hunt Lane" and declared, "Here is my Peasant Village."

1940s Postcard of Peter Hunt Lane (now Kiley Court). Courtesy of the Provincetown Heritage Museum.

"So, tell me, Madame, what do you hear from Europe?" Peter leaned back in the Victorian settee in the drawing room of Helena's Park Avenue apartment.

"Princess," Madame scolded. She wore a richly embroidered Persian caftan and bedroom slippers. Peter, on a quick trip to New York to check his department store inventories, had called to invite himself over for drinks "But, from you, 'Madame' sounds more appealing. Less girlish."

Madame's new husband came on the scene just in time, Peter thought. Had she been alone to deal with the Paris shop in the middle of the war, Madame probably would have tried to stay on too long, before transportation out of the city was cut off.

She, too, had done well financially, even after her Paris shop was destroyed and her London salon bombed. Madame had set up a permanent home in Paris 10 years earlier, in 1920, when she sold her cosmetics empire to "preserve my marriage." It was too little too late, and Edward Titus filed for divorce less than a year later. Nine years later, when the American stock market crash in 1929 severely undercut the value of her former empire, Lehman Brothers sold it back to Madame at a bargain basement price. In a few years, Madame had rebuilt the business until it was stronger and bigger than ever, with salons in London, Paris, New York and other large cities around the world.

She met Prince Archtil Gourielli-Tchkonia of Georgian Russia in 1935 over a game of bridge at a mutual friend's home. They married in 1938, a year before the war drove Madame, her husband and her sons first from Paris, then from London, to the United States.

Once settled back in the U.S., Madame focused her energies on her branches in America. Lately, she and Archtil had been planning a gentleman's salon, fronting on Fifth Avenue, offering massages, hairstyling, accessories and skin treatments for men, much like she offered in her women's salons, which they would name House of Gourelli.

"My deepest apologies. Princess Gourielli, of course. What do you hear from Europe?"

"Nothing good." Madame frowned. "German soldiers are encamped at my country place at the Combs-la-Ville. I fear they will take everything and burn it down. This war is breaking my heart. I worry so about my family. It's so hard to get word. Ganna, too, is frantic about her people in Poland. She hasn't heard anything in weeks."

"Ganna Walska? Where is she?"

"You don't know?" Madame's eyebrows arched in surprise. "Just go to the movies."

Peter laughed. "Oh, that. I saw *Citizen Kane*. How awful. Do you think Orson Welles really modeled that poor opera singer after Ganna?"

"Of course, darling. He said so himself, to the Hollywood press. And the press never lies."

"What must Ganna think!"

"It's a mystery. A dramatic, off-key mystery." Helen's bracelets jangled as she held up her glass for Peter to refill. "She's probably drying her eyes with dollars at her new place. Did you hear? She calls it Tibetland." Helena snorted with derision. "She's making it a spiritual center for seekers of enlightenment, she says. She's all blah blah blah about that sort of thing. Santa Barbara is probably reeling."

Peter stopped pouring. "Santa Barbara?"

"Of course, darling. Didn't you hear? Ganna bought Cookie's house when she left the country."

Cookie's life had gone through sea changes since she and Colin had moved to Campbell Ranch in 1933. Though she delighted in their daughters, Alison, born soon after they arrived, and Juliet, born two years later, Cookie was lonely and bored. "If we want to go to the theater, we have to stay overnight in Santa Barbara," she complained to Peter. "Nobody can just drop in and we can't just scoot out for drinks. Colin thinks that's perfectly fine. He loves mucking around with his horses. But I could just scream."

All that changed when an old friend of Colin's from England, Sir Humphrey Clarke, came to visit. "How did it happen? How does it always happen? A bored wife, a dashing stranger. I feel hopelessly plebeian on that count." Cookie told Peter. After a hurried divorce from Colin, Cookie and Humphrey married in a small ceremony attended only by their witnesses and the girls, ages seven and five, at their new home, an enormous mansion in Santa Barbara called Cuesta Linda.

The newlyweds had barely settled in when the war in Europe erupted, and Humphrey's homeland needed its fighting men. Colin refused to allow Cookie to take their daughters to England, fearing for their physical safety, and took custody of Allison and Juliet. After Colin installed the girls in a Chicago mansion on the lake, he had Campbell Ranch and all its contents auctioned.

So, with their newborn son, Toby, Humphrey and Cookie traveled to England. Cookie and Toby were settled in Humphrey's country house in Norfolk while he went with his regiment to fight the dreaded Rommel in Africa.

"So, Ganna's the one who bought Cookie's house. What a small world!" Peter exclaimed.

Madame heaved herself out of her seat. "Peter, darling, come look in my gallery." She led him up the curving stairs. "Tell me what you think."

"Oh, Madame, doesn't it look well!" On the wall facing the Dali mural, between a collection of African masks on one side and a Picasso sketch on the other, hung Peter's latest discovery. "You have such excellent taste, you know. That's the best one of the lot."

Madame crossed the gallery to sit on a bench directly in front of the painting. "Now tell me the story again, darling, so I may tell the Prince over dinner."

Peter drew close to the painting and used the eraser end of his pencil to point as he spoke. "This is *The Revelers*, a wonderful primitive of an imaginary theatrical performance painted by George Edwin Lothrop. He, ma cher, was a self-taught painter and lunatic from Boston.

"He called himself the Poet King, and he used to rant around Greenwich Village before the war. I never thought of him as a painter until the big show in 1917. Remember? The first show of the Society of Independent Artists? Back then, I thought his paintings were ridiculous. But, since Pa . . . " Peter cleared his throat. "Well, our views of art have certainly broadened since then, haven't they?"

Madame pointed to the painting. "Good colors, quite strong, reds and yellows and blues. And I like looking for the hidden faces he puts in the sky and the sea."

"What do you think of the paste rubies and sapphires he's glued onto the dancers?"

Madame clapped. "My favorite part of the painting!"

Peter tapped the frame with the eraser. "See the detail in the frame? He carved it himself. He was trained as a piano carver when he was a lad, and applied those skills to make his frames."

"Very good, darling. Now tell me again how you discovered him."

Peter rubbed his hands. "Ah! This, I think the Prince will find amusing. I was at a thrift shop in Boston, doing my usual rounds for bits and sticks to decorate, when I stumbled on a stack of paintings. It turns out they were donated when some unpaid storage lockers were cleaned out. What a windfall! Nobody recognized the talent, the brilliance! Nobody but me . . . and now you." Peter bowed to Madame's applause.

"Wonderful! I wish I could spin a tale as well as you, darling. Now, where is our genius lunatic? Can we get more?"

Peter shook his head sadly. "No, that's the tragic part of the story, Madame. He lived on the streets of Boston the last few years of his life, begging for drinks and food. Two years ago, he was found dead on the street."

Madame took Peter's arm. "Qu'elle dommage! Such a loss. But such a wonderful story. I can't wait to tell the Prince. Now, darling, let's have another drink, shall we?"

Princess Achille Gourielli (Madame Helena Rubenstein) and Ladislas Medgyes, Princess Gourielli's art director, showing Peter Hunt how they have hung his two collage pictures, "Magazin des Antiquities" and "The Art Gallery" in her home. From Peter Hunt's How-to-do-it Book. Prentice Hall, 1952.

"Peter! Where are you?"

He appeared slowly, yawning and stretching.

"Where have you been? I haven't seen you for days!"

Peter blinked. *"I fell asleep."*

"Asleep? You sleep after you die?"

"I suppose you do." Peter looked around my study as if seeing it for the first time. *"Why did you call me?"*

"Oh. I was thinking."

"Why start now?" Peter seemed to float across the room. He eased himself into the overstuffed chair.

"Ha. Funny. You're a funny guy, Peter. I'll make sure that comes across in the book."

"Book?" Peter wrinkled his forehead. *"Oh, right. The book. How is it going?"*

I felt like he'd slapped me. "You don't know? You aren't reading along?"

Peter lifted his legs onto the hassock and crossed his ankles. *"Not lately. Is there a problem?"*

"Problem?" My voice rose. "Problem? The only problem is you nagged me and pushed me for months to write the damn thing, fussed at me over everything I wrote and didn't write, and, after all this time, you're losing interest."

Peter was unperturbed. "Are you?"

"Am I what?"

"Losing interest? You don't have to do it if you don't want to."

Was this another of his mind games? "Don't want to? Don't want to?" My voice was shrill in my ears. "I'm in way too deep now, Peter. You know that. I have to do it until it's done."

"Then, do it. It's your book. What I say now doesn't much matter, does it?"

Stunned, I stared at him. What was going on here?

Peter's smile was tranquil. *"So, what did you want to talk about?"*

"Oh. Right." I struggled to remember why I'd called for him. "I wanted to ask you something. Why, when you were doing so well with the peasant decorations, did you keep on making up stories about your past?"

"What stories?"

"You told one of your clients that your family had to flee Russia during a coup, and another that you were born to a banker in Manhattan. You bragged about working with the Ballet Russe, and you did no such thing. Why? Those people already liked you. You were in high demand, commercially and socially. You could quit making up stories, but instead, you made them even wilder."

"I was in high demand, as you say, because my stories amused people. Nobody took them seriously. I made people laugh. I entertained them. What's wrong with that? The more fun they had, the more invitations I got. The more invitations, the more clients. It was good business. And, it was fun."

"But if somebody caught you in one of your lies? Wouldn't that have ruined you?"

Peter sighed. *"You really have no sense of the times then, do you? Sometimes I was caught. I'd make a joke of it. Nobody cared."*

"How would you make a joke out of it?"

"Oh, let's see. Once somebody asked me if I really came to Provincetown on Scott and Zelda Fitzgerald's yacht. Before I could open my mouth, one of the other guests jumped in and said I came on a bicycle. I said, of course I didn't, I arrived on roller skates."

"That is funny."

"That was the point. People got together to laugh, to have fun, especially as the war loomed. It didn't matter what anyone said. What mattered was wit and dash."

I thought for a moment. He made sense. "Still, it sounds pretty shallow."

"It was tremendously shallow. But I wasn't like that all the time. Just when I needed to make an impression. I had some very close friends, even intimate friends." He looked at me meaningfully. *"Some even you don't know about."*

I laughed. "Ha! Maybe I don't want to know."

Peter raised his hand to quiet me. *"I was much more than what people thought of me. You should know that by now."*

"Oh, Peter, I believe you. But, I wonder, did you think that if they knew you, they wouldn't want you? Or did you think you could be anyone you pretended to be?"

Peter faked a yawn. *"I think you're taking my little fictions much too seriously."*

15

PERILS OF PRINT

JUNE 1944 - NEW YORK

B*ang! Bang! Bang!*

Peter's head jerked up. Good Lord! Who was pounding on Macy's big display window?

There stood Helena Rubenstein, wearing an orange wool suit and her signature bowler hat on top of her severe chignon. She waved when she caught Peter's eye and signaled for him to come outside.

Peter gestured to the people surrounding him, all waiting for him to begin his demonstration, then held up his hands, helpless. Madame motioned even more insistently for him to come out.

Babbling a stream of apologies, Peter extricated himself from the knot of people, promising to return in a moment. A few looked to see the cause of the commotion and recognized Madame. Peter heard their whispers and smiled in satisfaction. Perhaps Madame's rudeness would actually help boost sales. Yet again.

Peter bowed over Madame's hand, aware of the crowds inside and outside the department store window watching them. "Madame, what a delightful surprise."

"Good, good, good," said Madame in her heavy Polish accent. "You are not too famous to stop and chat with an old friend, yes?"

The people around them chuckled. Madame was the one they all recognized, her picture on all of her cosmetics advertisements and in every New York society column. Really. Who was too famous for whom?

Madame glowed at the crowd's reaction, but pretended she didn't hear it. She loved the spotlight, and it followed her wherever she went. She enjoyed the attention enormously.

"Darling, what is going on here?" she said. "I come out shopping, looking for a new handbag maybe, and see my friend Peter in the window at Macy's. What are you doing here? Why aren't you at the Cape?"

She knew perfectly well what he was doing, Peter realized. Madame was playing to the crowd. He went along. "Why, Madame, do you see? My newest line of decorated furniture, floor coverings and table settings are being featured in Macy's summer event," he said in clear voice, to make sure everyone heard. "And as part of their annual antiques show, Macy's is showing paintings by my father."

Madame's eyes twinkled. Peter was always good at this game. "You mean, the primitive painter, Pa Hunt?" she replied. "Why, I love his work!"

Both grinned at the rising murmur of the crowd. Madame was promoting Peter more effectively than the full-page ad Macy's that had run in the New York newspapers. "I'm honored you think so. Would you like to see them?"

Madame waved away Peter's proffered arm. "Maybe later, darling. I am in a rush." She peered through the window. "But that dining room set is charming. It's as pretty as the lovely chairs and tables you made for my Park Avenue terrace. Don't you think my little 'farm in the sky' looked well in *House Beautiful*?"

Peter fought to keep from laughing, and could see Madame was doing the same. "May I escort you to your car then?"

"No, no, I'm walking," said Madame. "It's so good for my skin to get a little fresh air every day."

"Well, as everyone knows, Helena Rubenstein is the best expert on maintaining a good complexion."

They were about to explode with laughter. "Excellent, my darling," Madame managed to say. "Stop by my apartment for drinks when you're done here."

Peter bowed over Madame's hand and turned to go back into the department store when he glimpsed a face in the crowd. He stopped in his tracks and looked harder, but the face was gone. Peter shook his head. It couldn't be.

"Now, ladies, where were we?" Peter swept back into position in the Macy's window. "Ah, yes, the Basic Stroke." He lifted his brush and approached his easel. "See, here? What does this look like?"

"An upside down tear!" said one of the women.

"An exclamation point," said another, "without the dot."

"Exactly! But when I make several, gradually making them smaller...."

"A flower!"

Peter's brush flew over the canvas. "Put two of them together..."

"A heart!"

"And if I bend it, make several in a row, we have a nice border. You see?"

A heavyset woman in a green suit shook her head. "It looks so easy when you do it. But I couldn't draw a straight line."

"Dear heart!" Peter put down his brush, walked to the woman and took her gloved hands into his. His smile was flirtatious. "Who wants to draw a straight line, anyway? Straight lines aren't very interesting at all."

Peter was putting his hat on outside Macy's revolving door when the department store's lights were shut down for the night. What a wonderful day. Macy's full-page ads had drawn countless shoppers to his demonstrations, boosting sales and orders for his furnishings and accessories even higher than the Home Department manager had hoped.

Now, for a pleasant drink at Madame's apartment. A cab approached just as Peter stepped to the curb as if waiting for the chance to pick him up.

In fact, the driver had been waiting for Peter for almost an hour.

"Cab, mister?"

Peter slid into the back seat and gave Madame's address.

It took Peter a couple moments to realize the cab driver hadn't moved. He looked forward. Peter could see the driver's eyes fixed on him in the rear-view mirror.

Peter froze.

Tebbs.

Peter saw the eyes wrinkle from an unseen grin. "I figured you'd remember your old pal, eh Schnitzer? Oh, I mean, Hunt. Yeah, Peter Hunt."

Peter sat ramrod straight, his fists balled at his sides. "Tebbs. Is this some kind of a trick?"

Tebbs put his arm over the back of his seat and turned to look at Peter. He looked different somehow. His face was clean and his shirt had been ironed. "Trick? Yeah, I guess it is. Good one, huh?"

Peter could feel his heart pounding. With an effort, he kept his voice under control. "Good one. So, then, I'll be going." Peter wrapped his fingers around the door handle.

"What? Aw, no Schnitzer, you got me all wrong. I'll take you where you wanna go. I just wanted to talk to you first." As if to prove his words, Tebbs turned front and shifted gears. The cab lurched forward to the sound of squealing brakes and honking horns. "New York traffic, huh?" Tebbs said pleasantly. "All that racket." He changed lanes, wedging himself between a bus and another cab. Without signaling, he jerked the cab to the right, down a side street.

"Tebbs, this isn't the way to Park Avenue." Peter tried to flatten the fear in his voice.

"I know. You think I don't know? I just thought we'd go the long way so we could talk."

Peter's eyes darted around the cab and into the traffic surrounding them. The taxi was moving too fast for him to jump. "Talk about what?"

"Hang on." Tebbs took a sharp left, narrowly missing a shop girl, then a right into a dark alley that was barely wide enough for the sides of the cab to clear. He slammed on the brakes. "Here we are."

The brick walls on either side of the cab were too close for Peter to force the door open and run. He took a deep breath. *Well, if this is how it's going to be, I guess I better get ready to defend myself,* Peter thought.

Tebbs left the headlights on and the engine running. He turned again, putting his arm over the back of his seat. His wide grin made Peter sick to his stomach.

"You know, it's funny the way things work out. I been wanting to talk to you for a while, now, and whaddya know? There's your ugly mug all over the papers. Only you ain't Freddy Schnitzer no more. Now, you're Peter Hunt and you're some big deal at Macy's."

He didn't call me Shits-ner, Peter realized. "That's how you found me?"

"Yeah. I checked you out this afternoon, when you was talking to that little lady with the accent."

So, just as Peter suspected. "I thought I saw you. I wasn't sure."

"Yeah, well, that wasn't the time or place to say what I need to say." Tebbs fished in his shirt pocket, and Peter's stomach turned over. Tebbs pulled out a pack of cigarettes and offered one to Peter. Peter shook his head and watched as the kitchen match illuminated Tebbs' face.

"What do you want to say to me?" *Might as well get this over with.*

Tebbs blew a thin stream of smoke and turned back to Peter. "It ain't as easy to do as when I was thinkin' about it." He flicked the cigarette out the window.

"Here it is then. I wanna say thanks."

Thanks? "Thanks?" Peter thought he was ready for anything Tebbs could pull, but not this. Was Tebbs drunk? Drugged? Peter couldn't smell any alcohol.

Tebbs held up his hand for silence. "No, hear me out. Remember that time I beat the crap out of you, back in the neighborhood in Jersey City?"

Peter nodded. The memory was painfully clear.

"That money I took? And those clothes? And your shoes? They was real nice. Made me feel like I was somebody. People don't look down at you so much when you got good clothes. You know that, right?"

"Well, yes, I suppose so."

"Sure. You always have nice clothes. But me, that night, that was the first time I ever wore clothes that nice. Made me feel like a new man. Made me feel so good, I decided to take myself to the city with that money you give me . . ."

"I didn't give you the money. You stole it."

"Yeah, well, it was enough for me to get here. What a city! I found a job, washing cabs. Wasn't great work, but it was steady. A fellow with one leg can't be too choosy. Anyway, while I was working there, I got it in my head to learn to drive. 'Course, a one-legged guy shouldn't be able to do that. Can't work the pedals, right? Look at this here." Tebbs motioned for Peter to look up front. Peter leaned over the seat and looked where Tebbs pointed. There, by the dim indicator lights, he could barely make out a jury-rigged affair of wood and straps that went from the stump of Tebbs leg down to the floor pedals.

"I made that myself." Tebbs worked the contraption up and down, showing how it depressed and released the brake. "Pretty good, huh?"

"Very creative." Peter's head began to throb. "Now, Tebbs, if you don't mind . . ."

"I gotcha. I'm almost done. Anyway, the guy that owns the cab company, he lets me get the cabbies to teach me how to drive and when I got good enough, he let me drive for him. Not bad, huh?"

"That's terrific. But . . ."

"Once I start drivin' I start meetin' all kinds of people. Some folks were nice, too. Like Sal. I met her when she was trying to get home after her shift at the hospital."

"Hospital?"

"Yeah, she's a nurse. Well, she was a nurse. Now she's my wife, mother of my kid. Now do ya get it?"

Peter rubbed his temples. "I'm not quite sure . . ."

"You're the one that made it so I could get here, get a job, with your clothes, your shoes, your money. You're the one who made me mad about how you was makin' it and I wasn't. That's why I came to New York. I figured if you could do it, so could I. Now you see?"

"I suppose." Tebbs circuitous logic was exhausting Peter. His back ached from his rigid posture.

"So, when I saw your picture in the paper, I figured now's the time. So thanks, Freddy." Tebbs held out his hand. "No hard feelings, right? Thank you and we're done."

Dazed, Peter accepted Tebbs' outstretched hand and felt his head bounce as Tebbs' shook it vigorously. "You're welcome?" Peter managed. "Now, could you take me to Park Avenue?"

After the second martini at Madame's, Peter couldn't resist feeling pleased with himself as he stood in the middle of her terrace. Paper lanterns brought out a cheerful glow from the deep purples, lipstick reds and creamy whites of the peasant-decorated furniture he'd created for her.

In one corner, a small gazebo festooned with images of peasants picking grapes and pouring wine, served as a bar, and decorated milk cans with padded lids acted as bar stools. A wooden rocking horse had been fitted with a ledge around its decorated body so it could serve as an end table. Here and there were the chairs made from barrels, and painted with red hearts, blue and yellow flowers and purple flourishes. This is some of my best work, Peter thought with satisfaction.

Madame's redecorated terrace was the talk of the town after it was featured in *House Beautiful* the year before, creating a welcome surge of business for Peasant Village and heightened demand for Peter's demonstrations.

Two years earlier, in 1942, DuPont's advertising agency took full advantage of World War II to push its line of interior paints, and Peter right along with them. Building a campaign around the tightened wartime economy and the lack of imported goods from Europe, DuPont made it sound positively patriotic to learn how "to make old furniture new."

A nationwide campaign was built around Peter's instructions on decorating furniture, including the color booklet *Transformagic*, a 100-city tour of demonstrations and classes by Peter, and an avalanche of press releases to magazines and newspapers across the country.

Life was the first of many magazines to seize on the notion of creating a multi-page photo spread centered on rebuilding and redecorating old furniture. In their November, 1942 issue, they devoted several pages to showing Peter sorting through piles of old furniture and remaking apparently useless pieces into charming home accents. The magazine cover showed a fierce-looking uniformed chaplain with the heading "Praise the Lord and Pass the Ammunition." Inside, the article, entitled "Made-over Junk," included "before" and "after" shots of a battered piano stool converted into a candelabra, a broken mirror into a sleek-looking end table, and a tarnished gilt frame into a coffee table complete with paintings of coffee cups, a pot and a plate of cookies painted on the surface.

Public response was incredible. Paint sales skyrocketed and soon DuPont had to replenish the fast-dwindling supply of *Transformagic* booklets with a new edition, this one keying on a story about two couples who visit Peasant Village, learn peasant decorating from Peter and go home to launch a frenzy of fixing and painting. Dubbing their latest effort a "Furniture Conservation Program," DuPont advertisements declared, "Make the best of the shortage of new furniture."

Peter had just finished working on Madame's terrace when *House Beautiful* called. Madame, in a fit of patriotism fanned by a note from President Roosevelt thanking her for her efforts to beautify a war-weary nation, had decided to plant a victory garden at her penthouse apartment and insisted Peter apply

Life *magazine presented a photo feature on Peter Hunt in its November 2, 1942 issue. Here is his Peasant Village Shop with junk waiting to be re-made.* ©1996 Time Inc. *Reprinted with permission.*

his "furniture conservation" skills to creating a village theme. Delighted with the possibility of a society exclusive along with a highly illustrated how-to article, the magazine editors lost no time in sending photographers to Peasant Village and Park Avenue.

"Here's my answer to those idiots saying I shouldn't sell luxury items!" Madame announced when the issue was released. She waved the magazine like a flag in a parade. "You see? I am not even American, yet I support the United States with all my heart! Here, see! I am a good patriot!"

House Beautiful ran both photo features in their August, 1943 issue. The first was a four-page photo spread, "Summer Home Life Al Fresco: Peter Hunt Salvages Cast-Offs for Helena Rubenstein's Terrace," declaring "Miss Rubenstein's farm in the sky has many devices which could be transplanted successfully to a down-to-earth garden spot."

In the pages immediately following was a glorious photo feature, "Revealing the Secrets of Peter Hunt, America's Most Imaginative Furniture Magician." Pictures detailed how a radio cabinet could be converted to a toy box and table legs into lamps, along with an illustration of Peter's brush strokes filling a third of a page. "*House Beautiful* believes that, with the principles explained here, people who can't even draw a straight line can be both creative and proficient," the article stated. "It's fun, and it's patriotic, too!"

In eighteen months spanning 1942 and 1943, Peter and Peasant Village were featured in *House & Garden* (Sam's favorite, as he was pictured in several photos), *Mademoiselle*, *McCall's* magazine, *Home Crafts* and *Nancy Craig's Digest*, along with countless newspaper features, most leading with Peter's personal appearances in cities in the 48 contiguous states.

For the first time in his life, Peter had more money than he had bills, so he immediately bought up the last few buildings he didn't own adjoining Peasant Village. Despite the oppressive economy and restricted gas rations that flattened the tourist industry for several years, Peasant Village was bustling. The teen-age apprentices he'd hired, "my little peasants" he called them, worked rapidly and well, most of the time sitting in the sun of his terrace with Ma perched on a nearby bench, her face half-hidden in the shadow of a large straw hat. Peter's shops were filled with all manner of trays, lamps, dressers, tables and peasant-decorated what-nots. To complete the village effect, Peter even had a young man cobble custom-made sandals under the willow beside his house.

At a lobster-and-champagne party thrown for Peter by collector Hudson Walker at his Provincetown home, they talked about the surprising demand for Christmas decorations painted in the Hunt style. Walker's twelve-year-old daughter, Berta, piped up. "You should make a Christmas Shop, Uncle Peter, where it's Christmas all the time."

"Why that's a fine idea!" Peter said. By the summer of 1943, Peter Hunt's Christmas Shoppe took a corner of the Commercial Street house, with a four-foot folk art angel hovering over the arched doorway.

But the highest point of his career seemed to start here, on Madame's terrace high over the city. I wonder if I could see all the way to Jersey City, Peter mused as he wandered about, straightening a plant here, adjusting a chair to a better angle there. But why would I want to look back on that? My dream's come true, even better than I imagined.

"Darling, there you are. Have you fixed yourself a drink?" Madame swept onto the terrace, her sheer lounging dress whirling around her, its gold threads glittering in the lanterns' light. "How lovely and cool it is up here! I brought you a surprise." She thrust the brown paper-wrapped package at Peter as he handed her a glass of champagne. "Ah, thank you. You're so generous with my fine wines!"

Madame lighted on one of the now-famous barrel chairs Peter had made for her and Peter sat opposite her. "What's this? Oh my! Is this the book with Pa in it?"

Sidney Janis, the art collector who befriended Pa, Peter and Helen, had been working for more than a year to put together his latest exhibition called *They Taught Themselves: American Primitive Painters of the 20th Century*. Considered the nation's expert on American folk artists, Janis had one of the largest collections of that genre, rivaled only by Abbey Aldrich Rockefeller, a passionate collector with bottomless pockets. Prominently featured in Sidney's collection (after Henri Rousseau and Grandma Moses) were paintings by Pa Hunt and Peter's latest discovery, George Lothrop.

"Sidney dropped this by today," Madame said. "Can you see? He spared no expense. Beautiful color plates, lots of pictures. He says he will sell the book at the exhibition in the fall."

Peter peered at the pages in the low yellow light. "Goodness! He's pulled out all the stops! He must have seventy-five pieces in the show! Morris Hirshfield, John Kane, P.J. Sullivan, all with pictures and biographies. Sidney must have been writing for months!"

Madame sipped champagne as Peter turned the pages. "Here he is! Here's Pa in that ridiculous picture we took, making him hold a palette!" Peter's eyes danced. "The joke is Pa never used a palette! He squeezed his paints right on the brush."

Madame leaned forward and tapped the book. "Do you see? Your Mr. Lothrop is there, too. Sidney took the painting you found for me." She settled back in her chair. "Now, you, Peter darling, tell me about your work."

Peter looked up from his book and smiled broadly. "Business is booming, Madame. People are pushing so much money at me, it's almost obscene. Almost."

Madame raised a plump, jeweled finger. "No, no, darling, not business. I can see you're doing well. What of your painting? Your art?"

"But my business is my art. I put my whole heart in creating those designs."

Madame shook her head so hard, her earrings danced and jingled. "That's not what I mean. I know business, yes? And I know art. A business thrives only if it keeps renewing itself, doing new things. That's why I spend hours working in my laboratory, pushing myself to find something new, a new cream, a new skin treatment. That is my art. Are you telling me you are finished with your designs, your pictures? That this, this Peasant Village, is the very best of what's inside you? There is no more? Pah! Peter, you are more than a shopkeeper!"

Madame slammed her drink on the table and her champagne splashed like a small fountain. Peter withered in her glare. Only Madame knew him well enough to badger him so. "To stay in one place, to not push, that's bad for business. That's bad for your art."

Peter hung his head. "I've been so busy with all the appearances and the shops. Well, I simply haven't had time to do more."

Madame sat ramrod straight in her chair, her hands on her knees. "You are the boss, are you not? Then you make the time. Simple." She snapped her fingers.

Peter sighed. "Not so simple. Even if I could make the time, what would I do? I haven't any new ideas lately, except for my decorations."

"Fool." Madame held out her glass for Peter to fill. "Do that then. Work on new decorations. Do something or you do nothing. You become stale. Work on your decorations. See where they take you. Experiment. Grow your art."

Peter poured the champagne too fast and foam overflowed the lip of the glass. He licked the foam from his fingers after handing Madame the glass. At her hard look, he pulled a handkerchief from his pocket and wiped his hands.

"No, not art. Not anymore. Back in the Thirties, maybe. That's when my work was something. Then, I was even named as a juror for the Art Association Show in Provincetown. Twice! But now, the artists look at my work as if it was done by one of those sidewalk sketch artists that draw the tourists on Commercial Street."

Madame burped loud and long. "Who cares what those Cape Cod artists think? They can't even find a way for the modernists and the traditionalists to exhibit together. Separate shows. What nonsense. What do they know about art?"

Peter looked at her, startled. A smile flickered across Madame's lips, giving her away. They burst out laughing.

"You may have a point," Peter said finally. "I hear they're calling Hans Hoffmann's paintings 'mere decoration.' And his work is awfully good."

"They're just a bunch of snobs," Madame sniffed. "Do you ever notice how people with the least money are the most snobbish? Think about it." She put down her empty glass and rose. "Now, you walk me downstairs, yes? I must change for dinner."

"What do you hear from our Cookie?" Madame asked as she slowly made her way down the spiral staircase. "Will she come back to the States soon? England is a frightening place to live right now."

"She and Humphrey live out in the country. They're much safer there." Peter helped Madame down from the bottom step. "Funny you should mention Cookie. Just before I left for New York, I got a package from her. No letter, just a little note."

"What was it?"

"Well, that's what's truly odd. She sent me Willy Maugham's new book, what's it called?"

Madame's eyes darkened. "*Razor's Edge*."

"That's right! *Razor's Edge*. Odd name. But Cookie knows I won't read Willy's drek. I'm done with him. What a waste of money."

"What did Cookie's note say?"

"Oh, something silly as always. What was it? 'You need to read this. I wish you wouldn't.'"

Madame frowned. "That's not as silly as you might think darling." She took Peter's arm and walked him to the door. "You do what I tell you, yes? This is important. You read Willy's book and throw it away. Then you must paint, paint, paint. Don't let success stop you. Push on."

Peter kissed her hand. "As always, Madame, I will do my best. May I call your car? I'm done with cabs tonight."

Madame frowned at the closed door. She kissed her fingers and patted the door as if it were Peter's cheek, then turned to shuffle to her room.

Ma heard Peter's grunt from the window above her head. Then she saw the book flying end over end over the terrace in a flapping arch. The book struck the back of Peter's gift shop and dropped to the ground face down, its cover splayed open.

"Son of a bitch! You can't steal my life!" Peter hollered before he slammed the window shut. Ma heaved herself off the bench Peter had made her, painted with peasants dancing, and shambled to where the book lay. Good thing it was too early for the girls to be here, otherwise Peter would have to talk pretty fast to explain this one. He must have been up all night reading. Ma picked up the book and dusted the grit from the pages with her hand. *Razor's Edge.*

Ma turned a few pages. She wasn't much for reading. It gave her a headache when the lettering was so small. Closing the book, she read from the cover, "W. Somerset Maugham."

Somerset? What kind of a name is Somerset? Why in the world would Willy choose to use that name over a perfectly good "William"? Ma recalled seeing Willy at Helena's Fourth of July party, so many years ago. When was that? Nineteen-thirty-two? Thirty-three? He was a strange fellow, that was for sure. A dandy who thought an awful lot of himself. He hurt Cookie's feelings, too.

Well, time to look after Peter. He must be in a state.

Ma knew last night that Peter would need her when he left the big house and headed down the alley, taking only the book. Usually, when he left to sleep at the other house, he had one of his boyfriends and their laughter and loud whispers ricocheted off the houses and up through her window. She never said anything. She didn't have to. She and Peter had an unspoken understanding ever since Pa died. Peter would follow his heart wherever it led him, and she would take no notice. He didn't want to talk about it and she didn't want to hear about it. Life was simply more comfortable that way.

But when Peter came home after one of his trips, he usually spent the first few nights in his bedroom in the Commercial Street house, "settling back in," he called it. Peter would stay up late, sorting through his mail and the business accounts, humming to himself. Ma liked falling asleep to Peter's contented humming.

This time, however he picked up the package from Cookie, pulled out the book, and looked at it with a puzzled expression. Soon after Ma headed upstairs for bed, she heard the front door creak and saw Peter's silhouette in the moonlight, walking with only the book to the Peasant Village house.

He must have had a sense even then that something was wrong, Ma reasoned. Why else would he need to read in such solitude? He didn't like Willy anymore, Ma was sure of that. Whenever Willy's name was mentioned or someone asked after him, Peter's relaxed smile would tighten to a thin line and he'd talk as if they hadn't said a word. Ma stayed awake all night, watching the yellow glow from Peter's window down the alley. Just before sunrise, she'd let herself out of the house and went down the alley. Peter's light was still on, so she sat on her bench under his window. Just in case he needed her.

Ma could hear Peter slamming around upstairs, probably washing up and changing his clothes, she guessed. She heaved herself up the kitchen stairs and let the screen door slam behind her so he would know she was in the house. Ma put the book on the kitchen table and set about making coffee. She heard Peter thundering down the steps but didn't turn from her work as he banged into the kitchen.

"Good morning, son. Coffee?"

"What's that book doing in here?"

Ma turned and held out a steaming cup. She saw the vein in Peter's taut neck throb and his fists clench. He ignored the cup Ma held out to him, his eyes fixed on the book. Ma set the cup on the table in front of him. "Found it outside."

"Then put it back outside." Peter's voice was low and threatening. He reached for the book, but Ma slammed her palm on the cover.

"That stays right where it is until I know why it should be thrown out." Ma's jaw was set and her words were firm. "You sit down and you talk to me."

"Dammit, Ma, no! Get that book out of my sight!" Peter lunged for the book, but Ma was even faster. She yanked it off the table and set it in her lap.

"That's enough. Sit down and talk. There's nothing you can say that'll surprise me. I'm old now. I've seen everything. Tell me what's bothering you."

Peter's eyes darted from the book in Ma's lap to her face. His eyes had the look of fury and fear Ma had seen on circus lions when folks yelled at them, poking sticks between the bars or throwing things in the cage. She expected Peter to start pacing like one of those lions. But something let go in his face and he sagged into a chair.

"I'm too mad to talk right now, Ma."

"Well, then, we'll just sit here until you're ready to talk." She recognized the long-forgotten tone in her voice, the one she used when he was a headstrong youngster. He could almost wear her out, then. But she always managed, in the bitter end, to outlast him. She was ready to outlast him again, if that's what it took.

Ma heard the clock ticking, the birds chirping outside and Peter's ragged breaths. He wouldn't look at her, but stared at the handle of his coffee cup. Ma saw how much his hair had receded in the past few years, early, just like his Pa. She settled in her chair. Might as well get comfortable. She opened the book, curious.

"Ma, don't. Please don't." Peter's eyes were still fixed on the cup handle. She closed the book. "Tell me."

Peter drew a long, deep breath, and then slowly let it out. "That book, Ma. Willy wrote it."

"I can see that much."

Peter held up a hand. "In it, well, he put me in there. Or somebody who's supposed to be like me."

"How can you tell?"

"I can tell. First of all, the character is called Elliot Templeton. Templeton. My name. Remember?"

"All right, maybe he just likes the name."

"No Ma, it's more than that. He writes about . . ." Peter faltered. "Oh, God, what if they read it?" He buried his face in his hands.

"Who? What are you talking about?"

In halting words, Peter told his mother about the Elliot Templeton character, a fellow who established himself by selling antiques and helping arrange the homes of wealthy women. Templeton was lavish with flowers, gifts and flatteries to high society matrons, becoming the pet of many mansions. The ladies would, in turn, introduce him into their social circles. He used them as stepping-stones to ascend into richer and more prestigious circles. Like Peter, Templeton served in the ambulance corps in the first World War.

Peter paced around the kitchen table. Templeton would swallow any rudeness to be invited to a certain party or meet a person of rank. People laughed behind his back, calling him a colossal snob. "Willy even wrote that he doubted whether it was possible for Templeton to be a friend because he took no interest in people aside from their social position. His dying wish was for an invitation to a party!" Peter stopped by the kitchen window and looked out, unseeing. "Am I that shallow?"

"Sounds to me like Willy was writing about himself," Ma muttered. She turned the book in her hands and opened it. She lifted a page by the corner and slowly pulled down, ripping it out. She placed the page on the table and began ripping another page.

"People will know. People will see it right away," said Peter. "They'll hate me. I'll be shunned. Despised."

"Don't be silly, son." Ma was ripping out pages a handful at a time. She kept her eyes on her work as she spoke. "That could be anyone."

"No, Ma, it's in the details. The details are all there. And everyone knows Willy takes his characters from real life. Cookie saw it, didn't she?"

"Maybe so, and maybe he was writing about you. But you did those things a long time ago. To survive. A lot of people did. That's how things were done.

Still goes on, as far as I can tell. Besides, you don't act like that Templeton person now, do you? That was long ago. Why, you don't even use that name anymore!"

"But, Ma." Peter turned and his mouth dropped open in astonishment. "Ma, what are you doing?"

She pulled the last few pages from the cover, set them on the pile on the table and rose. She moved to the fireplace, pulled back the screen and tossed the cover on the glowing logs and waited for the cover's edges to burst into blue-green flames. Ma picked up the pages. She looked at Peter, her eyes shining and her chin high.

"Don't mind about Willy. He's a small, mean man. He wrote a book that likely nobody will read." She held up the sheaf of pages. "But that doesn't mean it can't be useful."

Ma turned back to the fire and dropped the top page into the fire. She watched as the edges darkened and curled and dropped another page on top.

Ma's head swiveled towards Peter. "There's nothing like a nice, big fire to lift your spirits when the world's looking gray." She held out the remaining pages. "Care to help me stoke it up?"

"I like Ma's style." Peter and I were sharing the glider in the back yard. I pushed the grass with my foot so we could rock a little.

"She had her moments."

"But, you know, Peter, years later, Willy said the Templeton character was based on Jerome Zipkin, that society moth in Manhattan. Another time he claimed Templeton was really Chips Channon, the American who wanted to be a European royal. Willy never, ever said it was you."

"He didn't have to. That was part of the game he played with me. I never moved with the Zipkin crowd or the Channon ring. But I would have loved to. No matter what I did, the furthest I could get socially was the fringes. Willy moved on the inside, with them. He knew it made me crazy."

"So?"

"So, the differences are in the details. I served in the Ambulance Corps, Channon never did. Zipkin didn't. I loved antiques and haggling over prices. They wouldn't be caught dead bargaining. I had a sister that lived in Chicago! Don't you see?"

"I see you still get angry about it."

Peter's face grew thoughtful. *"Not as angry as I used to."*

I turned to get a better look at him. "What's going on with you? You're forgetting things. You used to check on the book every day and now weeks can go by before you show up. You don't nag me about the box anymore. It's like you've forgotten. I can't even get you riled up like I used to."

Peter's eyes seemed unfocused as he looked at me, as if he were looking through me. *"Don't you know? No, I suppose you wouldn't. I'm letting go."*

"Letting go? Letting go of what?"

"Letting go of life."

"Life? But you already let go of life! You're dead!"

Peter shrugged. *"You're right."*

"I don't get it." I stopped the glider. "Are you saying you're not going to be a ghost anymore?"

"That's how it feels. I'm not sure."

I pressed my palms on my knees. "Does this have something to do with the book? With what we talked about before? About reviewing your life?"

Peter put his hands behind his head and stretched out his legs. *"How would I know?"*

"What happens after you're done letting go?"

"What difference does it make?"

"My God! If people knew the truth about what happens after you die, it would change everything!"

Peter yawned. *"No it wouldn't"*

"Of course it would!"

Peter chuckled. *"You want to know what? The truth? The truth about life?" His eyes narrowed and his voice grew hard. "I'll give you truth. The truth is, you're alive, right now. You want another truth? What you do or don't do in this life is strictly up to you. No matter what happens in your life, you alone control how you'll respond."*

I opened my mouth, but stopped when Peter held up his hand for silence.

"No, no, no. You always tell me you're searching for the truth. Well, you're getting it. Here's another truth: In the end, you'll die."

"But..."

Peter stood and faced me. His expression softened to the look an adult might give a child. *"Do you believe me?"*

"Yes, but..."

He put his finger to his lips, shushing me. *"It doesn't matter if you believe me or not. If you believe me, that's because you choose to believe me. If you don't believe me, well, then I'm just a figment of your imagination, and one that lies, no less."*

Peter started fading into the twilight, and I thought of the Cheshire cat in Alice in Wonderland. Would only his smile remain before he disappeared completely? "Wait!..."

He wasn't listening to me. *"I can't tell you what happens when you die. I'm not completely dead yet. I'm still letting go of my life. Bit by bit, I've been letting go. You've helped me do that with your book – your book, not mine – making me look at things and release them. Once I've let go of everything, well, then I'll know what happens I suppose. But by then, I won't be talking with you. I'll be dead. You'll still be alive."*

No, he didn't go like the Cheshire cat. He simply faded, letting the twilight fill the place where he stood until he was completely gone.

I stared at the place where he'd been standing. I couldn't absorb all that he said. Finally, my mind settled on this: I didn't want him to get the last word. Again.

I spoke to the spot where he'd stood. "So, I guess you don't care about the box anymore."

16

HUSTLING AND BUSTLING

JUNE 1950 - PROVINCETOWN

"I can't stand it, Peter. When did we get so old?"

"'We'? Speak for yourself."

Peter and Cookie spread their towels on the sand at the foot of Peter's house, and unceremoniously flopped down on them. Cookie kicked off her sandals. "I mean it. We're in our fifties! When we first met, did you ever think about what we'd be like when we hit fifty?"

"Never." Peter pulled his Panama hat down over his eyes. "Really, Cookie. I think Alison's graduation has sent you right over the edge."

"Oh, Peter, you should have seen her. A beautiful young woman with the loveliest manners. I was quite intimidated." Cookie touched her face, tracing the fine wrinkles around her eyes and mouth. "She was poised and graceful. All grown up."

"Too bad we can't say the same for her mother."

The soft roar of the surf filled Cookie's ears and the warmth from the sun settled on her like a silk sheet. The problem with children, she decided, is that they get older and grow up and make their parents feel old. It used to be when Cookie looked in a mirror, she didn't see a middle-aged woman. She simply saw herself, as she always was. But since her daughter's graduation, Cookie's reflection startled her. When had those wrinkles started at the corner of her eyes? Was that gray blending in with her blonde hair? She looked so . . . so . . . .

"Cookie, wake up! You're going to burn if you stay out much longer."

Cookie squinted up at Peter, who was little more than a hatted silhouette standing above her. "I must have dozed."

"Dozed? Darling you were snoring! That was no doze." Peter took Cookie's hand and helped her to her feet. "It's time for tea. Let's go inside."

Laughter and chatter filled Peter's kitchen. Four paint-spattered teen-age girls sat at the kitchen table or leaned against the counters as Ma handed around plates of finger sandwiches and cookies. "Peter, we're trying to figure out why you call this tea when you never serve a drop of the stuff," one said cheerfully. "Shouldn't you call it 'soft drinks' or 'milk'?"

"Because, dear one, tea is a matter of form, not substance," Peter retorted. "Have you managed to leave a little for us?"

After the plates were picked clean and the glasses drained, Peter shooed the gaggle of girls through the shop and out to the alley. "Let's see what you've been up to while I've been away."

Cookies' eyes flew here and there, trying to take in all the changes to the place since she'd last been here, when was it? Just before the war. Like mushrooms, shops had sprung up along the alley, all decorated with Peter's distinctive peasant motif. At the head of the alley was a large sign atop a pole holding up a wagon wheel supporting a merry-go-round horse, all painted a sunny yellow with peasant flowers and hearts covering every inch, declaring "Peter Hunt's Peasant Village Shops."

Beneath the sign was a storybook cedar-shingled cottage covered with rambling roses, and on its doorstep and inside the windows were jammed small tables, firkins, trays, lamps, plaques, and cabinets, all festooned with peasants, angels, flowers and hearts in crimson, fir green, violet and orange, all done in Peter's signature technique.

Inside, the shop was a cacophony of bright colors. As Cookie looked around, a young man, about 15 years old she guessed, waited on a thin elderly gentleman. "This will tell me how to make these designs?" The gentleman peered through wire-rimmed glasses at the open book. Cookie tilted her head slightly to read the title: *Peter Hunt's Workbook*.

Oh, yes, she remembered. After the success of the *Transformagic* brochure, Peter decided to write a full-sized book so he could expand on instructions about creating his designs. Sales were brisk, not only in Provincetown, but across the country. With the war over and women home from the factories with extra time on their hands, a wave of home crafts and decorating had swept the country, and Peter was riding the wave.

"I'll take it. And those decals, too." The man pointed at a rack behind the boy's head. There hung two dozen packets of peasants, angels, hearts and flow-

Peter Hunt demonstrates his painting style. Peter Hunt's Workbook, Ziff-Davis Publishing Company, New York, 1945.

ers: "Peter Hunt Designs for Meyercord Decals."

In the center of the room was a round table, set with plates embossed with peasant flowers and borders. Cookie turned over a dish and read: "Peter Hunt Designs, Rideau."

Good Lord, he's got his hand in everywhere. Cookie recalled what Peter had said over coffee the night before. "It's a scandal the way people fling money at me. I have more than I'll ever spend. And I'm just too busy to spend it!"

"And what news of Judith and Vickie?" Cookie inquired. Peter shook his head. "No news, I'm afraid. We've completely lost touch. I'm too busy with my business now and they're too busy throwing parties." Cookie noted the hurt in his voice. Had he offended them? Or had they grown bored with him? Looking through the shop, Cookie realized it was likely neither. Peter was simply not chic any more. His pieces were no longer unique and exclusive, but now mass-marketed.

Cookie stepped out to the alley. An olive-skinned man with longish black hair in his early twenties, Cookie guessed, bent over the leather sandals he was making for a heavy woman in a loud floral dress sitting next to him. "Cookie, that's Menalkis. Nephew of Isadora Duncan. Wonderful custom-made sandals," Peter sang over his shoulder. Menalkis looked up and grinned, his dark eyes twinkling. Peter, ever the name-dropper, Cookie thought.

By the time Cookie caught up, the teen-age girls were already seated on their small stools on the terrace, loading their old magazines with paint. Next to a potting shed-turned-studio that Peter had decorated with great blue swags and garlands of painted flowers, the day's work had been stacked. Peter moved through the larger pieces first, paintbrush in hand, adding a flourish here, correcting an expression there, and then signing his name or "Ovince."

"These are very nice, girls," Peter said. "Carol, you did this child's chest?" Carol Whorf, Peter's first apprentice, looked up and nodded. "See, Cookie? She has the angels with brushes and combs on that drawer, dainty underthings on this drawer, blouses and skirts on this one. That helps a child know where to put away their things."

Workers at Peasant Village. Peter Hunt's Workbook, Ziff-Davis Publishing Company, New York, 1945.

Peter bent over a blanket chest painted a deep blue with two-and three-masted ships on the top. "Wendy is this yours?" A tawny-skinned blonde with a wide smile looked up and nodded. "Did we get a little bored with this one, dear? The sails are a little lackadaisical. And it could use a few more embellishments in red here, yellow here, and more yellow here." Magazine palette in hand, Wendy ambled to the chest and saluted. "Aye, aye, Cap'n."

"Oh, look, sweetheart, here are the young artists. Just like in *Paintbox Summer.*" A woman in bright green culottes with a matching scarf pulled her pre-teen daughter towards the painters. "Could you show my Irene how you make those lovely flowers? She has quite a bit of talent, you know, from my side of the family." As the woman bent over Nora, who was working on a tray, Wendy whispered to Peter with a wicked grin. "That's the third one, today. Last one bought her daughter a whole bedroom set, and you weren't even here to schmooze."

"Certainly a woman of outstanding taste," Peter whispered back. He sailed towards the mother and daughter. "Did someone mention *Paintbox Summer?* Welcome to Peasant Village. I'm Peter Hunt."

Cookie edged towards Wendy. "*Paintbox Summer?*" she said in a low voice.

Wendy looked over to watch Peter in an animated exchange with the mother as the daughter sat cross-legged next to Nora. "It's a book, written for girls. One of the summer people in Chatham, Betty Cavanna, wrote it." As Peter turned to check on the girls, Wendy dabbed her brush in her paint, pretending to mix colors. "It's a romance, of course, but the main character works here, in Peasant Village, with Peter. He did all the illustrations for the book, too."

"Do you have any extra copies of the book, Mr. Hunt? I'd love to have you sign it for me, uh, my daughter."

"Certainly! And I'll rustle up something cool to drink so you can relax in the shade of my little shop," said Peter, leading the woman up the alley.

"And relieve you of all that heavy money that's weighing you down," Wendy muttered.

Cookie snorted.

"Sshhh," said Carol, nodding at the girl sitting by Nora. Nora looked up briefly, grinning. "So how do you spell your name? I'll put it right here on the tray and you can show it to your mother."

Peter returned to the terrace twenty minutes later, humming. "What a lovely woman. Came here all the way from Virginia. Bought the *Workbook*, a tray and a wall mirror just like that! Didn't have to push her at all." He patted Nora's shoulder. "Nicely done with the little girl."

Nora looked up. "Well, I was trained by the master."

"I have no idea what you're talking about." Peter took Cookie's arm and led her to the tiny studio. "Come, I want to show you something."

Leaning against two walls were two framed pieces that filled the studio, each as tall as Peter and about five feet wide. Cookie sidled between them to see better as Peter pulled the cord of the ceiling light.

"These are glorious," Cookie said after her lingering examination of first one, then the other. One was of a gallery with decoupaged paintings and people, cut from Victorian etchings and seriographs. The columns, frames and details of the gallery were drawn in ink and enhanced with gouache. A brass plate in the massive gilt frame said *Art Gallery*.

The other, done in a similar paint-and-decoupage style, pictured a bustling street scene or marketplace with peddlers, shoppers and goods created from carefully trimmed and colorwashed engravings. Its brass plate read *Magazin de Antiquities*. "Where did you get these?"

"You don't know?" An impish grin played on Peter's face. "You can't guess?"

Cookie turned back to the paintings. The hand that drew the gallery was deft and precise. The colors, though subdued by the underlying inks, were strong blues, mauves and golds. She leaned down to peer at the signature, and jerked back up.

"You?"

Peter laughed. "You should see your face! I can't tell you how many people have reacted just the same way when they've seen these."

Encouraged by Madame to expand his artistic horizons, Peter had at first been stumped as to what to try. Landscapes? Portraits? Sculpture? He thought of all the artists he knew and their wide variety of approaches to their work.

What can I do that they haven't already explored and done better, he wondered. Where do I even start?

Slowly, the idea of a gallery of different styles of art evolved. He was working on preliminary sketches when he decided to trim pictures out of magazines to give the sense of the different works of art so he could render them later.

He liked the effect, and searched through old books, periodicals and almanacs for more images. That's when he came across different pictures of people that he thought would work splendidly as attendees of his painted gallery. For weeks, he searched and cut, arranged and rearranged, drew and re-drew the gallery, the frames, even the potted plants. When he was finally done, Peter realized those who thought him a decorator, not an artist, would surely sneer at his use of outside images.

Funny, he hadn't even considered their reactions until after he'd put on his signature. By then, what they thought didn't matter so much. He was pleased with the work.

Peter started anew, this time developing his decoupage-and-paint marketplace. "See? In this, I added more dimension to the background, and let the articles dictate what the drawing would do."

"Peter, these are quite good. They're fresh, charming and witty," said Cookie.

Peter stood next to her and surveyed the *Magazin de Antiquities*. "Madame liked them, too. She insisted we hang them both in the foyer at her Park Avenue place, one over the other, right by the spiral staircase. They looked quite important there. She's had them for two years now. You know Madame. That's about as long as any piece stays in one place around her."

"Are you still working with the decoupage?"

Peter crooked his finger and moved it so Cookie would follow him. All the way at the back, a figure stood shrouded in a sheet, standing about five feet tall. Peter carefully pulled off the sheeting to reveal a cigar store Indian painted blue, his shirt and one pant leg covered in different patterns of cigar bands and tobacco cards. "This is a work in progress, of course. I pester everyone in town who smokes so they keep me in cigar bands and cards. Someone will have to drop dead of a coughing fit before I have enough to finish."

Cookie lightly touched the hawk-faced carving. "I've never seen anything like it."

"Good! Then I'm on the right track." Peter threw the drape back over the Indian.

"Now, of course, I'll have to get other people excited about what I'm doing. I have to make a living, you know."

17

ALONE FOR THE FIRST TIME

JANUARY 1955 - PROVINCETOWN

Peter stood on the deck of his house overlooking the bay, a musty beach blanket pulled over his tuxedo to protect him from the icy wind coming off the water. The sky over the horizon was pearly gray with thin mare's tail clouds. Dawn would break within the hour.

The first dawn of the New Year. Time for some resolutions.

The wind tugged at Peter's blanket and he pulled it tighter around his shoulders.

Nothing. I can't think of a thing.

Well, that's just fine. Here I am, 59 years old, finally free of my parents, and I can't come up with one single idea on what to do this year. Or next year. Nothing.

Peter turned on his heel and stalked inside, the door slamming behind him. He looked at Ma's chair by the table. Still empty. She was still gone. How could one short woman fill a house like she did? Fill a life the way she did mine?

Peter shook his head, hard. He'd promised himself he'd quit doing that, quit mulling over Ma's absence. There, that was a resolution, wasn't it? Stop thinking about what isn't and start thinking about what will be.

His head ached. He'd lost count of the martinis, the flutes of champagne he'd gulped at the McKains' New Year's party. He drank and drank and couldn't get drunk.

That never happened before.

Peter slumped in the Windsor chair beside the hearth. Mary Souza, his housekeeper, must have built a fire before she left. Peter stirred the embers and fed the rising glow a piece of driftwood. As the fire blazed up, he shook off the blanket.

All right. Where was I? Ah, the new year. Time to take stock, make a plan. Decide what to do.

The past year had been consumed with tending to Ma. At 88, she was still strong-willed and stocky, but she had trouble getting around. She'd grow breathless crossing a room or scolding Mary. Ma's heart would flutter and sometimes "seize up," as she said.

Peter and Ma knew that her time was running out, but they never spoke of it. Ma simply carried on as always, puttering around the kitchen, whiling away sunny days on her bench on the terrace, chatting with the Portuguese wives who came every few days with fresh loaves of bread and gossip.

When Peter and Ma planned a spring trip to Europe, she was excited at the thought of seeing Dorothy in Naples and Madame at her Paris apartment. Peter hired a companion for Ma, just to make sure she didn't overextend herself. But, by the time they reached their first stop, Naples, Ma was exhausted and spent the first several days after their arrival in bed in Dorothy's guest house.

"Ma doesn't look good. What does her doctor say?" Dorothy had asked, alarm widening her eyes.

Doctor? Ma would have no truck with doctors. When Dorothy tried to insist on bringing her personal physician, Ma yelled for everyone to leave her alone, then lapsed into a coughing fit that lasted a good ten minutes.

Despite Ma's protests, Peter cut the trip short and brought her back to Provincetown. He declined any major out-of-town jobs and arranged for people to keep an eye on Ma when he had to go to New York or Boston.

Aside from that, life went on pretty much the same as it always had. Peasant Village was thriving, and its demands, along with overseeing the third printing of his *How-to-do-it Book* (an expanded version of *Peter Hunt's Workbook*) and the publishing of his new *Cape Cod Cookbook* kept him pleasantly busy.

How Ma bristled at the notion of Peter writing a cookbook. "What do you know about cooking? The idea!" she railed. Peter smoothed her ruffled feathers by telling her it was a collection of other people's recipes, Ma, and I was wondering if I could use a few of yours, like the fish chowder you make.

All right, she said, but I know you'll pass it off as your own.

Don't I always?

Last summer, she'd preened in a shower of compliments given her when the local newspaper ran a story about Peter decorating the ceiling of The Moors, a restaurant owned by his friend, Maline Costa. Ma was there, sitting in a chair, watching Peter work when the reporter and photographer arrived. Peter made up a story about how this was her 70th anniversary of graduating finishing school, and the reporter lapped it up. Ma took the clipping with her everywhere, tucked in her handbag.

Their friends kept daily life fluid and amusing. Artists Bruce and Amy McKain often stopped by, regaling Ma and Peter with stories and jokes as they barbecued shish kebob or played cards. Hudson and Ione Walker regularly invited the Hunts for Sunday lobster brunches or cocktail parties. Ione's parents, Harriet and Harvey Gaul, came to Provincetown every summer from Pittsburgh and delighted Ma and Peter with their penchant for sing-alongs. Even artist Jack Amoroso had dropped by to say hello while on a visit to his parents in Eastham.

Dear Jack. A witty and warm man with an immense artistic talent, Jack had walked into Peter's life three years earlier, in 1952, asking for a job as one of Peter's apprentices. Imagine! When Peter saw Jack's portfolio, he refused to hire the young, dark-haired man as a furniture decorator.

Instead, Peter opened a small shop just for Jack in Peasant Village. Peter could almost see himself in Jack, young and hungry to make his way in the world with his art.

Now, Jack was living his dream in Coconut Grove, Florida, where demand for his work was rising, and every canvas he touched was brilliant with his evolutions in color and form. Before he left, Peter bought one of Jack's paintings, a scene of Beacon Hill.

Was it so long ago that Peter was Jack's age, wooing the patronage of the Beacon Hill dowagers? Remember how life was exploding with ideas and possibilities? There was so much to learn, so much to try. And then . . . and then.

I've spent my entire adult life here in Provincetown, taking care of my parents, Peter realized. I had dreams when I was a young man, of freedom and passion, of making a grand living as an artist.

Certainly I do make a living by my art. But why don't I feel the same excitement, the same drive? The last time I'd even come close was when I'd done those decoupage paintings for Madame. Then, life encroached. The business. Wooing clients. Making deals. Selling, selling, selling.

Despite all his efforts, Peter had noticed the slip in sales and demand for his work. People once charmed and delighted by his peasants, angels and flowers had tired of them, had moved on to newer designs. Intellectually, Peter knew this time might come, but now, with Ma gone, he felt as if all the fixtures of his life were slipping away.

He'd been so busy, he hadn't noticed how people he loved were fading, disappearing, leaving only Peter and Ma. Then only Peter.

Where was everybody?

Peter didn't recognize his life anymore. So many people were gone, so many came in their place.

Peter's friend, Colin Clements, was the first to go, back in 1948. The hard-drinking over-eloquent screenwriter died of alcoholism on the heels of his only playwriting triumph, when Helen Hayes starred in *Harriet* on Broadway. His wife, Florence Ryerson, screen writer for several successful films including *The Wizard of Oz*, was at Colin's side in the hospital for the three weeks it took for his liver to finally collapse. After she buried Colin, Flo closed up their Hollywood house and moved to Mexico.

Dottie was gone, too, living in Europe with her husband, first for a few years in Paris, then on to the villa in Naples. Dottie wasn't one to keep in touch, except for greetings on holidays and birthdays.

Cookie was now settled in England with her son and husband, hostess of the grand manor, she wrote, and delighted with annual visits from her daughters and their husbands. Lately, she hadn't felt any strong pull back to the States, and was quite content with trips to France and Italy.

Judith and Vickie had gently pulled away from Peter when the war ended, leaving him to sell his pieces to more middle-class buyers as they sought out new, modern designers and artists in Europe to "bring along."

Madame, though still his dear friend, was especially busy with her shops in France, England and the United States, frantically trying to make even more money for the ever-outstretched palms of her children and relatives.

The girls – Carol Whorf, Nora Haspell and Wendy Hackett – had grown up and become artists in their own right. Nancy Whorf, the youngest, who made Peter so nervous with her 14-year-old antics he had to fire her, was back, decorating pieces in his style even better than he could. Nancy was grown now and showed an exceptional ability in her oil-painted landscapes. Peter wondered how long she would stay with him.

His life was slipping and sliding, and Peter had no sense of where it was going, or how. What if all he was, all he had to offer, meant nothing now that Ma was gone, that Peasant Village had lost its novelty?

The fire in the hearth was out. Sunlight streamed in the window. Day had broken and Peter hadn't even noticed. Just like that day a few weeks ago, when Peter had looked in Ma's room to see why she wasn't up and dressed by 5 a.m. as usual. Curled on her side, Ma's cheek was cradled in her hand. Like a child, Peter thought, and he knew she was dead. He sat next to her on her bed, afraid to touch her. He studied her face and her hands for minutes? Hours? Until Mary Souza rapped at the door, looking for Ma and Peter. Day had broken, and sunlight puddled on the floor by Ma's window. He was mildly surprised that another day could dawn as usual, when Ma wasn't alive to watch it.

On the table was a card from Jack, sending his sympathies. *I need to write him back. Maybe I'll tell him about going to Coconut Grove when I was a young man, and the lavish parties Jim Deering threw at Villa Vizcaya, and how, as people danced and laughed, the servants unobtrusively swept away the snakes that slithered across the terra cotta tiles. Yes, that would amuse him.*

When I was a young man, life stretched out before me, and I was eager to seize every day.

Now, I am not so young, and life stretches before me and I wonder how many days I have left.

Why was I so happy then, and so unhappy now?

Peter started at the sound of keys rattling in the front door. Mary Souza, coming to fix breakfast, make the bed. He hurried through the kitchen and upstairs. *Not now, not now. I'm not ready yet.*

He stretched out on his bed, not bothering to take off his clothes. *Wouldn't it be lovely to just lay here and sleep and die and not have to worry so?*

No!

Peter sat bolt upright. *No, it wouldn't be lovely, not at all. I still have things I want to do.*

What things? What things indeed?

My art. It always comes back to my art, doesn't it? But haven't I lost my art? Canned it and sold it until nothing remains?

In a flash, Peter knew what he had to do. As he did when he was young, he would go to Europe, take his time, see everything. He would visit Madame, Cookie, Dottie, accept their comfort and heal.

Like before, Peter knew, without any reason to believe it, that something, some design, some dance, some teacher would reignite his passion for art. He would find something that sang to him, that he could make his own.

Only when that happened, Peter knew, could he come back to the States and start life anew.

"Peter! Peter! Are you there?"

"Yes."

"What do you think of the book so far?"

"What do you think?" Peter sounded remote.

"Really, Peter, please tell me. What do you think?"

"Has the writing become a chore, or are you having fun?"

"Fun? Well, yes. I'm really enjoying it. When I get up in the morning, I can't wait to start working on it."

"Well, then, you should know what I think. I think it's grand." Peter's voice softened to a whisper.

"But, Peter, am I on track? Is this what you wanted to say?"

"Peter? Peter? Are you there?"

18

PEACOCK ALLEY

NOVEMBER 1963 - ORLEANS, CAPE COD

"Jack! You're here!" Peter burst through the door of his shop and seized Jack Amoroso's hand with both of his. His eyes took in Jack's broad grin and deep tan. "You look wonderful! Florida must agree with you."

Jack laughed and gave Peter a bear hug. Peter was thinner since the last time they'd seen each other and he had less hair. Peter wore large, black-rimmed spectacles and Jack noted he was sporting a mustache. Peter smelled of sea spray and paint thinner, and telltale dots of paint were splattered over his white duck pants and yellow cotton shirt.

"Peter! Look at you! Look at this place! So this is your Peacock Alley."

It was an enormous, rambling old house, likely fashioned in the Cape Cod manner of cleaving two smaller houses to make one large one. Painted a deep Delft blue with bright white trim, the house sported an outdoor deck on its second floor, bordered in white pickets and oversized finials framing a shop sign: New Horizons Gallery. Below, on the first floor, the wide porch surrounded another shop, its windows glittering with multi-colored glass dishes, goblets and vases. The sign read, "Bill Sydenstricker, Glass."

Peter's shop was in the bottom of the ell of the house, facing the street. At the doorway stood a blue-painted cigar store Indian with glittering accents on his headdress, face and clothes (on closer examination, Jack realized the accents were actually cigar bands). A glory of flowers grew in front of the shop windows: hollyhocks, lady's slippers, rambling roses and narcissus, giving off a jumbled, heady scent. Jack could see a profusion of stools, birdhouses, chairs, paintings and firkins, all decorated in Peter's well-known peasant style.

"I'm so glad you came," Peter said as he led Jack around the house. "You must see my cottage, and we can talk business there." Tucked in a grove of pines and cedars behind Peacock Alley, on the edge of Town Cove's waters was a bungalow, painted in blue and white to match the shop. The front of the bungalow looked like it could have come out of a fairy tale, with an arched door almost hidden by morning glory and rambling rose vines. Once inside, though, the cottage took on a more modern look. The side wall, overlooking the cove, was made almost completely of glass and light filled the living room, dancing across Peter's "rogue's gallery" of paintings. Hung side by side was a Picasso sketch, an abstract painting signed "Rhodes," Jack's own Beacon Hill scene and a large canvas with an electric blue cat with wide red eyes dressed in a wedding gown and veil.

"That's my latest, the *Pussycat Bride*," said Peter as he handed Jack a glass of cold white wine. "Wild, isn't it?"

Peter had tried to make a go of it in Provincetown after Ma died in 1955, but his heart wasn't in it. The kind of tourists that flooded Commercial Street in the summer had somehow changed. Many came in buses or on boats offering group tours. Rather than savor the charm and idyll of the town, they shopped, boated and partied as fast and hard as they could, demanding every moment be filled so they got their money's worth of fun.

One by one Peter closed the shops on Peter Hunt Lane, leaving only the Commercial Street shop and his new shop in Orleans, Peacock Alley.

Peter rented out the rooms upstairs on Commercial Street, Pa's bedroom to jovial Bruce McKain, who had to move his enormous canvases with rope and winch out the window; and Ma's room to quiet, frail artist Milton Avery.

Peter enjoyed Bruce and Milton enormously. Bruce boomed through the house with his laughter, and Milton's quiet manner was soothing. Still, business continued to wane. Peter's designs, that not long ago could be found in almost every department store in America, were now "old hat."

Peter had the nagging sense that he might thrive better away from Provincetown, but stayed only because it was familiar to him. That he'd succeeded there once, and it might happen again.

Then, near the end of the season in 1959, Peter was tending his shop when he overheard a remark by an tourist wearing a straw hat, a soiled white tee shirt, green plaid shorts and black socks with his rubber sandals. He was holding up one of Peter's Christmas ornaments, decorated with an angel carrying a wreath.

"Two dollars and fifty cents for a Christmas ornament? That's pretty steep, dontcha think?"

"That's when I knew there was no more money in Provincetown," Peter told Jack. He sold the Commercial Street house and consolidated his shops at his Orleans location. His friends, Harriet and Harvey Gaul, spotted the house in Orleans where they summered, and told Peter it was about to be put up for sale. He bought it in 1952.

Peter decided Peacock Alley would be an artist and artisan showcase. He'd rent space to other Cape artists, not just any artists but good ones, who could sell as well as create so he wouldn't have to worry about their rents. Peter would have his own shop, too, at the center, where he'd display his newer works, the cigar band decoupages and his experiments in oil paintings. He'd carry peasant pieces so he could entice his longtime clients to Orleans. Nancy Whorf, now a wife and mother, would continue to decorate for him, carting the pieces from her home in Provincetown to Orleans.

In short order, Peter found artists he admired who were willing to rent space at Peacock Alley. Bob Osterhout would sell his watercolors and Cape-related gifts upstairs, where he would also rent a small apartment. Next to Bob's shop, Nancy Ann Norton opened her New Horizons Gallery, selling works she'd created along with pieces by other Cape artists. Downstairs, next to Peter's shop, Bill Sydenstricker sold designs in glass, using his innovative technique of pressing colored powders in the glass to create intricate designs.

Peter couldn't believe his good fortune. He, Bill and Bob became close friends and, for the first time since Cookie had left the States in 1941, Peter found himself opening up, talking about his youth in New Jersey, the Bohemian days in Greenwich Village, the hardscrabble early years in Provincetown.

Across the street, Eva Rich ran the stately Southward Inn where Peter often dined, and she looked after him, sending soup when he had a cold or hors d'ouerves (once, even a gypsy violinist) when he hosted parties in his cottage.

Muriel Strout was a widow who took a shine to Peter and often stopped by the shop to help out and once wrote a brochure for him.

"How's life? Why it couldn't be better," Peter said to Jack as they sat in facing fanback wicker chairs. "I thought it couldn't get better than the salad days in Provincetown, but look! People are pushing money at me until it's positively vulgar."

Jack had accepted Peter's invitation to manage Peacock Alley while Peter took a long trip to Europe, where he would drop in on Cookie in England, Madame in France, and Dottie in Italy.

"I'm so thrilled you could do this, Jack. I just heard about your painting being chosen for the World's Fair next year. What's the title again?"

"*Exploration.*"

"Well, I just can't wait to see it." Peter watched Jack's eyes as they traveled around the room. They stopped at a tromp l'oeil bookcase painted on the wall. Jack chuckled at the "book" titles: the *Kama Sutra*, D.H. Lawrence's *Women in Love* and Arthur Miller's *Tropic of Cancer*.

They turned at the sound of a tapping on the large glass window. Bill Sydenstricker waved. "Peter, someone at the shop is asking for you. A hot ticket from the city."

She stood tall, almost six feet in her Italian pumps. Her auburn hair was pulled back into a sleek French twist, the color enhanced by a forest green designer suit, Chanel perhaps? that fit her angular body to perfection. Peter saw her upper lip curled in distaste as she looked at his just-finished armchair, completely covered in designs made with cigar bands. He cleared his throat to announce his presence. She smoothed her lips into a cool smile. "Mr. Hunt?"

"Peter, please. Welcome. Won't you have a seat?" he gestured to the chair she'd been examining, a wicked twinkle in his eyes.

"No, thank you. I won't be staying. You see? I have a cab waiting."

In the parking lot, in the shade of a willow tree, Joe Martin was hanging out his cab window, ogling the woman in Peter's shop. Peter was suddenly aware that he must look a sight still in his painting clothes, wine on his breath. He took a step back.

"I had quite a time finding you. The only address I had was in Provincetown. Luckily, that cabbie seemed to know you."

"Joe? Oh, he and I are old friends. He's been cabbie on the Cape for years. Now, what can I do for you? Are you looking for furniture?"

"Oh, dear, no, not at all." She suppressed a shudder. "I'm here to give you something." She gestured to a paper-wrapped box she'd placed on a table Peter had decorated with birds and flowers. "I'm Adrianna Tebbs."

"Tebbs?" Peter couldn't stop the rush of blood to his cheeks and forehead, the buzzing in his ears. After all these years, the sound of that name could still rattle him. But certainly, this chic cosmopolitan was no relation.

"I'm the daughter of Albert Tebbs. Do you remember him?"

The pounding in Peter's chest slowed. "Albert? I know a man named Tebbs, but I don't believe I ever knew his first name."

"Papa said you two grew up together."

"That would be the Tebbs I know. Last time I saw him was 20 years ago. How is he?"

Adrianna's face was impassive. "He's dead. He died three weeks ago."

"Oh my dear, I'm so sorry." Peter was at a loss for words. "Please accept my condolences. Your poor mother. And your sister." Peter recalled the black and white photograph Tebbs had shown him that night in the cab. A smiling, round-faced woman held a laughing, curly haired toddler. "That's my Sal and that's little Elsa." Funny that Peter recalled those names after all these years.

Peter had long ago stopped searching the faces of the cabbies in New York, checking to see if the driver was Tebbs. He hadn't even thought of Tebbs since Ma died.

"My mother passed away five years ago." Adrianna's eyes softened. "But I don't have a sister. They had only me."

"Oh." Peter was confused. "What about Elsa?"

Adrianna's cheeks reddened, and she averted her eyes. "Oh, Elsa."

Peter caught on instantly. "Oh, I see. You're Elsa. Never fear. Your secret's safe with me." He lightly touched the sleeve of her jacket. "I changed my name, too. Long ago. It used to be Freddy Schnitzer."

Adrianna giggled. "I don't blame you. Out there," she gestured towards the door, "I'm called Adrianna Worthington. I only used Tebbs so you'd know who I was."

"Worthington? Oh my. You are certainly a Worthington. Tebbs doesn't suit you at all." Peter pulled the wildly decoupaged chair out, inviting her to sit. "I'm a firm believer that you are who you decide to be."

Adrianna sat gracefully. "My father, well, he didn't see things that way."

Peter perched on a decorated piano stool facing her. "Oh, believe me, I know all about his thoughts on the matter. He was, shall we say, painfully clear."

Adrianna looked down at the floor. "Yes. Well. He and I were not close at the end. He was very angry with me." She looked up at Peter. "I changed my name when I was at college. I think it helped me get a job at *Vanity Fair*. I'm an assistant editor."

"He must have been proud of that."

She shrugged. "I don't know. Whenever I saw him, he'd take me to task for 'putting on airs,' he called it." Adrianna cleared her throat. "He didn't call for me until the day before he died. He was in a hospital. Cancer. At first, he didn't know me. He thought I was Mama."

"Oh, you poor thing."

Adrianna rose. Peter watched her fight to compose herself. "Yes, well, he didn't talk much. But he did tell me that I was to find this box and to take it to you. That it was very important." She picked up the box and handed it to Peter. "There, now it's done. We're done."

"But, what is this?"

Adrianna was headed for the door. She paused and turned. Her expression was distant once more, her voice cool. "I have no idea. But, tell me. Is it true Helena Rubenstein lives here somewhere? I was hoping to somehow arrange to run into her."

"Sorry, dear, she's in Paris. But I'm sure she would have liked you."

Peter waited until Joe drove Adrianna away in a spray of gravel before he turned his attention to the box. He hesitated, not sure he wanted to know what was inside.

Finally, Peter ripped off the paper and opened the box. A shoe box. In it was one shoe, an old-style leather wingtip that looked as if it had hardly been worn.

Peter dropped it as if it burned. That's my shoe! The shoe Tebbs took that night, the night he took my clothes, my money. What was it he said? Peter's forehead furrowed. "I'll keep this one for a spare." That was it. And there was something else Tebbs said. "I know who I am. Who the fuck are you?"

Peter looked in the shoebox and spied a piece of paper.

On it was scrawled just a few words.

"Didn't need a spare after all."

Peter?
Peter?
Are you there?
Peter?

19

A Fine Day for April

April 1967 - Orleans

Peter stepped back from the easel to survey the day's work. Grinning back at him was his latest version of *Happy Lion*, a bright orange and yellow creature that Peter hoped caught the spirit of the psychedelic paintings he'd seen in Provincetown, while maintaining a sense of lighthearted folk art.

He was fascinated by the "hippie" art coming from Cape Cod studios, with its blend of brilliant colors and explosive forms. Peter felt it was the newest evolution in folk art, and he wanted to see if he could make it his own.

He was pleased at the reaction last year to his psychedelic owl, with its fire-engine red, burnt orange and pale yellow feathers, and images of Don Quixote in the eyes, Peter's vision of blending wisdom with fearless folly. Immense prints of the painting, almost three feet in height, sold almost as well as his more traditional peasant prints of the four seasons.

This was his fifth try at *Happy Lion*, Peter's notion of joy and strength. The face and mane were painted in tangerine, rust and butter yellow like the sunbursts Peter had seen in Mexico. Sitting on a tiny oasis, the lion grinned beneficently as a cascade of stars drifted from the melon-colored sky and onto his back.

Peter had Cookie in mind as he painted. She seemed so frail when he saw her last week in Key Biscayne.

Instead of taking his annual winter trip to Europe, Peter traveled to Florida to see his sister Dottie at her new house in Palm Beach. It was Dottie, now lean and tanned with peroxided hair and bracelets that jangled when she golfed, which was almost daily, who told Peter that Cookie was in Florida, too, staying with one of her nieces. In two days, Peter was in Key Biscayne, sipping iced tea under a green-and-white striped umbrella with Cookie.

Peter's heart ached when he first saw Cookie. Her hair had whitened to the color of French linen, and her pale skin was almost translucent. A web of wrinkles stretched around her eyes, lips and throat, and age spots mottled the back of her arthritic hands.

Still, the blue of her eyes was as deep as the ocean and her laugh as merry and ribald as when they first met.

"Oh, Peter, we've gotten so old!" Cookie was startled by how thin he'd become, how sparse his steel-colored hair. His fine long hands had a bony look to them, and his cheeks were sallow.

Still, Peter's grin was as broad and his step as light as when they danced away the evenings in Greenwich Village. He was well turned out, too, in a pale yellow sport coat, taupe slacks and a blue, yellow and green dotted scarf knotted at his neck.

"Speak for yourself, darling. We seem to have this conversation every decade or so!" Peter kissed her papery cheek.

"Did you ever imagine we would get this old?" Cookie's voice quavered.

"I never gave it much thought. Why be depressing?"

Peter rummaged in his jacket pocket and pulled out a yellowed black and white photograph. He held it out to Cookie. "I brought a present for you."

Cookie pulled a pair of glasses from her sweater pocket and settled them on the tip of her nose. She craned her neck to see the photo better. "Oh my God. Look at that."

The moment came back to her in a flash. It was on the beach by Peter's house in Provincetown, back in the Thirties, the summer when Willie had been so cruel and spiteful to her on the wharf. The picture was taken the next morning, just before Willie left. Clustered shoulder to shoulder were Pa and Ma, Hoppy and Peter, Cookie and Willie. Paolo was holding the camera. Cookie was rigid standing next to Willie, but she put on a good face and tried to smile when the group said "Cheese." Cookie's smile was like that of a death mask. Willie's smile was that of a cat who'd just finished a lunch of canary.

Peter leaned over the table and looked at the picture in Cookie's hands. "I didn't know it back then, but that was the only time in my life when all the people I loved were in the same place at the same time."

Cookie dropped the photo in her lap and covered her face with her hands. "Oh, Peter. You don't know."

Peter pulled a monogrammed handkerchief from his inside pocket and handed it to Cookie. He waited quietly as she softly cried. When she had dried her eyes, he spoke in a kind voice. "I think I do know, Cookie, but you tell me and we'll see if I'm right."

Cookie gripped the handkerchief in one hand and picked up the picture with the other. She set it on the table and turned it so it faced away. "Willie's book."

"Yes, Willie's book. *The Razor's Edge*. I remember."

"You were so angry about the way he wrote that Templeton character. But I thought you'd be even angrier as you read about the other characters, the old girlfriend and the fiancé."

"The old girlfriend, she was the one that still loved the main character, Larry, even though she dumped him for someone rich? So, when Larry fell for a recovering alcoholic, the old girlfriend tripped up the alcoholic fiancé, leaving her alone in a room with some incredible wine. The girlfriend knew the fiancé couldn't resist the temptation."

Cookie, her head down, nodded. "Willy was writing about me, Peter, and Hoppy. He just shifted things around a little."

"You have a drinking problem?"

"Stop!" Cookie slammed her palm on the tabletop. "Listen to me."

Her eyes locked with Peter's. "I'll stop when you quit talking nonsense."

"It's not nonsense, not all of it." Cookie's eyes brimmed with tears. "After all these years, Peter, I have to tell you what I did. I'm so afraid you'll hate me for it."

Peter opened his mouth, but Cookie held up her hand for silence. "I was jealous of Hoppy. I don't know why. Well, . . . I do. I felt no one could love you, appreciate you, as well as I could. I didn't want you to let anyone else as close as you let me."

Cookie took a deep breath. "I hired Paolo, Peter, and this is the awful part. I hired him thinking he would tempt you, that you wouldn't be able to resist him. And when that happened, Hoppy would find out, or you'd let go of her." Cookie covered her face with her hands. "Somehow, Willie figured it out." A sob escaped.

When Cookie lifted her face again, Peter was looking at her with sympathy. "You're not finished. Tell the rest of the story."

Cookie shook her head. "I don't know what you mean."

Peter stretched his hand across the table and, with a small hesitation, Cookie took it.

"I remember why I was so angry about Willy's book. It wasn't just that he modeled a character after me. It was that he got me wrong. Yes, the affectations were horribly accurate. But, inside, if I had ever been like Templeton, I'd long outgrown that kind of shallow ambition. I was angry that he showed it to the world."

Peter squeezed Cookie's hand. "I've always wondered about the girlfriend and the fiancé in the book. I couldn't help but see the physical resemblances. But, I've always thought it likely that even though Willy got the features right, he didn't get at the entire truth."

Cookie stared at Peter's hand holding hers. She felt like his hand was somehow a lifeline, keeping her from drowning in shame. But he couldn't save her from the truth. "Yes and no. Willy told me what he suspected the night before he left. I was angry at first, but then I was mortified. When he put it out in the open like that, I saw that what I was doing was so selfish, so hurtful."

Cookie tried to pull her hand back, but Peter held on. "Go on."

Cookie looked at Peter, her face weary. "In the end, I didn't want to do that to you. I didn't want to hurt you like that. That's why I left so suddenly. I tried to fire Paolo, but you'd already asked him to stay. So you see, Peter, what happened with Hoppy, it really was all my fault."

She pulled her hand and Peter let it go. She sat, her head bowed. Now, Peter would leave. He had to. The one person he trusted had betrayed him, and then hidden the betrayal. Cookie's shoulders sagged. What would she do without Peter?

"That's it?"

Cookie nodded.

"Good."

"Can you ever forgive me, Peter?" Cookie slowly raised her head, and was astonished to see Peter grinning from ear to ear. His finger tapped the photograph.

"It's all right here. I could always see it. You weren't smiling, you were grimacing. I'd never seen that expression on your face before, and, until the book, I couldn't, for the life of me, figure out what was going on."

"Well, now you know."

"But, what you don't know, is after Hoppy left I had it out with Willy. He blamed you for what happened, told me about your hiring Paolo to ruin things."

"You didn't say anything to me!" Cookies eyes were round.

"Why? You didn't make Hoppy leave. You didn't make her fall for Paolo. She did that all on her own. The only person I blame is myself, for not doing enough to keep her."

"But..."

"But, when I read Willy's stupid book, I realized how he perceived you. I thought about that summer, how things came about. I knew when Willy left, something had happened with you. I knew he'd said something that troubled you."

Peter rose from his chair and creakily knelt at Cookie's feet. "You didn't just leave, either, you tried to fire Paolo. For me. You did that for me."

Cookie stroked Peter's cheek. "Do you know, that was the first time, ever, I put someone else first? I think that opened something inside me. Changed me. In a good way. I was learning about love. So when Humphrey came into my life, I had to risk everything for his love."

Good old Humphrey. Peter picked up a paint-spattered sheet and draped it over *Happy Lion*. Cookie almost snorted when Peter inquired after her husband. The knight in shining armor had certainly suffered a few dents.

After years of arduous work translating some Tibetan spiritual writings, Humphrey finally published *Message of Milarepa* in 1958, causing a decided slump in the number of invitations they received from his austere circles. It had been one thing for their circle to put up with his fascination for Tibetan teachings, but publish a book? That was simply too much.

Chastened, Humphrey sought the counsel of a Brother Gerald, and leapt into Christian worship with unmitigated fervor.

Cookie was untroubled, either by the book or Humphrey's subsequent conversion to Christianity. What maddened her was Humphrey's decision to publish his poetry.

"He put every single poem he ever wrote into one volume," Cookie spluttered. "Not just his new Christian poems or his droll verse. He included every single word he'd ever written to me, back when we were first lovers." She couldn't resist a wink, "Some of it is quite racy, you know."

"You can't imagine the odd looks I get from the other ladies in the garden club."

Despite her embarrassment over *Love in Majorca*, Cookie was quite content with "my Humphrey." "I just wish he'd leave me out of all his fuss."

Peter poked his head into his Peacock Alley shop and, satisfied there were no customers, moved back to the studio. I've never been so productive, he thought as studied his canvases. He'd surprised himself with his experiments over the past several years, finding unexpected wells of inspiration as he worked.

Peter's paintings were diverse in style, from the whimsy of the *Happy Lion* and *Blue Pussycat* series, to the primitive *Lady in Red* and the reverse painting he'd tried in *Children in a Baroque Landscape*. Although his sharp eye saw flaws in each of his works, Peter viewed them with satisfaction. He was stretching and growing as he never had before. Is this how Pa felt when he painted? Good Lord, I'm older than Pa was when he died, Peter realized.

No matter what his approach, Peter always tried to convey a sense of joy. If I have any message at all, he often said, it is to greet all the things you do with a blithe spirit and a happy heart.

Peter tugged the chain of the ceiling light and easily made his way through the dark to the back of the shop, where Nancy and her husband had unloaded a truck full of her latest decorated furnishings. Good, good. Strong colors, good balance to the designs. He picked up a brush, dipped it in a dark green paint and began signing the pieces. What a fine stroke Nancy has. Why she's as good as me. Better.

"*Anno domini '67*" Peter wrote on each dresser, chair and chest Nancy had brought. On a table, he added "*Duc d'Orleans*" and on a wardrobe "*Pierre le Chausseur.*" I really must remember to send Nancy a check for these. When she'd come in the rattling blue Ford, Peter was on his way out to dinner at Chillingsworth, fluffing the kerchief in his dinner jacket as he stepped out on the patio where his dinner companions were waiting.

Nancy looked like a ragpicker's daughter as she stood next to them, with her paint-smeared overalls and her hair wild from driving with the windows open. "Shall I write you a check, darling?" Peter asked, his voice light.

Nancy, saucy as always, waved him on. "Oh, no, that's all right. Just drop it in the mail." Peter admired her spirit. He knew very well her family lived hand-to-mouth. Once, when Nancy had brought her children along on a delivery, they squealed with delight at the sight of stale crusts Peter had just left in the grass for the birds. "Look, Mama, raisin bread!" Yes, he better get to it, first thing in the morning.

When Peter was done signing, he dropped the brush in a jelly jar of turpentine and looked out the loading bay to see that twilight was descending. Time to close up. Not one soul had visited the shop all day. Still too early in the season for tourists and the Cape Codders were off on the mainland or in Europe to shake off the winter doldrums.

What a fine day for April. So mild.

Peter heated a can of soup for supper and ate sitting in his wicker chair, watching boats bob on the quiet cove waters. He washed his bowl, fixed himself a martini and settled in front of the television. Nothing interested him, so he turned it off. Peter wanted to call somebody, but no one was around. Maybe he'd cross the street to the Southward Inn, have a chat with Eve. No, he was too tired.

Glass empty, Peter made another martini and took his drink with him out onto the patio. The cove was wrapped in a soft darkness, and water lapped softly at the neighbor's small dock. Pine needles stirred in the boughs over Peter's head, and a grackle called for a little quiet. Another grackle across the cove answered, and they fell silent.

Peter shivered. The Cape could still get pretty cold on a Spring night. He went inside and put his glass in the sink. He'd wash it in the morning.

He went into his bedroom and changed into his favorite blue pajamas. I really should tear these up for rags. They're so frayed, he told himself for the hundredth time. But they were so soft and familiar, he could never bring himself to do it.

Peter turned off the light and lay down on the bed. He pulled the covers up to his chin, burrowing under the woolen blanket, and turned onto his side, pulling his knees toward his chest. He sighed and fell asleep.

Afterword

Peter Hunt was found dead a few days later, on April 11, 1967, still curled on his side in bed, wearing his blue pajamas. Orleans Medical Examiner Joseph Kelly determined that Peter died in his sleep of a heart attack.

Peter's friend, artist and gallery owner Bruce McKain, saw to the arrangements with the Nickerson Funeral Home in Orleans. Peter was cremated before funeral services at the Church of the Holy Spirit in Orleans. A reporter from the *Cape Codder* who attended the service wrote that the mourners who filled the church "ran the gamut of social and economic extremes. There was at least one beach-comber and one millionaire." After the service, Peter's ashes were strewn on the waters of Town Cove in Orleans.

Peter's sister, Dorothy Heist, tried for a while to operate Peacock Alley, but eventually offered it for sale. Peter's estate, including his paintings, his household furnishings and his shop's inventory, was auctioned off by Cape auctioneer Robert Eldred in July, 1968, bringing in about $40,000. In the course of that auction, a Sheraton-style sideboard decorated and signed by Peter went for $130. That same piece would sell today for $5,000-6,000.

After Peter's furnishings and store inventory were disposed of, Nancy Whorf Kelly (who never got that final check) and Muriel Strout set about gathering all the remaining sketches, artwork, clippings, scrapbooks and photographs they could find in Peter's home and studio, and sent them to the Smithsonian Institute in Washington D.C., where they are now protected in the Archives of American Art. (Yes, that's the box I told Peter about.) At the time, a museum official suggested a showing of Peter's work at the Smithsonian, but that show has yet to take place.

A few years after Peter's death, Nancy Whorf Kelly set up her own shop filled with peasant-decorated furnishings and gifts in Wellfleet on Cape Cod. Decorative artist and writer Priscilla Hauser was so taken with Nancy's abilities, she produced a book called *The Painting World of Nancy Whorf* in 1976. At the time of this writing, Nancy is alive, a grandmother and a well-respected modern impressionist painter, as is her sister, Carol Whorf Wescott. Both women still live in Provincetown.

The Museum of Modern Art in New York still has Pa Hunt's painting, *Peter Hunt's Antique Shop* in its collection. It's been in storage since its single 1938 showing.

In 1971, Parke-Bernet auctioneers in New York sold a collection of folk paintings by Peter's "discovery," George Lothrop, the Poet Prince, for prices ranging from $225 to $1,700 apiece.

Lothrop is still recognized as an American folk artist of note, and his painting, *Buttercup*, is in the collection of the Museum of American Folk Art in New York. Lothrop's *The Jewels* is in the collection of the Addison Gallery of American Art in Andover Mass.

The Provincetown Art Association, which has two Peter Hunt prints in its collection, ran a local artists retrospective in 1983 that included a Peter Hunt work. The Provincetown Heritage Museum, curator of a substantial standing display of Peter Hunt's furnishings, has been closed for renovation and the pieces may presently be viewed during the summer at the Pilgrim Monument Museum in Provincetown.

The only other permanent public display of Peter's work is a decorated cabinet and three-drawer dresser at the Decorative Arts Collection at the Museum of Decorative Painting, sponsored by the Society of Decorative Painters in Wichita, Kansas.

Helena Rubenstein died in 1965, leaving behind her autobiography, *My Life for Beauty*, (Simon & Schuster, 1964), and one of the world's largest collections of primitive art. Cookie died a few years after Peter, of age-related ailments. Her self-published book of poetry, *Rose in the Sand*, is occasionally found at used bookstores, most often in California. Cookie's husband, Sir Humphrey Clarke, died in England in 1973.

In her nineties, Ganna Walska was a renowned gardener at the Santa Barbara mansion she bought from the Clarkes, which she renamed Lotusland. Walska died there in 1984, and her lavish gardens are now open to the public and famed for their rare species of flowers.

W. Somerset Maugham died in Nice, France in 1965, one of the world's wealthiest authors, his passing notable in its caustic tributes. It is said that as he lay dying he asked athiest philosopher Sir Alfred Ayer to visit him and reassure him that there was no life after death. One acquaintance said Maugham was "the milk of human kindness half-soured." Maugham himself once said, "I have always been interested in people, but I don't like them."

Peter never commented publicly about Maugham's character, Elliot Templeton, or his book, *The Razor's Edge*.

Jack Amoroso is alive and thriving in Coconut Grove as a well-known and respected Modern impressionist artist.

Peter's three books, *Peter Hunt's Workbook*, *The Peter Hunt How-to-do-it Book*, and *Peter Hunt's Cape Cod Cookbook*, are all out of print, but turn up from time to time at used bookstores and online auctions. The same is true for his *Transformagic* brochures and the Betty Cavanna book set in Peasant Village and illustrated by Peter, *Paintbox Summer*.

Signed Peter Hunt pieces now command impressive prices at auctions and sales of both folk art and antiques. Even works by his apprentices, especially Nancy Whorf Kelly and Carol Whorf Wescott, are in demand by decorators and collectors.

Peacock Alley in Orleans still stands, but Peter's home in back is gone. His shop now houses a discount clothier, and the only traces of him left are two barely perceptible decorations on red panels at the front of the building.

What was once Peasant Village is now Kiley Court. If you keep your eyes open, you may spot the last vestige of Peasant Village: an exterior door decorated with Peter's charming characters and designs, now faded by weather and time.

That's where I come in.

I saw my first Peter Hunt piece on my wedding day in 1994, a dresser at my mother-in-law's summer home on Cape Cod. I've been chasing him ever since.

My mother-in-law, Barbara Weller, knew Peter Hunt, as did her mother and many of their friends on the Cape. It was through them I learned how much fun he could be, and how wide-ranging his circle of friends. A bookseller drew my interest a step further when he showed me the books Peter had written, on decorating furniture and cooking (especially ironic since one of his friends, Cape Cod artist Walter Hyde, noted Peter couldn't cook a TV dinner without burning it).

Peter's former apprentices showed me the other side of Peter: his penchant for making up stories about himself and his family. "He lied all the time," Nancy Whorf Kelly said. "He was as phony as they come. But he had an ability to make you feel like you were the only person he ever wanted to see." She was the person who told me about the box at the Archive of American Art.

After an article I wrote about Peter appeared in *Yankee* magazine in 1998, I thought I'd learned everything there was to know about the artist. But I soon realized I'd barely scratched the surface.

My brother noted the resemblance between Peter Hunt and Elliot Templeton in Maugham's *The Razor's Edge*. That remark started me on years of researching Somerset Maugham, then Helena Rubenstein, Ganna Walska, Elisabeth Cook, Sir Humphrey Clarke and so on. By putting together a 15-page timeline tracking all their lives and events on Cape Cod and around the world, I was able to piece together more and more of Peter's story, and the stories he invented about himself.

I combed through his box at the Archives, traced every arcane scribble, every name, every clipping I could find.

After seven years of research, I finally had enough for this book, *The Search for Peter Hunt*. Even after I'd handed the manuscript to the publishers, I still heard new stories and anecdotes about Peter Hunt.

That's the magic of the man and his art. Once you meet him, he never stops changing.

Peter Hunt in his Peacock Alley shop photographed for Cape Cod Compass, *1964. Courtesy* Yankee *magazine.*

Bibliography

Sketch by Peter Hunt for Cape Cod Compass, *1963. Courtesy* Yankee *magazine.*

Books

Andrew, A. Piatt, Introduction. *Friends of France: The Field Service of the American Ambulance described by its members.* Houghton Mifflin Company, 1916.

Barr, Alfred H., Jr., ed. *Painting & Sculpture in the Museum of Modern Art.* Museum of Modern Art, 1942, 1948.

Barr, Arthur, foreword; Rubin, William, introduction. *Three Generations of Twentieth-Century Art: The Sidney and Harriet Janis Collection of the Museum of Modern Art.* Museum of Modern Art, 1972.

Beebe, William. *Zaca Venture.* Harcourt, Brace & Company, Inc., 1938.

Bihalh-Merin, Oto and Tomasevic, Nebojsa-Bato. *World Encyclopedia of Naïve Art: A Hundred Years of Naïve Art.* Chartwell Books, Inc., 1984.

Birmingham, Stephen. *California Rich.* Simon & Schuster, 1980.

Bossert, H. Th. *Peasant Art in Europe.* Ernest Benn Ltd., 1927

Bossert, Helmuth T. *Peasant Art of Europe and Asia.* Frederick A. Praeger, Publishers, 1958.

———. *Folk Art of Europe.* Rizzoli, 1990.

Brookhauser, Frank, ed. *These Were Our Years.* Doubleday & Co., 1959.

Cahill, Holger, Gauthier, Maximilien, Cassou, Jean, Millwer, Dorothy C., et al. *Masters of Popular Painting: Modern Primitives of Europe and Asia.* Museum of Modern Art, 1938.

Cavanna, Betty with decoration by Hunt, Peter. *Paintbox Summer.* Westminster Press, 1949.

Churchill, Allen. *The Improper Bohemians: A Re-Creation of Greenwich Village in its Heyday.* E. P. Dutton & Co., 1959.

Clarke, Sir Humphrey O. *Love in Majorca: Poems.* Favil Press, 1960.

———. *Message of Milarepa.* John Murray Publishers, 1958.

Clements, Colin Campbell. *Plays for a Folding Theatre.* Jacket design by Hunt, Peter. Stewart Kidd Company, 1923.

Cook, Elisabeth. *Rose on the Sand.* Self-published, 1938.

Crocker, Templeton. *The Cruise of the Zaca.* Harper & Brothers, 1933.

Crotty, Frank. "Provincetown Profiles and Others on Cape Cod." *Barre Gazette*, 1958.
Douglas, Ann. *Terrible Honesty: Mongrel Manhattan in the 1920s*. Farrar, Straus & Giroux, 1995.
Goddard, Donald. *American Painting*. Beaux Arts Editions, Hugh Lauter Levin Associates, Inc., 1990.
Greeman, Edward. *Grandpa's War: The French Adventures of a World War I Ambulance Driver*. Writers and Readers Publishing, Inc., 1992.
Hansen, Arlen J. *Gentlemen Volunteers: The Story of the American Ambulance Drivers in the Great War*, August 1914 - September 1918. Arcade Publishing, 1996.
Hatch, Robert. "At The Tip of Cape Cod." *Horizon*, American Heritage Publishing Co., Inc., July, 1961.
Hauser, Priscilla. *The Painting World of Nancy Whorf*. Self-published, 1976.
Hunt, Peter. *Peter Hunt's Cape Cod Cookbook: A Cape Cod Treasury of Favorite Recipes Illustrated by the Author, Peter Hunt*. Hawthorn Books, Inc., 1954.
———. *How to Transform Outdated Furniture*. E. I. DuPont de Nemours & Co., 1943.
———. *Peter Hunt's How-to-do-it Book*. Prentice-Hall, Inc., 1952.
———. *Transformagic*. E. I. DuPont de Nemours & Co., 1944.
———. *Peter Hunt's Workbook with Text and Pictures*. Ziff-Davis Publishing Company, 1945.
James, Robert Rhodes, ed. *Chips: The Diaries of Sir Henry Channon*. Weidenfield & Nicolson, 1967.
Janis, Sidney. *They Taught Themselves: American Primitive Painters of the 20th Century*. Originally printed by Museum of Modern Art, 1942; reprinted by Hudson River Press, 1999.
Kellner, Bruce, ed. *Letters of Charles Demuth: American Artist 1883-1935*. Temple University Press, 2000.
Kuchta, Ronald A., ed., text by Seckler, Dorothy Gees. *Provincetown Painters 1890s-1970s*. Visual Arts Publications, Inc., 1977.
Maugham, Robin. *Conversations With Willie: Recollections of W. Somerset Maugham*. Simon & Schuster, 1978.
Maugham, W. Somerset. *The Razor's Edge*. William Heinemann Ltd., 1944.
———. *The Summing Up*. William Heinemann Ltd., 1938.
———. *A Writer's Notebook*, William Heinemann Ltd., 1949.
Meeker, Arthur. *Chicago, With Love: A Polite and Personal History*, Alfred A. Knopf, 1955.
Moffett, Ross. *Art in Narrow Streets: the First Thirty-Three Years of the Provincetown Art Association*. Provincetown Cape Cod Pilgrim Memorial Association, 1989.
Morgan, Ted. *Maugham: A Biography*. Simon & Schuster, 1980.
O'Higgins, Patrick. *Madame: An Intimate Biography of Helena Rubenstein*. The Viking Press, 1972.
Parke-Bernet Galleries, Inc. *American Painting and Folk Art by J. O. J. Frost and George Lothrop from the Collection of Betty and Albert L. Carpenter*, public auction catalogue of Parke-Bernet Galleries, Inc., 1971.
Rosenak, Chuck and Jan. *Museum of American Folk Art Encyclopedia of Twentieth-Century American Folk Art and Artists*. Abbeville Press, 1990.

Rubenstein, Helena. *My Life for Beauty*. Simon & Schuster, 1965.
Sarlos, Robert Karoly. *Jig Cook and the Provincetown Players: Theatre in Ferment*. University of Massachusetts Press, 1982.
Shaw, Jackie. *The Big Book of Decorative Painting*. Watson-Guptil Publications, 1994.
Sorel, Cecile. *Cecile Sorel: An Autobiography*. Translated by Philip John Stead, Roy Publishers, 1953.
Spurling, Hilary. *La Grande Therese: The Greatest Scandal of the Century*. Harper Collins Publishers, 2000.
Tebbel, John. *An American Dynasty: The Story of the McCormicks, Medills and, Pattersons*. Doubleday & Company, 1947.
Time Life Books, eds. *American Painting 1900-1970*. Time-Life Books, 1970.
Tompkins, Walker A. *Goleta: The Good Land*. Goleta Am-Vets Post No. 55 with the Santa Barbara News-Press, 1966.
Vorse, Mary Heaton. *Time and the Town: A Provincetown Chronicle*. Originally published 1942; reprinted by Rutgers University Press, 1991.
Walska, Ganna. *Always Room at the Top*. Richard R. Smith, 1943.
Whorf, Nancy, with Snow, Marynell. *The Painting World of Nancy Whorf*. Priscilla Hauser, 1976.

MAGAZINES

Chesy, Judith. "Peter Hunt: A Village Within A Village." *Cape Cod Antiques & Arts*, September, 1982.
"A Christmas to Make and Remember" and "How to Paint the Peter Hunt Way." *McCall's*, December, 1943.
Hunt, Peter. "Peter Hunt's Painting Magic." *Design*, November, 1950.
———. Prints and cover design. *Lorelei: Journal of Art and Letters*, August 1924.
———. "Victorian pair" set decoration. *Vogue*, April 15, 1940.
———. "Winter is Best." *Cape Cod Compass*, 1963; cover art *Cape Cod Compass*, 1964.
"Made-Over Junk: Provincetown artist shows how to transform dark, ugly furniture into gay modern pieces." *Life* magazine: November 2, 1942.
"In Peter Hunt's Studio Overlooking Provincetown Harbor, Girls Make Rugs in old Portuguese style." Photograph for "Cape Cod People and Places." *National Geographic*, June, 1946.
"Revealing the Secrets of Peter Hunt, America's Most Imaginative Furniture Magician," "Summer Home Life al Fresco: Peter Hunt Salvages Cast-Offs for Helena Rubenstein's Terrace." *House Beautiful*, August, 1943.
Ruoff, Abby. "Brushing Up on Peter Hunt." *Country Living*, May, 1990.

NEWSPAPERS

Boston Globe: May 2, 1954
Boston Herald: Nov. 22, 1922
The Cape Codder: April 20, 1967; July 6, 1968;
New York Times: articles, reviews and obituaries from 1938 through 1967
Provincetown Banner, August 22, 1996
Tech magazine, Massachusetts Institute of Technology, Nov. 21, 1924

INDEX

Page nmbers in italic indicate illustrations.

Ambulance Corps, 48-49, 51, 60, 200, 203
Amoroso, Jack, *vii*, 215, 221, 238
Annie Spindler, 89
Anno domini, 108, 234
Apprentice(s), 137, 194, 209, *210*, 215, 239
Archives of American Art, 116, 237, 240
Arden, Elizabeth, 71-72
Argonaut Club, 148
Armory Show, 28-29, 37
Armour Family, 39
Arras, France, 51, 53
Art Gallery, The, by Peter Hunt, *183*, 211, 238
Austrian Village Ball, 167
Avery, Milton, 222

Ballet Russe, 43, 186
Basic stroke, 122, 170, 188
Batik(s), 43, 64-65, 70-72
Beacon Hill, 215, 222
Beardsley, Aubrey, 135
Beers, Richard Cameron, 140
Bloomingdale's department store, 178
Blue Pussycat by Peter Hunt, 234
Bohemian(s), 35, 41, 80, 223
Bombois, Camille, 144
Boston, MA: 80, 89,106, 114, 139-142, 145, 148, 153, 166-167, 170, 176, 182-183, 214; clients, 64-65, 67, 88; Hunt, as a young man in, 40, 42-43, 47-48, 108
Boston School of Practical Arts, 42
Brunswick Cellar (Hotel), 148

Campbell, Alison, 181
Campbell, Colin Leiter, 146-148, 156-157, 181
Campbell, Elisabeth Cook, *see* Cook, Elisabeth
Campbell, Juliet, 181
Campbell, Nancy Leiter (Mother Campbell), 156-157
Campbell Ranch, 147, 156-157, 181
Cape Cod Cookbook, Peter Hunt's, 214, 238
Cape Cod, MA: map, *viii*; 81, 85, 177; art and artists, 196, 229, 237; hurricane 167, 171; life on, 95, 98, 162, 165, 239-240; move to, 89; Orleans, 221; Rubenstein, Helena, 73
Cape Codder, 163, 237
Cape Cod Compass, 116 - 117, 240-241
Cape Cod Room, Drake Hotel, 145, 147, *158*
Cavanna, Betty, 210, 239
Channon, Sir Henry (Chips), 203
Chatham, MA, 162, 164, 210
Chicago, IL: 166; Campbell, Colin, 146-148, 156, 181; Cape Cod room, Drake Hotel, 107, 145, *158*;

Cook, Elisabeth, 39, 96-97, 109-110, 114, 126, 203; Rubenstein, Helena, 66, 69, 77; Schnitzer, Dorothy, 83
Children in a Baroque Landscape by Peter Hunt, 234
Chillingsworth restaurant, 234
Christopher Street, 36
Church of the Holy Spirit, Orleans, 237
Citizen Kane, 181
Clarke, Elisabeth Cook Campbell (Cookie), *see* Cook, Elisabeth
Clarke, Sir Humphrey, 181, 238-239
Clarke, Toby, 181
Clements, Colin Campbell, 59-62, 64, 80, *116,* 130, 216
Coconut Grove, FL, 215, 217, 238
Commercial Street, 85, 103, 140, 142, 162-163, 165, 195-196, 198, 222-223
Communist Party, 37
Cook, Elisabeth (Cookie): 95-99, 103-104, 239; Boston, 42-45; Cape Cod, 95-99, 103-104, 106-114, 125-133, 140-141, 149-153, 155, 158, 207-212; Campbell, Colin, 146-148, 156; children, 157, 207; Clarke, Sir Humprey, 181, 197, 233, 238; cousin, 81-83, 130; death, 238; Greenwich Village, NY, 36-40; Key Biscayne, FL, 229-233; Lynch, Edward, 81; poetry, 238; Razor's Edge 197-198, 200, 231; Walska, Ganna, 181-182; *see also* 216-217, 223-224
Crocker, C. Templeton, 60-61

Decorative Art Collection, Museum of Decorative Painting, 238
Decoupage, 211-212, 215
Deering, James, 217
Dodge, Mabel, 37, 64
Don Quixote Owl by Peter Hunt, *116-117,* 229
Drake Hotel, 69, 83, 107, 145, 147, *158*
Duchamp, Marcel, 28
Duncan, Isadora, 209
Duncan, Menalkis, 209
DuPont Nemours, 93, 122, 124, 177, 179, 192-193

Eldred, Robert, 135, 237
Ellis Island, 7
Ellsword, Richard, *115*
England, 41, 54, 67, 127, 156, 165, 170-171, 181, 197, 216, 224, 238
Erté, 135
Exploration by Jack Amoroso, 224

Fitzgerald, F. Scott, 67, 130-131, 186
Fitzgerald, Zelda, 67, 186
France, 29-30, 44, 47, 67, 73, 108, 166, 216, 224, 238

245

Gaul, Harriet Avery, 215-216, 223
Gaul, Harvey, 215, 223
Gimbel's department store, 178
Gourielli-Tchkonia, Prince Archtil, 180, 183
Gourielli-Tchkonia, Princess Archtil, *see* Rubenstein, Helena, 180, *183*
Great Depression, 176
Greenwich Village, 27, 29, 35, 41, 68, 127, 165, 182, 223, 230
Grosse Pointe, MI, 162, 166-167
Guilbert, Yvette, 65, 87
Gumaer, Lucia, 121

Hackett, Mary, 174
Hackett, Wendy, 179, 216
Happy Lion by Peter Hunt, 229, 233-234
Harriet by Colin Campbell Clements and Florence Ryerson, 216
Hartley, Marsden, 29
Haspell, Nora, 179, 216
Hauser, Priscilla, 237
Hawthorne, Charles, 68
Hayes, Helen, 216
Heist, Dorothy or Dottie, *see* Schnitzer, Dorothy or Dottie
Heist, Robert, 84-85, 145, 223, 234, 237
Hirshfield, Morris, 195
Hoffmann, Hans, 197
Home Crafts magazine, 194
Home for Working Women tavern, 36, 38
House & Garden magazine, 194
House Beautiful magazine, 188, 192-194
How To Transform Old Furniture, 122-123, 123, *124*, 178
Hunt, Ma (Anna Lowe Schnitzer): Cape Cod, 96, 104-107, 112-113, 16, 128, 131-132, 142-143, 146, 148-150, 158, 161-165, 168-171, 176-177, 194, 208, 230; death 213-217, 222, 225; Pa's death, 139-140, 175; peter, 38; Razor's Edge, 197-201; Schnitzer, 5 - 12, 15, 21-23, 25, 40-41, 79-83, 85-89
Hunt, Pa (Edward Schnitzer): Cape Cod, 104-107, 110-114, 128, 131, 230, 222; death 139, 175, 198; painter, 114, 125-126, 136, 139-146, 148-153, 158, 163-164, 182, 188, 195, 234, 237; Schnitzer, Edward, 5, 9, 11-12, 15-17, 19-23, 40-41, 79-83, 85-86, 88
Hunt, Peter (Frederick Lowe Schnitzer), *209, 240*
Hurricane of 1938, 161, 163, 167-168, 171
Hyde, Walter, *118*, 239

Italy, 60, 108, 216, 224

Janis, Sidney, 140, 148, 164, 195
Jeanne d'Arc by Peter Hunt, 135
Jersey City, NJ, 7, 35, 79, 106, 140, 191, 195
Jones, Guy Pearce, 42-44, 64

Kane, John, 195
Kelly, Joseph, 237
Kelly, Nancy Whorf, *see* Whorf, Nancy
Key Biscayne, FL, 229-230
Kiley Court (see Peter Hunt Lane), *119*, 179, *179*, 239
King Soloman, 109, *118*

La Grande Therese, 73-74
Lady in Red by Peter Hunt, 234
La Reine Saba et Soloman by Peter Hunt, *118*
Le Petit Gallerie, 64
Lehman Brothers, 70, 180
Leiter, Joseph, 156
Life magazine, *115, 193*
Lindenmuth, Todd, 140
London, England, 180
Lowe family, *see* Hunt, Ma
Lorelei, Journal of Arts & Letters, 135
Lothrop, George, *see* Poet Prince, 148-149, 182, 195-196, 238
Love in Majorca by Clarke, Sir Humphrey, 233
Lynch, Edward Allen, 81, 96
Lynch, Elisabeth Cook, *see* Cook, Elisabeth

Macy's department store, 178-179, 187-190
Mademoiselle magazine, 194
Magazin de Antiquities by Peter Hunt, 211-212
Marseilles, France, 51, 53
Marshall, Benjamin, 145
Martin, Joe, 224
Masters of Popular Painting, Exhibition, 163
Maugham, Syrie, 128-129, 154
Maugham, W. Somerset (Willy), 27-36, 38-39, 47-55, 57-58, 60, 126-132, 136, 153-155, 167, 197-198, 200-201, 203, 231-233, 238-239
Mayflower Heights, 110, 112
McCall's magazine, 194
McCormick Family, 39
McCormick, Harold, 88
McKain, Amy, 215
McKain, Bruce, 140, 215, 222, 237
McMillan's Wharf, 104, 141
Medgyes, Ladislas, 183
Mentor magazine, 64
Message of Milarepa by Clarke, Sir Humphrey, 233
Meyercord decals, 209
Moffett, Ross, 140
Moors, The, 215
Moses, Grandma, 195
Museum of Decorative Painting, 238
Museum of Modern Art, 163, 237
My Life for Beauty by Helena Rubenstein, 238

Nancy Craig's Digest, 194
Naples, Italy, 214, 216
New Horizons Gallery, 221, 223
New York: 2, 7, 13, 48, 67, 85, 88, 110, 146-148, 154,

158, 170, 176, 214; advertising, 177, 179; Armory Show, 28; art and artists, 21, 61, 80, 107, 114, 127, 136, 237-238; Greenwich Village, 33, 40-41, 44, 166-167; Pa Hunt, 139-140, 145, 152, 164; Rubenstein, Helena, 59, 64-65, 73, 77, 180, 187-88, 192, 197
Nickerson's Funeral Home, 237
Norfolk, 181
Norton, Nancy Ann, 223
Nude Descending a Staircase by Marcel Duchamp, 28-29

O'Neill, Eugene, 113
Orleans, MA, *115, 119*, 221-223, 229, 234, 237, 239
Osterhaut, Bob, 223
Ovince, 108, 209

Paintbox Summer by Betty Cavanna, 210, 239
Painting World of Nancy Whorf, The, by Priscilla Hauser, 237
Palm Beach, FL, 229
Paris, 21, 43, 55, 60, 62, 73-74, 86, 136, 143-144, 153, 180, 214, 216, 226
Parke-Bernet, 238
Parrish Family, 65
Peacock Alley, *115, 119*, 221-224, 233, 237, 239-240
Peasant Village, 2, *115*, 159, 165, 173, 175, 179, 192-194, *193*, 196, 198, 208, 210, 214-216, 239
Peinture d'instinct, 144
Peter Hunt Lane, see Kiley Court, *119, 179*, 222
Peter Hunt's Antique Shop by Pa Hunt, 141, 237
Peter Hunt's Christmas Shoppe, 195
Peter Hunt's How-to-do-it Book, 124, 238
Peter Hunt's Workbook, 120-121, 123, 208-210, *209-210*, 214-238
Petrograd, 63
Pilgrim Monument Museum, *118*, 238
Plays for a Folding Theatre, by Colin Campbell Clements, *116*, 80
Poet Prince, *see* George Lothrop, 148-149, 182, 195-196, 238
Poland, 60, 109, 177, 180
Polly's Restaurant, 35, 42
Portmanteau Theatre, 61
Primitive painting, 53, 108, 143, 145, 182, 188, 195, 234, 238
Prohibition, 80, 89, 103-104
Provincetown Art Association, 148, 196, 238
Provincetown Heritage Museum, *118, 179*, 238
Provincetown, MA: *99, 115, 118-119, 179;* arrival in 67-68, 104-105, 186; art and artists, 88, 103, 108, 177-178, 215, 229; Hunt, Ma, 175-176, 213-214; Hunt, Pa, 110-112, 139-143, 145-146, 148-149; hurricane 161, 167; life in, 85-86, 89, 95, 128, 147, 176, 207, 222-224, 230; O'Neill, Eugene, 127; Peasant Village, 159, 165, 179, 208; Rubenstein, Helena, 73, 76-77, 127; Walker, Hudson, 194; Whorf, Carol and Nancy, 237

Provincetown Theater, 42
Psychedelic art, *116*, 229
Pussycat Bride by Peter Hunt, 222

Race Point, Provincetown, MA 89
Raymond, Sam, 153
Razor's Edge by W. Somerset Maugham, 197-198, 231, 238-239
Reed, John, 36-37
Revelers, The by George Lothrop, 182
Rich, Eva, 223
Rideau pottery, 209
Rockefeller, Abbey Aldrich, 195
Romania, 108-109
Rose in the Sand by Elizabeth Cook Campbell, 238
Rotonda Café, 60
Rousseau, Henri, 144, 195
Rubenstein, Helena, *see* Gourielli-Tchkonia, Princess Archtil: 110, 176, 183, 226, 239; Chicago, 88; death, 238; New York, 59, 62, 64-65, 187-188; patriot, 194; Princess Archtil, 180, *183;* Provincetown, 73, 76-77, 126-127
Rubenstein, Horace, 59-60, 62-66, 75
Russia, 63, 67, 73, 80, 180, 186
Ryerson, Florence, 130, 216

S-4 Submarine wreck, 98
Salon des Independents, 144
Santa Barbara, CA, 147, 181, 238
Schnitzer, Anna Lowe, *see* Hunt, Ma
Schnitzer, Dorothy (Dottie) (Heist): 141, 145-146; Jersey City, NJ, 8, 21-22, 41; marriage to Heist, Robert, 83-85, 107; Naples, Italy, 214, 216-217, 224; Palm Beach, FL, 229
Schnitzer, , Edward, *see* Hunt, Pa
Schnitzer, Frederick, *see* Hunt, Peter
Smithsonian Institution, *116*
Society of Decorative Painters, 238
Society of Independent Artists, 182
Somerset Ballroom, 167
Sorel, Cecile, 87
Southward Inn, Orleans, 223, 235
Souza, Mary, 214, 217
St. Louis, MO, 39, 82
St. Mary's of the Harbor, 176
Strout, Muriel, 223, 237
Sullivan, P.J., 195
Sweden, 60, 166
Sydenstricker, Bill, 221, 223-224

Taylor's Funeral Chapel, 139
Templeton, Elliot, 200, 238-239
Templeton-Hunt, Peter, *see* Peter Hunt, 2, 63, 66, 71, 87, *116*, 135, 239
They Taught Themselves by Sidney Janis, 195
Tibetland, 181
Times Gallery, 145
Titus, Edward, 69-70, 180

Titus, Horace, 59-60, 62-66, 75
Town Cove, Orleans, 237
Transformagic by Peter Hunt, *124*, 179, 192-193, 208, 239
Truro, MA, 68, 176

Vanity Fair, 225
Villa Viscaya, FL, 217
Vivin, Louis, 144
Vorse, Mary Heaton, 68, 140

Walker, Berta, 194
Walker, Hudson, 140, 144, 148, 164, 194, 215
Walker, Ione Gaul, 215
Walska, Ganna, 71, 88, 180, 238-239
Waugh, Coulton, 140
Waugh, Frederick, 19, 88, 140, 176
Weber, Max, 148
Weller, Barbara T., *121*
Welles, Orson, 181
Wellfleet, MA, 237
Wescott, Carol Whorf, *see* Whorf, Carol
Whorf, Carol: *123-124*, 140, 146, 173-174, 178-179, 209, 211, 216, 223, 237, 239
Whorf, Jack (John), 36-38, 108, 140, 146, 173, 178, 195
Whorf, Nancy, *124*, 216, 223, 237, 239
Wichita, KS, 238
Wizard of Oz, 216
Woods End Lighthouse, Cape Cod, MA, 95
World War I, 47-50
World War II, 192

Zaca, 131
Zipkin, Jerome, 203

QUANTITY SALES

This and other books from The Local History Company are available at special quantity discounts for bulk purchases or sales promotions, premiums, fund raising, or educational use by corporations, institutions, and other organizations. Special imprints, messages, and excerpts can also be produced to meet your specific needs.

For details, please contact us at:

Special Sales

The Local History Company
112 North Woodland Road
Pittsburgh, PA 15232-2849
412-362-2294
info@TheLocalHistoryCompany.com
www.TheLocalHistoryCompany.com
Please specify how you intend to use the books (e.g. promotion, resale, fund raising, etc.)

INDIVIDUAL SALES

To order this book, use a copy of the order form at the back of this book, or for an up-to-date listing of our books and information on how to order, contact us at:

Sales

The Local History Company
112 NORTH Woodland Road
Pittsburgh, PA 15232-2849
412-362-2294
info@TheLocalHistoryCompany.com
www.TheLocalHistoryCompany.com

ORDER ADDITIONAL COPIES OF

THE SEARCH FOR PETER HUNT
by Lynn C. Van Dine
(ISBN 0-9711835-4-6)

from THE LOCAL HISTORY COMPANY
Publishers of History and Heritage
www.TheLocalHistoryCompany.com

ORDER FORM - PLEASE PRINT CLEARLY

NAME _____
COMPANY (if applicable) _____
ADDRESS _____
CITY _____ STATE _____ ZIP _____
PHONE _____ PLEASE: include your phone number so we can contact you in case there is a problem with your order.

Please allow 2-4 weeks for delivery. Prices are subject to change without notice. All book sales are final. US shipments only (call or write us for information on international orders). Payable by check, money order, or Discover/Visa/MC in US funds (no cash orders accepted)

PLEASE SEND _____ copies at $34.95 each .... Subtotal: $_____
Sales Tax: PA residents (outside Allegheny County) add 6% per copy
                      Allegheny County, PA residents add 7% per copy $_____
Add $5 shipping/packaging for the first copy and $1 each additional copy $_____

                                                TOTAL AMOUNT DUE: $_____

PAYMENT BY CHECK/MONEY ORDER:
___   Enclosed is my check/money order made payable to *The Local History Company* for the total amount due above.

PAYMENT BY DISCOVER, VISA, OR MASTERCARD:
Bill my __ Discover __ Visa __ MasterCard   Account # _____
(Address above must be the same as on file with your credit card company)

Expires _____   Name as it appears on your card _____

                           Signature _____

Mail or Fax your order to: *The Local History Company*
(Fax 412-362-8192)   112 NORTH Woodland Road
                                                 Pittsburgh, PA 15232-2849
                                                 Or—call 412-362-2294 with your order.

QUANTITY ORDERS INVITED

This and other books from The Local History Company are available at special quantity discounts for bulk purchases or sales promotions, premiums, fund raising, or educational use by corporations, institutions, and other organizations. Special imprints, messages, and excerpts can also be produced to meet your specific needs.

For details, please write or telephone:
    Special Sales, *The Local History Company*
    112 North Woodland Road, Pittsburgh, PA 15232-2849,   412-362-2294.
    Please specify how you intend to use the books (promotion, resale, fund raising, etc.)